ing George Singleton's hilarious short-story collection *The Half-Mammals of Dixie*. Again and again Singleton stirs empathy for characters with physical and mental limitations. And he keeps the humor volume on high."   —*The Seattle Times*

"A book by turns raucous and enigmatic, and by and large inspired and inventive...An attuned Singleton captures in just the right words the vicissitudes of life and the resilience of individual, often off-kilter lives."   —*The San Diego Union-Tribune*

"Sly, intelligent, hilarious."   —*The Charlotte Observer*

WORK SHIRTS FOR MADMEN

ALSO BY GEORGE SINGLETON

WORK SHIRTS
FOR MADMEN

GEORGE SINGLETON

A HARVEST BOOK
HARCOURT, INC.
Orlando Austin New York San Diego London

Requests for permission to make copies of any part of the work should be
submitted online at www.harcourt.com/contact or mailed to the following address:
Permissions Department, Houghton Mifflin Harcourt Publishing Company,
6277 Sea Harbor Drive, Orlando, Florida 32887-6777.

www.HarcourtBooks.com

This is a work of fiction. Names, characters, places, organizations, and events are
the products of the author's imagination or are used fictitiously, and any resemblance
to actual persons, living or dead, events, or locales is entirely coincidental.

Chapter 14 previously appeared as "Director's Cut" in the
2005 Summer Reading Issue of the *Atlantic Monthly*, and in
New Stories from the South — the Year's Best — 2006.

The Library of Congress has cataloged the hardcover edition as follows:
Singleton, George, 1958–
Work shirts for madmen/George Singleton. — 1st ed.
p. cm.
1. Sculptors — Fiction.   2. South Carolina — Fiction.
3. Self-realization — Fiction.   I. Title.
PS3569.I5747W67   2007
813'.6 — dc22   2006101572
ISBN 978-0-15-101307-4
ISBN 978-0-15-603439-5 (pbk.)

Text set in Electra
Designed by April Ward

First Harvest edition 2008
A C E G I K J H F D B

For Brent Burry and Dale Ray Phillips

"Shame reveals to me that I *am* this being, not in the mode of 'was' or 'having to be' but *in-itself*."

—Jean-Paul Sartre,
Being and Nothingness

PART ONE

PART ONE

1

YOU'D THINK THAT, being a saturated and memory-lost drunk, I would've been the one who stole the twelve snapping turtles, but it was my wife Raylou behind the entire operation, from original vision to relocation. I didn't even know she had an interest in the plight of nontraditional lab animals, never mind the moral bridges certain toxicologists were choosing to cross. Maybe I didn't pay enough attention. Raylou shook me awake from the floor of my Quonset-hut workspace one dawn and told me she needed a steep-sided three-foot-deep pool chiseled into our yard by the time she got home that night. She told me to line it with plastic and the ceramic earthenware tiles she'd fired in the electric kiln a week earlier. She said she had enough for about a 240-square-foot area. I, of course, opened my eyes, tried to remember the past twenty-four hours, and thought about how this was too much math for me to ever remember. Raylou said she'd written out the phone number of her lawyer friend Darren — a man who over the past ten years had bought more than a hundred wood kiln–fired scary-face jugs from my wife — on the To Do list stuck on our refrigerator, should she get caught and need bail money. Raylou would have her cell phone with her, she said, but asked me not to call in case she needed to quietly stake out this female biotoxicologist somewhere between the Lester Maddox and George Wallace boat landings on the Georgia/Alabama border, far from where we lived.

I nodded, but tried to think if "biotoxicologists" really existed. And I pretended to know exactly what she was talking about, seeing as I felt sure she'd told me all about this particular ploy some time within the previous week, month, or year. That's how I operated back then, mostly. I'm not proud, embarrassed, or ashamed. At the time, I figured that drinking helped me to conceive the original ice sculptures that I sold and displayed at weddings, corporate functions, and the occasional bar or bat mitzvah down in Charleston.

I don't think that my wife kissed me good-bye there on the cement floor, but she didn't cluck her tongue in a your-reputation's-been-ruined way, either. After I heard her drive my refrigeration truck down the driveway I got up, walked past an unused shovel, and grabbed work gloves, two chisels, and a twelve-pound hammer. It seemed right to have a project.

Now, our chosen homestead stood atop a mica-flecked and pine tree–deficient granite hill known as Ember Glow, a bulge in upstate South Carolina that, according to past settlers and present-day aviators alike, sparkled even on sliver-mooned nights. Raylou and I bought twenty acres of what Hollywood sci-fi movie directors dream about—our place didn't look dissimilar to Saint-Exupéry's Asteroid B-612, is what I'm saying.

The previous four or five generations of owners, a family named Coomer—of questionable genes, moral standards, and rational capacities—spent their time believing that they'd find a vein of gold somewhere on Ember Glow. I wished that they had dug three-foot-deep holes instead of the narrow bores that were twenty feet deep and wide enough only to be a danger for mis-stepping stargazers, drunks, blind people, and awkward stray dogs. They didn't find gold, of course, and over the years they got buried, from what I understood, standing straight up in the graves that they unknowingly dug in their youth. One remaining Coomer named Jinks finally decided to give up the family dream, and sold us the house and land for the same amount of money his great-grandfather spent on the place during the Reconstruction. Then Jinks Coomer moved to Nevada because, according to him, he could get a civilian job with the government seeing as he had firsthand knowledge of missile silos and barren landscapes.

I chiseled and pried and scraped and tossed chunks of granite, releasing amber bourbon toxins out of pores I had never noticed before, until the sun stood halfway between me and the horizon. Who sweats from his elbows and the tops of his feet? I went inside to get one of Raylou's crystalline-rock–aquifer, double-oxygenated, reverse-osmosised bottles of spring water that cost something like five bucks a pint because a special order of monks siphoned and blessed the stuff down in Louisiana, and saw her refrigerator notes — one for the lawyer, another reminding me that I promised to *check myself into outpatient rehab* before I got fired officially and lost my insurance.

I said out loud to no one, "Oh, man, those hot television lights did me in," and started remembering everything that I hoped wasn't really true. Like only a worthwhile desperate guilty drunk can do, I got in our other car, drove down Ember Glow's hard, shiny road, and didn't stop until I found a pet-supply joint thirty miles away that sold the Whisper Internal Filter System 10-20 with its large carbon ultra-activated cartridge, so Raylou's newly rescued snapping turtles wouldn't have to live in their own waste.

I bought a dozen, and put in an order for more.

When I got home I would've installed the things, too, had I not found one last bottle of Old Crow stashed behind my ice-sculpting tools back in the Quonset hut and then taken a nap on the same spot where I began the day.

It's not like I ever kept a diary of my drinking escapades, but it wasn't hard to recall that I'd gone from drinking mostly beer when I could get it, back before I was fifteen, to nothing but bourbon by college. And then from graduation until age thirty-eight I went from not drinking until after five o'clock in the afternoon all the way to drinking as soon as I woke up. I went from taking days — even weeks — off to being able to fit three good drunks into one twenty-four-hour period. Sometimes a fifth didn't seem to affect me; other times I got wasted on two or three drinks.

My liver went from confusion to apathy, it seemed.

I went from receiving regular outdoor-metal-sculpture commissions from various cities — walk around Atlanta, Savannah, Richmond, Charlotte, Nashville, Cincinnati, and Greensboro, for instance, and more than likely you'll bump into a giant Harp Spillman structure that's usually in front of a bank or CVS Pharmacy — to not being able to think of anything new whatsoever. As Raylou's reputation as a traditional potter grew nationwide, my reputation as an avant-garde welder diminished. It took fifty hate letters detailing everything I said and did in a drunken stupor at a particular unveiling before I said fuck it all and threw my acetylene torch down one of the man-made mini-caves on Ember Glow.

This might've been around the Ides of March, 2001. Within the year I was pretty much broke, so I contacted Ice-o-Thermal, a chain of ice-sculpture fabricators that hired artists, caterers, florists, butchers, and interior decorators who either couldn't make ends meet in their chosen field or had fallen to has-been status. Ice-o-Thermal sent along instructional videotapes and a dozen molds. Its employees provided their own workspaces, which meant someone like me had to convert part of my Quonset-hut studio into a deep freezer.

I don't want to brag, but within eighteen months Ice-o-Thermal executives were impressed by my freestyle ice sculptures. I didn't use those little ice angels in a punch bowl or dolphins in midair above a tray of sushi. No, I received work orders from the home office, brainstormed the best I could in my condition, and invented one-of-a-kind sculptures to fit any occasion. For one particular wedding reception I learned that the bride and groom both took ROTC in college and that they would be joining the army as first lieutenants directly after their honeymoon. It took some time and experimentation, but I carved out an ice howitzer that — using the same techniques as that of a potato gun — fired a plastic bride and groom right onto the wedding cake. At a fund-raiser for a history museum down in Greenville I built an ice replica of Stonehenge at half-scale, which was still so big that I had to set up the thing out on the front lawn. When it finally melted a couple days later, the water clogged up the storm drains out on the street and a road crew had to show up.

The bottom line goes something like this: The CEO of Ice-o-Thermal, Fulton Dupont — oh, he liked to point out immediately that he could've gone on with his life as part of the family's giant chemical company, but early on he got himself disowned — drove down from the home office in Dover, Delaware, and offered me a regional vice-president position overseeing all of the

7

ice sculptors in the Carolinas, Georgia, and Tennessee. I, of course, declined, seeing as I still, through bourbon haziness, saw myself as an artist, not a corporate type. But I did threaten to quit unless I got some benefits, most importantly health and dental insurance.

Fulton Dupont looked across our top of Ember Glow. He said, "My people have done some things to the earth to make it resemble this place. What did y'all do here? Was there a giant spill somewhere along the line?"

That's right, he said "y'all." It happens all the time.

I said, "Nothing. It's just the way the land ended up, I guess. Ember Glow's kind of the last little bubble of the Blue Ridge, in a way."

"I can get you benefits," Fulton said. "I'll get you benefits, and I'll up your percentage to fifty percent." He looked over at the Quonset hut, then to Raylou's wood-firing kiln. "The only thing I ask of you is honesty, Harp. If you get contracted out for something all by yourself, and if you end up using our molds, then you need to send me the company half of your net profit."

I shook his hand. I tried to inhale constantly so he couldn't smell my breath, which would certainly let him know that honesty wasn't one of my best qualities at this point. Raylou wasn't around to chide or cover for me on this day. Thankfully, she taught a group of senior citizens how to make face jugs of their extended families as an alternative way of writing their autobiographies. Raylou'd gotten a giant grant from the arts commission. I said to my boss, "This is an exciting time for ice sculptors, isn't it?" I didn't know what else to say. I wanted a drink something fierce.

Fulton Dupont scanned his surroundings again and said, "You do ice, and your wife does pottery. You should put a sign down at the end of your driveway advertising 'Fire and Ice.'"

I tried to smile. I thought, *What an idiot.* I thought, *I might be drunk most of the time, but I'm never going to name our land after a Robert Frost poem.* "The Dead by the Side of the Road," maybe. *The Waste Land.* I said, "I never thought about that," like any other suck-up employee might be prone to say.

We shook hands. He said he'd get his HR person to send along the paperwork. When he drove away I noticed how he kept his eyes in the rearview mirror, and I swear he shook his head in a way that only meant Man, I'm glad I don't live here.

I went directly into the nonfreezing walled-off space of my Quonset hut, opened a metal file cabinet, pulled out a Dukes of Hazzard lunch box, rifled through some old savings bonds that wouldn't mature until I was fifty-five if I lived that long, and uncovered a pint of Ancient Age.

I wasn't hiding it from my wife. I just liked to keep pint bottles in lunch boxes and tin Charles Chips containers that I embedded in pink fiberglass insulation behind trick walls—I promise.

With all that talk of upcoming health insurance, I sat down on a stool and started feeling persistent throbs and pangs in most of my vital organs.

Raylou and I bought our place on Ember Glow only six years after we both finished art school. I had completed a giant welded piece made up entirely of nuts and bolts for the city of Pittsburgh, and worked on a similar piece for one of those smaller Rust Belt towns in northeastern Ohio. This rich Japanese guy associated with the automobile industry somehow came across Raylou's work and ordered a thousand face jugs he wanted to give to the assembly-line workers at one of his plants. Already she and I lived in South Carolina where—although no one appreciated our work or success—it didn't take but something like $800 per month for us to live, as long as I didn't go out to bars nonstop with a credit card.

We bought the Coomer homestead, which more or less resembled a miniature version of the Winchester house out in California, and took to gutting it. We turned four added-on rooms that faced the south into one normal-sized den. Raylou and I tore down an odd makeshift staircase with different-width risers and treads that began in the middle of the living room and led to a mere crow's nest. I assembled an equally mismatched spiral staircase, but it took up less room and seemed more artistic and less Dr. Caligari. In the chiseled-out cellar, we put down a plank floor and drew Lascaux-like images on the rock walls.

We replaced the badly shingled room with tin, replaced the clapboard with cedar siding, replaced the hole in the floor with an actual toilet. We didn't raze an old outhouse we found still standing in a copse of hardy tulip poplars that somehow took root and emerged from the granite a hundred yards away.

Then, from what I hear, I started to drink harder, and my welded pieces took on what might be considered as post-post-modern-avant-avant-garde qualities. Let's just say that more than a few old-fashioned lightning rods cropped up around the Quonset hut, which probably weren't the safest things to keep around. Maybe I had the self-destructive death wish of a true fatalist, I don't know. That's what any booze therapist steeped in the ways of the creative arts might say. Will say. Said later.

And Raylou continued with her face jugs. How many different goofball faces are there on this planet? I often asked myself, peeking out the one window of my own studio as my wife produced one bucktoothed miscreant after another. This was a time before the Internet and eBay, and she got phone calls and orders by mail daily, not to mention what she sold at hillbilly craft fairs where she put on overalls and hairsprayed her head silly into high, tight bouffants.

Sometimes I wondered whatever happened to the woman I fell in love with in class, the woman who threw regular bowls and vases and urns on an old-fashioned kick wheel, the woman who — despite being named halfway for her daddy Raymond and halfway for her mother Louise up in Tennessee — could've been a senior ceramicist at Hull, McCoy, Pfaltzgraff, Watt, Lenox, or even Limoges. What happened to the woman who could've hand-thrown her way to the covers of both *Art in America* and *Playboy*? And when did my wife decide that rescuing imperiled snapping turtles hovered above even the importance of face-jug production?

Maybe Raylou asked the same things: Whatever happened to the man who could've been on the cover of *ARTnews*, *Modern Welder*, and *Esquire*? When did Harp Spillman's liver become his most utilized organ, ranked above brain, lungs, or pecker?

Fuck it, I thought, seated across from the refrigerator at midnight on a specialized stool I'd constructed myself, wondering if it was time to call Raylou's attorney. I breathed out hard twice, jerked my face forward, and sniffed. Then I heard my truck's squeaky horn from down Ember Glow, the celebratory honk of a woman who had completed her mission. I walked to the bathroom, gargled twice, found some breath mints, and chewed a half-dozen down to pebbles. Raylou parked in front of my snapping-turtle pond — half aquarium, half terrarium — and kept the headlights on. I flipped the front-yard floodlights, came outside, and said, "I was going to wait one more hour to start calling.

Are you okay?" I heard those cooters scratching on the bed of my refrigeration truck, imagining that we had some pretty riled, mean reptiles.

Raylou threw her arms around my neck and kissed me hard. She held her mouth open wide, then said, "Well I don't think we'll have any problems with those Republicans coming up here to lynch you like you've been saying. Hotdamn, a couple of these snappers must weigh forty pounds!"

I didn't say, "What? What's that you said about Republicans?" I thought, *Goddamn blackouts*, and knew that my time had come, that I would soon be speaking in the bumper-sticker language of recovery: One day at a time. What's the next right thing to do? Grant me the serenity to blah, blah, blah. Whenever I drink I break out in handcuffs.

Raylou said, "Hey, go get a couple pieces of rebar from your shop and let's get these things into their new home." She looked down at the habitat I had chiseled out during the day. "I would've gotten here sooner, but I stopped in at the farmers market outside Atlanta and got some free-range chicken necks and milk thistle for these bad boys. I'm going to get their systems cleaned out, one way or the other. Are those filters? Where'd you get all the filters and the power strip?" She followed the extension cord back to our outside outlet, right above a piece of ground where I'd been promising to build a paving-stone patio.

I said, "Hey, I had a dream about chicken necks one time." Raylou turned her head upwards and close to my face. She said that my teeth looked like the chipped porcelain shards she used for her jugs. I said, "Oh. Breath mints."

My wife offered up a half smile. The first snapping turtle to emerge out of the truck's bed hissed, spat, and jerked its head in and out. My wife said, "I'll be able to live around temperamental and irrational animals, don't you think, Harp? Don't you think?"

I didn't say, "Subtle, Raylou, subtle."

Here's what I pieced together the day after we got our bale of turtles: At some point when I was either pretending to work or had passed out in a variety of possible locations on our property, Raylou watched a local news item about a biologist from Clemson University who used snapping turtles to measure PCB levels in lakes and rivers throughout the Southeast. According to this woman, snapping turtles proved to be resilient to the worst environments in regards to toxins; they absorbed and retained said toxins for long periods of time without dying off; and, relatively speaking, they weren't difficult to lead to water or to corral back up for a return trip to the lab in special porous diving chambers with holes in the tops just big enough to let them crane their necks out. The biologist's name, according to Raylou, was Dr. Nerine Nodine.

Well it didn't take my wife much of a prod to notice that "Nerine" meant "of the sea, or swimmer," according to her *Name Your Baby* book, which she quit looking at once she had convinced me that even if my semen wasn't fried up completely, any progeny spawned from my loins might end up on the same level as that silo-yearning Coomer man. Secondly, she noticed how there were six letters in each of Dr. Nodine's names, including her middle and maiden names, too.

My wife and I sat in the kitchen drinking coffee, of all things, only four hours after dropping the snappers into their new home. I said, "I'm listening. Six letters. Six-six-six. Water liver," and then cringed, hopeful that she didn't hear what I said, knowing that the mention of "liver" might set her off on my condition.

"Her downfall occurred when she sought the spotlight. I'm telling you, scientists shouldn't ask people to feel free to come watch them work. That's why they usually don't—people would show up and start dicking around with the Bunsen burners. I know I would."

I said, "No lie," and waited for Raylou to clue me in.

"I mean it. The worst thing she could've done was say, 'Any of y'all who want to see my snapping turtles in action, drive on over next weekend to the Alabama side of the Chattahoochee River on Goat Rock Dam and I'll be glad to show you science in action.' I probably wouldn't have gone if she hadn't said, 'I know some people are against using animals for science, but when you die from eating poisoned fish, don't blame any of us who are trying to help out.'"

I had a funny feeling that Raylou made that last part up. I couldn't imagine a real biologist—especially a bio*toxic*ologist— saying something like that into a camera. Plus, Raylou scratched the palm of her hand, the same thing she always did when she said something like "I'm positive that you'll get back in the real sculpture groove pretty soon, Harp" or "I didn't hide your bourbon" or "Yeah, I'm still glad we got married."

The snapping-turtles' tissue also held other poisons, I supposed, seeing as Raylou walked over to the window, looked out at our pets, and chanted, "Pesticides. Herbicides. Insecticides. Raw sewage. Fertilizer. Hog shit. Radioactive isotopes."

I said, "I still can't believe you got away with it. Tell me again how you went about stealing the turtles without her knowing." In my mind, I saw the slap-nut face I wore, trying to be both ultimately interested and on top of the entire story's continuum.

Raylou said, "I haven't told you the first time, Harp. Don't pretend to know what's going on, or what went on. My nerves are so bad right now I feel like I need a drink."

"Go on and get you one," I said. "I ain't feeling so hot myself."

Raylou leaned against the refrigerator. She stuck her right hand up against the To Do list, but said nothing. "It wasn't that hard. The woman drove her turtles around in what looked like the bed of a pickup truck lopped up from its cab. You know those things I'm talking about? It was like a homemade version of a regular U-Haul trailer you hitch to the back of a truck. There was hurricane fencing covering over the top. I drove up and eyeballed the situation. Nerine Nodine got out, unhitched the trailer, and leaned it down on the cement. Then she walked down the boat ramp to look across the water, but I figured that she was waiting to see if anyone would come and watch her in action, you know."

I drank from my cup of regular coffee. It tasted different than usual, seeing as I hadn't dolloped some Jim Beam into it. I said, "Did she wear leather gloves? Who would deal with those turtles without wearing leather gloves? They say that if one bites into you, you have to wait for sundown for its jaws to release."

Raylou tapped her finger next to the "You promised to go to outpatient rehab" reminder. She said, "That's a myth about the jaws. Yeah, she wore leather gloves and blue jeans, and some kind of gag T-shirt that read BIOTOXICOLOGISTS DO IT WITH TRAINED LAB ANIMALS. I'm sure it got a lot of laughs over in the biology department."

I should mention that in my mind I understood how too much information got packed into too few hours, either in memory or *wanting* memory: the turtle rescue, my drinking problems, remembered or not, the history of Ember Glow, the Coomer family, fixing up our own homestead, and the complications with Ice-o-Thermal. Raylou's face jugs and her odd career that out-shone mine. I made a point to concentrate.

I said to Raylou, "Yeah. I'm betting those people have no sense of humor. You need to have an open mind about both evolution and creationism to have a good sense of humor." It occurred to me that I had a habit of spouting out anything that came into my head.

"So I got out of your truck and walked down to the woman. Wearing my most concerned face, I said, 'There's a man up there with three or four snapping turtles he's caught, and he's holding an ax.' I pointed in the opposite direction from where I planned to go. Well, this woman didn't even say thanks. She ran up to her own truck and drove off. Me, I sauntered back, hitched the turtle wagon, and drove away until I found a dirt road off the main highway. I pulled in, found a thick limb, and started transporting the snapper cages into the back of your truck. Later on maybe I'll make an anonymous call and tell the university where they can find their missing trailer."

We walked outside and looked down at the pit. All of the snapping turtles had their heads above water, retreating beneath the surface at our approach. I said, "It's like looking at dinosaurs."

Raylou stared down for a while. She didn't respond as she picked up a piece of rebar from the night before. When one of the turtles grabbed ahold of it she pulled him up, placed him on the ground, and turned him over. It didn't take a biotoxicologist to understand that the quarter-sized gizmo attached to the underside of the turtle's carapace right above the base of its tail probably worked as some kind of monitoring device, in case they got out of their cages or in case they underwent tests involving migratory habits. It didn't take a paranoid ex–ice sculptor, who had recently offended the state's entire Republican Party at a fund-raising function he'd been hired out to decorate with busts of famous Southern public servants, to understand that Dr. Nerine Nodine could probably track her turtles right on up to Ember Glow.

I said, "I'll get some pliers and a chisel and hammer."

Later that afternoon with the turtles back in their new home and free-range chicken necks scattered atop Raylou's tiles, my wife and I drove all over South Carolina, skipping little tracking devices across various lakes, rivers, and creeks, knowing that a deranged scientist might be following us zigzagging from one two-lane state road to another. I saved one last disk and, finding ourselves near downtown Greenville, tossed it up on the roof of the Republican Party's headquarters. What the hell.

Rehabilitate *this*, I thought.

I'd like to say that the one thing you could count on was my word, but that's not true. I'd spent my lifetime telling lies — well, that's an exaggeration, really; let's say I'd started lying about the same time I took my second drink at age thirteen, came home, and told my mom the smell on my breath was a new hard candy sold over at Riley's Market that came in bourbon, vodka, and gin flavors. Hell, when I woke up six out of seven days in the Quonset hut, Raylou would ask me if I had been drinking all night or had I started back up first thing in the morning — or did I plan on working on one of a hundred half-finished metal sculptures scattered around our lunar-landscape homestead — or had I listened to the answering machine and written down notes about the next ice-sculpture orders. I looked her straight in the face and answered that No, I didn't drink all night, and No, I waited a good hour before pouring the first bourbon, and Yes, I had some new ideas about the half-sculpted pieces, and Yes, I'd get right on that series of ice ruminants due for the Weight Watchers' national convention up in Asheville — even though none of what I said held anything close to veracity.

"If you say it's time for me to check in to the rehab place, then I'll take your word for it," I told Raylou the night after we distributed our turtles' man-made parasites. "I ain't had a drink today. You can drive me down Ember Glow to that Carolina Behavior place in the morning and drop me off."

Raylou didn't hold my hand, or give me hugs and kisses like some dreamy-eyed, dupe-worthy wife might do in a made-for-TV miniseries. She hadn't called me on my pulling the truck over earlier in the day with the excuse that I heard a ping from the engine and a whump-whump from the rear wheel wells while I was actually sneaking two or three bubbles from a bottle duct-taped to the windshield-wiper-fluid reservoir. "I'm just thinking about the future twice," she said. "First off, I'm afraid your liver might be shot, and your brain's not lagging too far behind. Second, I'm betting there's going to be some action taken against you, and it'll look good in a judge and jury's eyes if you've taken steps to improve yourself and stop the inevitable shuffle straight to prison."

Again, I wasn't quite sure to what Raylou alluded. Was she being sarcastic? Did she find it necessary to stick her toe into the waters of hyperbole?

I stood up from my seat at the bottom of the spiral staircase and said, "I told you I'd check myself in tomorrow morning, goddamn it. Jesus Christ, woman, do you want me to go down there tonight and sleep on the front steps?"

I realized that I couldn't control my anger — believe it or not. Poor Raylou sat there staring at me, accustomed to such behavior. I walked out of the house, intent on locking myself inside the Quonset hut, and fell straight into the snapping turtles' chicken-neck-supplied lagoon.

Under water, and almost hoping to get clamped hard, I heard my own blood surge. But it might've been the filters running.

2

"HELLO, HARP, I'm Vincent Vance. Have a seat and let me ask you some questions about what brought you here today. I ask that you be completely honest. We can't help you unless you want to help yourself, I'm sure you understand."

I had filled out a ten-page questionnaire printed in about four-point type in the waiting room of Carolina Behavior Center, a five-winged facility made up of in- and outpatient services. Vince Vance looked over my answers, which were as honest as possible—I mean, who actually kept track of the dates they had red and German measles, mumps, minor concussions? I said, "Evidently I'm having a hard time remembering things. I think the technical term is 'blackout.'" I said, "I'm talking about recent events."

"How long have you been drinking, Harp?" Vince Vance wore close-cropped gray hair, and kind of looked like he'd pumped himself up with good amphetamines. He didn't blink. "Hey," Vince Vance said, "that came out funny. It came out sounding like 'How long have you been drinking Harp lager.' Your folks didn't name you after an Irish beer, did they?" He laughed. Rehab humor.

"Quarter century," I said. To me it sounded shorter than twenty-five years. "Not hard all the time. I mean, I started sneaking my father's beer and vodka. I guess I didn't start drinking hard until high school."

"How much are you drinking nowadays? What's your normal drinking day?" A group of what I assumed to be qualified nurses laughed on the other side of the wall. Vince Vance reached down from his Queen Anne chair and flipped the switch on a white-noise machine. Or maybe it was an air filter. I kind of had the feeling that I reeked, seeing as I had got up earlier than Raylou and left on my own. I'd dried out from falling into the snapping-turtle pit, but I'd not taken a shower, only thrown on a union suit and a pair of blue janitor's overalls.

I said, "Understand that I'm not proud of this, and I'm not sure when I kind of lost control. I usually get up about an hour before dawn and make a pot of coffee for my wife. Then I go to my workspace and start drinking bourbon. On a good—or I guess from your point of view, a bad—day, I can fit a few drunks in. I'll drink and work from six until about eleven, then take a nap. Then I'll work and drink from say one until five and take a nap. Then after supper, if I eat, I'll go at it again until midnight or thereabouts."

"And this has been a relatively new schedule for you?"

I said, "I have to tell you right now, Dr. Vance—is it *Dr. Vance?*—that I want to quit drinking 'cause I figure my liver's pretty shot. But I have a million things to do, and I can't afford to come as an inpatient."

Vince Vance took notes. He said, "It's not 'doctor.' I have a master's in social work. And I've been working with addicts and alcoholics now for about twelve years here. Before that I concentrated on other kinds of counseling. I'm an LISW. Most everybody in the addiction field is an LISW."

I said, "Good," because I couldn't think of what else to say. "All right. I see."

"This schedule of yours is relatively new? Kind of like you used to be able to control"—he looked down at my answers—"bourbon, but now it seems to be in control of you?"

I said, "Uh-huh. It's a relatively new schedule in regards to the age of the universe. I've been this way a good fifteen years."

Later on I would tell people that Vince Vance's jaw dropped to his lap. In reality, he only kept staring. He said, "I'm glad you chose to come here. Can I see your insurance card?" He got up out of his chair. "I'll be back in a minute."

His office was decorated in a modern Alcoholics Anonymous motif. There must've been two dozen of those sappy cross-stitched framed dictums on the wall—LET GO AND LET GOD!, ONE DAY AT A TIME!, STAY SOBER!, IT'S BAFFLING AND CUNNING!, EASY DOES IT!, YOU CAN'T TURN A PICKLE BACK INTO A CUCUMBER!, and so on. I stood up and rubbed my kidneys. When Vince Vance returned, I said, "Do y'all have some kind of arts-and-crafts classes that are part of everyone's recovery process?"

"Well, we have good news and bad news. The insurance company says they won't pay for inpatient anyway. And they say that you'll be cured in sixteen three-hour sessions. That's about what every insurance company is saying these days. And it *does* work for some people, at least if they follow the steps."

I sat back down after he handed me the insurance card. "I have to make a confession, Vince Vance. I know this'll sound sacrilegious and/or defamatory, but if this program's one where Jesus gets shoved down my throat, it ain't going to work for me. If this is one of those places where everyone's going to say Jesus is the only way to stop drinking, I'll drink more, goddamn it. If Jesus can't keep his followers from starting wars all over the place, I doubt He'll be able to stop my Adam's apple. Oh, I believe in a Higher Power, just like you've got up on the wall two or three times, but my Higher Power might be Buddha, for all I know. It might be that Trickster fellow in Native American myth. I'm from fucking South Carolina, so I've had the Jesus stuff pounded into me enough, and I kept drinking all the while. Maybe I need a *higher* Higher Power, you know. It seems to me if a Higher Power were in charge, our country wouldn't have poverty-stricken, uninsured, poorly educated people voting for Republicans who want to keep them down all the time no matter what."

Vince Vance kept eye contact and nodded during my minia-ture diatribe. He said, "What kind of art do you do, Harp? You don't work with a lot of lead-based paints, by any chance. Do you work around a lot of fumes?"

Vince Vance laughed, and slapped me on the shoulder. He said, "I used to work in New Orleans. I've seen that giant sculp-ture you made down by the Custom House. What is that thing, anyway? I remember it being gigantic, and wonderfully—what's the word?—*graceful*, and your name down at the base."

I'll be the first to admit that maybe I changed my mind about Vince Vance and his outpatient program only because he re-membered my sculpture. I said, "I think the politicians down there started calling it *Our Ship Comes In*. It kind of had a nau-tical theme, you know, with exposed ribs made out of threaded nuts and bolts I got down at a junkyard in Jacksonville, plus some long old rebar left over from one of those stadiums torn down in Atlanta. Originally I titled the piece *The Twenty-first Amend-ment*. It was New Orleans, man. I guess some do-gooder idiot down there caught on and looked up the Constitution."

Vince Vance said that my first meeting would begin at six o'clock that night, and that I'd be in group therapy with about half addicts and half drunks like me. He also referred me to a psychiatrist who honored my insurance company and specialized in clients angry at the government.

I shook his hand, said I'd be on time, and didn't mention how I had a theory about the government and the insurance industry.

Raylou tried to hide our only real car—a 1979 Citroën I bought drunk—behind the clinic's short bus. I walked out of Carolina Behavior and pretended to look toward the horizon, but peripherally I saw Raylou parked there, slumped in her seat, making sure that I didn't really drive down Ember Glow and end up at a liquor store, or Scatterbrain's bar. I got in my refrigeration truck and drove out of the lot; I turned left and started north on the Old Walhalla Highway, keeping an eye on Raylou lagging a quarter mile back. Finally I sped up, rounded a curve, turned into a red clay loggers' road, and let her pass. When I got home, she stood next to her kiln, looking at my Quonset hut.

"Hey, honey," I said. "Are you firing that thing up? You want me to go down and get you some more wood?" Of course I wasn't going to let on that I saw her tailing me. That's how alcoholics are, I was soon to learn. Some people—usually family members—have a technical term for people like me when we're acting thusly: Manipulative pricks.

"How'd it go?" Raylou asked. She began walking my way.

"Pretty cool. I liked Vince Vance a bunch. I guess you know what I mean—he told me you had come by there earlier and talked to him about me. I thought he was pretty cool."

Raylou came up and kissed me on the cheek. "Well, I had to go in there and tell him about you and your ways, or else he would've tried to lock you up for good, Harp. I thought it was the right thing to do."

I thought, *Ha ha ha ha ha ha ha.* I might be a drunk, but I still had that little conniving part of my brain working full force. I said, *"He didn't tell me you'd been up there to talk to him.* I just made that up! You told on yourself, Ray. Maybe I'll have a little talk to the group tonight about wives who're always playing tricks on their husbands, and how that might shove the man to wanting a drink."

Raylou shook her head. "Excuses. You aren't going to be able to stop unless you stand back and see how you're always finding excuses—it's a good day, it's a bad day; Raylou's not paying me enough attention, Raylou's hanging around too much; the sun's come up, the sun's gone down."

I nodded and smiled. "I know that you're right. Let me go on record right now as saying that I know you're right. And I appreciate your going down to Carolina Behavior and making sure I went in for the assessment. I saw you parked down there, so that's why I fucked with you on the drive back."

Raylou walked over to the snapping-turtle pond. "I need to get a book and see how much these bad boys eat."

"I know that I left before you did this morning. So you couldn't have talked to Vince Vance this morning before I got there, or while I sat in the waiting room. When the hell did you go down there?"

Raylou took a piece of rebar and stroked one of the turtles. It retracted its head, and didn't hiss or bite. "About three years ago. Two years ago. Last year. Last month. Last week. I've been down there a bunch of times, every time you made a promise to check in."

I didn't say that I'd never recalled making such vows. I said, "I'll be damned."

My wife said, "I think he likes to be called *Vincent* Vance, Harp. Not Vince Vance. You might want to stay on his good side."

I walked back to my refrigeration truck, opened the passenger door, and pulled out an inch of reading material Vince Vance wanted me to pore over before I came to my first session. I looked at my watch. "I need to read over some stuff about alcoholism before I go in tonight. I'll be in the hut."

Raylou smiled, set the rebar aside, and nodded. "I'm going to load up the kiln and fire it up. I don't know if you remember or not, but I'm supposed to be up in Sylva this weekend for that mountain-arts festival. Unless it'll mess with your recovery. I have to say that I'm not going to be your biggest cheerleader until I see that you're serious about this. I'm going to be as supportive as any wife in the history of living with an alcoholic, but I have to be realistic, Harp. Vincent Vance will tell you that you're going to want to do this for yourself—not me, or your people at Ice-o-Thermal."

I felt myself edging toward the Quonset hut as she spoke. I'm not proud to say that I wanted to ease back my secret wall, pull out the fiberglass insulation, and just make sure I had a backup plan in case I took to shaking uncontrollably. I said, "I'm not coming up with ideas drunk, so I might as well try it sober."

Raylou stared at me in much the same manner as Vince Vance. "I threw your bourbon down the mountain." She pointed to where Ember Glow's rounded slope accelerated.

When she walked away, I noticed how her rear end could've been used for one of those bottle openers on the side of a cold drink box. I thought, I could stick an old-fashioned non-screw-top Pepsi right up there and unhinge the top. What a nice body my strange face-jug—making wife has, I thought. "I'll do it for myself," I called out, but I don't think she heard me. One of the snapping turtles, though, stretched his neck and head a good six inches past the edge of its boundary.

The outpatient group-therapy sessions took place for three hours, three nights a week, in a doublewide portable between the fourth and fifth wings of the facility. Also, on Sundays Vince Vance held a nonmandatory, but highly-urged-to-attend "Family Day at the Rehab Center" discussion group, so friends and loved ones could come in and learn about the intricacies of the alcoholic mind and liver, plus—as I learned later—get in as many cheap shots as possible. Sixteen three-hour sessions, according to the insurance company, should heal anyone who'd spent, let's say, the last decade in a blur. I'm no math genius or abnormal psychologist, but right away I was willing to bet that forty-eight hours wouldn't constitute a cure-all.

I drove down to the clinic alone, checking the rearview mirror about every tire rotation for Raylou sightings. Then I passed the rehab center, drove twenty miles past the Pickens County line, drove around aimlessly, pulled into a couple do-it-yourself car washes, and finally returned to my first group-therapy session fifteen minutes early. As I drove behind the place to the parking lot for outpatients, I thought that maybe either Raylou had indeed shown up and started a makeshift raku firing or the doublewide trailer was burning uncontrollably. Then I saw my new group of ex-mercenaries, somehow alive after dodging so many bullets, huddled beneath a picnic shed, smoking two or three cigarettes apiece.

"My name's Harp and I'm an alcoholic," I said as I approached. "I guess I might as well get used to saying that. It's what we're supposed to say, right?" I'll admit now that I didn't quite take it seriously at this point. No one laughed, but they smiled. I would learn presently that all of my new comrades — there were a dozen of us — were in various stages of official outpatient rehabilitation. They nodded, or held up helpless palms in some sort of I-give-up recognition.

"Like the musical instrument? That's all right. Harp. I'm Bayward," a fellow wearing a work shirt said. Over one pocket it read NUCLEAR WELDING. Above the other pocket it read WAYWARD.

I reached in my pocket and pulled out a little Camel, then took the wooden match Bayward or Wayward offered. "Thanks, man. Yeah, like the old stringed thing. Vince Vance pointed out there was a beer called Harp. Might explain some things."

"He's a good man," a woman said. She held out her hand. "I'm Tammy," and we shook. She might've been either thirty or sixty years old, with eye bags that could've been used for pole-vault pits. Then she pointed to the door at the end of Wing 5. "I guess it's time. Here he comes." Vince Vance smiled at us, sidestepped an invisible puddle, and made his way toward the portable. "Tonight will be your worst night. But we're a good group of people. And there's about twenty boxes of Kleenex in there, unless that girl used them all up on Monday. I guess she ain't coming back. I had a feeling she wasn't ready to get off the crack rock just yet." She put out her cigarette on the half-melted top of a plastic garbage bin. "I'm going to get my pocketbook out of the car in case she shows up later and relapses into robbing everybody."

The outpatient portable wasn't decorated as homey as Vince Vance's office. The walls were painted pastel blue, which I figured right away was supposed to add a calming effect, but there were fist- and foot-sized holes in the walls. A fifty-cup coffee urn stood on a table that was bolted down to the floor, and a grated metal box surrounded the canister, maybe so no one could lose control, pick up however many gallons of hot coffee, and throw it onto fellow brothers and sisters in the recovery process. Plastic chairs—the cheap stackable kind usually seen for sale on the sidewalk in front of a discount department store—stood in a circle. Vince Vance said, "I'm going to pass around two sheets for y'all to fill out—the attendance sheet, and the one noting your progress or lack thereof. While we fill those out, we have a new member to the group, Harp Spillman. Let's introduce ourselves to Harp."

Everyone sat down. Bayward started off with, "I'm Bayward, and I'm an alcoholic." A young woman said, "I'm Abby, and I'm an addict." Tammy came in with her pocketbook and said, "Tammy, alcoholic." A guy wearing a flight jacket, though it might've been eighty degrees outside said, "Gene, addict." Another middle-aged woman said, "I'm Carol, and I'm an alcoholic," and so on. I nodded at each of them, smiled, and tried to keep my foot from bouncing up and down.

Vince Vance said, "Harp, why don't you tell us what brought you here."

I cleared my throat twice. "Evidently I'm blacking out more often than a normal person should. Of course, I wouldn't know, seeing as I'm always blacked out. I'm not proud of it, but that's the way it is."

Vince Vance said, "Name off some of the bad consequences you wrote down on that sheet I had you fill out earlier today." He looked at the class and said, "Harp wasn't in inpatient. He checked himself into this program on his own."

I tried to remember what I'd filled out earlier. "Well, I can't remember when I had the measles, if that's what you mean. I told you that I had some memory problems."

"No," Vince Vance said. "You wrote down that you were concerned with your job. And your relationship with your spouse. Stuff like that."

I said, "Job and wife."

"Yeah."

Bayward held his forehead up and said, "Did you come here because your boss man suggested it?"

"We pride ourselves in being honest here, Harp," Vince Vance said. "And what goes on inside this room should stay in this room. I need to fess up and say that Harp's wife — Raylou's her name, right?—has been coming to see me for about three years. Evidently Harp will decide that he needs some help, she comes by to make sure we have room in the program, and then Harp decides otherwise. Does that sound about right to you?" he asked me.

I felt sweat going down the insides of my upper arms. I took a Kleenex from the empty chair beside me and wiped my forehead. "I kind of learned about all that just this afternoon when I came home from here. To be honest, I don't remember ever blurting out that I wanted or needed to quit. But I believe Raylou. And I appreciate it." I set an unlit cigarette in my mouth. "I'll go out on a limb and predict that you never really saw my sculpture in New Orleans, that Raylou told you about it or something."

Vince Vance kept eye contact and said, "We pride ourselves on honesty within these walls, Harp. I didn't say anything about the walls of my office." He laughed and scanned his group members. "I guess I'm learning how to be a con man, too. Maybe I should thank y'all for that."

"Raylou's a cool name," Carol said. "I like that name."

I said "Okay," to Vance and "Thank you" to Carol. "From what my wife says, I'm about to get in some trouble from my boss. Y'all might've seen it on the news a few days ago. I'm an ice sculptor, among other things."

Vince Vance said, "I saw it on CNN."

"That was you?!" Bayward said. "I seen it on the local news about three times. Down in Columbia at that big old party for rich people?"

I shrugged. "I guess so. I kind of remember having the idea. And then I guess I went through with it." To Vince Vance I said, "I know that a certain paranoia probably comes with alcoholism, Vince, but I don't think it would be a bad thing to lock the door when I'm in here."

Mr. Dupont had called me up in January excited and said that we had a $20,000 project that only I could pull off, for some kind of Republican fund-raiser down in Columbia in February. They wanted busts of all the famous Southern politicians, past and present, which would be scattered around the ballroom inside the Adam's Mark Hotel and convention center. Now, I kind of remember listening to Mr. Dupont warn me not to screw up and play any practical jokes. He said, "I totally understand that your political livestock might graze in a different kind of pasture, but if we can get this account every year, I think it would be beneficial to both of us. Hell, you could probably live all year long in Ember Glow on what your take will be from this job, man. What's a loaf of bread cost in South Carolina, a dime? Is it true they just hand out cigarettes down there when you walk into the store?"

Since the entire event—which at this point wasn't but three days old—I kept telling myself that it was only a dream, that it wasn't as bad as the newspeople kept saying. I tried to convince myself that everyone *laughed* once the busts began to melt, that they didn't turn my way and point fingers, make threats in ways

31

that only Republican donators know how to do, and finally escort me out of the hotel. The last thing I heard, some fellow named Karl yelled out that I could forget about getting paid, and that there might be a class-action lawsuit coming my way should any of the fainting women decide to press charges for inducing long-term mental suffering, and inciting a riot.

I had driven my refrigerator truck home on autopilot, 140 miles on interstate, then two-lane, then rocky path, just in time for Raylou to point at the television set and say, "I told you not to do it. Are you trying to kill yourself? I really want to know, Harp. Are you trying to get me to leave you or something, or do you just want me to shove you in the kiln, cremate your sodden self, then throw your ashes in one of the leftover Coomer holes. Sober up sometime and tell me, honey."

I looked at the screen. The Karl guy said, "Chances of this being coincidence are pretty slim. This has all the markings of an inside job by the Democrats. They're always talking about conspiracies, but I think we have rock-solid evidence against them this time."

The reporter, a woman I'd seen at three in the morning sometimes when I made Raylou's coffee, said, "Until they melt completely, I guess you'd have to say."

The Karl guy stormed off.

Here's what I had done, and I can't believe I pulled it off: I carved out some ice sculptures, then set them in square bins of water, two at a time, in the deep freeze. When that water froze up into blocks of ice, I carved out busts of Strom Thurmond, Jesse Helms, Lester Maddox, Trent Lott, Newt Gingrich — all of the Southern senators and representatives that meant so much to the national Republican Party post-Kennedy, when the region I lived in and loved turned radically red.

On the afternoon of the fund-raiser, I set my ice sculptures up on chunks of granite pillars that stood shoulder-high. Karl told me it was supposed to represent the "rock-solid commitment" of the party. Karl asked me only two things beforehand: "Have you been drinking?" and "Will the ice make it through the evening without making a mess on the floor?"

I said, "No. Yes," but didn't go into detail how I might not be answering his questions in order. Most of my sculptures could handle room temperature for at least eight hours; I understood the importance of a deep carve in working anything outside of a mold so that the inevitable melting process didn't keep a viewer from still knowing what he or she looked at. And long before the fund-raiser, I understood that a room full of Republicans might increase the room's temperature a good ten degrees. In reality, I thought my little stunt wouldn't happen until the last of the partygoers stood around drunk, and that they would only blame it on the booze.

It didn't occur to me that the networks might be there with all of their camera equipment and necessary lights, speeding up the process. Hell, the $5,000-a-person fete began at 6:30, and two hours later Jesse Helms had melted down to the ice sculpture I had fitted underneath him—namely, a Grand Wizard. Strom Thurmond transformed into Mussolini, and Lester Maddox into Tito. I'd brought along a three-headed bust of Reagan/Bush/Bush that didn't quite fit the prescribed "Southern politician" theme, but everyone allowed me to set it right in the middle of the room after I announced that it was my free contribution to the shindig. I'd brought one of Charlton Heston, too, knowing that all the NRA hammerheads would want to get their photos taken beside it, just like in a wax museum. Well, they weren't so happy when *that* particular ice sculpture turned into Lucifer.

They seemed more upset with what I'd done to Moses than when the three presidents transformed into a perfect rendition of the Three Stooges.

Karl and his henchmen escorted me out of the ballroom just as some woman screamed, "Newt Gingrich has melted down to Koko the gorilla!"

On my way out I tried to explain that it was supposed to be a Neanderthal man, that I would never insult Koko.

Back at the rehab center, I finished up my long story about my last real blackout. "An episode like that might challenge your sobriety," Vince Vance said to the group and me.

I said, "I'm not proud of what I did. Or what I've done over the years, even though I don't remember most of it."

Carol said, "I think you *are* proud of it. *I* would be. I'm sorry, Vince, but I think it's probably a jolt of reality that those people needed — to know that not everyone out in the real world sees their party as a bunch of saviors. You're always saying that we need to take up new hobbies and leisure activities in order to forget about wanting to drink. Maybe I'll take up ice sculpting."

I said, "There'll probably be an opening real soon."

Vince Vance went through the room and asked how everyone did over the last couple days. No one slipped, lapsed, or relapsed. He said Good, then had us watch a videotape of a priest scratching out words on a chalkboard, talking about how sane people don't request ether every day, seeing as too much ether can only lead to death.

At least that's what I got out of it.

At nine o'clock Vince Vance said, "Okay. Don't forget that you signed a form stating that you wouldn't use any mind-altering substances of any kind during your time in the program. And that you'd attend meetings on your off days."

Everyone got up to leave. I said, "Say that again. Say that again, what you said we signed?"

Vince Vance said, "Raylou told me you might have a problem with this part."

In the parking lot, Bayward waited for me. He said, "It won't be as bad as you think. Just go and sit there and let those people tell their stories. I go to a good meeting over near Travelers Rest. They got everybody from doctors and lawyers to you and me telling their stories. Believe me when I say you'll feel better about yourself oncet you pick up your surrender chip. And then before you know it you get your thirty-day chip."

We walked toward my refrigeration truck. I said, "You're a welder?"

"I'm taking some time off from work. Boss man said I can't come back until I graduate from here."

I said, "What if I get a bunch of those chips and then become addicted to tiddlywinks?"

Bayward didn't laugh. He rotated his neck a few times. "I'll meet you down there tomorrow at noon. They got meetings at eight, noon, three, and six. I usually go to all of them, just to keep myself out of trouble. If you hate it, I can get you in touch with some old boys who've gone to some crazy extremes so's not to drink. They say they smarter than everyone, but I'll let you make your own judgments. You heard of the Elbow Brethren? — that's them. They benagle the pure-tee hell out of me, but what do I know?"

Benagle! I thought. Perfect. "I'll see you there," I said, and couldn't wait. I said, "How long have you been in this program, Bayward?" and opened my door.

He shook my hand. "This is my fourth go-round. I swear it works. I'd be dead drunk and dead if it weren't for Dr. Vince. I can get about six months under my shoelaces, and then out of nowhere I'm driving the company truck right up to the red dot store when they open at nine. Without Dr. Vince, I don't think I could wait two days between drinks."

I didn't mention how it must *not* work that well if it didn't take on the first three check-ins. I didn't mention how he might want to rectify his misspelled name on the tag above his pocket if he wanted to be taken seriously. Nor did I bring up how I could feel half of my internal organs throb. Instead, I wondered why I'd not ever been pulled over by a highway patrolman, why I had never fallen into one of the granite sinkholes on my land, how much longer I would've lived before hemorrhaging, and how I ever talked Raylou into marrying me.

I turned the ignition. I accidentally put the engine in reverse, stepped on the accelerator, and bumped into what turned out to be Vince Vance's little hybrid car. In the old days, I would've driven off. The new Harp Spillman, though, got out, noticed how a thick red crayon could fix the scratch, and *then* drove home unused to clear eyesight and top-notch reflexes.

3

RAYLOU SAT IN THE DEN, reading a book by, of all people, William James. I don't want to say that my wife seemed incapable of grasping philosophical treatises, but for the most part she read thin biographies of self-taught folk artists who tended to believe God directed them straight toward divine artworks. Sometimes, I had said often, people shouldn't listen to that voice they think's God's. Anyway, Raylou read some fat book about different types of religious experiences when I came back from Carolina Behavior. I said, of course, "I haven't been drinking and driving," which I always said, no matter the truth.

Raylou closed her book. "How'd it go?" She didn't say how she figured I would hate it and give up, that I thought I was smarter than everyone else in the program, that I figured I could stop drinking on my own, et cetera.

"I still like Vince Vance. And I really like the people in the group. There's this country boy I liked a lot named — get this — Bayward. What kind of name is *that*? He's a welder, too. I didn't tell him that I used to weld art. I don't want to presume anything, but I'm figuring he'd start hitting me up for work, you know, if I let on what I did."

Raylou got up and walked to the kitchen. I think she said, "I'm proud of you for going." She might've said, "You wouldn't think a person could go downhill in regards to employment, unless he decided to work for you, Harp."

I said, "I need to go get some chocolate if I'm going to quit drinking. You want to go down to the grocery store in Easley? If we left now, we could get back home before midnight."

Raylou said, "I want you to sit down at the table. I have some things to ask you."

Fuck, I thought. Here we go—another heart-to-heart, wherein I would have to be truthful. How many times in the same day do people have to regurgitate their horrific deeds and actions? I said, "I have to think about my recovery first. Vince Vance said we all have to think about our recovery first. It might trigger my wanting a bottle of booze if I sit down at the table. The same goes for doing the dishes, mopping the floor, taking the garbage down to the recycling center, changing the oil in your step van or my truck or the Citroën, sweeping the front yard, and splitting logs for the kiln. Oh, I can't do much. It might be a trigger."

More rehab-vocab seeped into my brain than I thought.

Raylou said, "I went grocery shopping while you were gone. I got you a bunch of sweets, but you need protein more so. Here." She came into the room with a YooHoo Chocolate Drink, a cardboard sleeve of Little Debbie's Jelly Creme Pies, and two cooked pork chops. Then she returned to the kitchen and came back with a bottle of ginseng iced tea for herself. "This ginseng's supposed to be good for memory, by the way. You might want to take it intravenously pretty soon."

I looked out the back sliding-glass door, pretty certain that I saw a snapping turtle jump out of the water. "What now?" I asked, whining it out. "Did Mr. Dupont call up? Did those Republicans find our phone number?" I said, "Tell me again the significance of the snapping turtles."

Raylou smiled. She pulled her hair back with one hand and tied it in a knot, somehow. "Harp, when I say 'Birmingham,' what comes to mind?"

I said, of course, "A town in Alabama. And in England."

"Anything else?"

"Raylou, my nerves are kind of shot. Could you get to the point? Did I black out in Birmingham one time when I didn't even know I was there? Where's my bourbon, goddamn it."

I started to stand, but lost my balance slightly and sat back down, trying to hide it. Raylou said, "Do you remember ever applying for a commission down there in Birmingham, Alabama? Something about a bunch of angels welded from nuts and bolts, each one about ten or twelve feet high? You would've sent down a prospectus back around the first of the year."

I said, "Oh, man! I almost forgot all about that thing!" because it's how I always answered anything to which I had exactly zero memory. I would've said the same thing if Raylou had asked if I offered my kidneys to a poisoned stranger.

"Michael Heatherly brought a big envelope up today, and I went ahead and opened it. I know that it wasn't addressed to me, but I thought I might have to run interference, what with your condition, if you know what I mean."

I didn't know what she meant. I said, "Who the fuck's Michael Heatherly?"

"The UPS man. He comes by here, oh, maybe twice a week. He brings me my clay, and he used to bring you welding rods. I send off my face jugs through Michael. You talk to him every time. You like him."

"I'm kidding with you." I looked down at my shoe. "Go on. Birmingham."

"There's also a message on the machine. Whatever it is that you promised to make, you got it."

I looked up at my wife, who sat there scumbled-looking from my point of view, the lights behind her fuzzing out any perceptible edges. She reached over to an end table and handed me the envelope. I looked over the terms I had evidently set out for myself: I could have the angels delivered by Thanksgiving, the angels would be placed on concrete pedestals provided by the city of Birmingham, and so on, right there outside of Sloss Furnaces National Historical Landmark. A dozen nuts/bolts/cogs/sprockets angels for a hundred twenty grand, bought by the city through grant monies, to be placed along both sides of Forty-second Street to symbolize "the steel industry's importance to Birmingham, and safe travel for those in need of guardians," my words. I said, "Man, I must've been drunk when I sent this proposal off. Hotdamn. There's no way I can do this between now and then. It used to take me almost a month full-time to make one sculpture that size. There's no way to make twelve between now and November. I guess if I don't get an ice-sculpture contract I might can do it. I don't know."

Raylou leaned over and kissed me. "Personally, I think it's the best thing that could happen. There's no way you can drink hard and get this finished."

I set the envelope down and looked at the answering machine. In my mind I tried to figure out what it would cost in raw materials—Frank and Joe's Nuts and Bolts charged eighty cents a pound, and the normal twelve-foot sculpture—like the one I made fifteen years earlier for the city of El Paso depicting a Day of the Dead–like skeleton to scare off illegal aliens—weighed in at just under half a ton. A thousand times point eight, I thought. "Fucking A, if I need to hire a welder for this little project, I'd still come out making a killing," I said.

Raylou wrinkled her forehead. She said, "How bad does this Bayward fellow shake?" She handed me two Little Debbies with a pork chop in the middle. "Happy Valentine's Day, by the way," she said.

One of the rules of that most-famous nondrinking institution that holds meetings throughout the United States goes like this: No one will talk or write about it, good or bad, ever, for any reason. With the backlog of bad karma I had stored up and forthcoming, I didn't want to break any sacred bonds. So let's say that I met Bayward the next afternoon, as part of my agreement with the Carolina Behavior counseling program, at a Sots Pseudonymous gathering in a cement-block building that also served as the VFW, DAR, 4-H, Narcotics Anonymous, Junior Achievement, Rotary, Lions Club, Kiwanis, Jaycees, and Shriners meeting venues, right on Main Street in the middle of Travelers Rest, a town once known for welcoming anyone who crossed the Blue Ridge Mountains, or hoped to do so the next day.

They called it the Alcohell Club.

Bayward met me in the gravel parking lot and said, "I didn't think you was going to make it, Cuz." He wore his Nuclear Welding shirt again.

I looked at my watch. The drive from Ember Glow on the map isn't but an inch, but no straight roads led between the two places. It took an hour, but it still wasn't but a quarter until noon. "I'm early," I said.

"We like to get here about an hour early and shoot the shit. We also check on each other to make sure we have enough cigarettes." He put his arm on my shoulder and said, "How long's it been since you quit drinking now?"

"Today's day two."

"They don't have a two-day chip. You want to get you a surrender chip for the first day sober. If you'd've come here yesterday, you could've gotten a surrender chip. Just keep it in your mind that now you can get your thirty-day chip in twenty-nine days."

I looked at the men standing around hunched over the sand-in-a-drywall-bucket ashtray, as if they were guarding it. No women seemed to attend this particular meeting. I said, "I'm ready. I'm committed. I figure I drank my share of booze, and now it's time to let other people pull up a stool."

We walked inside. The folding tables and hard-back chairs weren't set up in any discernible formation. A man sat in front of a caddy of poker chips and a stack of paperback books. Bayward looked at him and said, "Billy, this is Harp."

"Hey Harp!" Billy screamed out. I figured he must've been half deaf.

"This is Harp's first meeting."

"Welcome, and keep coming back," Billy said.

The smokers wandered in and took seats. Some of them approached Billy and picked up one of those paperbacks. Bayward said, "Remember what I told you: Don't feel obligated to speak."

Billy welcomed everyone and got a few friends to read some things, something about tradition, something about steps, some kind of daily reflection. He said that there would be a hot-dog supper on Friday, a dance on Saturday—I kind of wandered off with this announcement, thinking about a bunch of grown, shaking men dancing with each other—and a series of yard sales each Saturday on up to April 15 for anyone who needed to make some money for the IRS. He said, "Anyone visiting from out of town? Anyone here for the first time?"

Bayward said, "I'm Bayward and I'm an alcoholic."

"Hey Bayward!" everyone yelled out.

"I brought me a friend here, Harp. It's his first time."

"Hey Harp!"

So much for my sitting back and not talking, my camouflaging into the woodwork anonymously. I raised my hand and waved. Billy said, "Since Harp ain't ever been here before, let's introduce ourselves and then tell him what brought us here and how our lives've been changed."

There might've been twenty-five or forty men in attendance, all of whom appeared to be disabled, unemployed, or retired. Who else can meet at noon every day? They started at one end of the room saying their names and stating they were alcoholics, and everyone blurted out, "Hey," whatever, in greeting: "Hey Leroy, Hey Kenny, Hey Michael, Hey Jasper, Hey Kevin, Hey Will, Hey Baker, Hey Randy, Hey Dave, Hey Lester, Hey Dale, Hey Parker, Hey Fred, Hey Stuart, Hey Terry, Hey Brandon, Hey Will, Hey Jeff, Hey Bryant, Hey Charlie, Hey Daryl, Hey Rick, Hey Will, Hey Bayward, Hey Harp, Hey Will, Hey Clyde, Hey Tony, Hey Chris, Hey Craig, Hey Phil, Hey Will," and so on. Go watch a documentary concerning mentally challenged adults, listen to the way they talk to one another, and you'll pretty much hear this particular sound track. There seemed to be a lot of guys named Will, I thought. Anyway, everyone appeared to be genuinely pleased to have a beating heart.

And all of them wore used work shirts once owned by someone else. I checked. When, say, one of the Wills said he was an alcoholic, I looked down to read FRANKLIN on his shirt, right across from VANADORE'S LAWN CARE. And although they might be dancing with one another on Saturday nights, they didn't seem to be into shirt-swapping. There was no Franklin there, is what I'm saying.

Billy said, "I'm Billy, and I'm an alcoholic."

"Hey Billy!"

"I 'member how I woke up in a hospital bed. It's been eight years now. I had tubes sticking out of my nose. Out of my mouth. In my arms. I didn't know how I got there. But it had to do with blacking out behind the wheel of my old DeSoto. Thanks for letting me share."

"Thanks, Billy!"

One of the Wills said, "I'm Will, and I'm an alcoholic. I been declared dead three times legally! Thanks for letting me share."

No one had time to yell out, "Hey Will!" like that. I thought about asking him how many times he'd been declared dead *illegally*, but said nothing. Everyone looked in my direction. I thought about how I would kill Bayward later.

"I'm Lester, and I'm an alcoholic." Lester held his head halfway tilted toward the rafters. He slouched in his chair and waited for everyone to quit saying, "Hey Lester!" "I don't know if you looked around you when you realized that you'd reached the bottom, but if you did, I know that you saw some footprints around you, even though nobody stood around. Well, let me tell you right now that those were the footprints of *Jesus*. Jesus has been with you, Harp, all along the way! I want you to know that. Just give us ninety days here and see if your life ain't better. Hell, I'll go buy your first drink on day ninety-one if you think otherwise. But let me tell you something: you gone *die*! You have one more drink, and you gone *die*."

I nodded. I started to say, "Thanks, Lester," but wasn't sure if he was done. Everyone else, I figured out later, knew that he wasn't finished yet, that he had told this story every day for as long as he'd been coming to these meetings. "Now, Billy asked us to relate to you how our lives was better. I got cancer right now and the doctor says I ain't gone live another six month. I got the cancer in my limp nodes, in my rectal, and in the bone marrel. You'd think I'd have it in my liver, but the doctor says somehow I excaped that one. Anyway, I just want to say that my life is so much better now than it was when I was drinking twenty-four beer a day. Thanks for letting me share."

I thought, Your life is better *now*, with all those cancers? Give me a break. I thought, What zombies have overtaken this group? Man, I wanted a drink more than I'd ever wanted one in my life, even after Raylou said that she married me because if she ever ran out of ideas for face jugs she could always have me model for her.

The congregation got silent for a moment. Then Billy said, "I hope this helps you out, Harp. I'll pass around a phone list so you can call any of us up should you feel desperate and want to crawl inside a bottle again."

I said, "Okay."

The Will guy said, "Did I say 'three'? I been pronounced dead legally *four* times."

Billy said, "Okay. Bayward, you want to help hand out the chips?"

Bayward stood up from beside me. He walked to the front table, took five different-colored chips out, and offered explanations as to the first white one, the thirty-day, ninety-day, nine-month, and full-year chips. Bayward looked at me and said, "Is there anyone here who would like to admit that he or she had a problem with booze, and he wants to surrender right now today at this time."

I stood up and took the chip from him. Everyone clapped. Somebody yelled out, "It works if you work it," which I recognized as one of the mantras cross-stitched on Vince Vance's office door.

It wasn't anyone's anniversary for any of the other chips, so Bayward said, "Okay. One last time. Does anyone want to reconsider, and get you a white first-day chip." Billy got up and walked to the coffee urn. Bayward said, "Well, I guess I do. I kind of had a slip last night." He held his white chip up for the rest of us to see.

"It works if you work it!" everyone, except me, yelled out. Then they went into individual favorites: One Day at a Time, Keep Coming Back, and so on. I closed my eyes and thought about a documentary I watched one night about people speaking in tongues.

I met Bayward at a place called Shaky's, a coffee joint inside an old bank building. This wasn't one of those cool, modern coffee joints with a hip name. Shaky the owner got his name early on in life due to epileptic seizures and went on to a logical, rational career. The menu consisted of scrambled and over-hard fried eggs, regular American coffee, and hash browns. It didn't take a logician to understand that Shaky understood his limits.

Bayward was sitting at the counter when I arrived. I plopped down next to him and said, "What do you mean, you slipped last night? Please tell me that you picked up a white chip only because you collect the things for poker night."

"Hell, no. I wish. I got out of the meeting at Carolina Behavior, you know, and I don't know what happened. One minute I was driving back to Powdersville where I live, and the next thing you know I'm pulling into the parking lot of the Slabtown Bar

46

and Grill. Karaoke night got the best of me, I guess. I won the $25 prize, but I ain't proud of it. I sat down and knocked off about six gin and Cokes, then got up onstage to sing Johnny Cash's 'Jackson.' I even did the high-voiced June Carter parts all by myself. That's probably why people voted me the winner."

I looked at Shaky standing in front of the stove. He clapped two spatulas together and blinked hard and fast. "I just want some coffee," I said. Back to Bayward I said, "Man. I thought you were one of those people who wouldn't drink again, really. I just had this feeling about you. I'm not so much disappointed as surprised."

"It's a disease."

I didn't go into my own thoughts on the subject: that drinking too much booze too often got tabbed a disease so that insurance companies would get involved. In my mind, smoking cigarettes wasn't a disease, but people had a hard time quitting and it could *lead* to a disease. Banging your head on a brick wall wasn't a disease, but it wasn't good for your health if you kept it up. "Well, I won't tell on you tomorrow night when we see Vince Vance. It's up to you."

Shaky spilled half of my coffee onto the Formica. He refilled Bayward's cup and said, "No charge on refills up to a point."

"My boss man can't find out," Bayward said. "They won't let me back at work until I get a clean good-to-go."

I turned around to see if there was an insane person at a booth behind us, but it was only a woman saying, "I can do that. I can do that. I can do that," into her cell phone.

To Bayward I said, "That's a nice segue, that shit about your boss. Before I became an ice sculptor, I welded giant sculptures—you would probably say that they were modern art that didn't look like anything else, and I understand that—usually for parks inside big cities. Anyway, I'm supposed to be welding these

47

giant angels for Birmingham, and they're due there in a couple months. I was wondering if I could hire you on — pay you under the table, you know — to come run my other mig welder. I'll have drawings and whatnot, and I'll be there to tell you what goes on next."

Bayward leaned away from me and smiled. "I had a good feeling about you when you showed up in the smoking area last night, Harp. All right, buddy. I'm about to run out of money what with having to take a leave of absence, no paycheck." We shook hands, then Bayward reached into his pants pocket, pulled out a handful of nickels, and said, "I'll buy the coffee. You and me's going to be good for each other. I'll be a good influence on you, and you can be a good influence on me."

I gave him directions to my house and told him how I liked to start work at daybreak. As I drove off, he might've yelled out to me something about friends of his he wanted me to meet. I looked in the rearview, saw Bayward reach into his car, and shook my head. "That was just glare coming off his wristwatch," I said to myself. "That wasn't a bottle."

My wife's butt stuck out from the front of her wood-firing kiln. She extracted and stacked a good fifty new face jugs, wiped off stray ash with a rag, then stood up and backed away. I honked my bad horn and drove crazy into the yard, happy to be alive and ready to follow a new routine, namely to finish a project before I started another, and another, and another, and trying not to be overwhelmed to the point of drinking to forget. Out of all the cross-stitched dictums I had seen over the last forty-eight hours, the only one that made sense went something like "What's the Next Right Thing to Do?" Or it might've been "What's the Right Thing to Do Next?"

"Come look at this new batch and tell me what you think," Raylou said. She paddleboated her hand for me to join her.

Because, even though I had hardheaded myself into believing that I wouldn't touch another drop of bourbon—that I would prove to everybody that when my thirst got quenched then I no longer needed brain-and-liver–damaging stimulants in order to weld or ice-sculpt whatever came next—it still came natural for me to insist on my sobriety. "I went straight to the goddamn meeting, and then that Bayward fellow and I went out for some coffee. I'm going to hire him on, Raylou. As long as you don't think it's a bad idea. I'll do whatever you say. Hey, he didn't even make it a full day without booze. He went straight from the rehab-group therapy meeting to a bar. He likes to sing karaoke. Not me. I mean, not me, I didn't go have a drink last night, and not me, I don't sing karaoke."

My wife turned and looked at me. She said, "How much coffee did you drink? You don't have to make excuses, Harp. I know this might seem to be a lose-lose situation for you. I don't want you drinking, but I don't want you thinking that you have to talk about it all the time, either. I fucking hate those people." She picked up one face jug and pointed it my way. "Those people obsessed with their recovery are just like, well, *people*."

Most face jugs feature broken, half-missing, crooked teeth fashioned from shattered porcelain or china. Bug eyes, big ears, and long hooked noses are the genre of face jugs, normally. Sometimes the jugs have devil horns. You can always tell a really bad or neophyte folk artist—he'll make face jugs that either out-uglify anything beyond belief or vessels that look exactly like him. Raylou pointed her new creation my way and said, "What do you think?"

It was a really elongated jug with what appeared to be chevrons beneath the poked-out eyeballs. The flat forehead looked entirely different than anything Raylou'd done before—and I mean she must've thrown ten thousand jugs since we'd married. I said, "What's that thing between its eyes and the spout? It looks like a playing card."

"That's exactly what it is. I'm glad you could tell, Harp. This particular one's the one-eyed jack, but I also have queens, kings, and deuces. Do you get it?"

I didn't. And I tried hard, because I didn't want to disappoint Raylou for one, and I needed to prove that my brain still worked. "Is it supposed to be a football player? Like a gambling football player. Those marks below the eyes look like shoe polish to cut down glare."

I put one arm around my wife and took the jug with my left hand. Between us and the house, the snapping turtles sunned themselves. "I'm going to that big folk-art show up in Sylva this weekend, remember? Sylva's the next town to Cherokee. I figured I'd make some Native American face jugs. These boys here are supposed to look like they're playing Indian poker. Those are cards on their foreheads."

Even dead drunk and blacked out working on autopilot, I would've had enough sense to tell my wife that it wasn't a good or safe idea. I said, "Lord knows I don't have the right to question your abilities or motives or history"—I waved in front of my face at some lingering smoke from the kiln—"but it seems to me you might offend a chief or two up there with these things. It would be kind of like making a bunch of face jugs to look like Charlie Chan and taking them to Chinatown."

Raylou took back her jug and placed it on a row of kiln bricks lined up on the ground. By the look on her face, I couldn't tell if I hurt her feelings, or if she knew something that she didn't want to divulge. "In the old days I didn't want to take you along with me to one of these shows because I thought you'd get roaring drunk and embarrass me. You're really sober today, aren't you? Now I don't want to leave you alone because I might come back to find you dead. Or that if you go with me, you might start getting the shakes so bad you'll drop all my work."

I took my wife's hand and led her toward the house. "I need to go down to Frank and Joe's Nuts and Bolts to buy up some stock and put in an order for more. You want to go with me?"

Raylou looked back at her Native American face jugs. "I don't have anything else to take up there. I have to take these things. I'm betting they'll sell like crazy. Regular white people are going to be at the show, not just Cherokee Indians."

We walked inside. The message machine didn't blink, but it showed that we had one message. Raylou must've listened to it beforehand. I pointed at the telephone and said, "From what I understand, Jeep is changing the name of their bestseller to 'Jeep Native American,' what with all the political correctness. Hey, who called?"

Raylou kept holding my hand. She walked through the den, through what used to be a dining room, through what used to be a living room, and into our bedroom—which used to be either a mudroom attached to the house or some kind of abattoir where the previous generations of occupants slaughtered livestock and wild game.

My wife slid off her blue jeans and smiled. She said she didn't expect much out of me, that she figured I could blow a legal drunk with what my blood still held, but she wanted to at least be next to me on the bed. "Do you remember the last time we made love, Harp?"

I tried to think back. Surely I got it up once or twice over the past year, I thought. "Was it before or after I gave up real art in order to make ends meet with the ice?"

Raylou pulled off my shirt and stuck her nose to my mouth, which I thought odd. Maybe I had forgotten the rules of foreplay. She said, "Pre–Ice Age." Raylou pulled up her own work shirt and said, "I smell like smoke. At first I thought I smelled it on you, but it must be the kiln."

I should mention that I had almost quit smoking some decade earlier, had bought my cigarettes on the way down to the rehab clinic the night before only because I had read up on how people needed the nicotine while undergoing painful inward self-evaluations and humiliating public decrees. I had made a promise to Raylou years earlier in our marriage that I would quit smoking, and I had signed some kind of document for Ice-o-Thermal's insurance company, too, stating that I'd stopped and never planned to take up the habit again.

The old Harp Spillman might've said something like, "You *do* kind of stink, Raylou. Why don't you go take a long shower?" and then I would've brushed my teeth for ten minutes. But Vince Vance, somewhere along the line, insisted on honesty. I said, "I've been smoking since I quit drinking. And I'm a little worried I might take up gambling."

My wife stuck the pillow over her head, but I could still make out, "That settles it. You're going with me."

I said that I could get Bayward to feed the turtles, run the mig welder alone, and so on. Then I got up, re-dressed, went out to my Quonset hut, and stacked up what ice molds I needed to send back to Mr. Dupont. I could tell that he'd called in order to let me go while I was at my first meeting.

4

BAYWARD DROVE UP on a moped thirty minutes past dawn. I stood in front of the Quonset hut, stacking my nuts and bolts left over from the last project, which may or may not have been a disastrous experience involving the University of South Carolina and their mascot, a gamecock. I waved at Bayward and said, "Don't you have a regular car?"

I remembered talking to him in the parking lot at the rehab clinic, and how he kind of wandered off while I backed into Vince Vance's car. I thought about his reaching into a car and pulling a bottle the day before, there at Shaky's place. "It matters what you mean by 'have,' I guess. I ain't supposed to be driving one. Sometimes this buddy of mine lets me borrow his, but he needed it today. The state of South Carolina says I'm a menace on the roads, you know, so I usually let them have their way about it."

Bayward stepped on his kickstand there on top of our granite yard. He walked my way, looking left and right. "You ain't got no dogs left up here, do you?"

I shook my head. I dropped a handful of five-eighths compression nuts onto the ground in front of me. "We can't keep a dog up here for some reason. We got turtles. But every time we go get a dog from the Humane Society, it runs off like crazy. We always end up catching it somewhere down the road and having to take it back. Raylou says a dog's better off waiting for a nice home than being chained up here."

Bayward shook my hand. He still wore his Nuclear Welding shirt. "I know why." He scanned the top of Ember Glow again. "Dog don't like to live where he can't shit on soil. You just got this quaquaversal acreage ranging out everywhere. Dog don't like to squat on such a terrain."

I looked past Bayward and saw my wife pouring coffee in the kitchen. She didn't have on a shirt. "Say that all again?"

"That's why I said it. I bet you didn't think I'd know a word like 'quaquaversal.' Learned it in inpatient when they made us play Scrabble. We got to use dictionaries and all, seeing as the nurses said it took too long otherwise. One time I got stuck with the Q, and I looked up every word they was. I didn't get to use 'quaquaversal' seeing it's more than seven letters, you know. But I've always remembered it. And I made a vow to use it one day."

"Well, you got your wish," I said. Raylou waved at me and jiggled her boobs, then walked back to the bedroom. "Listen, come on into my shop, and I'll show you around. We'll go into the house in a few minutes and get some coffee."

Inside the Quonset hut I had my molds piled up ready to ship in the same crates in which they'd been delivered. Up to this point, except when I felt rushed and figured no one would mind a replica of Neptune or Snow White and the Seven Dwarfs, I kept them off in the corner. For the most part, they became hiding spots — a quart bottle of Old Crow could be slid perfectly into the hollow mouths of the donkeys and camels that I'd done for a giant manger scene. Bayward walked around touching everything until he got to my mig welder. He studied the coil of wire inside, the ON/OFF switch, the nozzle. He said, "Hotdamn, this is one fancy air pump. Does it seal tires automatically?"

Raylou came in with a clay serving platter, three mugs, a sugar bowl, and a creamer, all of which she'd fired herself. "I take it you're Bayward who Harp's been talking so much about." Understand that I hadn't said all that much about him, but Raylou liked to make people feel welcome and comfortable atop our hard granite abode. "Is Bayward a family name?"

Bayward said, "Nice to meet you, ma'am."

Raylou placed the platter down on the mig welder. She said, "Y'all help yourself. The floor in here stays cold even in the summer until about noon, Bayward. You might want to wear an extra pair of socks."

I wished that my wife had put on a brassiere. Bayward said, "It ain't a family name I know of. I always meant to ask my folks how they come up with it, but I never got around to it. I never met another Bayward, but I guess whoever used to own this shirt might've had that name." He pointed at his cigarette pocket. "When I was a kid they always called me Wayward, you know."

If I were drunk, I might've missed the implications. "Wait a minute. That's not your shirt?"

"It is now. I've had it about, oh, two, three year. Got it off the rack over at the Goodwill store. At the time I was looking for one oncet owned by a man named Tucker. The way they stitch those things onto the labels, the Ts look like Fs."

"Okay, then you *don't* work for Nuclear Welding. A couple nights ago you said that your boss wouldn't let you come back to work as a welder until you passed the rehab classes."

Raylou sat down on a stump I had chainsawed into a type of chair. At one point, right after we bought the place, I planned on setting stumps all over the yard so it looked like trees at least once stood here.

Bayward scooped about four tablespoons of sugar into his mug. "I never said anything about being a welder. It's true my boss man won't let me come to work. That's all I said to you there after your first meeting. I'm a roofer by trade. Boss man said he couldn't afford me falling off one more time."

I thought, *Twelve angels by November.* There was no way to get it done on time. Raylou said, "You ever have to do any spot welding on your job? Learning how to use a mig doesn't take a whole lot of brains."

This from a woman who made mud pies into goofy faces, I thought. "Well, I can still hire you to help me out with some of the nontechnical stuff. I need help down at Frank and Joe's Nuts and Bolts. You can cold-bend the rebar for the initial forms, I guess."

"I never said nothing about knowing how to weld. I think you said something about needing some help, and I said okay. It's just like what Dr. Vance says—I'll bring it up tonight so's he can say it again: 'You can't turn a pickle back into a cucumber.' What he means by that is, us drunks hear what we want to hear, and see things the way we want to see them, no matter what's the reality. At least that's how I interpret it all."

"That sounds about right to me," said Raylou. She got up and pulled a splinter from her back pocket. "I need to go do one more firing. I'm glad you got up here fine, Bayward. A lot of people can't seem to follow the directions."

Bayward said, "Dr. Vance also says we got to be honest from here on out, so I might as well tell the truth. I got lost, but your neighbor down there told me where to turn."

I'm not proud to say that Raylou and I didn't know our one

56

neighbor. The closest house, down at the bottom of Ember Glow, was a shingle-sided leaner with a yard full of dogs, bicycle frames, tillers, lawn mowers, and barbecue grills assembled from fifty-five-gallon drums. Whoever lived down there kept a sign in his yard that read OPEN WHEN NOT FLOODED. I always had a feeling that the guy blamed me for Ember Glow's runoff during downpours. Past this guy—and halfway to Pickens—stood a sad trio of singlewide trailers that would make a perfect set for any movie that involved characters who didn't give a damn but didn't know any better.

Raylou took her coffee and walked to her kiln and adjacent shed. I said to Bayward, "The guy who says he fixes things?"

"Name's Mr. Poole. I asked him where you lived—he was out there in his yard with a flashlight, looking for something. He said, 'You talking about the crazy guy? When you see him, tell him to build a wind-wall or something to stop all the howling at night.' Then he told me I could take any rock-slab path that appeared to go up. That's when I started to think about my old word. Goddamn, I can't even remember it now."

I said, "Quaquaversal."

"Well. I feel bad about you misunderstanding what I could and could not do, Harp. Let me make it up to you. Is there a red dot store anywhere around here?"

Frank and Joe split up some two years earlier. That's how long I'd been out of the loop in regards to giant commissioned welded sculptures. When I still bought my art supplies from the brothers, they forever wanted to come up Ember Glow and see what I was welding up. Frank took great care in weighing my truck when I drove in and after I loaded up. Joe didn't seem to care and always asked me what I thought I owed him.

"Frank and I had some disagreements as to how to run the business. Me, I believe like our daddy did, that giving customers a break brought them back for more. Anyway, if you want bolts, you need to go over to his place down on Old Old Dacusville Road halfway between Hogback and Pumpkintown. I understand he ain't doing too good. If you see him, tell him I said ha-ha-ha."

I said, "This is Bayward," and turned my thumb toward my new worthless employee. "Don't let his shirt fool you any."

"Anyway, it's Joe's Nuts and Frank's Bolts. In the end, we plain old divided up our business half and half. You can get your nuts here, but you have to get your bolts there. Oh, there might be another nuts-and-bolts operation somewhere within the tri-state area, but don't quote me on that."

Joe stood six-two and weighed in at about 110. He sported those sinewy-type arms that appeared to be more veins than muscles. I thought to myself, Tristate area? What was the tristate area — the Carolinas and Georgia, the Carolinas and Tennessee, the Carolinas and Virginia? I said, "You've been watching the Weather Channel."

Bayward wandered off and picked up scrap pieces of metal from the hard red clay that served as both parking lot and loading dock. I opened the back of my refrigeration truck and, for the first time, understood that I might should go ahead and turn it back into a regular pickup, that I more than likely wouldn't be hauling ice sculptures around to any ballroom venues soon.

Joe said, "You finally going to make that big windmill you used to talk about? You finally saying to hell with Duke Power not being able to keep your lights on up Ember Glow when the wind blows?"

I didn't say, "When did I ever say that I was going to make a windmill?" because I knew that I probably harped on it at one time. "No, sir. I got this big old commission to make a slew of sculptures, and I'm going to have to dust off the welder. Bayward here," I looked over at Bayward and said, "I'm not offering you any workmen's comp, buddy. Drop that piece of rust. Bayward here was going to help me construct the things, 'cause I thought he was a welder."

Bayward walked back over. He said, "I never said anything about being a welder. Tell Joe the whole story." To Joe he said, "We met at Carolina Behavior 'cause we both drank like crazy and couldn't stop."

I made a point to remember to bring up to Vince Vance the importance of anonymity later that night. That is, I made a point to tell on Bayward.

Joe looked at me. "Yeah, word is you can't handle the booze. Or that you handle way more than what normal people think's proper. You still got that good-looking wife?"

Bayward said, "Hotdamn, yeah."

I motioned for Joe to find his hand trucks and start moving some new shiny nuts my way. I walked into the crumbling-down redbrick building and said, "Make it a mixed bag, I don't care," and pointed to his boxes of five-eighths, halves, three-eighths, and so on. Joe loaded box after box, and Bayward and I lugged one at a time.

I bought a half-ton to start, and asked Joe to order at least that much every week until I told him to stop. He said, "What's the word on the street about ball bearings? I was thinking about diversifying a little. I don't want to go into bolts again, seeing as Frank might lose his balance and kill me. Last family reunion

Labor Day, I know for a fact he kept trying to hit me in the head with a horseshoe. So I ain't going to test him no more. But Joe's Nuts and Ball Bearings has a ring to it, don't you think?"

I handed Joe five twenties. "What's it cost altogether, eighty bucks? Keep the rest for a tip. Please don't let me down ordering more. I'll see you." I looked at my watch, which didn't have a calendar on it. "Next week this time, if everything goes as planned. I'll call otherwise. It might be a day before or later."

"I got some steel dowels six, eight, twelve inch around if you could use them," Joe said. He looked at Bayward and said, "You say she's still hot?"

"Hotdamn, yeah."

"You want, Harp, I can deliver the next load myself."

On the drive back up to Ember Glow, I answered Bayward. I said, "No, there's not a liquor store within twenty or thirty miles. A good drunk like you should know that. Back in the day, I sometimes drove all the way to Columbia to load up. It was worth the gas money."

Bayward grabbed my wrist and looked at the time. "Boss man always gave us a coffee break about this time. Don't forget we got group therapy tonight." He said, "Say, do you think you could get me a little advance? I been working now, what, three hours? I guess we never officially set down exactly what my salary would be."

I honked the horn and laughed. I swerved away from a dog, then a dead opossum. "I pay twenty bucks an hour for qualified and licensed welders. And experienced. For everyone else, it's called gofering, and that pays about a quarter more than minimum wage."

Bayward stared forward. He said, "Dr. Vance says it takes six months for a good alcoholic to really start thinking straight. You pay me what you think's fair now, and then in six months I'll see if you'll consider giving me a bonus."

I said, "I would say that that sounds fair, but I'm not six months in. So I'm not thinking straight."

Bayward rolled down his window. He spit twice. He said he didn't like this dry way of life. I didn't mention how I'd been sober, officially, longer.

When we got to Mr. Poole's house, I rolled down my window and waved at him standing there in his fouled habitat. I yelled out, "Hey! I might be down later to look over some of your lawn mowers," like a fool. He knew that I owned no lawn whatsoever.

Mr. Poole stood there shirtless. He pointed at a roll of silt fencing first, then some gutters he had stacked up between a plastic Bi-Lo bull with a bullet hole in its neck, and two orange-and-white roadwork barrels.

Bayward said, "He looks like the kind of man could turn on you fast. I bet he either drinks hard, too, or goes to one them new churches where the preacher only named himself a preacher."

I put the truck in low gear, careful not to spill and dent my hardware.

My father quit drinking the year I celebrated my bar mitzvah. We weren't Jewish, but my mother and father thought that it was time for me to be a man, et cetera, and there weren't such traditions in our Scottish/Irish heritage. I slaughtered Hebrew in front of friends and strangers alike, there in a Moose Club hall in Augusta, Georgia. We lived on the other side of the Savannah River outside the unincorporated town of Murphy Village, a place known to Americans only because a bunch of the national news organizations uncovered what most of our neighbors did for a living—namely, scam people throughout the Southeast who needed their driveways sealed, roofs fixed, houses painted. My parents and I lived smack in the middle of the Irish Travelers nation—the non–Irish Travelers in this part of South Carolina called them "gypsies"—and we watched in awe as they lived in trailers parked behind giant under-construction houses that would be painted in pastels later, Virgin Mary statues scattered all over the lot. These paradoxically devout and chronically lawbreaking Catholics wouldn't move into their new 5,000-square-foot houses until their priest blessed the place. They homeschooled their children long before it became an American pastime. Their daughters got prearranged-married before puberty, to men three times their age.

Me, I learned all of this later in art school in Florida when I had to take a handful of electives at a nearby liberal-arts college, which were supposed to make me a better artist. This particular class concerning the Irish Travelers took place in a Sociology 101 course taught by a Marxist-feminist man named Dr. Shulty who became obsessed with the Amish in Lancaster County, the Mennonites of Ohio, a group of Baba lovers down on the coast of my home state, survivalists in Idaho, Melungeons of eastern Tennessee, and some Sufis camped out somewhere in the Ozarks. I doubt Dr. Shulty really toted the "Marxist-feminist" luggage, but he understood that if he wanted to keep his job, he better label himself as such—something not done, obviously, among the Amish, Mennonites, survivalists, and so on. When Dr. Shulty questioned me about my accent, I told the truth about my place of upbringing. I'm not sure, but I think he opened up his grade book and placed a red A next to my name immediately—or at least right after I promised to infiltrate the Irish Travelers over the summer and return with a tape recording of their conversations, which I never did, knowing that if I got caught I would end up rolled inside tar paper and thrown into the Savannah.

Anyway, I underwent my odd rite of passage, and the next thing I knew my father packed up his bags and moved to New Orleans with a woman named Gorman who'd escaped her clan of Travelers somehow, left her husband and children, and promised that she would do all in her power to let the world know what went on in Murphy Village. His leaving came down to my discovery, one day, of a Kleenex in the toilet bowl, with a round red mark on it. My mother came home from work — she taught seventh-grade civics — and said she would quit if the Irish Travelers ever infiltrated the schools, seeing that she had "a hard enough time getting fucking kids to understand that Washington, D.C., and Washington state weren't the same place," her words — and I said, "I think some woman's been in our house." I took Mom to the toilet and showed her what I discerned rightly as a woman's blotted lipstick staining the Kleenex and floating in our unflushed commode.

When Dad came home, she brought this up and showed him the evidence. For a good two weeks, my father said, "I got hemorrhoids, goddamn it. That's from me wiping my ass. Leave me alone."

I believed him. As a matter of fact, I went around with a Lysol-soaked rag and scrubbed down any chair that he sat in earlier, because I couldn't stand the thought of sitting on top of bloodstains. For a while there it smelled like all of us mopped the floors with our butts.

My mother never said, "So you sit down on the toilet, wipe your ass, and never flush?"

As it ended up, we pieced together later, this Gorman woman snuck out of her house and/or work — this was spring, when Irish

Traveler menfolk take off, change their license plates and identities, and head off to trick Midwesterners — and met my father at his job. My father, of all things, worked for the South Carolina Department of Agriculture, and spent most of his days traveling around a three-county area "maintaining the state's primary standards" — his words — for peaches, pecans, and eggs. Everything got graded and labeled through my father. When Mom came home and said something about how important grades were to students hopeful of getting into college later, my father said something like "Well, they wouldn't even live long enough for college if I graded their breakfast eggs wrong and killed them off."

My parents had no other children after me. It might've been, as they say, serendipitous.

So my father claimed hemorrhoids for two weeks, and then, finally, that Gorman woman came visiting again and left her lipstick blot floating in the toilet. I came home at three fifteen and saw it. My mother came home at four o'clock and saw it. My father returned "from the field" whistling a James Brown tune, and Mom asked if he'd come home to eat lunch. He said he didn't. To me she asked if *I* had hemorrhoids, or if I played some kind of transvestite dress-up in my spare time.

My father said, "Tell the truth, Harp," and winked at me. "See if you can look me in the face without your eyes cutting up to the ceiling. It's okay. Not every boy in Edgefield County has what it takes to grow up and be an ag inspector. You got a sissy talent for drawing, but that's all right, son."

Lookit: I figured this out later. Before I started drinking, I had this nervous affliction wherein I kept my face pointed at an inquisitor, but slanted my eyes up the entire time I talked. I've seen other people do it. Somehow that particular habit and/or

64

defense mechanism retreated at the same time I started hitting the bottle, about age thirteen.

And lookit some more: I didn't play football because there weren't twenty-one other boys in the area available to field two teams. There might've been nine other kids for basketball, but one of the Irish Traveler kids would be watching from somewhere, and eventually run over and steal the ball. So I learned to draw. I watched this guy on ETV with funny hair, and I self-taught myself how to shade, and the importance of negative space. It didn't seem like such a "sissy" hobby to me. It's not like I sat around in my room alone at night, jotting down poems.

I said, "I'll tell the truth. I got sick at school today. Mom and Nurse Loretta didn't believe me. So I skipped second period and came home. But I didn't come in because I saw Dad here. I saw him leave the house, and he wasn't alone."

I lied. I figured I could go ahead and solve what became known as "the mystery of my father's hygienic habits."

My dad held up one hand to hit me across the face, but Mom stood in front of me. She said, "It's not like no one knew about all this, you son of a bitch. I've known all along." To me she said, "Go on to your room, Harp. Draw your mother a picture of a dead mule." I still have no idea why she chose a mule — I'd drawn horses before, and goats, but never a mule. I went to my room, not crying but hurt about what my father said. I heard Mom say, "I guess you felt a need to inspect something a little bigger than eggs or peaches, is that it? Well, good luck with that. And if I ever, ever hear you say something derogatory about Harp again, I'll hire out some of that Gorman woman's kin, and I'll pay them good money to kill you dead three times."

And that was that. My father left for New Orleans, I supposed, that night. He sent me a letter about a year later and said that what he'd done was wrong, but that he'd since learned that it was the booze making him do it—that he was genetically inclined toward alcoholism, et cetera—but now he lived with a clear head and recognized the harm he'd done. My father wrote, "I'm in a program now where I have to make amends to everybody I've hurt. I'm to ask forgiveness. So I hope you forgive me, Harp. And I hope you understand why I did what I did. It wasn't you or your mother. It was my addiction that made me do it. By the way, there are a bunch of men who dress like women down here. Some of them are in my meetings."

Over some time I would hear more people talk like this— blame everything on their so-called disease and, in a more-or-less passive-aggressive way, say that they understood if everyone couldn't comprehend the situation or forgive the drunk who'd finally dumbed himself down to a non-free-willed, powerless, nonhuman zombie.

I never saw or heard from my father again. My mother exchanged all of her S&H Green Stamps for a fancy frame, and mounted what I finally finished drawing on the night that I became the official man of the house: a dead mule, toppled over in a pecan orchard, with a man and woman drinking moonshine from Mason jars, seated atop the poor animal. When Raylou and I drove to the outskirts of Murphy Village a few days after our impromptu and secretive marriage, my new wife asked about the drawing. My mother said, "I don't want to speak for Harp, but early on he understood symbolism. I think the mule stands for a stubbornness only found in the South. The pecan trees stand for how it's nuts. The man and woman stand for everyone in the history of the world except for Adam and Eve. But I may be wrong."

I took Raylou by the hand and said, "Okay. Time to go. I'm sorry we didn't have a big public shindig, Mom, but I figured

66

that you'd agree that it's best to save the money. Just wanted to let you know that I'm trying to show some responsibility. We need to get to a travel agent's place and make some decisions about a honeymoon."

My new wife looked Mom straight in the face, smiled, and said, "Don't believe him, Ms. Spillman. Responsible men don't marry women who stand too close to raging fires more often than not."

I think Raylou made a reference toward her kiln. My mother interpreted the comment as having to do with mistresses.

I didn't hear from her again.

"My parents were twice-a-week Baptists who didn't drink at all," Bayward said as I parked the truck. "That thing about it being genetic, well — if my parents were inclined to be drunks, they sure held it back."

I got out of the truck and said, "Or hid it. I'm not so sure I believe that genetic thing, even though my parents and grandparents on both sides, from what I understand, drank like all get-out." I didn't know why we brought the subject up. Had I been thinking aloud while driving up Ember Glow? Was I doing more than daydreaming about my upbringing near the Irish Travelers?

Bayward said, "You got the hand trucks around here?"

I walked over to Raylou's kiln and shed. She sat on one of my old stump chairs, surrounded by her Native American face jugs. "You might be right," he said. "But it's too late to go back now." Bayward said, "Good morning, ma'am. I'm Bayward," as if he hadn't met Raylou before. I realized right there that wasn't a good sign.

"They look cool," I said. "But I don't know." I picked up a beautifully ugly jug with turquoise stains running below the eyes. I knew enough about her techniques to know that she'd shoved glass—probably old little Coke bottle shards—into the clay before firing it. I said, "Trail of Tears, this one."

Bayward looked around his feet. "I seen some of these before one time when we put on a bunch of roofs the other side of the Chattooga. Whole families over there made these things. They say they worth a lot of money. I don't want to hurt no one's feelings, but I don't get it."

My wife laughed. She stood up, kissed my cheek, and said, "Sometimes I don't get it, either. Maybe face jugs will one day run out of their popularity. Hell, the clay and plates I use to make one doesn't add up to fifty cents, probably. Even the firing wouldn't cost me anything if we could ever grow trees on this weird land."

I walked behind Raylou's shed and rolled a homemade dolly back with me. Bayward said, "I just don't understand why people would pay—what do you get for yours, like a hundred dollars?— that much money for a jug, when you can go down to Big Lots and buy a whole case of twelve new Mason jars with lids for $16.59. I know. In my spare time, I do a little canning."

Raylou had heard it before. She turned and shook her head.

I said to Bayward, "What do you can? You don't can. In all my life of knowing roofers—and I've known some roofers down when I lived amongst the Irish Travelers—none of them canned anything outside of moonshine." I looked at Bayward, then said, "Oh."

He grabbed the handle of the dolly from me and pushed it out from beneath the overhang. On his way to the truck I looked at my wife and said, "I got me a good helper."

Raylou turned her head and spoke in a whisper. "Do you think you can trust him to take care of the turtles? If he can take care of the turtles, maybe you could go with me up to Sylva this weekend."

I looked at Bayward. He unloaded the boxes of nuts and loaded them on the dolly. "I feel pretty sure he can be trusted. He's a little bit nutty, though no more than I am. But you know I can't go with you, seeing as I have rehab on Friday night, then again on Sunday afternoon. I know you don't believe me when I say this, but I've been thinking nonstop, and I'm committed to stopping. Stopping the booze, not the rehab."

Raylou pointed at Bayward. He overloaded the dolly and couldn't move it. Raylou said, "I know you're serious this time, Harp."

She didn't tell me that Vince Vance had called to let her in on how she could read my body language. She also chose not to mention—I found out later—that I wouldn't be attending any more rehab-clinic group-therapy sessions after that night.

5

WHAT EVERYONE seemed to know, except for me, was that my employer, Mr. Fulton Dupont of Ice-o-Thermal, got pressured by the Republican National Committee and had no other choice but to let me go. They said that they wouldn't press charges against his company if and only if I got fired and if I never got a good letter of recommendation from him. Evidently that guy named Karl actually sent letters, faxes, e-mails, and made phone calls himself. From what I learned much later, this Karl guy made it clear that he could make an IRS investigator hang out at the Dupont household more often than the maid. He said that the government would rather have a guy like Harp Spillman on the unemployment line than gainfully employed. I'm sure there were other threats, and that somehow the government had other information on Mr. Dupont. Luckily I learned the full details months into my sobriety, or I would have, if I know me, acted out irrationally, et cetera. I would've suspended my entire Birmingham angel project for one of Karl and his superiors welded entirely out of nuts, except where nuts counted.

I got to Carolina Behavior before anyone else and walked into Vince Vance's office. I said, "I suppose you've already talked to Raylou about how I did over the last forty-eight hours. I did great. I didn't drink. I went to one of those smoke-and-doughnut meetings and thoroughly hated it, pretty much. I'm not going to lie to you and say that some kind of Higher Power came down on a sunbeam and struck me silly upside the head. What's with everyone repeating everyone else's name? That's weird. It made me feel like I was at the annual awards presentation for the Special Olympics." I crossed and recrossed my legs. I reached over to his candy dish and pulled out a Walnetto and a Chic-O-Stick. "Then I hired on Bayward to work as my welder for this new project I got that'll have me so busy I won't even have time to think about drinking, but as it ends up your boy Bayward only wears a shirt from some welding outfit. If he ever comes in here wearing a doctor's smock with a stethoscope around his neck, don't think that you can hire him on to do preliminary physicals over at the hospital wing of Carolina Behavior. Hey, I've been wondering. What exactly goes on inside over there, you know, with the inpatient people?"

Vince Vance stared at me intently until I realized that I was speaking like a maniac. He leaned over and said, "I take it Raylou didn't tell you about the phone call I received yesterday."

I thought back. I remembered seeing the answering machine lit up but never listening to it. I said, "Not that I know of."

"We got a call from your insurance company and they said you'd been fired. And because of that, they won't be paying for any more of your sessions."

I placed my two pieces of candy back in the bowl. "I've been fired from Ice-o-Thermal? How come they didn't tell me? Shouldn't my boss tell me I'm fired, and that I don't have insurance?"

Vince Vance nodded, smiled, then shook his head sideways.

"You're kind of scary, Harp. Maybe your boss is afraid that you'll snap and take it out on him."

Scary? I thought. I'm not scary. Outside of the old burn marks on my arms from welding, I figured I looked about like everyone else, even though I didn't have an abnormally large forehead sloped down like Cro-Magnon man. They should've seen me when I always talked to people while looking at the sky, I thought, then rolled up my sleeves and said, "Did you say 'scary' or 'scarry'? I'm scarry, but it's not as bad as it used to be. I put aloe on my arms for about a year."

I can admit now that I felt as though my sixth-grade teacher had told me I needed to be left back another year, as though a driving instructor had told me I couldn't come back until I learned how to parallel-park, as though my wife had said she needed to leave me for a man with at least a three-inch pecker.

Vince Vance said, "I don't know what you're like completely sober. But I imagine even running on pure blood you might intimidate some people. It's not your size so much as it's your eyes. Charles fucking Manson would quiver in your presence, Harp. And that actor who talks funny."

This from a man who didn't blink, I thought. I said, "I don't know what I'm like completely sober, either," and for a microsecond felt as though I might cry. Was this part of the program? In some kind of bombardment-therapy treatment did booze therapists across the country belittle their patients?

"All is not lost. If you really want to quit drinking through this program, you can pay out of your own pocket. It'll cost you a bunch of money. You might want to go up to the front desk and check into exactly what the price would be for twenty-nine more sessions. And I want you to be in tonight's group, so we can explain to everyone else what happened. It's not good for the group's

morale when someone drops out." Maybe I made a scary face—
I don't know—but Vince Vance added, "If you don't mind. I
don't want to pressure you. Whatever you think's best."

I sat there trying to think of an actor who talked funny, and
figured out that it was a "psychological ploy" to divert my attention somewhat. From behind me I heard the door beeper go off
twice. Bayward came into Vince Vance's office and said, "Hey,
Harp. Hey, Dr. Vance." We looked up at him. "Y'all are supposed
to say 'Hey, Bayward!' like that, you know."

I said, "Man, I just found out that I got fired from doing ice
sculptures."

"Because of what you did on the TV to all those old dead
guys?"

Vince Vance said, "Let this be a lesson to us all. If we do
or say something, and then keep saying to ourselves 'That was
funny' or 'That was the right thing to do' or 'Goddamn, can't
anyone see how I'm right about this?' all the time, then we
should be prepared to eat a shit sandwich before long."

I didn't want to leave the group, above all else, because I
liked a booze therapist who would say "shit sandwich," I realized. Bayward said, "Fuckin' A. Does this mean I get fired, too?"

I didn't pay much attention during my final official group-
therapy session. Everyone seemed genuinely sad about the
demise of my job and insurance. Vince Vance said it wasn't impossible, though he'd been taught to never admit it, to quit drinking without the help of therapists, spiritual organizations, and a
readily available and eager Higher Power, amen. I began daydreaming about another non-art class I took outside of my college,
a Religion Department course in the New Testament I accidentally undertook that was listed right below Natural Unbelievable
Wonders—some kind of history/anthro/biology team-taught class

73

that would, as a needful artist, acquaint me with everything from Stonehenge to hermaphrodites. I'd been in New Testament a week past drop/add day before I recognized my mistake. Hell, there were plenty of natural unbelievable wonders going on up to that point, what with virgin births, guys who came back from the dead, magic tricks involving bread, people who thought myrrh was a nice gift, lepers, magic tricks involving fish, that guy who got his head cut off, magic tricks involving water and wine. Understand that my mother wouldn't allow me to attend church in my early days for two reasons: because my father did, and because the Irish Travelers did.

Anyway, I sat in class three times a week and listened. Dr. Hannah must've been meta-emeritus — he was that old — but to me, at the age of nineteen, anyone over thirty seemed ready to move into a grave plot. I kind of got the feeling that my professor actually knew some of these characters he spoke about as if they were old playmates. There were no tests or papers. The guy genuinely only wanted us to grasp and embrace a book that, obviously, kept him living. For the final exam, he handed out one page. At the top of the paper he wrote, "Did Jesus Say These Things? — Mark True or False."

Then he pretty much went straight down the fifth chapter of Matthew: "Blessed are the poor in spirit," et cetera; "Blessed are they that mourn," et cetera; "Blessed are they which do hunger and thirst after righteousness," et cetera; "Blessed are they which are persecuted for righteousness' sake," and so on.

I wrote "False" beside each dictum and handed in my paper first. Dr. Hannah looked over his half rims, then down to my paper. He followed me outside into the hallway and said, "Son, is this some kind of joke?"

I said, "I thought it was a trick. I went to every class and I listened. I even took notes."

"Why would I trick you? I want to give everyone an A. 'Judge not, that ye be not judged. For with what judgment ye judge, ye shall be judged,' you know. I learned a long time ago not to cast aspersions."

I said, "I still think it's a trick."

"Do you not remember that Jesus said everything that I typed out on your exam?"

I shook my head. I said, "Not in English. He didn't say all those things in *English*."

Dr. Hannah closed the door to the classroom, put his hand on my shoulder, lifted a leg, and farted one of those old-men made-up-sounding farts. He said, "Well, there *was* no English back then, Harp. Of course He didn't offer up all those beautiful parables and blanket statements and such in English. But He could've said it in English if He wanted." Then he laughed, patted my head a few times, and walked to the stairwell carrying my exam. For all I know he never even took up the rest of my classmates' papers. I indeed received an A that semester for my elective course. I made a B in sculpture, and a No Credit in ceramics — but that's because I stared at Raylou's hands on the wheel more often than I paid attention to what whirled around on my own wheelhead bat.

I sat there in the group-therapy room thinking about whatever happened to Dr. Hannah when Vince Vance said, "Okay. So, after the break, I want to hear from Tammy, and then we're going to talk about the stages of change."

I walked out with Bayward. He said, "You okay, Cuz? You seem kind of out of it. As a matter of fact, you kind of look drunk, if I didn't know better."

I lit a cigarette and coughed three times hard before gasping. A middle-aged man who wasn't at my first meeting said, "The only thing I can figure out is, when my buddies came over maybe some of the cocaine flew into the air and went up my nose. There ain't no way my drug test should've come back positive."

I said to Bayward, "I've always been a little hardheaded, and I've told myself that I can quit drinking all by myself. I'm not one of those people who thinks he's powerless. I can close my mouth and refuse to swallow. I can keep my arms from bending, you know. If I should ever go into a town big enough to support a bar, I'm sure my legs won't involuntarily take me inside. But now that I'm out of the program, unless I want to pay for it myself, it's making me wonder."

Tammy came up to the man with flying coke and said, "You better come up with a better excuse than that. Vince Vance isn't going to buy it. None of us are, either. You can't bullshit bullshitters. We're a bunch of lying con artists who've spent our whole lives thinking up better excuses than that."

Bayward said, "Uh-huh," to her, and to me said, "Listen. I got this idea." He took my tricep and led me out from beneath the gazebo. "I'll bring in a little tape recorder and tape what went on in the meetings. Then I'll come by each day to work with you, and we can play the thing. So it'd be kind of like getting the therapy that you need, you know."

"That's not a bad idea. It would be against the law, seeing as there's a sign in the room saying no cameras, or cell phones that take pictures, or taping devices. I tell you what, you can come work for me and just tell me what went on."

Bayward nodded quickly. He said, "I'll do my best. It'll give me a reason to take better notes. And I won't have to hit you up for money to buy me a tape recorder."

The guy who'd missed his previous meeting went on and on about how the drug test wasn't a hundred percent accurate, that he'd read an article about how some crazy lab techs have been known to manipulate results just out of plain meanness, and so on. As Bayward and I walked back to the portable, the Tammy woman yelled out, "I used to be a palm reader. I used to be a seer. You can't keep telling your lies. I can see right through you."

When I walked back inside Vince Vance jerked his head for me to follow him into the second meeting room. "I can't tell you how bad I feel about all this. I wish we could find a way to allow everyone in, like they do in Canada and Holland. You're a smart man, I know, but let me reiterate one more time what it says in all the literature, Harp: You need to stop thinking so much."

I said, "That's what got our president elected, and what will probably get him reelected, too many people deciding that *thinking's* a bad thing."

"I'm serious, man. The more you think, the more you're going to think that it'll be okay to have just one beer. Then you're probably going to have some kind of setback or pitfall — or maybe even success and a pink cloud. Then it won't take long before you'll be pouring bourbon in your morning coffee, and acting out in ways that, eventually, will either get you thrown in jail or punched in the nose."

I knew that he was right, outside of the thinking part. I said, "Well. I'm not sure what to do. What I think right now is, I'm going to white-knuckle it for as long as I can. If it doesn't work out, I'll recheck myself back in and pay for it myself."

"That sounds like the only kind of plan there is left," Vince Vance said. "Keep it in mind that if you're like the rest of us, you'll either want to drink when you're having a great day or a bad day. There's no in-between, besides maybe a coma — even with a coma, though, you'll be drug dependent. There's no winning this fight, I guess, unless you have professional help. If they paid me more money here, I could trade out my knowledge for a sculpture, but that isn't a possibility right now."

I looked at the empty blackboard. "I'm going to drive into Greenville and buy up some books. Certainly there are books out there." I thought, of course: Make a point not to have good or bad days. Become a zombie.

"And you can always go to noon meetings at the Alcohell Club for free." He laughed. "I've already heard about what you thought about those things." Then he stood up and said, "Let's go listen to Tammy. She's going to tell a story you're not going to believe."

Back in group therapy, Vince asked Tammy to tell her story, seeing as some of the newer people hadn't heard how she got to where she was. Tammy started off by saying, "I'm an alcoholic for a number of reasons. I started drinking gin when I was about twelve in order to fight off the cold. You see, my father had this golf-ball–cleaning business, and he would get my brother and me to dive into all the golf-course lakes because, I'm pretty sure, he was so afraid of snapping turtles."

She went on and on. Bayward leaned over and whispered to me, "I'll bring over some of the Elbow Brethren. I'm not ready to go as far as they have, seeing as I still plan to hammer a nail every once in a while, but what you said out there about keeping your mouth shut and not bending your arm — that's how they feel, too."

I put my finger up to my lips for Bayward to shut up. Tammy said something about putting a hex on her father that actually might have worked, and how it made her so guilty she drank even more. I thought about Dr. Hannah's exam again: "Ye are the salt of the earth: but if the salt have lost its savor, wherewith shall it be salted?"

As a child, my wife killed her brother Sammy unknowingly. The story—as far as I could ever make out, though she only told me once while we sat on a bench during college—involved a little brother who wet the bed, and a time when Raylou's mother made my wife-to-be poke the kid with a stick in order to keep him awake. Maybe Raylou made it up, I don't know. It was such a grim story that I never brought it up again. Sometimes I had been involved with women who made things up, I figured, just to see how I would react. Well, maybe not women. Woman. One girl, in about seventh grade, who told me a story about her cat and a car engine.

I recalled sitting there with Raylou, both of us scared of art school, then reaching inside my coat pocket to pull out a flask. I offered it to her, but she shook her head and told me to feel free to partake.

I said, "I thought I had a fucked-up childhood. Outside of almost getting kidnapped by Irish Travelers one time because my father ran off with one of their women and some kind of payback needed to take place, my childhood was normal. My mother framed some things that I drew and put them up on the wall."

Raylou said, "True story. I think about Sammy every day. I should've untied him, and let him run away, or something."

I said, "Where was your dad all this time? Were your parents already divorced?"

Raylou shook her head. She turned to me and said, "Drunk. He didn't even know what was going on. He told the social workers that he thought my mother was playing Cowboys and Indians with us."

I kissed her, and prematurely told her that I loved her. We began walking south, carrying our duffel bags, picking up off the sidewalk and sand whatever we thought we could use later.

Now, much like Raylou, I felt haunted by her tragic upbringing almost daily. I mean, I thought about it *all the time*, and wondered what it would be like to have a brother-in-law come visit us down on Ember Glow, whether he peed in the guest bed or not. And as I drove home from Carolina Behavior, I thought about how it might be comforting to come home after being kicked out of group-therapy booze rehab, call him up, and ask for his advice.

Raylou met me at the door and handed me some hot chocolate. She said, "I didn't follow you down there, but I thought about it, I'll admit. I'm sure you know that I know that you know that I know." She set the mug down — a face mug she'd fashioned with her own hands, a sad-faced guy with crazy teeth and a cigar stub sticking out of his lips. It looked like it might've come from the Red Skelton Collection, or any of those other old-time clowns before clowns got frightening.

Raylou hugged me like never before, like — I imagined — how she hugged a stuffed animal after the death of her only brother. I said, "You know that I'm not one of those guys who thinks that bad things happen for the best, but I'm feeling positive that all of this has happened for the best. Out of plain meanness, I'm not going to drink, just to prove it can be done without a 'Kumbaya' sound track playing around me. Without a ghost choir chanting the Lord's Prayer twenty-four hours a day."

Raylou eased up but held on. She said, "I went down to the store while you were gone. I got Mallo Cups, Hershey's Kisses, more YooHoo, and every kind of Little Debbie cake. I also stopped by and got the smallest bottle of brandy Mr. Francis had to offer, in case you want it. You wouldn't be disappointing me."

I kissed my wife on the forehead and leaned back. I said, "I don't want to get maudlin or anything, but I'd like to take care of you for a while. You've been the designated driver and CPR expert for long enough. I want you to drink the brandy. I'll eat some of those oatmeal pies. Come on."

I opened the door and led Raylou out to two chairs on the edge of our new turtle pond. She said, "If that's what you want. I know you're going to hate my saying this, Harp, but you're being kind of romantic, and awfully thoughtful. Are you sure about this? I want to be honest with you—I kind of wanted a glass of brandy before you even returned; as a matter of fact, I kind of got scared that you'd just drive off into the sunset somewhere."

This, of course, broke my tiny hardened heart. I started to say how this was a new Harp Spillman, that I would be my wife's keeper and perhaps turn really effeminate and redecorate our house. Right away I knew that my best defense when confronted with life-changing situations occurred in the arena of humor, of self-deprecation, of the absurd. But I couldn't talk. Instead I hung my head down halfway to my lap and cried, cried, cried.

6

BECAUSE I NEVER got the shakes like everyone else, Raylou let me help load up her step van. She had built the shelves inside, bolted right into the metal and poking out on the exterior. From a distance it looked like Raylou's van had warts, or herpes. Any vicious, jealous face-jug competitor could, if he or she wanted, take some channel locks and unbolt the shelves from outside, thus causing any jugs inside to topple over. According to my wife, the face-jug world didn't think like that.

"Even though I think these things are politically incorrect, I really like them," I said, placing two at a time up, divided by chunks of foam rubber, then strapped in with bungee cords.

Raylou wiped off her wares with an old kitchen rag, then handed them to me. She wore a red and white checked shirt, tied up at her midriff. She looked like one of those women from *Hee-Haw*, or any hillbilly siren in the eyes of a Hollywood director. "If I asked for wampum, then it would be politically incorrect. If someone came over and asked a price, and I offered a peace pipe first, then it would be politically incorrect."

Half of the jugs held the same visage as the Cleveland Indians mascot, if that same face were seen through a hotel room's fish-eye. "You could've put a one-armed-bandit thing on the sides of these heads. Like up at the Cherokee casinos."

We loaded up sleeping bags, pillows, a battery-operated TV, my old Coleman cookstove, two suitcases, a cash box filled mostly with tens and fifties, and an armful of books for me: *The Small Book, Drinking: A Love Story* by Caroline Knapp, *The Thirsty Muse* by some guy who said artists weren't great because of their addictions but in spite of them. Raylou had ordered the books long before I decided to quit, evidently, and kept them boxed up and waiting for me. More than a few of them were self-published, with titles like *Either Me or the Globe Must Quit Spinning,* and *The Bottle's Full Because I'm Not,* and *Drinking and Deriving: Notes from a Cerebral Stock-Car Driver,* et cetera.

We waited for Bayward to show up. He'd agreed to look after the place for three days. I would let him use my truck if and only if he didn't drink and drive. Joe from Joe's Nuts had called to say that he'd gotten a giant shipment of what I needed, and Bayward was to load and unload my needed art supplies, stack them neatly in the Quonset hut, fetch rebar from down at a building-supply company in Greenville, cold-bend what he could in ways that I had drawn out on graph paper, and so on. He was to enter our house—Raylou tried to talk me into moving our refrigerator out to the Quonset hut, but I felt like Bayward's knowing our slight mistrust would only send him out to liquor stores—grab chicken necks out of the freezer, and throw them into the turtle pond daily.

When my wife and I returned from Sylva, and when I had a good seven days of sobriety stored up, I would shove on my welder's mask and set to work on what Birmingham needed in November. Bayward would help me until he got the go-ahead to roof again. And he would offer up Cliff's Notes versions of group-therapy sessions every Tuesday, Thursday, and Saturday morning.

We heard the moped long before he entered our compound. Bayward honked his tinny wheezing horn, I supposed, at Mr. Poole down at the base of Ember Glow, then weaved his way up our driveway. He set down his kickstand and took off his helmet—a cyclist's helmet with the numeral 3 painted, in black, on both sides. "Shew. I was afraid I was late. I'm glad y'all didn't leave without me 'cause I thought up a couple questions about taking care of the place."

I said, "Hey, Bayward."

Raylou said, "Hey, Bay. Thanks for helping us out here."

"Do I have to force-feed the snappers? I don't mind doing it, if you could show me to the steel-reinforced gloves. That's my first question. My second question is, Do y'all mind if I bring a couple old boys up here with me? We won't mess with anything, I swear. I got these couple buddies—I've mentioned them to you, Harp, and you'll meet them eventually. They ain't got much to do most of the day. And they ain't on the sauce anymore, if that's what you're thinking. As a matter of fact, they've gone as far ways possible to never be able to drink again, outside of sewing their mouths shut completely after taking a bellyful of Antabuse."

Raylou sat down on the back end of her step van. "We don't have any money hidden inside the house. You'll be responsible for anyone you bring up here, Bayward. Y'all can sleep inside if you want, or build a fire in the kiln and sleep outdoors. I don't care. Just don't let people touch the clay."

"I'll keep an eye on them hard," Bayward said. "Yes, ma'am. I will admit that these fellows do have a tendency to bump into things accidentally. But I'll watch them close."

I said, "Okay. I think we're ready to head out."

I handed Bayward directions to everything possible, written out by my wife. She said, "The cell-phone number's on there if you need to call. And we'll be staying at a campground called the Great Smoky KOA. I don't know if there's a phone there. If there is, I'll call from my cell phone and give it to you."

I didn't say anything about how it wouldn't matter if they had a phone or not, et cetera. Bayward said, "If all else fails, I'll send some smoke signals." Then he stumbled a little bit on the hard earth and knocked over his own moped. He held one palm to the side of his head and yelled, "Hey, don't drink any firewater while you're gone."

I never judged Raylou for never wanting to hang out with other artists, especially ones who participated in small towns' arts-and-crafts fairs. Back when I was still half sober, meaning where I could maybe stay away from the booze for at least a twenty-four-hour period of time, I went with her probably once a month between March and October, to six-block hamlets scattered, usually, on the edge of the Blue Ridge or Appalachian Mountains—places like Pound, Virginia, or Helen, Georgia. My wife forever sold enough goofball face jugs to put us up in the finest motels the areas had to offer, but she always found a campground where most of the other artisans stayed, and she did her best to act interested when they brought over horrendous watercolors to show off in front of a campfire.

"If I stayed in a fancy hotel, word would spread, and the next thing you know I'd have a booth filled with broken jugs. And I wouldn't mind talking to people at the campsites if they could think up a conversation that veered into something other than the high price of table rent, or how no one understood their work, you know," Raylou told me back then, before she quit inviting me. I think the last time she offered up her explanation was in Mars Hill, North Carolina, right before I got in a fistfight with a man who insisted that he carved some nice fishing lures himself, but I knew for a fact that they were factory-made and manufactured by the Harry Comstock Company out of New York. I never did recapture exact memories of what happened right there beneath a platoon of tiki lanterns in a mountainside campground so steep that goats couldn't pitch a tent there, but I think I said something about how he could brag about his craftsmanship about as much as God could brag about His work directly after molding the fellow's brain.

"I don't know if you remember a few things I used to tell you," Raylou said as I turned left into the campground. Below the sign welcoming RVs was another one welcoming gamblers. An arrow pointed toward Harrah's Casino, with 1 MILE! printed inside it. When I say "arrow," I mean like "arrowhead on the end of a stick."

I said, "I'm so worried about letting Bayward inside my studio I doubt I'll think of much else."

"You know you'll be better off not mentioning how you are a sculptor, or that you went to a real art school. I wouldn't even mention that you did ice sculpting, seeing as someone's going to want to challenge you. If it's at all possible, don't say anything to anyone about his or her work, good or bad. Good only gets you hounded to buy some, and bad causes hurt feelings and fights, and then the probability that my work will get damaged somehow."

I said, "Look at that totem pole! What's that thing on the top? It looks like a video-poker machine." We pulled into a space in front of the Tuckaseegee River. A woman hung dream catchers on a makeshift clothesline two sites down. Past her I saw a shirtless man seated atop a chain-saw-carved creature that might've been a bear or Buddha.

Raylou said, "Did you see a Welcome Center anywhere around here? Usually you have to pay at some kind of little guardhouse."

Somewhere off in the distance a person screamed out, "Those goddamn things are rigged. Deuces wild without any deuces? I don't think so. I know I'm supposed to feel guilty about what the white man did to the Indians, but I just paid off my restitution, goddamn it."

"It's ten dollars a night," a young man said from above us. I looked up to see what could've been either a half-built tree house or an economy-style deer stand. The man jumped down. He appeared to be Native American, but perhaps it was his getup: fringed hide jacket, moccasins, a leather loincloth. "If you need anything, just honk your horn. I like to stay up in these things." He pointed around to show off a good six or eight structures in the trees. "I'm finishing up a Ph.D. in economics at Stanford. My dissertation involves both trickle-down theory and migratory-bird depletion. It's February. The birds never left, per my hypothesis."

I thought, I can get along with this dude. I thought, *Don't ask him about his outfit; don't say anything wrong.*

Raylou said, "We're here for the art fair over in Sylva. We'll have to take the van back and forth for a couple days, so should we put an orange cone or something here to mark our space?"

A hummingbird flew right up to my nose. I said, "Stanford's mascot used to be an Indian. Now they're called the Cardinal. Do cardinals migrate?"

Raylou yelled out, "It's a miracle! He was a deaf-mute until this very moment."

The economics-studying Native American campground-monitor guy held out his palm. "What are you people talking about? I hope you're not trying to make fun of me and my people somehow. I'm only doing this because it's the family business. My dad died, my mom took off, and my uncle needed some help. I figured that I could still finish up my dissertation and see what's going on with the casino."

I opened up the back of the step van, pulled out a face jug, and handed it to him. "No. No, no. Listen. My name's Harp. This is Raylou. I want to give you this. Raylou, put it on my tab. I'm good for it."

"I'm William."

Raylou pulled out an ice chest and set it down on a small cement patio. "You should've brought your fly rod. When's the last time you went fishing, Harp?"

"I'm no economist," I said to William. "Hell, I can barely figure out a checkbook. But let me guess: You're saying—because the casino brings an economic boon to the area—people are at these campgrounds. If they're at the campgrounds, then there's food around all the time. Birds that normally head farther south in winter stick around. Birds that go north in the summer stick around."

William turned the face jug around a few times and smiled, then placed it on the picnic-table seat. "That's pretty much it. I also look into how people don't buy birdseed or sunflower seeds anymore, at least in about a four-county area, because birds don't frequent their feeders as much. It goes on and on. In the end it won't be good for the birds because they'll still freeze in winter."

Raylou said, "I need to drive into Sylva and check out my booth. I can set up what the tables and shelves will hold and lock it up until the morning."

I said to William, of course, "So you'll finish up your dissertation. Then what'll you do?"

Raylou handed William thirty dollars. When William took
the money and went to sit down, she said, "Don't sit on my face
jug." He placed the jug on the tabletop.

He said, "I tell you what animal has rebounded from the
casinos. Black bear. Say, you might want to put that ice chest on
a rope." He pointed to a high limb, above his lookout. "Bears
come out at night like picnic ants." He stared at us about five seconds too long, then meandered off to collect someone else's
campground fee.

I wanted a drink. I got in the step van, rummaged around
Raylou's bag, got the cell phone, and called Bayward. He answered on the first ring—which meant he'd lounged around
four hours—"Wayward Bayward's Turtle Paradise."

I said, "Give me one of those little bumper-sticker sayings
from AA. I can't think of one."

"'If you don't think, you won't drink. If you don't sweat, you
won't stink.' I kind of made that last part up."

I said, "That's it. I'm not supposed to think. Hey, is everything okay down there?"

Bayward said, "Who is this?"

We set up Raylou's booth in downtown Sylva, went back to
Cherokee, ate supper at a place with tomahawk-adorned walls,
and returned to our campsite. No bears showed up, I assumed,
for a couple of reasons. First off, all of the casino people kept
Coleman lanterns lit throughout the night. The artists and crafts-
people moseyed from one site to another, swapping stories, lying
about how much money they made at the last festival, making
bets with one another, and sharing speed-trap locations all up

and down the back roads of the eastern seaboard. Secondly, I shook so much inside the step van, it sounded like I was a palsy victim trapped inside a diving bell.

At about midnight Raylou said, "Do you want to go? Are you shaking from no liquor, or are you cold?" She lit a candle and sat on a canvas-seated foldout stool. What face jugs still stood in rows stared down at us in a way as if we huddled inside a wig shop for the damned.

I threw my blanket off, reached over for my down vest, put it on, and stood up to look out the front windshield. At first I thought a bear looked in, but it was only William the Stanford economist, with his hands to both sides of his face, spying in. I yelled out, "Hey!" like anyone does when there's an unwanted voyeur hanging around the premises.

William rapped lightly on the glass and said, "I have something for you, man," without raising his voice. He pointed for me to come outside, which of course I did seeing as, at that particular moment, a good knock upside the head might stop my shaking.

Raylou said, "Be careful. Economists can be sneaky."

I stepped out and William said, "I know this may sound crazy, but I come from a long line of what the Cherokee call *didanawisgi*. I come from medicine people. Long before I got forced to undergo public education I learned to look into a man's face and see what he suffered from. You, my friend, are in need of this." He handed me a foot-long bundle of roots the circumference of a pickle jar. It appeared to be tied up with raffia. "Kudzu root. Trust me. Just chew on it until you feel better."

I shrugged. I pulled out one stem and stuck it in my mouth like a stalk of childhood sweetgrass. "What's that Cherokee word you said earlier? Something about *whiskey*?"

When I woke up seated upright in the passenger seat some six hours later, I made a point to ask Bayward to ask Vince Vance about delirium-tremens visions and hallucinations, about notions of supply and demand, or theories of unintended consequences.

Raylou had gotten dressed in what she wore best, namely a giant T-shirt with a simple print on front that cost something like three hundred bucks, made by some company called Blue Fish. She sat in the driver's seat. "I was going to make coffee for us, but there was already a pot on the campfire over there. Did you bring that old splatterware percolator?"

I turned my head and focused outside. I looked past the bundle of kudzu vines, then picked a piece of viny sinew from my teeth. "Don't drink that coffee," I said. "There's no telling what the psychopathic economist used for grounds." To my wife I said, "There's no possible way you could've gotten in touch with this William guy over the past few years, the way you did with Vince Vance. Was this all a setup so I'd come up here with you and undergo some kind of tribal cure? No way!"

I took off my vest, for I felt overly warm even though it wasn't forty degrees outside on this crisp late-winter morning. Raylou laughed and laughed. She said, "Did you have some bad dreams last night?"

I shook the kudzu in her face. "Well, where did this come from, huh? I don't think I dreamed it straight into life."

Raylou shrugged. "I'm having a problem following you, Harp. Listen, are you going to go with me into Sylva? We need to get going pronto."

I shook the kudzu roots. "I *caught* you on this one, Ray. I caught you at one of your little cause-and-effect strategies."

She turned the ignition. "Don't you remember? We walked around looking at other people's booths last night, and that woman who wove baskets out of vines handed them to me? She said they were left over, and she handed them to everyone who came by saying it made good tea and whatnot. I set the bundle outside before we went to sleep because I figured even a bear wouldn't cross a line of kudzu shit."

I stared at my wife a good thirty seconds. "I knew that. I remember that," I said. I tried to see if her eyes rattled back and forth in mid-lie. Again, I still felt ashamed of my faulty memory. I said, "Huh. Well. I'll be damned." Deep down, though, I figured that Raylou made all this up. I tried not to look confused.

"Run over to the bathhouse and wash your face off. Give yourself a whore's bath. Brush your teeth. Then get right back here. We can get you some coffee in town."

I slipped on my shoes and grabbed a towel and shaving kit. I thought, This is how all interventions start—with people making you think you're crazy. I thought, Somehow Vince Vance and Bayward and William the Cherokee economist/ornithologist are going to be huddled inside a stall with a straitjacket.

I only feigned going to the public restrooms. I circled around, found a regular family of unlucky gamblers, and offered them five bucks for the river water they boiled on their fire. The father said, "Five bucks is a hundred plays on the nickel machine. You can come buy our water anytime. Say, you wouldn't be interested in some genuine, honest-to-goodness mountain honey, would you?" The man reached over and uncovered a bucket. "We ain't got no jars. You'd have to bring your own jar, or jug." His son came out of the tent, his face swollen worse than mine ever got on a two-year binge. "Little Judge got it hisself. We're saving up for some those beekeeper uniforms so he don't get stung as hard."

I said, "Oh, I got a jug. I got a set of jugs that'll break you out in night sweats," and went back to buy another of my wife's wares.

I'll be the first to admit that there's not much worse than an artist working in public. It's not a spectator sport. Over the years I had gone to one of those Wal-Mart–like bookstores only once, because every supposed customer in there sat in the coffee shop — or right out in the middle of the racks between Self-Help and New Age — writing a memoir, or the Great American Novel, or, worse, poetry. What good would working in public do for these people? The only thing it made me think was that they were so poor, they couldn't afford their own desks back at home.

Now, these arts-and-crafts festivals seem to invite people who can only be watched. I left Raylou at her booth there on Jackson Street — which as far as I could tell was one of only two streets in town, running parallel — oriented myself, and decided to check out what these people tried to sell. I passed by a woman who sketched charcoal portraits while her subjects sat there on a bearskin-covered chair. I saw a man who tumbled his own gemstones, drilled tiny holes in the middle, then strung them into necklaces. About another hundred men and women exhibited horrific watercolor scenes that could've been the Oconoluftee and Tuckaseegee rivers, or they could've been Rorschach tests from bygone years.

There were other potters displaying pinch pots they'd raku-fired, and a couple oil artists who showed off their paintings of deer and wolves, bobcats and beavers. A group of mentally handicapped adults from a nearby vocational center yelled at passersby to come check out their wind chimes, dream catchers,

93

and string art. I thought to myself, What does Raylou think, paying good money to rent tables at these fairs?

"You look like the kind of man who could use some change in your life," a man said to me in about the same low growl as any child molester offering candy. I turned around from looking at what I think might have been a Play-Doh bust of General Custer with an arrow in his eye socket, and was confronted with a wall full of stuffed jackalopes and their odd cousins: otters, barn owls, woodchucks, tabby cats, a poodle, and rattlesnakes, all adorned with antlers. This guy even had a smoked ham, for some reason, mounted on a piece of inch-thick stained pine, deer antlers stemming from what used to be a hock. He said, "What's that you're chewing on?"

I didn't even remember sticking a kudzu root in my mouth. To look like a rube in the middle of an arts-and-crafts festival in the middle of western North Carolina took some work, but I'd managed, evidently. I said, "Are those real antlers? How can you do that?"

He looked a lot like Bayward, only more grizzled. "I don't kill no deer. That's against my ways. Buck sheds his antlers come after rutting. November. December. I got me some favorite trees out in the woods where I know. Well, I guess they's the buckses favorite trees first, where they go scrape. Then they mine."

I thought, of course, I need a drink, I need a drink, I need a drink, I need a drink. "Is *that* right?" I said. "How about that!"

"I get my antlers, then I attach them on what's around. Used to be I'd stick them on, say, these rattlers, and then the weight would knock off my snake head. So I got smart. I glued the antlers onto the wood, then I glue the top of the snake head onto the base of the antlers. That's how them work."

94

I said, "I've seen jackalope before," and pointed to the rabbits. "That's pretty interesting, those other animals. Are they still considered jackalopes?"

I clamped down on the kudzu root. I felt my liver cry out for help. "Beavalope. Chuckalope. You know." He turned and pointed at the poodle. "Wifealope, seeing as it was her dog when she took off with my old business partner."

I looked down at the last two booths down Jackson Street. An albino woman sold moccasins at one, and a man showed off his stained-glass-from-a-kit windows, plus some colorful crack pipes. I meant to say, "Well, I better get back to my wife. She's down there selling face jugs." Somehow it came out, "I need a drink, I need a drink, I need a drink, I need a drink."

"That's why I'm here. The famed jackalope wards off both evil and bill collectors. You put one up in your bedroom, and it'll only bring peace and serenity. You get you some peace and serenity, you won't crave no more."

"Peace and serenity from a mythical beast. It must go to AA meetings or something."

"Go ahead and scoff, scoffer. I can tell on your face you could use you one. Or two. One for your house, and one for your workspace. One for your liver if that's why you chewing kudzu."

Hell, it couldn't hurt, I figured—and it's this kind of irrational thinking that drunks will continue to percolate, Vince Vance told me through Bayward much later. I said, "How much?"

"The beavalope brings you uncommon power in the world of convincing people. The owlalope is the hardest to say, and that's why it's known to bring the owner great powers of communication."

"I want the rabbit with the antlers," I said. "I got to get back."

"Fifty dollars. Two for ninety-nine."

I pulled out the money and didn't say anything about how he needed to offer better deals on larger quantities. "What do you call the antlers on that salt-cured ham? Is that salt-cured, or smoked?" I held my new fake good-luck trophy in the crook of my arm. I looked down at the back of the pine to see "Jackalope/ trapped by Rembrandt Rash/January 1, 2004."

"You stuffed this thing on New Year's Day?"

"I caught it on New Year's Day. Got one I just sold, caught on Valentine's Day a year ago. It's red."

"Okay. Listen, there wouldn't happen to be a launching pad nearby, would there? I need to catch a rocket back to planet Earth."

Rembrandt Rash said, "Salt-cured. I'll call it 'lunch' in about four hour."

I liked his answer. I bought the antlered owl for Bayward. When I gave Mr. Rash a fifty-dollar bill, he said, "Should've bought both them at the same time. Would've saved you."

I couldn't have been away from Raylou more than ninety minutes. I wove back to her booth, armed with my jackalope and owl, all the while looking for an open bar on Jackson Street. I could even envision myself seated upon a red vinyl stool, my new antlered friends on either side of me. I would order a Pabst Blue Ribbon and a shot of bourbon. Or a PBR and a shot of vodka. Hell, I'd drink one of those fruity umbrella-garnished drinks if that's all the place offered up.

But there were no bars. I stopped at the bookstore and poked my head inside. I said, "I'm not crazy. Just because I'm carrying these things, I'm not crazy. Listen, is there a bar anywhere nearby?"

A woman behind the counter, holding a copy of *Don Quixote*, of all books, shook her head and smiled. "We finally got a microbrewery, but it's not open this early, I don't think. And as you know, unless you're just visiting, the surrounding area's dry." I guess I made a visible what-the-fuck-kind-of-place-stays-dry-nowadays-outside-of-Mormon-territory? face. She said, "You're just visiting. Kind of like Don Quixote." She held out the book.

I said, "I read that a long time ago. I think it took. Maybe I should read it again, though." I walked in, placed a twenty on the counter, and said, "Keep the change. Put the change in some kind of fund to attract more bars to the area," like an idiot, then I shoved and balanced the paperback between the rabbit's antlers and continued down the street.

Raylou sat on the back edge of the step van. I smiled at her and placed my trophies down, unwedged the book, and looked around. Her booth was empty. She said, "I can tell that you're going to have a weirdo story for me." She stood up and kissed me, and I easily heard the long nasal breath she took, in search of booze. "But I get to go first. I'm sold out, Harp. We can go back home. I sold every face jug." She reached in her pocket and pulled out enough hundred-dollar bills to wallpaper a walk-in closet or an outhouse.

You know that I only saw this as some kind of trick, as part of Raylou's as-yet-undiscovered overall plan, that she somehow got that fake economics warrior to come pick up everything and either hide the jugs or mail them back to Ember Glow. "Every one of them," I said. "While I was right down there," I pointed not an eighth of a mile down Jackson Street, "and pretty much noticed that hardly anyone even attended this half-ass arts-and-crafts festival, much less buy anything for sale, some wild pack of folk art–loving clay collectors swooped right down to your booth and

97

bought you out. You know, they say that drunks have a hard time with reality, and sometimes they convince themselves into believing big old self-contrived stories. Maybe it's *you* that's got a drinking problem."

Let me say here that I wore a funny face when I said all of this, and rolled my eyes and neck around a bunch. It wasn't like the old fights I invented and waged so readily.

Raylou closed the back of the van and walked toward the passenger side. She said, "Yeah, I'd rather spend a lot of time and money pretending to sell my work than actually sell it. Look. I know you have a hard time accepting the fact that what I do isn't 'high art,' Mr. Ice Sculptor, but I have a name of my own out there. If you'd ever pay attention and listen to my stories..." She went on and on. I caught the keys when she threw them my way, and got in the other side.

"How much money is that?"

"And it's not like a pack of people came down. I wish they had, and maybe I could've jacked up some prices. One guy bought everything, and handed me six thousand in cash. I didn't even know him, but he said he'd been following my work on the Internet, or something." I backed out and drove out of Sylva, back toward the campground. "Said he needed to take up a hobby, according to his therapist. Said his therapist kept face jugs in the office, so this guy wants to one-up him."

I said, "Did you give him your card? I hope you gave him your card."

"Where are you going, Harp? Home's that way." Raylou slid her door wide open and pointed past a mountain, toward Asheville, in the direction of I-40.

"Didn't we leave something at the campground?" I looked at

the near-empty back. Our clothes and sleeping bags and ice chest stood neatly in the corner. My jackalope and owlalope slid around. "I thought we left a bunch of stuff, seeing as we'd be going back."

My wife said, "Nah. Say, it's been five days since you've had a drink. You think the big boy can come up yet?" Raylou kind of leaned my way and put her left hand on my upper thigh.

I veered late on an exit ramp in order to cross back over the highway and turn around. I said, "Shoney's Big Boy? You want a hamburger? I didn't notice one when we drove here yesterday. Is this the same road?" This is how long I'd been drunk, blacked out, and unphysical with my wife.

Raylou laughed and shook her head. She leaned back, slid the door shut, and turned the radio dial to a local mountain evangelist. The preacher kept screaming about salvation — what else? — and then the station faded into some woman on Wall Street explaining how important it was to have health insurance, but that — for the price of a passport, airline ticket, and course in Spanish 101 at the community college — Americans could receive above-average care at a number of Central American clinics.

I said, "That dude from Stanford bought all the face jugs, didn't he?"

Raylou said, "William said that he could sell them for twice as much at a local apple stand on the side of the road as long as he could convince people from up north that Raylou was a traditional Cherokee name. He said all the money came to him last week because one-eighth Cherokees get annual checks from the bingo parlors and casinos."

I honked the horn and stepped on the gas. "Ha ha ha," I said.

"My brain's coming back! You can't trick an old trickster, Ray-lou, especially when his head starts to clear."

I think she mumbled something about how lucky she felt. She said something about how she's so lucky, maybe we should turn around and try out some video poker. I shook my head and drove forward, for we needed to get home, and I called her "Pancho" until she told me to shut up.

7

BECAUSE I UNDERSTOOD that my entire new nondrinking existence had become a series of planned and barely concealed tricks invented by my wife, it didn't bother or surprise me to find three men standing like coatracks between the snapping-turtle pond and Quonset hut when we came home early from Raylou's arts-and-crafts festival. The men held their arms locked at the elbow, pointing, I supposed, *quaquaversally*—my new word. One guy looked like he just called a base runner safe at home plate. Another might've posed for a yoga documentary, doing the Warrior. The third man held both arms in front of his chest, shoulder-high, the classic sleepwalker look. I slowed down the step van, but didn't act surprised to Raylou next to me. The umpire-looking fellow seemed more purple than black, and he would've stood out even if he were a half shade below burnt sienna, seeing as few African Americans, and, more than likely, *no* Africans, ventured onto Ember Glow, which might've been the variety I had missed most and which caused me to drink myself over the years straight into rehab. It's a theory to consider, I thought.

Bayward's moped leaned on its kickstand, next to an El Camino, right in the center of our so-called yard. Bayward came out from behind Raylou's outdoor studio, zipping his fly. He walked through his apparent buddies and waved at us. "You home early, you home early!" he yelled. The three other guys smiled and waved, their arms still locked. Bayward walked past his moped, smiling. "Shock absorbers ain't having to put up such a fight as when you left. I take it you sold out or something."

Without moving her lips, Raylou said to me, "Who are these freaks?"

I shrugged and turned off the ignition. To the left I saw two snappers slide off rocks that weren't in their pond the day before. To the right I noticed my boxes of nuts, stacked perfectly, ready to be welded into giant metal angels. I got out.

Bayward said, "Harp, I want you to meet a few of my friends. A few of *your* friends. I've kind of mentioned them to you before, but I don't know if you were really listening." I could smell gin seeping from his pores. If you're ever feeling nauseated and you're unable to throw up, lock a good gin drunk in a small room overnight, then go in and take a few deep breaths.

All three men said, "Hey. Keep coming back. It works if you work it," which seemed to crack them up. I'd heard those words once before, but couldn't place it at the time.

Raylou said, "Everything work out all right?" to Bayward.

He said, "I got up on your roof and patched a place where the vent had popped up too much. A good wind and rainstorm would have your ceiling damp. These guys were just about to do something, as soon as they could figure out what they could do here without causing damage, you know."

I said, of course, "What the hell do y'all do? And what's with the arms?"

Raylou said, "I need to go check the messages. Y'all make yourselves at home," which wasn't like her, normally. Back when

I had a slew of drunk friends, acquaintances, and complete strangers coming over, Raylou found ways to make them feel unwelcome. I'm pretty sure she ground up some Antabuse one time and stirred it into my pot of chili one Super Bowl Sunday, because everyone spent the day in the emergency room.

Bayward said, "Last night at rehab, Vince Vance said that the one thing I could do for you is what I'm doing right now. Oh, we spent some time talking about you, Harp. Probably way too much for some people's tastes. Any insurance-company rep would think so. Anyway, Vince Vance said he'd only run across one other guy in the past like you. Well, he either said 'one' or 'one thousand.' I tend to drift off, you know, but I believe he called you hardheaded. Unable to believe in a Higher Power. You know—*you*. Vince Vance said he hates to admit it, but you might be one of those rare people who can quit drinking without spending half of every day in a meeting with a bunch of ex-drunks talking about liquor all the time. But he still thinks you need sponsors. So I brought out the Elbow Brethren here to make your acquaintance. You get to pick one. They've all agreed, and no one's feelings will get hurt. It'll be like a beauty contest, only without any crying or foot stamping."

I thought, *Hallucinations—the hallucinations have set in.*

I walked to my studio and ran my hand on the boxes stacked outside the door. I invited Bayward and his friends inside to sit down because I didn't want these folks inside my house. They introduced themselves as Vollis, Brinson, and Kumi.

Vollis said, "I'm Vollis. I'm forty-five years old and I've been sober for about six years now. I quit counting. In the old days I worked in banking, but then I was unemployed for five years because I kept going to so many AA meetings, I couldn't keep a steady job. It was kind of hard to get up in the middle of a loan application in order to, you know, eat doughnuts, drink coffee, and smoke a pack of cigarettes. Anyway, for the last year, I've been working for Cone and Barrel Manufacturing, kind of in an advisory capacity. And I'm an on-call bus driver for the South Carolina Secretary of Education's School of the Arts and History. The S.C.S.E.S.A.H. Most of the day I sit around in the parking lot, waiting for one of the teachers to tell me where to go. The museum. Library downtown. Some kind of bad poetry reading at about a thousand coffeehouses and bookstores. The only time I'm not on the bus is when the director of the school wants me to leave so he can 'inspect the seats,' which means he wants to sit in back with the HR woman and this VP for finances so they can drink martinis and make out. Okay. That's it for me. So I'm able to talk on the phone most of the day if you're feeling like a bottle. I have a telephone at home, and a cell phone. You can call me at any time, day or night."

I looked toward the house. I tried out some ESP to call Raylou out here to check out what was going on. I said, "I got some ginger ale in the refrigerator over there. Who wants a good ginger ale? It's Blenheim's, the hot kind." I got up and got a bottle for myself. The stiff-armed men shook their heads. Bayward said, "You got any YooHoo?" I told him to go inside for that, and he did.

Brinson said, "I guess I'm next." He said, "I'm Brinson Delay. I haven't had a drink in about four years, but I wanted to drink hard up until when Vollis and Kumi and I went down to Costa Rica. Anyway, I think I might be the right guy for the job here. In the old days I was a regular public high school English teacher. And I advised the school newspaper. Nowadays I have about sixty industrial Maxi-Vacs that I need to go check on, you

104

know. You've seen them at convenience stores and car washes. Those are mine. That's my business now. I got a cell phone, too."

Vollis didn't start laughing when he said, "We either call him Brinson Sucks or Delay Sucks all the time. Get it? Because he owns a bunch of those vacuum cylinders. Get it? He don't mind. You don't mind that we say Brinson Sucks, do you Brinson Sucks? Brinson Sucks or Delay Sucks, he'll answer to both."

Brinson Delay said, "It's my job. I'm just glad that I'm not bitter about wasting my life drinking it away."

"Brinson Sucks is bitter that he never made it nationwide as an industrial-vacuum owner," Vollis said. Me, I wondered how I could get these people off my property.

Kumi held his arms up above his head as if to perform a high dive. "I'm Kumi!" he yelled out. "It means 'forceful' in my native Ghana! I came to America in order to catch the education! But instead of go to college, I drank! Kumi means 'forceful'! I am Taurus! You will not drink again with me!"

Let me make it clear that Kumi seemed like a caricature to me, right off. He yelled out his words not unlike this actor I'd seen one time years earlier, wherein the actor played an African king or prince, and came to the United States to look for either a wife, or friend, or food, or stylish clothes. My mind wasn't much better than Bayward's when it came to concentrating.

I interrupted Kumi by saying, "I knew you were from Africa. I told Raylou, I said, 'That guy there isn't from around here.'"

Bayward walked back in my studio and said, "I ain't ready to fuse my elbows, but I still like them. I admire their drive—you know what I mean?"

I coughed hard ten or twelve times from the ginger ale. "What? What about fuse?"

Vollis said, "We didn't get to that yet. What we did, Harp, was this: We didn't like AA. We didn't like therapists. We didn't like any kind of recovery groups whatsoever. Kumi and I met one time when I drove the South Carolina Secretary of Education's School for the Arts and History students to one of those poetry readings. He'd just gotten off the stage, and I recognized him from one of the meetings back in the old days."

"I write poems about my home!" Kumi said. "I write about the leopard that comes into the village!" He brought his arms down to his sides, and I noticed two-inch-long scars between his bicep and forearm.

Brinson Delay said, "And I met both these guys when Vollis came to clean up his own school bus—you'd think the state of South Carolina could afford to buy their own vacuum cleaner—at one of my locations."

"Kumi was along for the ride, picking up experience for a new poem," Bayward said. He came back from the house and had a brown crescent across his upper lip. "And Vollis needed to clean up the bus by more than sucking it out. Tell him, Vollis. Tell Harp how you get paid by keeping a log of how many cones and barrels you destroy 'by accident' in the middle of the night. When an asphalt company orders more, Vollis gets a percentage."

"I could use a helper," he said to me. "That's my other job I was talking about, with Cone and Barrel Manufacturing. I could use a good step van, for that matter. My Toyota's pretty beat up, and sooner or later I'll get caught for using the school bus."

I said, "I see," though I didn't whatsoever.

Delay nodded. I made a mental note not to think of him as "Brinson," seeing as there was already a Bayward in my life. Too many Bs. And that would remind me of "bourbon." Evidently unable to follow a story line correctly, Delay said, "We couldn't get a doctor in America to do what we wanted. At least, not a qualified doctor. So we started looking into Mexico and further south. There were plenty of doctors—"

"*Surgeons*, Delay Sucks. They were surgeons," Vollis said.

"There were plenty of surgeons who would operate on us. We wanted to make sure we didn't drink again. None of us thought of ourselves as powerless, like they always say..."

"I can close my mouth! My leg muscles do not direct me into the liquor store automatically!" Kumi screamed.

Delay Sucks said, "Anyway. We needed a backup plan. So we got metal rods inserted in our arms so we couldn't raise a glass or bottle to our lips."

Well, automatically I thought about how they could use straws. I thought about how they could hold each other's cups and bottles and pour good guzzles. They could pour booze in a pan and lean down. Certainly they drank water, right? How did they drink water? Kumi said, "I hear what you think—but we will not use those crazy straws. We will not drink from a pan, like a dog."

Vollis said, "We thought about getting it done to our legs, too—kind of like in defiance of the fucking worthless twelve-step program. But we didn't want to scare people by walking around like Frankenstein's monster."

I looked for my wife. I looked around the horizon for cameras. This was too much. I would've pinched myself, but it might've looked like I was showing off.

Delay reached down and touched my mig welder. He said, "We don't like to think of ourselves as in recovery. And we don't like to think of ourselves as recovered. We use the term 'upholstered.' We haven't recovered, but we've been reupholstered. 'Up' is such a more positive word, and from what Bayward told us, you, too, didn't cotton to all the negative talk and war stories of the traditional meetings."

I thought, Do they also eat facedown in a plate? Do they wipe each others' butts? I supposed that all of them could drive as long as the car seat was pushed back way past all the way, but it still couldn't be comfortable or adequately safe. "Why didn't y'all just devise some kind of elbow chastity belt and hide the key?"

Bayward's three men looked at me, then each other. They hung their heads. I think it was Kumi who said, "We must save up our monies again to see Dr. Sanchez of San José!" He jumped into the back of the El Camino as effortlessly as a gazelle might, or an Olympic high jumper adept at the Fosbury flop. His comrades got in their respective sides, and they backed all the way down my sad mound of acreage.

Then Bayward told me that I could weld up some armbands for his friends, burped, and said he needed to go get a white surrender chip from the six o'clock meeting. "I guess you can take up to about twenty-four hours before you pick which one's your sponsor." He walked out into the yard, picked up the owlalope without my ever saying it was his, got out a bungee cord, and strapped it to the front of his moped.

And I promise that, at this early point, I understood it all to be a ruse. I understood that people were only trying to keep me busy. I promise. Promise, promise, promise.

Raylou sat at the kitchen table, counting her money and taking notes. "I've been thinking about building one more outbuilding, and this'll be plenty enough for what I have in mind." She mashed off her calculator and turned over a sheet of lined paper.

I said, "Did you see those friends of Bayward? Good God. They went and had *stainless-steel rods* implanted into their arms so they couldn't bend them." I set my half-empty bottle of ginger ale down on the counter. I looked closely at her face to see if she'd give up the joke, the plan, the ridiculous premise.

She kept eye contact. "Zimaloy. I hope it wasn't stainless steel. I think they use Zimaloy for those kinds of rods and whatnot."

I pretended to turn my head away from Raylou, and sure enough she folded up her paper and stuck it in her shirt pocket. I thought, How can she know such things? "Anyway. Why do we need another outbuilding? I don't need more space. Do you need more space? Are you planning on bringing in a few million tons of sod, spreading it all over Ember Glow, planting grass, then needing a shed to house the lawn mower?" I wasn't being a smart-ass, I promise. I smiled throughout.

"I don't know. I guess you're right."

"You should put that money in a long-term CD down at the bank. I think they're offering point zero zero zero one percent interest these days." I poured out the ginger ale. "Hey, what happened to all those kudzu stems or roots? I probably need to chew on some root."

Raylou said, "I've changed my mind. You're not right. You can never have enough outbuildings. For *my* friends, this time." She got up, brushed past me, and opened the refrigerator. "We need to do some grocery shopping. The snappers are out of chicken necks, and I don't want to have dreams about them escaping in order to attack us in the middle of the night."

I said, "Let's go. I can't remember the last time I was in a grocery store sober. Let's splurge and go to that Publix way way out on Highway 25. There's that old-fashioned hardware store down the road from it, and I might need to buy some WD-40 in case Bayward's friends start hanging out up here." I wished that I hadn't poured out the ginger ale. "I also probably need to get some paraffin and make up some model angels so I can stay on course. Some wax. What the fuck's the word I'm supposed to use? There's a word for what I mean. From art school."

I think Raylou probably didn't mean to say, "Gingko's supposed to be good for people who've drunk away their memories," out loud. She skittered past me again—she was up to something, I knew that much—mumbling, "Cayenne pepper. Sweat out toxins."

In the Citroën, which I noticed had three hundred more miles posted on the odometer since when we left the day before, I said, "Are we keeping these turtles forever, or are you going to release them?"

"Maquette. The word you were trying to think of was 'maquette.'"

I didn't say anything about how Bayward must've driven somewhere that, oddly, was right about the same distance away as what Raylou and I drove to Sylva. I said nothing about her sudden need for more outbuildings. Let me take a solemn vow that I still didn't believe in all that Higher Power mumbo jumbo, but I realized that my wife kept hidden secrets and what I might have wrongly considered to be irrational plans. But deep down, even only five or six days in, I knew to "Let Loose and Let Raylou," so to speak. If there were some kind of fabric outlet somewhere between the grocery and hardware stores, maybe I would've bought some thick thread and cross-stitched a little piece of burlap with this saying, framed it, and nailed it inside the Quonset hut.

Who'd've ever thought that I had married my Higher Power? Not me. Goddamn, she poked a kid to death accidentally and never fashioned a face jug with a full set of teeth or eyes that didn't bulge crazy. She stood in the way of scientific discoveries, of ways to make humans understand lake toxicities. Somehow she snuck around collecting questionable men—Vince Vance, William the savage economist, Bayward, the Elbow Brethren, among others—whom she understood to be foolproof watchmen.

How was I to understand way back in art school that she had collected me?

I said, "That's the word. Maquette."

I woke up beside Raylou at three o'clock in the morning. I didn't tremble, sweat, or crave bourbon, even though the amateur tee-totaler might wrongly deduce such. It felt like the old days, maybe two nights after receiving the go-ahead to start a major commissioned project; say, a giant hollow steel ribbon slithering all over downtown Salley, South Carolina, to help reinforce the annual Chitlin Strut. Back before I succumbed to whoring my-self out for ice sculptures—back when it wasn't unusual to have three or four projects lined up—I'd drink hard in celebration for seventy-two hours, then ignite the mig welder. It's not like I went cold turkey, but I could at least tend toward moderation until the project not only got completed here on Ember Glow, but prop-erly installed on-site. What I'm saying is, I could wait between the first two nuts welded together all the way to a ribbon-cutting ceremony before I unscrewed a good quart of Old Crow, Jack Daniel's, or Jim Beam daily. It's not like I kept notes or a diary, but somewhere along the line it became Old Crow, Jack Daniel's, *and* Jim Beam *hourly*.

Then I kind of forget. I think I lost control somewhere be-tween an abstract outdoor sculpture of marijuana buds the size of grape clusters for the ex-hippie hamlet of Cohassett, California, and a ten-foot-high lifelike rendition of an old-school sweetgrass basket to be placed in the middle of Beaufort, South Carolina, for the Gullah Festival. It doesn't matter. What matters is, I woke up, shuffled out of the bedroom, put on a pair of flannel pants that weren't exactly pajamas, and walked out across the granite yard. I stopped at the turtle pond and wondered when I would ever find out the truth about why Raylou rescued the things, why she thought it necessary to bring them to our land and tantalize them with chicken necks daily.

I saw no one else on the property, but then again, I wasn't looking. In our twelve years atop Ember Glow we'd never had a trespasser, even accidentally. There was the UPS guy, and that was it. "You ain't thinking about drinking, are you?" someone said as I wandered in the direction of my Quonset hut.

Let me say right now that I didn't jump. As a matter of fact, I didn't even respond, seeing as I figured the voice to be just another specter, similar to the new ones I had in my oops-I-promised-not-to-drink dreams, and the ones I knew would be forthcoming. I said, in a normal voice, "No."

At first I couldn't tell if it was Vollis or Delay. Kumi would've yelled, and Bayward would've drawled longer. "It's my watch. This is Vollis. Seeing as you wouldn't pick a sponsor for official, we're dividing up the responsibilities," Vollis said. He came out from behind Raylou's kiln.

I thought, Fucking Raylou's going to spend all her money on hiring out night watchmen. "How'd you get here?"

"I was having car trouble anyway, so I left it at Mr. Poole's place down at the end of your drive. He's been working on my car now for years. Before and after drinking. Used to work on it more often back then, but I'm talking bodywork 'cause I kept hitting things. I left the car down there about midnight, and walked up here. It's a hike, I tell you what. It don't look like much of a hill, but it's gradual."

Again, I'd only been on the wagon a total of six or seven days. At the time I felt rejuvenated, clearheaded, and so on. But I feared, above all else, not being able to weld again. I said, "I don't want to be rude, but I have work to do. I don't know if y'all are getting paid by someone to keep an eye on me, but I'll be in the Quonset hut working. And I need to be alone while I do this, I swear. And as for the sponsorship, I absolutely detest the idea of picking a stranger to be my mentor. That's why I won't ever go back to one of those meetings, unless somehow I have a lobotomy." Additionally, I thought about how Mr. Poole—whom I'd never spoken to and rarely seen—had never shown off working on a late-model car with its hood up, either. I stored away Vollis's specious explanation.

He said, "Do you think your wife would mind my making a pipe? I haven't ever worked with clay, but I'm thinking I could roll out a long pipe, you know, even with my arms locked up and such."

I said, "I don't know. I guess," and eased open the door to my studio.

"You don't have to do the Twelve Steps according to us," Vollis said. "We made up some of our own. Seeing as we went so far as to do what we did down in Costa Rica with the arms, we say that you need to undergo the Twelve Curls. You get done with the Twelve Curls with enough weights, and you won't be even wanting to bend your arm."

I said, "Uh-huh. Okay. Maybe after I get done with these twelve angels, I'll get right on it."

I closed the door behind me. I shoved my miniature refrigerator, worktable, and the mig welder's tank up against the door. I closed and locked my four tilt windows. I said, "If there is a Higher Power out there anywhere, please keep these people away from me," like a fool.

Vollis, his voice muffled, said, "Okay. I'll be rolling out clay for the pipe if you need me."

I had taken my paraffin out the night before after Raylou and I came home from grocery shopping. Let me make it clear that there was exactly no reason whatsoever to make a maquette — I could close my eyes and see how my rebar should stand to form a skeletal frame, how the nuts would weld into wings, how I might be able to float a halo above each head. In the sour, buzzing fluorescent light of my workspace, I envisioned the Birmingham road where my sculptures would rest, and knew that — like any athlete who'd undergone rigor, pain, and injury decades earlier — my mind and body would easily reacquaint itself to labors it knew well in more sober times.

I sat on a high stool for a good hour, looking at a blank sheet of butcher paper taped down onto my drafting table.

I don't know if I spoke aloud to see if Vollis still eavesdropped on the other side of the corrugated metal wall. "I could go without maquettes and color studies if I had a few live models standing around here." No answer.

I unblocked my one entrance, slid back the sliding door, and looked up at the still night and non-light-polluted sky, connecting stars into how I imagined the major organs to appear. Peripherally I made out my own wife walking down the slick granite driveway, her arms in front of her, holding what in the darkness appeared to be a bale of hay.

Call me a visionary, but I understood what she took down Ember Glow to plant where the outcropping and soil met, how she planted these seedlings only for me, and how she and I might be swallowed up and strangled should I not finish the art project and get us out. My wife awoke early in order to shove live kudzu roots an inch into the ground on what, technically, belonged to

114

Mr. Poole on the western boundary of Ember Glow and to the South Carolina Department of Natural Resources–Wasteland Affairs on the south, east, and north. I thought, *What other man in America has a wife who would plant crops in order to strengthen his liver?*

Behind the kiln I heard that night's watchman grunt and imagined what he looked like rolling out raw clay without the use of forearms or biceps.

Raylou never took to Spillman as a last name. She's always been Raylou Hewell. Real women artists tend to keep their maiden names, and male artists hope all their careers to go by only one name. I'll admit that I want people to stand around cocktail parties saying things like, "I got my eye on a Spillman," or "If Harp dies, this big metal thing in our backyard should quadruple in value." Anyway, if the Internet had been around all along while we grew up, anyone who pecked in her name might have found two notable entries: the unnamed minor in a local newspaper who got sent off to foster parents because Mr. and Mrs. Hewell got deemed unfit, and Miss Calamine Lotion.

My wife—and she didn't tell this to me until we sat down and tried to figure out where to go on a honeymoon—won a national beauty contest the summer before she entered art school. Raylou's high school nurse nominated her most "sent to the nurse's office" student-patient for the Miss Calamine Lotion pageant. The nurse mailed off two photographs of Raylou's splotched face and arms, she got named one of twelve finalists, and during summer break she received an all-expenses-paid trip to Forty-Five, South Carolina, one of the eighty or a hundred small towns that called itself "The Poison Ivy Capital of America."

From what I could piece together as we sat in a travel agent's office in Augusta — not far from my place of upbringing, supposedly to introduce Raylou to my mother while looking for desert land to visit — Raylou's guardians had to sign some kind of waiver. And then Raylou and her competitors — all pretty-enough girls who couldn't come in contact with poisons ivy, sumac, or oak — got a rubdown of sorts, right in front of a slew of locals gathered at the annual festival. Raylou told me, "I'm not like one of those people who accidentally touches poison ivy, then breaks out two or three days later. If someone ran a push mower over a patch of the stuff and I breathed in the scattered molecules or whatever, then I got it in my lungs. Then I'd sneeze into my hand, touch my face or whatever, and there you go."

I said, "I'm almost sure Antarctica doesn't have any poison ivy. The Arctic Circle. Easter Island, more than likely. Tell me all of this again?"

It made sense: For a long time I thought Raylou sported the weirdest tan ever, as if she were allergic to the sun itself and instead of bronzing come the sunny months, she turned an off-pink seen mostly in sidewalk puddles outside of late-night bars. I thought that maybe she was a biracial mix that simply didn't work out.

"I won the contest, they put a sash around my waist, and I got savings bonds that added up to $2,000. And a couple cases of cheap calamine put out by Rite Aid Drugs."

The travel-agent woman had handed us a stack of pamphlets, brochures, and magazines. She said, "Are y'all having a big church wedding?"

Raylou said, "Can't. I'm allergic to those places, too."

We handed back over the information and said we'd come back later, though we wouldn't. Raylou said, "I thought you knew. As a matter of fact, I'm pretty sure I told you early on about my allergies."

I shook my head. I shrugged my shoulders. "Well. Maybe. Was I drunk or something? I promise to God I listen to your stories. Poked the brother. Drunken dad. Dave the Slave wrote on his jugs down in South Carolina even though he wasn't supposed to know how to read or write." I thought hard. "Something about how you could never have a pet seeing as you didn't know how long you'd stay with a certain family."

"I told you. Miss Calamine Lotion, 1984."

"Oh, now I remember!" I said. "Yeah, 1984." I didn't make eye contact and we walked down Broad Street, right past James Brown's radio station.

Raylou said, "That's the reason I fell in love and agreed to marry you, Harp. You were always so into your own work that you never even, as far as I could tell, noticed when I looked more polka-dotted than a Lichtenstein painting."

I didn't say, "Oh, I noticed, baby. I thought you had a rare skin disease." I said, "Sorry. I promise to be more observant."

And I meant it, for a while, I guess. That's why we moved to Ember Glow, I realized—there wasn't much chance of Raylou breaking out uncontrollably atop land that couldn't support a dandelion spore.

So Vollis worked on his long-stem pipe, and I stood there beneath fading stars. I thought about Raylou's patience, her forgiving nature, my slovenliness and inability to change social masks in an appropriate manner, how maybe I suffered from Asperger's syndrome. I thought of my good fortune, went inside the house, and got out the box of oatmeal. Because I knew that she'd come back itching, I ran my wife a warm bath, poured in the oatmeal, added some baking soda, and dolloped in white vinegar.

I learned all about this home remedy years earlier, when I tried to quit drinking without telling anyone, and garnered some odd symptoms that made chicken pox seem like a gentle breeze wafting over the skin. I never really learned if the bathtub concoction alleviated the outward effects. A good bottle of Old Crow, taken internally, did, unfortunately.

8

I BARELY HAD a hundred nuts welded to the first angel frame before Bayward said he needed to go help Raylou frame the new outbuilding. At the time, my helper's job consisted of reaching down in the box and handing me what I asked for. We both wore welder's masks, and Bayward sported work boots, two pairs of pants, a denim work shirt, and my leather industrial apron. He said that he couldn't take pain, that he kept a diary per Vince Vance's suggestion wherein Bayward listed every time he felt an irresistible urge to turn a bottle up for three or four bubbles. As I stood back, mig welder in hand, to envision what to fill in next, Bayward said, "Hitting my thumb with a roofing hammer. Stepping on a nail. Falling off the ladder. Scraping my knees on asphalt shingles. Getting sweat in my eyes. Twisting my back wrong while shouldering a bundle of cedar shake. Cutting my fingers on flashing. Cutting my fingers on metal bands. Hitting my thumb with a framing hammer. Breathing in fiberglass insulation. Paper cuts from rolling out tar paper. Breathing in asbestos when I take off my dust mask. Getting punched in the face by one of the Mexicans after I say something wrong in Spanish. Getting ball-foot blisters trying to stand on an eight-twelfths pitched roof. Spraining my wrists when a nail gun goes wrong. Cutting my fingers with a shingling hatchet. Accidentally sticking my hand in hot tar. Getting bit by a mean dog unused to having roofers in the yard. Getting punched in the face by the guy who hired on roofers, then got a nail in his tire when he backed out of the driveway. Sunburn. Frostbite."

I had on short pants and no shirt on a warm March day, and my shoes were still under the bed. As opposed to Bayward, when I went through pain, it kept me away from the bottle. Nothing could've helped my sobriety more than to get a good nut glowing red, then have it pop off and embed itself somewhere near my sternum. I said, "Shut up! You're driving me crazy, man, I can't concentrate. Go help Raylou do whatever she has in mind. Where are your buddies, anyway? Where's Vollis and Kumi and that other one?"

Bayward said, "So that's why I'm afraid of a spark flying off and burning my skin. If I get a burn, I'm going to want to drink hard again." He took off his welder's mask and said, "Don't light that thing back up just yet. There's no telling what would happen if I got blinded, you know. Anyway, they're on their way. From what I gathered, they were going to the noon Alcohell Club meeting."

Raylou came out of the house with a bandanna on top of her head. "I just got off the phone with the guy, and they're delivering. They're on their way, Bayward."

I shook my head and looked off in the distance. "I thought those Elbow boys didn't cotton to AA. I thought they didn't go to meetings."

Bayward walked around my naked angel as if it would topple over onto him. "They like to stand out front and wait for the right moment. If someone acts a little skeptical or tired, you know, they hand him a little tract explaining why they all went down to Mexico."

I said, "Costa Rica."

"I never read their bylaws and whatnot. Anyway, that's what they do. And because no one would ever turn them away, they like to go down there when it's Drunken Jeopardy day. I believe you might have a different opinion about that place where you only went once if you attended Drunken Jeopardy. You smart. They got real prizes!"

I looked at Bayward as if he spoke in an alien language and tried to imagine what occurred at Drunken Jeopardy. And I'll be the first to admit that I don't do well when Raylou picked up what I considered a needless project: When the lumberyard guys showed up, I'd have to drop my welder, help them unload, then waste my time framing whatever new outbuilding she had in mind. Somewhere along the line I would find it necessary to wash the turtles, water the kudzu seedlings down Ember Glow, and so on. I would find absolutely everything else to do besides the project I needed to finish.

Raylou said, "I talked to Vollis and Delay Sucks. They said they'd be glad to do what they could do. They said that they could hold boards while I hammered. They said they could raise walls."

I went inside the Quonset hut and flipped the welder switch. I checked the argon and CO_2 levels. Then I yelled back to Bayward, "Let me go put on some shoes and a shirt. Let me go dig around for a pack of cigarettes so I don't feel out of place."

He took a ream of documents off the "passenger seat" of his moped. "We can both ride on this, if you want. You can drive." Then he handed me the papers and said, "I forgot all about giving these to you. They from Dr. Vance. He said they should help."

I looked at the top photocopy. It read in bold letters, "Many People Have Successfully Quit Drinking Without the Benefit of a Structured Group Meeting: They Died."

I said to Bayward, "Nothing like positive thinking offered up by the addiction industry." I yelled back to Raylou, "I'm going off to become a game-show addict," and motioned for Bayward to get in the truck.

Raylou said, "I might start to work on the outbuilding, if you don't mind."

I didn't say, "Do I have a choice? Do I have a voice in the matter?" I said, "Don't bang your thumb and end up like this guy."

Not that I've ever read any Sigmund Freud or psychology texts, not counting *The Future of an Illusion* back when I took one of those elective courses outside of my art-school curriculum, but I've always hoped that there was nothing valid about all that you-are-looking-for-your-mother/you-hate-your-father line of thinking. Because I feared some truth to all of this, I strayed from any magazine articles that even remotely suggested such a topic. Goddamn, it seemed like every title or subtitle in any of the slicks might've veered toward psychotherapy, and the more innocuous and seemingly innocent articles almost inevitably got straight into discussions of psyche, id, collective unconsciousness, egos, archetypes, and the importance of eating plenty of fiber about two paragraphs past the writers' attempts to plot out a viable direction they purported to take. You start off thinking that you're going to read about the latest summer-blockbuster B movies, and you end up plodding through how a machete-wielding guy in a hockey mask out in the woods represents the American Male Shadow. Even in the art magazines, there's barely a column without some kind of art historian — and I'll be the first to admit that 99 percent of art historians know nothing about what it's like to be an artist, so you can't blame them for delving into something easy and improvable, like the apparent lack of superegos among drunken paint-thinner-sniffing men and women unable to finish their work — blaming carte blanche public education's need to slash programs because certain New York artists' behavior from 1950 onward (de Kooning, Pollock, Kline, Rothko, and any of those idiots who insisted that graffiti was art) represented, oh, I don't know, bipolar manic depression that shouldn't be recognized or taught.

It's not easy staying away from these thoughts creeping in, and I finally got to the point where I could simply let what was about to happen, happen. I offered up no fight. Growing up, my mother would do something like this: She would start talking about how she wanted, say, a new refrigerator about the first of August. She'd say, "I'm going to save up my spare change and get us a new refrigerator. We need a new refrigerator! I'm so tired of defrosting the freezer. They have new refrigerators that self-defrost! There are also ones out there with a bunch of special trays and bins, so you could keep all of your favorite foods stacked up together, Harp."

I never said anything one way or the other. I had enough problems, what with being the only fatherless boy at school while trying, simultaneously, to fend off local Irish Travelers wanting to lure me into their world of con games. Unless we had to keep our milk outside in an ice cooler, I thought the old boxy refrigerator worked fine.

My mom would bring up the refrigerator about twice in September, a few times in October, then pretty much daily right on up until Thanksgiving: She couldn't shove the turkey inside if she wanted to keep the jellied cranberry sauce cold, et cetera. Right about the first of December she would say, "I got this great idea, Harp. Let's you and me not get each other anything for Christmas. Let's pool our money and get a new refrigerator!"

I don't need to point out how I didn't care if we had a new one or not, and that this supposed "gift to ourselves" seemed a little lopsided in my mother's favor. Not once did I ever bring up in mid-November how I wanted a basketball hoop set up in the gravel driveway, then say, "I know what! Let's go halves on a hoop and post for Valentine's Day!" Or St. Patrick's, or Father's Day. In the history of the universe, I learned before I'd even sprouted hairs, it didn't matter, but I still thought of this MO on my mother's part as slightly passive-aggressive.

And I still thought that way with Raylou: This whole "I want to have another outbuilding set up between the house and your workspace" smelled more than faintly of what the psychology texts might call "ulterior motive." Over the years the same thing happened when we evenly split the costs for a new gas kiln, another new electric kiln, a new wood-fire kiln, the added-on room we needed so we could have a vanity, Raylou's step van, the convection oven, the microwave with convection features, and a raku barrel that, supposedly, also worked as a smoker.

My mother, my wife, my lack of backbone, my drinking.

I would be willing to bet that the guy who came up with the idea that no Little League T-ball team in America should ever lose — and that absolutely everyone got to play in the game — came straight out of a rehab program. Drunken Jeopardy notwithstanding, the Alcohell Club was all about no one feeling like a loser, which I found to be odd, seeing as I'd always thought of

rehab programs being for quitters, et cetera. In the one meeting
I attended with Bayward a blind man could've seen the forlorn
lost looks plastered on each attendee's face. So let me make it
clear that I wasn't all gung ho about going to the same club—
their group was called the Renegades, for some reason, which
didn't make sense to me—partly because I already knew I would
hear the same stories repeated, and partly because I felt guilty
about making fun of the men right after the first time: Maybe
they *didn't* sound like a documentary sound track of the mentally challenged; maybe I was wrong, and there was such a thing
as "bone marrel."

Bayward and I parked my truck in the last available space,
which happened to be right in front of the sand-bucket ashtray.
I said, "Okay. Here we are. If this is some kind of trick—or if you
insist on introducing me again as a newcomer—I'll kill you."

Bayward got out and said to one of the lag-behind smokers,
"Hey, Leroy. You ain't seen none of the Elbow Brethren, have
you? I thought they was supposed to be here handing out their
papers."

Leroy's face could've been used as a lifelike topographical
map of the shifting Sahara. He said, "Who?"

We walked in right as the same guy as before—Hey, Billy!—
read off the standard meeting opener, then got three volunteers
to read out the traditions, steps, and daily reflection. Bayward
and I sat down at a picnic table someone had donated, a heavy
redwood structure with burn marks pockmarking each two-by-
four. I looked down, but I swear to God I listened to what got
listed off, and might've even asked God—if there was one—to
make me a believer. I thought to myself, *If I fall down on the floor
like a jellyfish, then I'll admit that I'm powerless.*

Bayward said, "Shhh."

Billy said, "It's good to have such a large crowd here this afternoon for Drunken Jeopardy. For those y'all never done this here, we got it down to a science. I'mo reach in this-here bag" — he lifted up a brown paper sack that might've once held a meatloaf sandwich, what with the grease stain seeping through — "and pull out three numbers. Y'all look under your chairs and you'll see a number taped on the bottom. First three numbers — well, I think we all smart enough to figure this out. And I'll be the moderator."

Was there ever a question as to whether I'd be chosen right from the beginning? I reached beneath my seat cushion and found a tiny torn sheet of yellow legal-pad paper, the number 12 etched on it shakily. I looked over at Bayward, who had 11. I looked around the room and noticed that three or four of the men had already fallen asleep, their heads dangerously close to filled ashtrays, Styrofoam coffee cups, and day-old glazed doughnuts. Billy called out my number first, then 22, then 4. I got up and looked around for those fused-elbow dudes, but they still weren't around.

I got up at the front of the room and had to say, "I'm Harp, and I'm an alcoholic," to avoid getting shot, and after everyone said, "Hey Harp," my two opponents introduced themselves as Stew and Clem. Clem! I thought — who has named a boy Clem in the last two hundred years? No wonder the man turned to booze. Billy said, "We ain't got money for a board to look at or for real buzzers, so I pretty much just pull these questions face-down off the lecture here, and the money on back really only means points. Y'all hit your dinger in front of you if you think you know the answers. I'd like to thank Shaky over at his coffee shop for donating the dingers, as always. Okay, y'all set yourselves down there."

We slid back three metal folding chairs and sat at an institutional cafeteria table. The "dingers" were those silver bells that always went off before the words "Order up!" emanated from a short-order cook's mouth; they were those silver bells heard right before "Bellhop, get this man's grips" in old-fashioned hotel movies.

"At the end of all the questions, though, when it's all tallied up, the winner gets the prize. And as y'all know, the five-hundred-point question is harder than the four hundred, and so on."

Clem said, "Are there any discernible categories?" just like that, maybe even with a slight brogue. I realized that anyone named Clem could only become a drunk or a professor. What I thought was a weird bandanna around his neck ended up being a fancy ascot, of all things. A pipe stem poked out of his knock-off Barbour wool Harris tweed sport coat.

Billy said, "Uh-huh. They all got to do with what got us here." Louder, and to the audience, Billy said, "I don't know how many of y'all remember old T.C.B. — his first name was T.C. and his last name, what with us being anonymous and all — began with the letter B. Anyway, T.C.B. invented this game all by himself. We've been playing for more than ten years, I'd say, about oncet a month. T.C.B. wrote up enough questions and answers for us to play into eternity, or at least into the next generation here. Okay. Any more questions? Are y'all ready, Clem, Stew, Harp?"

Well, I started laughing because it sounded like "clam stew." I shook my head.

Billy said, "For one hundred points. Who's the most famous man to ever come out of Lynchburg, Tennessee?"

I went *Ding!* I said, "Jack Daniel. Who is Jack Daniel?"

Billy nodded. He said, "I forgot to introduce our score-keeper. Hey, who wants to volunteer to be the scorekeeper? It's got to be somebody knows how to add and won't cheat for his favorite." No one volunteered. Billy said, "Well, it might slow down the game some, but I'll do it." He looked around for a pencil until Clem pointed toward Billy's ear. "Okay. A hunnert points for you," he said. "For two hundred: Who's the most famous man to come out of Clermont, Kentucky?"

I hit the dinger and said, "Who is Jim Beam?"

"Correct," Billy said. To my competitors, he said, "It's obvious this-here Harp knows a thing or two about bourbon. Don'chall worry. We'll get to your favorites before long." He wrote down my score. "For three hundred points. Fill in the blank: 'I believe I might've poisoned myself last night because juniper berries is poison, and that's what *blank* is made of.'"

I'd never been much of a gin drinker at the age of sixteen, though one time my mother and I got tanked on the first spring-like day during an Irish Traveler parade that took place out on the road to Murphy Village. That's what my mom said, too: "Let's get tanked on some Tanqueray." We sat on our porch, armed with gin-and-tonics, and waved at men we knew were about to crisscross the nation, conning people out of their silver-ware, somehow. To Billy I said, "What is gin."

"I'll be damned," he said. He looked at Clem and Stew. "Y'all can jump in whenever you like."

I could smell beer on Stew's breath. He leaned over and held on to the table in front of us, his hands on both sides of his bell. Someone in the back of the room yelled out, "Go to the moon-shine questions. Give Stew a chance."

Billy didn't acknowledge Stew's fan club. He said, "I'mo go back to one of the hundred-point questions. Here we go." He picked up a file card from the lectern. "Budweiser likes to brag about its finest hops and what?"

It was only a hundred-point question. I held on for a moment, in order to allow one of my drunk brethren to answer. They didn't. Clem said, "I was always a Guinness man, myself. And martinis."

Ding! I hit. "What is barley?"

This went on forever. I'm talking I amassed something like 7,500 points at the end of Round One. I got the first nine answers in Round Two, also, which must've had a wild-animal theme — Old Crow, Wild Turkey, Black Dog, Grey Goose, Black Eagle, Cougar, Eagle Rare, Fighting Cock, and Beefeater — but then Stew threw up on the table and Clem walked right out of the meeting mumbling something about he must not *really* be an alcoholic if he didn't *know* any of these *answers*. I pictured him driving straight into downtown Greenville and bellying up to one of those microbrewery places, then pontificating about pubs he'd frequented in Ireland, Zimbabwe, and the Canary Islands.

Billy said, "Okay. I guess our winner today is Harp... Harp, I don't know your last letter. What's your last letter?"

I said, "Spillman."

He said, "Today's winner is Harp S." He reached into the paper bag and said, "Okay. It's time for three new contestants. Can somebody go get some paper towels out of the bathroom and come clean up this table? At the Christmas Alcothon we'll have a Tournament of Champions, you know, where there'll be a really big money prize."

I said, "Okay," and started back to the table. I wanted out of there. Let me say that I wasn't proud to know all of the answers. It made me think. It made me wonder what I'd missed out in regards to what I should've known over the last ten or twenty years of hard drinking, stuff like what went on in the art world, or how to make a woman know that you love her.

I said to Bayward, "I can't hang out for the next one. If you want, I'll come back and pick you up."

He said, "I knowed you was smart, but I didn't know what a big alcoholic you really was. I'm beginning to agree with you, too: This might not be the best place for you to hang out, talking only about booze twenty-four/seven."

Billy yelled for me to stop as I reached the door. He said, "Don't forget your prize," and handed me a small box. I thanked him and inched out the door, embarrassed that I got caught leaving early. He said, "Come on back and often."

Of course I expected a Bible, or one of about a million paperback books concerning sobriety. When we got to the truck Bayward lit a cigarette and offered me one. I shook my head and opened up my prize to find a Swiss Army knife—used, but in good condition. I said, "Oh, man, this is nice."

It would take another eight months before I learned that the bottle- and can-opener attachment had been broken off intentionally, like a possessed demonic digit.

In the old days, sometimes—maybe in dreams—I envisioned what it would be like to quit drinking altogether, and it never ended up like this. First off, I would be alone with Raylou after some kind of supernatural disaster wherein only liquor stores got leveled. Something like that. I never quit before because I thought that I'd be shaking nonstop to the point of heart attack, or that I'd lose my so-called artistic bent. More than anything, though, I thought that I wouldn't be remembering every fucking detail that occurred daily—shouldn't there be some kind of beneficial and protective haze so that an old drunk could bypass bad memories? Isn't that what happened to people who went into comas, shock, or paralysis while undergoing malpractical procedures at, say, Graywood Emergency Regional Memorial? I know I've read about it somewhere. Maybe I only thought up a theory, all slumped down next to my mig welder back when I never produced anything.

In the nondrinking days, whole months might go by, it seemed. For some reason I had a difficult time differentiating November from February, and March from May. But from that minute when I woke up on the cement floor, learning of the snapping turtles, and reminded of the rehab promise, the sun rose and the sun set, et cetera.

And I didn't like this endless process. It made me want to drink, contemplating the planet rotating so inexorably.

But none of this matters. What matters is, the entire Drunken Jeopardy expedition ended up a ruse, I felt certain later, so that Bayward's corpse-armed friends could come over and help Raylou erect that unnecessary outbuilding. We drove up to find my wife hammering a tin roof down on a sloped structure that might've been only eight-by-twelve. It didn't cost any $6,000 — that's for certain.

Vollis and Delay Sucks stood there looking like Scotland Yard fuckers. I stuck out my head, as a matter of fact, and said, "Remind me to buy y'all some shakos to wear around. You could start up dueling marching bands and both be drum majors."

Bayward got out and said, "Kiwi go on back down to see your old doctor?"

"Kumi," said Delay Sucks. He wore a nail belt halfway down his thighs, as did Vollis. "He's the only one of us could afford to take off. We don't make money like those performance poets. And we don't have the vacation time stored up."

Vollis looked at his wristwatch, the silver metal expansion band stretched out high on his bicep. "I imagine he should be arriving about now, getting the pins out about three hours ago as long as Dr. Sanchez of San José's not busy. There's a time change, you know."

"And he'll be laughing about it then or now," Delay Sucks said. "Finally get his funny bone back." I laughed at that one. Raylou laughed and said she never thought about them losing that little nervy area. The Elbow Brethren stared blankly.

"So what exactly are you going to use this little shed for?" I asked my wife. I reached in my pocket and pulled out the Swiss Army knife. "Hey, I won the grand prize in Drunken Jeopardy."

Raylou jumped right off the back end of the slanted roof, onto the hard ground. It wasn't a six-foot leap. "I thought we'd put a card table and some chairs in here. Seeing as no one outside Bayward really trusts going to the meetings, I figure y'all can have them here. We can run an extension cord from either your studio or mine. Or the house as long as it doesn't dangle into the turtle pond. And then everyone can talk about, I don't know, what happened and what's to come."

I figured Raylou understood that I'd done a majority of my drinking beneath the rounded corrugated roof of my Quonset hut. She understood that I needed new surroundings in order to start over.

Vollis said, "Okay. I think that's about it for us. Brinson Sucks needs to go check on his vacuums, and I'm supposed to take some of the arts kids on a field trip over to Spartanburg, where a one-armed woman's going to be giving a piano concert."

Raylou said, "I want to thank y'all for your help. And you know to come back anytime, especially when Harp's either working on his metal angels, or not."

I realized that I had never stood around in my yard so much. Is this what sober people did all the time? Delay Sucks said, "Bring the bus by my machine on Church Street and I'll clean it out for you. Those students over there don't deserve to sit on what you told me, Vollis. Tell Harp. Tell everybody about our taxpayers' money." He flapped his arms against his outer thighs.

Raylou said, "Y'all stand inside the shed and see what it feels like," then walked toward the house.

Vollis shook his head. "This story I'm about to say is nasty. I'm not too proud of what I did, either, if that matters. If I were still in AA meetings, I'd probably have to redo Step Four or whatever and make some amends. Anyway, you know how I said I'm always stationed at the bus unless the president of the school and the VP for finances come out there and have their afternoon drinks? Well, I set up a little spy camera I bought over the Internet, and it works like a charm. I set it up right above the EMERGENCY EXIT sign. Anyway, the president, that VP for finances—a woman who claims she's HR, but don't know what an IRA stands for—and this old boy, VP for furniture, evidently met in the bus and had some kind of I'll-show-you-mine-if-you-show-me-yours competition."

I said, of course, "You're crazy. I don't believe this one. I'm still not sure I believe in y'all's arms. Let me take you two through a metal detector somewhere."

"I can bring the video. It can be the first thing we watch in here once Raylou gets the cord run out. Long story short, the two women got bigger dicks than the two men. Enough said there. You talk about seeing something that made me want to take a drink—it made me want to drink Drano."

I looked at Bayward. He didn't seem to listen to his friend's story. He peered out the hole where a glass pane would be, and said, "Harp's got to get to work. I'm supposed to be in charge of his getting to work."

I said to Vollis, "I'm just going to play along and say that I believe whatever you're talking about. Let me say right now that I'll not be surprised that your weird spy-cam story comes back in my nondrinking life, somehow."

Raylou came out with a pitcher of iced tea. She said, "I'm so out of face jugs, I need to get to work, too. Hey, you want me to fire that clay cane you made, Vollis?"

He didn't tell her it was a pipe. Delay Sucks said, "I know the feeling, about nasty people. Back when I worked on a submarine, this fellow from California named Backsplash got a tattoo on his shoulders on down of a naked woman all sprawled out showing herself. She had her legs spread open all over the place. This guy used to take off his shirt and turn his back at night so guys could beat off right there. Oh, it cost them some money. Last I heard, Backsplash owned half of one of those big states out west. He went back to his real name, too."

I excused myself from the group, walked to my studio, and fired up the welder, intent on not yelling back over my shoulder, "I don't get it," or "You people can stop now," or "Someone please come take my Swiss Army knife from me before I jam the blades in my ears and eyes." And I didn't turn around when I heard two car doors shut, a moped rev up, or my wife stacking split oak into what I foresaw as my future funeral pyre.

9

MR. POOLE WALKED UP quietly from his house down Ember
Glow. I had finished up my first angel alone, a giant structure
weighing in at just under nine hundred pounds. Even with all
of the interruptions, I finally got into a good work ethic I'd not
felt since spending a summer working as some kind of fake
groundskeeper full-time down in Sarasota for a man who never
would tell me his name, instructed me only to cut the grass and
pick up palm fronds, and report back to him any car I saw pass
by his house more than three times daily. He lived in a gated
stucco mansion, wore standard plaid Bermuda shorts, black
socks, oversized sunglasses, a sweat-rimmed fedora, and paid out
in cash every third day. When I told him about the old VW bus,
or Dodge Dart, or Pinto going back and forth on the street in
front of his house, he would retreat into a hidden wall or trap-
door leading to a tunnel of sorts. Sometimes he tipped me an
extra fifty, said he liked to be considered an arts supporter, and
asked me if I could paint a mural in his dining room someday
of him, Frank Sinatra, Dean Martin, and some fellow he kept a
black-and-white picture of in his wallet who, I'm pretty sure,
ended up being Generalissimo Francisco Franco.

I said, "I might could do a sculpture, but that's about it. Painting's not my gig."

"What about that girlfriend of yours? She's in the art school, isn't she?"

"She's a potter. Well, they all call themselves ceramicists, but you know what I mean." I watched the man's face widen as he looked past me, out at the street. I turned to see a black Lincoln Mark VI limo ease toward the house at about five miles an hour. More than likely it was part of the Ringling clan, out on a joyride. By the time I said, "Don't worry, that's the first time that car's come by," he'd disappeared somehow into a bunker hidden beneath a bluejack-oak thicket.

From that day onward—he never asked me to find a portraitist—my pay came out backwards from the front-door mail slot. I never even heard footsteps in the house, as I didn't when my closest neighbor, Mr. Poole, sidled up to me and said, "I need to speak to the wife."

Luckily I'd turned the welder off, though I still held the gun, which knocked off my mask when I jumped uncontrollably. "Goddamn," I said. "Hey. I didn't hear you come up."

"I'm sneaky that way," he said. "Sometimes I pride myself on it, others I don't. I need to talk to the wife."

Mr. Poole and I had never met officially. I took off my gloves and stuck out my hand. He couldn't have been over five-five and looked like an ex-flyweight boxer, his arms pure sinew. "Harp Spillman," I said. "I would've been down earlier to introduce myself, but I didn't want to give you a bad impression. I was on a binge up until a few weeks ago."

Mr. Poole pronounced his name as "Poo." I didn't catch his first name, if indeed he actually said it. A lot of people went only by their last names in this area, anyway. He shook my hand and said, "Poo," just like that bear might say it, or a potty-training toddler.

"I take it you're worried about the kudzu Raylou planted. She promised me she'd groom those vines to come our way. In the long run, it'll slow down some of the runoff you get from up here when it rains like all hell."

Mr. Poole looked in his ramshackle house's direction back down my sloped yard. He said, "That's good."

"Raylou's not here right now," I said, which wasn't a lie. She'd gone down to the Pickens County Flea Market in search of makeshift fettling knives and other clay tools.

"Is this the thing?" Poole asked me. He put his palm against my first angel, pushed somewhat for give, then looked back at me.

I said, "It's the thing. I'm doing a commission for twelve of the bastards. This is number one."

My neighbor nodded. He turned his head around as if looking for the Elbow Boys. Then, speaking as if he got only a single chance to fill in as much information as possible, he said, "You get a chance tell her I got block and tackle we can rig up here using some these holes already drilled in the ground, plus a come-along, special motorcycle jack, hydraulic lift that'll mount on a cement floor or granite rock, I suppose, I might need to go back down and take some measurements. I didn't know what she talked about being this tall."

With that he offered me a half salute, swiveled, and walked down the driveway so bandy-legged it looked as if his legs were parentheses, his torso lurched so forward that I feared he'd end up rolling home.

Let me say right now he gave me ideas for the next eleven angels. I don't know why, but that unyielding slouch of desperation impressed me in ways I would never understand or explain. When Raylou returned a few hours later, her step van loaded down with everything except a fettling knife, I said, "Don't even try to pretend you haven't been talking to Mr. Poole or Poo over these years. He came up here and said he's got your 'block and tackle come-along hydraulic-lift jack.' Then he dissolved down Ember Glow."

"Good for him. I knew I could count on Mr. Poole," Raylou said. "Hey, I ran across one of those guys who sells shrimp out of a truck. I figured the turtles might like a treat." She threw me a ten-pound frozen bag.

I followed her inside. "I'm going to go out on a limb here. I never even applied for some kind of commission down in Birmingham. You made a decision that an intervention wouldn't work, you wanted to stop me from killing myself, and you made the whole thing up about twelve angels for an ex–blast-furnace site. Then you got Vince Vance involved, and he got Bayward involved, and Bayward got those crazy guys who may or may not really have pins in their arms. Mr. Poole. Somehow the entire Republican Party."

Raylou set the bag of shrimp in the refrigerator on top of a lasagna pan. She said, "I got other things to do, Harp. I'm not playing this game."

She didn't look my way. I said, "Let me see that contract again. Where'd you put that thing, anyway?"

Raylou said, "Are you finished with the first one?" She looked out in the yard, but the outbuilding blocked any view of it. More often than not, Vollis and Delay Sucks sat inside there, playing backgammon or spades, as if sitting sentry. "I like the way she's going to rust naturally."

I said, "Uh-huh. You've said that before. Come on, Ray. I won't get mad. I understand why you did what you did, if indeed you did it. Fess up, baby."

She shook her head. "The phone rang this morning for you but I didn't get it. You might want to listen."

I looked at the light flashing. I neared thirty days sober. "I know that trick, too," I said. "It's bad news. I ain't picking it up."

Raylou shrugged. She said she didn't know when she got so tired of everything, then took two steps and hit the PLAY button. A man said, "It took us some time to locate you. But now we have."

I could feel my face flush red. I hit *69, but got one of those "We're sorry, but the last number to call is unknown" mechanical messages back. I said to Raylou, "Who the fuck was that?"

"Who've you pissed off over the years? Besides me. Who's got it out for you?"

I sat down at our kitchen table and looked up at the ceiling, where a stain darkened from when I, drunk, tried to use a pressure cooker. "That Karl guy from the ice-sculpture thing. Any one of the higher-ups in Alcoholics Anonymous who doesn't like that I'm proving them wrong. Vince Vance, too, maybe." I went on and on, all the way back to a classmate we had at Ringling who blamed his later failures as an artist on me, even though I told him not to construct a low walk-through installation made of cement blocks and railroad spikes so close to the San Andreas Fault.

Raylou said, "I'm going to boil up some dug-up ginseng I bought from this mountain woman. She also sold me some yellow root."

I told Raylou that, if and when she spoke with Mr. Poole again, he could bring his hoist over.

It didn't occur to me then—and this, of course, is because all alcoholic drunks think only of themselves always, according to the industry's literature—that the person on the answering machine *could've been* looking for my wife.

Bayward showed up every morning and told me things I knew already because I spent most nights reading every possible essay, book, or pamphlet that Raylou squirreled away over the years in the attic. If alcoholism was genetic, then I probably wasn't that much of an alcoholic seeing as only my father drank, not his parents, not my mother's parents, and so on. And if alcoholism could be linked to a latent gene, then everyone in the goddamn world could be an alcoholic. If some people were susceptible due to stress and pressure, then maybe I had a drinking problem stemming back to the time I fell from the roof of the Forty-Five Little Theatre back in 1992 or thereabouts, working on the top of an abstract piece I called "Off-Off-Off-Off-Off-Off-Off-Broadway," wherein the form represented—in my mind—a giant misshapen ego, and the seven Offs stood for deadly sins. Anyway, I fell off the roof, landed on my back, and started drinking harder once the Percodan prescription expired.

If alcoholic dependence stemmed from inner demons, then I wasn't an alcoholic, seeing as I went to an Irish Traveler palm reader one time and she said I needed *more* inner demons if I wanted to live successfully in South Carolina.

I read old war stories told by homeless men who once owned giant industries, as well as men who became successful only after their drinking binges stopped. I pored over all of the homeopathic journals to see what kind of diet I should follow. The only thing I could figure out for certain was that total sobriety affected one's eyesight directly, for my vision blurred more each day.

"Vince Vance says you might want to write a Dear John letter to your best friend. Except instead of John, make it whatever your drug of choice was," Bayward said every morning. "Have I mentioned that before?"

"Memory," I said. "I guess long-term drinking affects the memory."

Raylou wore a pair of bib overalls with nothing beneath it, which I think she did on purpose to entice all of these drunks our way. She worked beneath her shed on an old kick wheel, spitting out face jugs about six an hour, it seemed. Although I never admitted it, I envied the way she could finish a jug in such little time and get it out on the market. Vollis worked on her Web site for free, something he learned, he said, while in the computer classroom at his arts school, when all of those administrators made him scram so they could make use of the party bus. I yelled over toward her, "Have I written a good-bye letter to bourbon, yet? I forget."

She laughed and nodded her head up and down. "You've written so many that if you mailed them all, the post office would be working in the black, all the stamps you'd have to use."

I said to Bayward, "As you may or may not recall, I've never given you much shit, buddy. But about every other day that you've come here, I've smelled booze on your breath. I don't know if you're collecting those white chips or what, but you might want to listen up more in those meetings. Why ain't it taking for you?"

I'd begun my second angel, this one a figure slouched over as if picking up aluminum cans on the roadside. Bayward said, "I admit it. But I'm powerless! You've been to enough meetings to know that we're all powerless to alcohol. So I can't help it."

I didn't say that he could ride his moped in a direction away from the liquor store. I didn't say that he could close his mouth, keep money out of his pockets, and so on. I said, "That's bullshit, man. If there are two things I've learned since deciding to quit, it's that the human will is powerful, and that we don't need to lock up our elbows. Me personally, I'm powerless to air, water, and food." I said, "I believe there's something else going on with old Bayward. Hey, hand me that nut there on top and wipe it off on your apron."

Bayward had turned into a good worker. Bending over eight thousand times a day didn't seem to bother him, I guess from his days on the roof. He handed me a giant lug nut and said, "I ain't studied up on the psychology as much as you have, but I'm starting to think that I got it figured out. Maybe I don't want to succeed. You know what I'm saying? First off, Vince Vance used to be an alcoholic, and now he's the addiction counselor. So's about another ten people working out there at Carolina Behavior. I don't want that to happen to me."

I triggered the mig and set the new nut in place, right where an angel's Adam's apple might be. I didn't tell Bayward that I didn't see him turning miraculously into a counselor. Like an idiot, I said, "You'd be a good counselor — about every other day."

"Roofing's hard, and I got a good boss man. Until Vance says I'm good to go, the insurance keeps paying up. Although from what I understand, they're getting somewhat impatient."

Raylou yelled over to us, "Are y'all about ready for lunch? I'm ready for lunch. Did we feed the turtles this morning? I'll fix some sandwiches if one of y'all feeds the snappers. We kind of need to clean out their pond, too, and change those filters."

I looked over at the face jug in her hands. She'd attached oversized stick-out monkey ears, and had bugs eyes above the nose and two in the back. I was about to say something about if she was selling to an art collector who worked for the CIA, but

Bayward interrupted everything by going over to the turtle pond, getting on his knees, jabbing his right arm in faster than a rocket-powered speargun, and pulling up one of the thirty-pound females by her prehistoric tail. The turtle kicked razor-wire–sharp claws out, then flapped her head hard and repeatedly on her shell — and I know it was a female because, in between all of the books on alcoholism I'd read, I studied up on Raylou's computer how a male turtle's cloacal opening extended beyond its carapace — or something to that effect. This snapper didn't seem to have anything extending, outside of its tail and Bayward's strong grip. She popped and popped and hissed hard. Any of all those middle-aged drumming-in-the-woods Iron John men would've been proud of the snapping turtle's rhythm.

Bayward said, "I got your lunch right here. Anybody up for some cooter pie?" He eased Raylou's unaffectionate pet back in her pollen-scummed habitat. I looked from him back to my wife. He said, "I've always meant to ask y'all why you keep these things. Vollis and Delay Sucks say they don't make good guard dogs at night, at least from what they've seen. Not like a goose makes a good guard dog. Or a dog."

I set down my welder and met Raylou in front of the turtle pond with Bayward. She said, "They've been rescued. I rescued them. Let's just say I got something against human beings testing animals that don't have a choice in the matter."

At first I thought Bayward shook only a little, that he underwent one of the numerous post-withdrawal-syndrome manifestations. In retrospect, though, I understand that his wheels spun, that he made some connections. He said, "Where I come from, 'rescue' and 'stole' don't necessarily mean the same thing so I won't go tell on you, Miss Raylou. I just want you to know that I've opened up both dictionary and Taurus before."

I went inside for the chicken necks. Maybe Bayward had picked up a dictionary of zodiac terms. I didn't follow his chain of thoughts at the time, but I'd forever been accustomed to not trusting my instincts. Somewhere along the line, too, signs, omens, and foreshadowing never made permanent marks on my ability to understand future relentless and unfailing events in the territory of aggravation.

I went down to Mr. Poole's house to buy a roll of chicken wire from him. I didn't have one step on his property when he yelled out, "I'm back here. Follow the path." I walked through a grave-yard of washers and dryers, metal clowns with holes in their mouths that must've been cast off by a third- or fourth-tier traveling fair, a pile of leftover copper wiring, an assortment of copper tubing, a driven-down dog stob with a metal chain that could've held a merchant ship to its wharf, and row upon row of upholstered bucket seats. I stopped midway to the back of his voice and looked back east. The kudzu, planted by Raylou not more than a month ago, crept up Ember Glow our way, perhaps twenty feet. "I'm back here. Follow the path," Poole said like a mantra, even when I stood above him. He slid across his own flat piece of granite atop a mechanic's old-fashioned wooden creeper, though no car stood ajack nearby. I underwent a horrendous flashback of a terribly deformed little person I came across one time scooting around my childhood's county fair on a motorized skateboard.

I said, "Mr. Poole, this is Harp Spillman from up the hill." I pointed. "How're you doing?"

He didn't get off of the creeper, but he sat up. Mr. Poole's family, like that of my home's previous owner, had lived in

Ember Glow proper since the days of trading with Cherokees. "Done better, done worse. Hard to tell." He squinted better than anyone in a spaghetti western. "I had a bad feeling if I come up to your house then you'd think we were friends."

I didn't say how one of the problems in America, as far as I could figure, stemmed from most everyone having garage-door openers; that people came home, beamed up their doors, drove in, and never had to have human interaction. I said, "I hate to bother you, but I wanted to see if you had a roll of chicken wire for sale. Raylou's got this irrational idea that hawks are going to swoop down and steal away her snapping turtles. Like a hawk could lift up a thirty-pound turtle."

Poole stood up. "Hawk ain't gone steal away a snapper. You put some trout in that pond up there, you might have bird-of-prey problems. Hawk. Falcon. Eagle. Turkey buzzard if the fish float dead on top. Wayward osprey." He said, "I'd invite you in, but the wife ain't feeling too good these days, and she goes on a scream party if I bring in the unannounced."

I thought, *Wayward. He's in on everything, too.* I thought, *I didn't even know you were married.* Although I'd not been the best neighbor, I usually made a point to look over at Mr. Poole's ramshackle abode, and I never saw a woman standing out there with a faggot of twined-together branches, sweeping the ground or whatever. I said, "I know about that. I know a little bit about that, man. Raylou's the same way," which wasn't true at all about her, of course. If anything, *I* was the person who couldn't stand friends or strangers showing up without warning. But I felt like I needed to bond with Poole.

"What makes you think I sell chicken wire, son? Do I have a sign out front advertising chicken wire? Have you seen rolls of chicken wire somewhere on my property? Is there something about the look on my face that makes a person think right off, There's a chicken-wire-selling man?"

Let me say right now that, in the old days, I kind of liked such confrontations. Over the years I'd relished yelling down someone who was being either impolite or irrational, and had thrown my share of drunken, wind-catching roundhouses. But without booze in my system, evidently, my behavior transformed. I didn't raise my voice. "Look, dumbfuck, you got about everything else strewn around this eyesore, so I just came down to ask. I figured you could use the money, shithead. Sorry to bother you. Go back to riding your sad little wagon."

I began my uphill trudge not ten feet before Poole yelled out, "I'm just toying with you, Harp. Goddamn. Come on back and I'll show you where I keep the wire." I turned around to find him half standing, crouched over, palms on knees. He said, "I promised the missus I'd try to get in shape, seeing as you've gone and quit drinking. At least that's the word around here: your stopping drinking. You ain't started back yet, have you? Not that I'd want anyone to start back up, but I'm tired of doing exercises."

I said, "I'm sorry. I didn't mean to snap at you, man."

Still, though, I didn't get him. I followed Mr. Poole back behind a shed where he had two rolls of chicken wire rolled and standing upright. Poole said, "Back in the day, I tried to raise some mink. Mink. Otter. Rabbit. You know. Fox. I had it in my mind that I could raise them up, bog them in the head, skin them, and sell to those fur people up north. Raccoon. This was back before y'all moved in. Long story short, most animals got enough teeth to bite right through chicken wire. And I never could hold a killing club above my shoulder, anyways."

I said, "Man. Me either. Good for you."

"Sometimes at night I imagine hearing those animals, or at least they great-great-great-great grandchildren, either thanking me for their freedom, or warning me that they could come back and get in the house anytime they wanted. You ever hear them animals screeching at night?"

I shook my head no, only because what noises I heard in the middle of the night—forever—seemed to be the voice of my liver calling for more. I looked back behind the shed. "How much land do you own, Mr. Poole? How far does this go?"

"I forget. I've been meaning to get ahold of a Bush Hog and make some trails out there." He pointed. "I've been thinking about starting a fruit stand down on the road. The blackberries back here are something, this time of year. I think a couple hundred acres. You want to buy some? I'm willing to sell." He leaned the roll of chicken wire to me.

"Maybe in the future," I said. "What the hell. Raylou and I are either going to leave altogether or dig in more so, I guess."

Poole stuck out his right hand to shake. "I'll save it till you're ready." Then he reached into his left pocket and extracted a pair of tin snips. "I'm figuring you'll need three four-foot widths, both twenty feet long. Am I right or am I right?"

I shrugged. He seemed to know more about the turtle pond than I did. He seemed to know ahead of time what I'd finally ask of him.

10

MY FATHER, WHOM I'd not seen since he left my mother for an
Irish Traveler's despondent wife twenty-five years earlier, didn't
look like the kind of man who would agree to help out the Alabama, Georgia, or South Carolina highway patrols in an exper-
imental and likely illegal ploy to raise traffic-violation accounts
receivable. He showed up unannounced at my home in Ember
Glow and, from what I could figure, kind of scared my wife in
the same ways that I did before I quit drinking. He stared off,
spoke in non sequiturs, and looked like he could lose his temper
at any moment. At first I thought that he'd been tracked down
and summoned here by Raylou, that he was joining the unend-
ing line of freaks, converts, and lawyers she had amassed over the
previous three months in an ongoing intervention process that I
promised her didn't need to take place. If I lapsed, it would happen only after I finished the commission for Birmingham, and
after the probable lawsuit brought on by the Republican National Committee. By then, I figured, my need for booze, I hoped,
would be nonexistent. And I wouldn't be out driving secondary
roads, a certain victim of the Rube Goldberg–like situation with
which my father affiliated himself.

"I've been able to keep up with your career on the computer," he said. It wasn't yet an hour past dawn. My father had found our sturdy home atop Ember Glow somewhere around midnight, seen the lights off, and slept in his car. "You were doing pretty good there in the 1990s, from what I could uncover. And I saw that big metal sculpture you made down in New Orleans. I think they took that down for some reason. Rats infiltrate barren lands, too. Probably didn't want it the only thing left standing should a hurricane drown the city. Probably want a Jesus statue to be the only thing standing."

I didn't know what that last part meant. Raylou stared at the coffeemaker. She crossed and uncrossed her legs, tapped her fingers on her thigh, and forced a smile every time I looked her way. My father wore khaki work pants and shirt, which made him look like a wild-eyed scout leader, as if he could lead his troop over Niagara Falls in barrels for a made-up badge. I said, "I don't want this to sound like I'm not happy to see you after all this time, but how'd you find us?"

Raylou said, "I hope you don't mind your coffee without milk. We're out of milk." She got up and walked away from the kitchen table. "It's been so hectic around here, I keep forgetting to go to the grocery."

"Black's fine with me." He patted his hip, the international sign for his carrying a flask. I shook my head. "And you, Raylou, when I was looking up everything about Harp, something in there had a little biography, you know, about how he was married to a potter, and I got to look up things on you. All those face jugs you sell. No offense, but I can't believe some of those things go for two, three hundred dollars. Clay's a fancy name for dirt, right? How much does dirt cost these days?"

Raylou made a noise in her throat. It wasn't a growl, exactly, but she didn't hum a happy song either, I could tell. I waited for my wife to say something like "Dirt costs more money than what you sent back for child support or college." She said, "Supply and demand, I guess. People want scary-face jugs on their mantels."

I looked out the window expecting to see my man Bayward showing up to help me weld the next twelve-foot angel. He'd never been later than seven in the morning, which meant he had to leave his house around six fifteen, seeing as his moped didn't top twenty miles an hour. I picked up the telephone and mashed out his number, then hung up after the tenth ring. "Bayward must be on his way," I said.

Raylou brought my father his cup and set it down. I got up and shoveled six teaspoons of sugar in mine. "And then I read up all what happened at that fund-raiser in Columbia," my father said. "They even got a videotape of the whole thing from one of the news shows. How'd you get that ice to melt down and look the way it ended up? That sculpture of Newt Gingrich turning into one of the Seven Dwarfs."

I didn't correct him. Gingrich melted down into a Neanderthal man. Strom Thurmond into Mussolini. Jesse Helms into a Grand Wizard. It was Dan Quayle—who wasn't even part of the prearranged commission, seeing as he wasn't a political leader of the contemporary South—who melted down into Dopey. His old boss turned into Moe, because that was the closest I could come to a man throwing up at a Japanese power banquet. I said, "Yeah, that kind of got me fired. I had picked up some work with a national ice-sculpture chain, you know. Up until that point, I'd pretty much turned into the best ice sculptor around."

My father pulled the flask out, pointed it my way, and raised his eyebrows. I said, "Seeing as everybody else seems to know that I'm on the wagon, I assume that you know, too. Don't think I don't know that this is some kind of test."

Raylou said, "I promise that I didn't have anything to do with this one, Harp," and got up from the table. "I need to get dressed and fire up the kiln."

"Your mother, of all people," my father said. "I found out where you lived from your mother. After about ten minutes of yelling into the phone, she told me. As it ends up, I'm staying halfway between here and her. My new line of work, I have to stay in out-of-the-way places. Right now it's the Gruel Inn down in Gruel. I imagine I'll be there about a month."

I got up from the table and opened the cabinet, pulled out my bottles of kudzu root, milk thistle, some kind of antioxidant, and an anti-inflammatory—every homeopathic capsule I'd invested in to heal my scarred and bloated liver. I said, "I haven't talked to Mom in a while. She's been angry since you left with Ms. Gorman."

"Although it's unlikely, a teakettle in the freezer might one day steam." My father took three hits from his flask, then poured a half jigger into the coffee cup. "I messed up back then. I know it might be crazy, but I think Flora Gorman put a hex on me. I'm serious. She got me to leave you and your mother, go all the way down to New Orleans, set up house and a joint savings account, and then the next thing you know I'm spending sixteen, eighteen years watching my back while she's milking the money."

I didn't say, "That's what you get." I didn't say, "You made your bed, now lie in it," partly because since I'd quit drinking I had a hard time remembering clichés. I said, "You stayed with her all that time?"

"So now I'm here, doing this. I started out in Alabama, and I got so good—and word spread—that other states started hiring me on. I got a patent pending on what I do. Copyright."

Raylou walked through the den wearing her overalls and leather gloves. "I might need some more oak split if you boys want to make yourself useful before noon." She didn't say anything about how she didn't want to break up a long-awaited homecoming reunion. She swished herself out the door, then went toward her work shed and adjacent kiln.

I said, of course, "How do I know you haven't picked up a bunch from Ms. Gorman, and you're here to swindle me? I mean, I got to tell you, showing up out of nowhere's not normal. And don't tell me all that crap like they do in the movies—like how you stood in the very back during my high school and college graduations, or sat in the parking lot at my wedding."

My father pulled the flask back out. He stood up and stretched, yawned, shook his head. "Anyway, I came up with the idea myself," he said, not answering my question. "It came to me when I was trying to escape Flora. I'd made it to about nowhere Mississippi and my transmission got stuck in first gear. I was on these back roads—which in retrospect wasn't all that smart, seeing as some of Flora's people only traveled back roads—going about fifteen miles an hour. People on tractors started passing me on curves, you know."

I thought back and tried to remember any movies where a long-lost father returns to his son, and how the interplay went. For some reason, Hollywood seemed to miss the ever-popular broken-down-Mississippi-transmission scenario. I said, "Maybe you shouldn't be drinking in front of me. I don't know if this is a test you and Raylou devised, but maybe you shouldn't be drinking in front of me."

My father looked up at the ceiling. He reached across the table, grabbed my spoon, and scratched the inside of his ear with its handle. "So I thought about how state departments of highway could put a double yellow stripe down secondary roads that have long straightaways. Then someone like me could intentionally drive back and forth on those roads way under the speed limit. There'd be a cop hidden at either end, waiting to see if people would pass on the double yellow. You know how much it costs here in South Carolina if you get caught doing that? It's a bunch, especially if you ain't from the same county as the arresting patrolman."

And I always wondered where I ever got the genes to talk city officials and arts commissions into buying monolithic welded public artworks that resembled nothing outside of giant piles of slag fallen from the sky. I wondered where I inherited my innate abilities to create melting politicians' heads down to obvious and recognizable *populi blasphematio*.

"Well, I had a friend who had a friend. Who had an uncle in Alabama. Next thing you know, I'm heading up a whole six-man team of slow back-road drivers. Alabama bled into Georgia, and Georgia to here. We're figuring we'll be working the asphalt of central Pennsylvania by this time next year."

I said, "Well, that's something to be proud of," though I didn't mean it. My father worked for the wrong side, which was the same thing he did before he left my mother and me, grading eggs and peaches with a deliberate squint.

"We keep in touch every night via e-mail. And we speak in code. It's only pig Latin, but you don't hear people using pig Latin all that much anymore, from what I've heard."

I got up, stuck my head out the door, and yelled for Raylou to please come back inside.

When it looked like my wife might open up her mouth and offer my father both food and a real bed for the night, I summoned up all the silent extrasensory intercommunication that married couples always develop between themselves, unless one of them went on a ten- or twelve-year binge. Raylou said, "Hey, Parker, why don't you bring in whatever you have out in the car and throw it in the guest room? I'll cook up a big batch of crayfish and cheese grits. There's nothing that gets a father and son back together like seafood."

First off, I didn't remember my father ever introducing himself by his first name. Even I had forgotten it. Second, Raylou had told me she'd gotten the crayfish—which possessed exactly zero saltwater connection—on sale to feed the snappers. I didn't know what she meant about the seafood/reunion connection. To me, it sounded like the beginning of a dirty joke involving incestuous shipmates.

My father said, "I didn't come to stay. I need to work the roads tomorrow. But I wouldn't mind peeling some tails. Boy, I sure learned enough about how to do that down in New Orleans, over the years."

Another dirty-joke premise, I thought. I said, "I wonder what happened to my help. I hope he hasn't fallen off the wagon." I grabbed the phone and called Bayward again. When he didn't answer I said, "He might be with Vollis and Delay Sucks."

My father stood up and unscrewed his flask top. He said, "I've been japing you on this one. It's just got iced tea in it. I wanted to see if you were like your mother." He put it under my nose to sniff. Raylou retrieved crayfish from the freezer and stuck the bag in a pot of cold water to thaw.

I said, "The only way I'm like Mom is that I tend to be hardheaded and faithful," the last part being a dig I didn't know if he'd get.

"Well, that's okay. Listen. I came here to tell you a story that

I never told. It's a story about how I quit drinking, and why I felt it necessary to take off before I killed your mother. I doubt you know any of this."

He sat back down. Raylou said, "I forgot to cover up my clay," and left.

I put my hands over my ears and tried to hum any song in the world, but the only thing that got in my head was "Have Love, Will Travel."

"Your mother started in on my drinking long before you were born, son. I'd stop for a month, or a couple weeks, and then start back again. I think I quit one whole year, but then I got the thirst again. You got born, and I would quit and start, quit and start. Hell, it was hard not drinking back then because all the egg farmers and peach growers would have a little something off to the side when I came to tour their operations. Well, your momma harped and harped about me and my ways. I'm the one who came up with your name, by the way. Reason why you're named Harp ain't because anyone in the Spillman family loved stringed instruments. I'm not proud of any of this, but I saw you as your mother's child, another harper brought into the household."

I didn't get up and slug him, but I saw it all happening in my imagination. What kind of gall did this stranger have to come to Ember Glow, track me down, and relieve his own conscience? I said, "I thought I was named after that woman who wrote *To Kill a Mockingbird*. I thought I was named after that place where John Brown attacked slavery." I sat there trying to remember all of my mother's stories, and for the first time realized that maybe she made some things up after Dad left.

"So I finally quit drinking. I quit for a long time. And when I wanted a glass of bourbon something powerful, I walked behind our house and followed a deer run that shot all the way out to where those Irish Travelers lived. There were blackberry patches ten yards deep on both sides, so I walked, and I picked blackberries. I ate them right off their prickly vines until I looked like I had the worst port-wine birthmark of all time, what I'm saying." He laughed. I stared at him. "I'd carry an old drywall bucket with me, bring back the blackberries, and then your mother would say something like 'I hope you don't expect me to bake a bunch of pies for you,' like that. I didn't expect it, I promise. Looking back, I'm figuring my body craved the sugar, you know. The booze-depraved body turns criminal, if you ask me."

At this point I got "Have Love, Will Travel" out of my brain, but it got replaced with "I Fought the Law and the Law Won." I needed to go outside, fire up my mig welder, and work on my next angel. I needed to stick my face straight down in the snapping-turtle pond and practice drowning.

"Anyway, the whole time, your mother kept saying, 'I don't know why you even bother—you're going to start right back up worse than before,' and stuff like that. Every day. She went on and on. I stayed out of the house more. Sometimes I came home from work, parked the car, and went straight to my path. Oh, I should mention that Flora Gorman had some troubles at home, too. She followed the deer run from her house toward ours. The first time I saw her, I thought I had withdrawal hallucinations, what I mean. She was allergic to getting pricked, so she dressed like some kind of spacewoman. She dressed like a beekeeper, I guess. You could only see her eyes barely."

I sat up. I grabbed my father's flask and drank iced tea out of it. Then I spun it on the table a few times. "I remember seeing her out there," I said. "That was Ms. Gorman? I thought it was somebody from the ag department where you worked."

My father shook his head. "Of course, when we met at the halfway point, I would turn around. It was kind of an unspoken thing. Even though neither of us owned the land, I felt like my section was up until I met her, and hers was up until she met me, if that makes sense."

If anyone else had been telling me this whole long-winded passage, I might've thought, What a great love story. I didn't. I said, "And then you started screwing her, and left Mom and me."

"No. No, son. And I didn't come here to tan your hide, like I'm figuring someone should've done a long time ago. Let me finish. I need to finish."

I can take a sixty-three-year-old man, I thought.

"About a month into this, Flora said, 'My husband beats me up at night.' Then she turned around and walked back home. The next day she said, 'If I eat enough blackberries, maybe my skin will darken enough to hide the bruises.' Then on the third day..."

I said, "It always happens in threes. Is this some kind of joke?" I turned toward the door and said, "Raylou! Come back in here. You don't want to miss the punch line."

"No. On the third day, she wore everything except for her head covering. She had black eyes twice. I mean, she had those black irises, and she had black eyes from getting beat up. Well, because I had connections from being a higher-up in the Department of Agriculture, I got someone sent over there on the guise of checking their house for weevils. Next thing you know, we got old Tommy Gorman in jail—and it's not an easy task catching an Irish Traveler and getting him thrown in jail. Well, that happened, and I told Flora all about my stopping drinking. Then she said something that's not all that bad an idea. She said,

157

'If you really want to stop drinking, then you should keep pictures of people you love tacked all over the house. Their eyes will tell you not to partake.'"

I'd thought of this, too. I had planned to dust off my old Nikon, uncover the back corner of my own Quonset-hut work studio where the darkroom cobwebbed, and try not to think about how I used the space mostly to hide bottles over the past decade. I would find some thirty-five millimeter black-and-white, and follow Raylou around a typical day. But fully knowing my obsessive tendencies, I feared that I'd stop my commissioned project and take up photography. Or that I'd start drinking the chemicals. I said, "I think someone said something about that when I was in rehab."

"She brought me a picture of herself, the next day. We met, both of us loaded down with berries, at the halfway point, and she handed me one of those Polaroid pictures she'd taken of herself. Naked. Flora said, 'Next time you think about drinking, pull this out.' I don't know if she still ran that Dial-a-Style beauty salon at this time. I don't know. Anyway, every day after that, until she finally began taking earlier starts and meeting me right in my own backyard while your momma taught school, she handed me another naked picture. Let me tell you, I pulled it out, if you know what I mean. Hell, if it happened today I could've started a Web site and made money."

I got up and said, "I really need to get to work." I looked at the clock and said, "I'm supposed to deliver a dozen twelve-foot-high metal angels to the city of Birmingham by November."

My father said, "I just wanted to let you know. When Flora and I finally split up, I found out that she was meeting up with some kind of Cajun fellow. I don't know exactly what demons he tried to rid himself of, but he followed a path and collected those little green lizards that change colors but ain't really chameleons."

"Anole."

"Yeah, he was."

I walked my father outside. He said, "Your yard is one piece of granite. It's like living on Stone Mountain." He stood at the apex of our land and said, "The term 'quaquaversal' comes to mind. I learned that somewhere. Maybe doing a crossword puzzle. I drive so slow on my job holding up traffic until drivers make a break for it that I can do crossword puzzles on the steering wheel."

We passed the snapping-turtle pond. I told him *that* story, concerning his crossword-puzzle word.

My father walked with a noticeable limp. He said, "Everybody's got a cause these days. Life was better before everybody had a cause, if you ask me." He stopped and looked straight up. "I wonder what this area looks like from an airplane. Probably like the moon."

I told him that one of the ten or twenty explanations for how Ember Glow got its name actually stemmed from the earliest aviators. I said, "Someone also said that Francis Drake's people didn't actually all die, that they took off from where their ship went down, traveled through here on their way to the mountains of east Tennessee, and came up this way only to say it looked like the remnant of a fire. The man I bought this house and twenty acres from said Ember Glow got its name from the Cherokee. He made a big production out of pretending to know the Cherokee language, and said that Ember Glow really came from the Cherokee words for something. I did enough research to find out that if the Cherokees called this place Dog Water, then he might've been right. 'Ember Glow,' said quickly, kind of sounds like 'dog water.'"

We walked past Raylou's latest outbuilding. I looked over and saw Raylou feigning to stick shards of a broken toilet bowl into the mouth of her latest face jug, for teeth. She had a mirror she kept beneath her open work shed so that, even with her back turned to me, she could know my whereabouts and doings. At the entrance to my Quonset hut, not a hundred feet from the house, my father said, "In case you ever want to know, the ring code for your mother is let it ring twice, then hang up. Let it ring seven times, then hang up. Let it ring three times, then hang up. She'll answer after that. Two, seven, three. It took me forever figuring it out. Math is hard."

"She's kind of a hermit. The last time I was down that way she was the only non–Irish Traveler living in Murphy Village. I guess she won't move out of meanness. I'm thinking the clan would probably pay her a million dollars to get her out of there."

Inside my studio, I showed my father the first twelve-foot angel I'd welded. I said, "Birmingham's trying to revitalize, I think. They want to pay homage to when it was the steel capital of the South."

My father walked around the angel twice, touched the nuts I had welded together. He said, "I'll be damned. They're paying you money for this? I'll be damned. No offense, Harp, but I guess I never got around to appreciating modern art. You say it's an angel?"

I wasn't offended. It's not like I hadn't heard such comments before, especially for a public-art piece I welded for Durham, North Carolina, that was supposed to mirror the Research Triangle's importance, but—I'll admit—kind of looked like a giant flatiron fell out of the sky and plopped down near I-85. I said, "Two wings, one halo challenged by gravity."

Raylou called out to us, "Two-seven-three must mean something to her, Parker. In police code, it means 'assault on a person.' Three-nine-zero means 'drunk.'"

I thought of one thing only: She couldn't have heard us only with her own ears all the way out from her work shed.

My father said, "Goddamn. That didn't even occur to me." He said, "I got this great idea. Let's you and me call up your momma. It'll be a historical day in the Spillman family saga."

We still stood in my studio. Raylou yelled out something about how the second telephone needed to be jiggled at times. "Even though this place looks convex, I think it's more like a bowl," I said. "At least for Raylou. She can hear about anything that happens. Hey, you want to go over there and look at some of her work? Man, I'm a little jealous, but she has a mailing list of face-jug collectors longer than the Savannah when it flowed." I stepped out of the Quonset hut and took three or four steps in Raylou's direction.

My father walked in the opposite direction. "I know," he said. "I'm on it, Slapnuts."

Raylou dropped her gloves. She walked toward us and said for my father to go over and see if that's what he had in mind. Raylou said she dealt only in cash these days, which wasn't the truth, as far as I could tell.

I looked down at the turtles, then off to the horizon, trying to piece everything together. Like any good old drunk, I pretended to know what went on as if I remembered their past transactions and correspondence.

My wife and I sat down at the kitchen table, as instructed. My father said that he perfected the art of peeling and deveining crayfish over the years, and that at one time he even considered opening his own catch-your-own restaurant down in one of the lesser-known parishes of Louisiana, wherein patrons scooped out crawfish from the belly of a Port-O-Let. He said, "I don't know if you'll remember any of this, Harp, but more than a couple times I used to take you down to one of those creeks that fed into a river that worked as a tributary into the Savannah. Do you remember? It was on old man Bagwell's property. We seined a bunch of crawdads out of there, took them home, and your momma threatened to kill me. Do you remember?"

I looked at Raylou and shrugged. My father's voice had turned into a dreamy slow accent. "I kind of remember. If it's the time we came home and you told Mom we knew where the baby lobsters lived, then I remember."

"Crawdads," my father said.

He wore Raylou's apron and—I'll give him this—could one-hand heads off a crustacean better than anyone on those food channels I used to watch drunk. Raylou said, "I'll wait till you're done before I start the cheese grits."

My father kept his back turned. "Harp, you know you come from a long line of men who suffered from SSS, don't you? I had it, and your granddaddy had it, and his father, and so on. I imagine none of us even knew that we suffered from this particular malady until we all quit drinking. One good thing about boozing up the bourbon daily—no SSS. So I'm wondering how you're coping."

I shifted in my seat. A family of wild canaries lit on my second twelve-foot angel, in the yard. I said, "I have no clue what you're talking about, man. Secret Service? Social Security?" For some reason, my father held an unpeeled crawfish up to the light and inspected it. "Cirrhosis starts with a C."

"I don't think it's an official scientific syndrome, really. I ain't so sure that the medical community has acknowledged it with a technical term named after the original sufferer and known to all. Hell, if they did, I'm thinking it would be SSSS."

Because my wife said nothing, I was convinced that no one in the room would like anything better than for me to pursue this conversation until my father explained whatever the hell he was talking about. I said, "Okay. Good. Aren't you afraid that there are speeders crossing double yellow lines between here and Gruel? Job like that, you must stay up nights worrying about the safety of our cement, asphalt, and macadam."

My father said, "Okay, Raylou. Now I just need a big pot to drop these in for exactly one or three minutes." She got up to grab what I normally used for making two batches of macaroni and cheese. My father said, "Yep. I'm surprised. Slow Sphincter Syndrome. They should change it to Spillman's Slow Sphincter Syndrome."

I didn't want to laugh, but did, probably out of incredulity. I said, "Shut up, Dad."

He turned around. Raylou filled the pot with water, then shuffled two paces over to the stove. My father said, "There you go, Harp. That's all you had to say. I just wanted to hear you call me that." He set the colander of peeled crawfish on the counter. "Y'all have a good lunch. If you want to get in touch with me, either call up the Gruel Inn, or call up the South Carolina Highway Patrol office down in Columbia and say you need to talk to the turtle. I came up with that myself—on account my job's to drive so slowly. 'The urtle-tay.'"

And with that, he walked out the door, got in his car, and backed all the way down our long granite driveway.

Man, I wanted a drink worse than ever. I said to my wife, "I don't know how or why you felt the need to pull that off. I don't know what self-help book you read that says making a man sober depends on screwing with him nonstop, but I'm willing to bet that this isn't really the way. Good God."

My wife shrugged and said she didn't know what I was talking about. She turned off the stove and poured out water that hadn't boiled yet, then went outside with the colander and tossed peeled crawdad tails into the turtle pond. Back inside she said, "Maybe you're right. But it could've been worse. We could've gotten sick from eating bad shell-things."

I heard the sputter of my helper Bayward's moped come up the drive. And I knew that he was in on this particular trick, too. Had he been waiting down at the bottom of Ember Glow until my father left? Was he staring at the sky in hopes of reading some kind of smoke signal emitted from my wife's wood-firing kiln? Had my imagination finally returned, but only to devise paranoid delusions of relatives wanting to bully me up?

I said to Raylou, "I need to get to work. I need to fire up the welder." When my one employee parked his moped and apologized for being late, I took a tip from my father and kept my back turned, and would do so until I got the information I needed. Bayward said he had to go get some film developed. I told him to take the day off, unless he wanted to follow a path down the other side of my quaquaversal tract, armed with a bucket, in search of any fruit drooping from barbed and tangled vines.

PART TWO

PART TWO

11

JOE'S NUTS RAN out of stock somewhere between my sixth and seventh angel, sometime in early July. He said that the steel industry wasn't as stable as the papers always purported, that there'd been layoffs and such. Joe didn't look like the kind of man who would know the day's weather, much less economic developments and forecasts, and I assumed that he'd probably forgotten to place an order. I knew for a fact that he could barely spell his own name, for on the second load of nuts he handed me a detailed bill of lading: "Ate Hunder Pown 3-8. Ate Hunder Pown 1-2. Ate Hunder Pown 7-16," and so on.

"Where's your helper?" he asked me.

I said, "Do you have a number I can call? I have a deadline for this project, man."

Joe looked up to the sky. A V of ducks flew toward Ember Glow. Although it didn't happen frequently, on some bright mornings ducks and geese landed in my yard, I assume mistaking the granite acreage for a clear pond. I looked at Joe and read on his face how he, too, wished that he could fly, probably over to his estranged brother's outfit to sully the mounds of bolts out back.

Joe looked back my way and stared at my truck. "I know a man can make that a six-wheeler. Make it easier to haul heavy loads."

"Well, it doesn't look like I'd need something like that if *I can't buy my nuts*, does it?"

Joe said, "Let me run back inside and give the man a call. Hell, maybe I plain forgot to turn in a order. That's happened before, I ain't proud to admit." He shuffled inside his shingle-sided office. From where I stood I heard the slow, slow rasp of a rotary telephone, and made a note that he dialed only seven numbers. He said, "Load of nuts" to someone, then back to me yelled, "You want to go ahead and order two tons?"

I did some math in my head. "That'll be just about right. I need one and a half, but go ahead and make it two in case I screw up."

To the person on the other end, I heard Joe say, "Oh he'll screw up. It's endless, these kinds of fellows."

Delay Sucks showed up alone. I came back empty, saw Delay standing at Angel #6, and figured that Vollis was taking a leak behind the Quonset hut. I walked over to Raylou and kissed the side of her neck. She stood back from a row of newly fired Siamese face jugs. She'd come up with the idea some weeks earlier, then sold the concept to the American Dental Association: She'd have one head with horrendously crooked teeth, the other with straight shiny porcelain. Before and After. "If this year's annual meeting was anywhere else, I probably wouldn't take the chance," Raylou said. "But what the hell. I got that one dentist who's a collector. I guess I can get him to either buy me out, or at least talk some of his scary colleagues to buy something for their waiting rooms."

At this point I'd been sober for four and a half months — 137 days to be exact. And six hours. I'd made a point to remember everything that occurred around me, from meeting Vince Vance on to my father's inexplicable visit. I said, "You didn't say anything about a dentists' convention. Don't go off saying something like we've been talking about it nonstop for months. I've been keeping track."

Delay Sucks walked over straight-armed and said, "I couldn't help but overhear y'all. You want to hear something weird? I was cleaning out one of my car vacuum cleaners last week over by one of the defunct mills. And there were *three teeth* inside all the lint and shit. I mean, I've found whole upper plates before, but these were three teeth extracted, roots and all. Those vacuums are powerful. Don't accidentally get the business end stuck up near your mouth — that's the lesson here."

I looked at him as if he beamed down from another planet. "Thanks for sharing," I said — which I couldn't *believe* I said, seeing as it was one of those ubiquitous transitional sayings between one drunk's ending testimony and another's beginning at every AA meeting. I said, "Where's Vollis or Bayward? Where's Bayward even been? Is he on another one of his every-other-day binges so he can collect white chips?"

"That's why I'm here alone," Delay Sucks said.

"Maybe I didn't tell you," my wife said. She held up one of her Siamese jugs by the bad-toothed one's handle-ear and tested the connection. "It's down in Charleston starting tomorrow morning. I'll only be gone tonight, then overnight, and not even that if I sell out right off. They got me a table there in the lobby of the convention center, right where the dentists have to come through and check in."

She didn't ask if I wanted to go along with her, understand. Even in the drunk days, she asked if I'd go along with her. Back then I acted the fool half the time, and there's no telling how many prospective buyers I scared off one way or the other. Because I wasn't paying attention to what I thought to myself and the conversation going on in front of me, I said, "I didn't act up in Cherokee, when we went to Cherokee." I said, "You still didn't answer the question, Delay Sucks."

He said, "Yes, I did," and walked away.

Here's what I pieced together for about a second: My wife missed the old, irresponsible, happy-go-lucky, irrational, quixotic (not a word I used every day drunk), temperamental Harp, and thus underwent a secret, torrid affair with Bayward, that Delay Sucks worked as some kind of lookout, and so on. I looked over at Delay in the makeshift clubhouse, seated, trying to shuffle a deck of cards with his arms stuck out mercilessly. I said to Raylou, "I like the conjoined jug heads," and started to walk to my studio, where I would tear the place apart in search of one forgotten mini-bottle of bourbon.

Raylou said, "Hold on a minute. I can read your face." I stopped and turned to her. "I'm not going down to Charleston by myself in order to hide something from you. And I'm not embarrassed to take you along. It's just that I know about a surprise that's going to happen to you — a really, really good surprise — and I had no way to change my plans. I couldn't reschedule the American Dental Association's meeting, is what I'm saying."

I said, "Does this involve my father? Is my father going to come up here and wait until I say 'Dad' so he'll feel better about himself? Here: Dad. Get on the phone and tell him I said it."

Raylou said, "It's not a trick. Help me load these heads in the step van." To Brinson Delay she yelled out, "Hey, Delay Sucks, you want to make yourself useful, will you haul those boxes of clay out of the van and set them under the shed here?"

He said, "Okay. I thought I'd be moving nuts, but they ain't showed up."

I made eye contact with Raylou for a time shorter than when I conjured up the scary image of her in bed with Bayward, the moped parked next to our nightstand. Raylou shrugged. "They say that people go on the wagon long enough, they pick up a sixth sense. I don't know what he's talking about. I have no clue, like I said." She walked in front of me, swishing her butt more than usual, like a vamp. Like an artist in search of collectors.

I should mention that I thought about booze about fifty-nine minutes out of every hour. I dreamed of being drunk, and felt guilty from the get-go each morning. I thought about the one-day-at-a-time reprimand, but wasn't sure if it should be amended to one-second-at-a-time, or maybe one-month-at-a-time in order to quit thinking about it constantly. If Raylou glazed a face jug the right amber color, I thought of bourbon. If the turtle pond got a little murky, I thought of mead. Every time I got stuck with Bayward and his elbow fuckers, the only thing they ever discussed was the old drinking days, which I found slightly boring. I'm sure that every old drunk thinks his fugues and antics top everyone else's, but from what I'd heard about mine from friends and strangers alike, mine did. Bayward didn't moon the forty-third president and his entire entourage riding in limos between Spartanburg and Greenville. Vollis and Delay Sucks didn't ever talk about the importance of rebar in their work with their zippers down to graduate art students at Clemson. I wasn't sure about my father's past, but I doubted that he got arrested for public nuisance, public drunkenness, and obstructing justice three days in a row while trying to help install a sculpture down in Meridian, Mississippi. I'd picked up dogs off the road and driven around drunk with them, knowing in my heart that a cop won't pull over a man with a big dog, that a man wouldn't even think to get drunk and take his pet for a ride, et cetera. If I drank on Day 137, I probably would've set the snapping turtles on my dashboard, or used them for hood ornaments.

Then there was the ice sculpture.

Raylou drove off for Charleston, a five-hour drive only because it took more than an hour to get from Ember Glow to a four-lane feeder into I-26. I stood there with Delay. I sat down outside on a glider Raylou had picked up somewhere. "So, Delay Sucks. Are you tired yet of people calling you Brinson Sucks or Delay Sucks?"

He said, "I think of it as a compliment. It's what I do. Well, technically, I don't vacuum. But I keep them so clean, it's what they do."

I nodded. Out of all the ex-drunks, Delay, I figured, was the one most likely to slip up and tell me what went on behind the scenes in this seemingly endless intervention of sorts. I said, "Whatever happened to that Kumi guy y'all brought over here about Day One. Did he ever come back from Costa Rica?"

He looked me straight in the eye. I could tell that Vollis and Bayward—maybe even Vince Vance, Mr. Poole down the road, Raylou, Joe from Joe's Nuts, et cetera—had schooled him on lying. It wasn't my usual paranoia, either. I could tell that he'd hold my hard gaze for hours at a time while step-by-stepping Kumi's new hard-luck stories involving questionable orthopedic surgeons, customs officers, newly developed arthritis, unfair poetry-slam judges, and a racist bus driver threatening to let him off somewhere in Alabama. He said, "No."

I said, "You want a drink? I know where Raylou stashed a bottle of gin—I normally don't drink gin, but on a nice summer day like this, a gin and tonic sounds good. We got some crazy-straws, too, so you could drink it."

"I don't drink anymore," he said.

"Listen. I know something's up. Just go ahead and tell me. I can't work 'cause I ain't got any nuts left, and I can't drink 'cause I ain't got any liver left. My blood pressure's out of the roof, and one more secret might send me over the side of Ember Glow."

"You'd just roll. It's not that steep a decline." Delay stood up. "Come on. I have to go clean up some vacuum cylinders. Maybe we'll find something worth keeping. You help me out, and I'll let you split the lost change."

I knew that trick. I said, "I know this trick. Because I mentioned the gin—and I was only bluffing, to see if you'd drink it, by the way—you're going to take me down to one of those god-damn meetings. No way, compadre."

"Stay here, then. I don't give a rat's ass. I was just being neighborly. It's not like I get paid to do any of this."

He drove off in his car, all straight-armed. I found myself talking to the turtles for about ten minutes, looked at my unfinished angel, then met Delay back at the top of my driveway when he returned to knowingly find out that I couldn't stand atop Ember Glow alone.

We drove to the first industrial-sized vacuum cleaner, at a Sav-a-Ton convenience store, which happened to be in Greenville pretty much right next door to the residential arts school where Vollis sat around waiting to take students on trips to the mall, grocery store, or arts-related functions within the state. Delay Sucks said, "After we're done here, what say we walk over and see what Vollis is up to? They're in the middle of summer sessions for another month, I think." He pointed, of course, at the school bus parked in what looked like a parking lot for an Italian prison. What I'm saying is, the buildings looked like some kind of Tuscan village, but I would've envisioned more windows for an art school. And maybe some weird naked kids running around.

Delay got out a key and unlocked the front cover of the vacuum cylinder. Inside, mostly, was a collection of lint and cigarette ashes. I handed him a long, special Hefty bag and said, "Shouldn't you be wearing gloves? What if there's a hypodermic needle in there? Or a diaper?"

"Oh," he said. "I always forget. Reach in the truck and get me a dust mask, too. And one for yourself." He said, "You want to see something cool? I like to think of it as the 'Circle of Life,' kind of." He put a quarter in the vacuum and sucked out what had been collected over the past week or so. As the innards emptied, they filled back up. "If there's a bunch of thick shit in here, I do this to puree it down. More will fit in the bag."

There was no spare change. We found no accidentally extracted molars, or dead babies, or winning lottery tickets. If Delay Sucks hadn't fucked around with the Circle of Life, it might've taken two minutes to clean the machine, collect the quarters, write down in a makeshift diary how much it cleared, and throw the half-filled bag in back of his truck.

I said, "This doesn't seem too difficult."

"We only have another hundred to go."

I've never thought of myself as a slob or a neat freak either way, but I couldn't believe that there were a hundred of these machines planted outside convenience stores, gas stations, feed-and-seeds, and at the back ends of Hardee's too close to the drive-through speaker. I watched Delay write down $22.50 in the ledger, then tried to do some math in my head. "Good God, man, does every one of them take in this much a week? Is this particular vacuum system average?"

"During summers it's a lot better. People like a cleaner car in summer. I've been thinking about writing a book on the things I've found, but I wouldn't want to deal with everyone calling up, saying I had what they lost. The engagement rings and whatnot. The glass eyeball. Blueprints to one of the local banks." He said, "Come on, let's go see Vollis."

We drove around a circle and entered the South Carolina Secretary of Education's School of the Arts and History, drove past two security guards staring at the flagpole, and parked. As we approached the one school bus — splattered in various paints to show off the talents of what students usually rode inside — Vollis opened up the door and said, "What are you doing away from home?" to me.

Delay and I trudged up the steps and sat down on two separate bench seats. The bus smelled faintly of ammonia, and not so faintly of gin. I said, "You been drinking?"

"Goddamn president, vice president of finances, the vice president in charge of the furniture, vice president of hallways, vice president of ceiling tiles, vice president of donated art, vice president of fountain, vice president of flower beds — hell, the entire administration, as far as I could tell — had a little private party in here yesterday and last night. They're all big about telling everyone else how bad it is to drink and smoke, but they don't have the balls to reveal their vices out in public." Vollis took a cigarette from Delay Sucks and said, "I ain't got to go any-where until tonight, some kind of piano concert by a Chinese woman says she can do more than 'Chopsticks.'"

Delay Sucks said, "That's a joke. That's a good joke."

"I don't get it," Vollis said. "I don't know what's happening to this country. They got a female dancer in there made all kinds of death threats against her teacher 'cause the teacher told her to eat more than celery. Then she's back after only ten days' sus-pension. Psychologist said she was normal. I guess these days if you don't threaten bodily harm on your teacher, then you're abnormal. I guess that's how it works nowadays. The whole ad-ministration's a bunch of shaky little pussies, scared some rich parent's going to sue the school. Scared a parent will call his red-neck state legislator, who'll then make a scene and cut some jobs. You see that Hummer over there?" Vollis pointed at the first parking space. "What principal did y'all ever have in school drove something like that? Answer: None. I think he drives it 'cause the name, like advertising for what he does best. And I don't mean throat noises."

I looked at my watch. I said, "Y'all want to come over tonight and play some poker or something? What happened to Bayward? Raylou's gone for the night. We can whoop it up and drink all the RC Colas we want."

Delay Sucks pointed, because he always pointed, at six or eight obese men and women walking side by side from the admin-istration building toward the courtyard. "That them?" he asked.

"That's the board of directors, showing up for their once-a-year meeting, acting like they knew anything about art or writ-ing or music. Fucking lemmings. They only know about sucking dick and kissing ass. Right now they're going to sit in the cafeteria for about two hours, eat up all the cakes and brownies, pretend like they give a shit about the students and instructors. Hey, I dare y'all not to think of that 'Elephant Walk' song." He went *Do, do-do-do-do-do-do-do, do-do.* He blew the horn and stuck his head out the small driver's window. "Hey! Hey, everybody! Don't think about diabetes! Save some ice cream for the tuba players!"

None of the board members turned around. They waddled onward, heads down. Vollis and Delay Sucks laughed. Delay said, "So you can help me move a bunch of my lint bags out to the recycling center if we're done cleaning up by three or four?"

"I'd even throw in some elbow grease of my own," Vollis said. "If I had any elbows left."

I swiveled in my seat and checked the bus's headroom. I said, "I wonder how much weight this bus could hold. Do these seats come out?" because I'm always thinking ahead, subconsciously, drunk or not.

My newfound love of cleaning up industrial vacuums waned by about the fifteenth one. All that talk of finding treasures didn't hold up. We uncovered a few dimes and pennies, but I don't think it was worth the cancer we'd probably contract from breathing in what detritus people offered from their floorboards and backseats. I said to Delay, "You suck, and this job sucks. Let's go back up to my house. I need to see if Joe got my order of nuts in yet. I need to see if Raylou called. I don't want her stranded on the side of the road." I said, "I think I still have a good length of rope I can attach to one of my rafters in the house and still have room for a noose."

He stretched out his arm and looked at his wristwatch. "Okay. It's time enough." He pulled out two moist towelettes from a dispenser, set them on the hood, and ran his arms across them. "I ain't so excited about it anyway. I can finish up my route tomorrow." He motioned for me to get in his pickup, then threw the last filled plastic bag in the bed. "We got one more thing to do, seeing as I won't be taking my bags for Vollis to truck off."

We drove through southern Greenville County, mostly looking at smashed-down orange cones and needless road repair. I said, "It seems like years ago, but didn't you or Vollis say you worked for the company mowing these things down?"

Delay nodded. I scanned his face and noticed broken capillaries on his right cheek. "Vollis does that. He don't talk about it much, but I know he still goes out at night running them over. I know this 'cause I drove by his house the other day, and he had a brand-new Evinrude on his ski boat. Another month, we can all go out to the lake. That's one thing our fused arms help us do better: waterskiing."

We took a series of two-lane roads, then turned into the satellite campus of a technical college. He put the truck in PARK and said, "Keep a lookout for me. Blow the horn if you see someone looks like he's in charge."

I turned on the AM-only radio and listened to one of those right-wingers talk about how there'd be no more money in the Social Security system come next week. Then he said it was all predicted in the Bible.

After Delay dumped lint, ashes, cigarette-pack cellophane, and common dirt into a number of unlocked vehicles, he came back and asked me to fold up the plastic bag. "People studying real estate and interior design," he said. "That's what they use this campus for. Used to be a Masonic temple, but now it's a college."

I said, "What are you doing, man?"

"Oh, it's okay. I know all the professors from back when I went to the Alcohell Club daily. They tell their students to go ahead and make a habit of keeping their doors unlocked, 'cause when they become bona fide agents they might have to take off fast from an angry seller, buyer, or bad neighborhood. They also tell their students that it's important to keep an immaculate car, for when driving clients around looking."

I, now clearheaded, said, "You muss their cars, and they go to one of those self-serve vacuums you lease."

"Damn right," Delay said, pulling out of the lot. "Circle of Life. It's endless."

Bayward stood sentrylike above the chicken wire–covered turtle pond. I asked Delay to leave me off down at the end of the drive-way, partly because I could use the uphill walk for exercise, mostly because I didn't want him hanging out. I could spend the night alone, I thought, finally. Bayward didn't look at me as if he'd been caught doing something wrong. He toed the edge of the turtle pond with his boots, veered my way a few steps, then sat down on the ground.

"Where've you been? On a drunk?" Bayward shook his head. I walked up closer and said, "Why're you wearing a turtle-neck? It's ninety-eight degrees out here," which was an exaggeration. It was about ninety, with eighty percent humidity.

In a whisper, Bayward said, "I didn't know about biology. I figured there was just one tube going down. You got any catgut around here?" He pulled his shirt down to show off a hole in his neck, maybe the circumference of a Bic pen.

I said, of course, "You need to get to a doctor."

Bayward stood up. He walked over to his moped — the owla-lope had lost most of its feathers and looked like some kind of animal that might guard over one of the circles of Hell—and sat down. "I thought if I gave myself one of them trach...trach..."

"You tried to give yourself a fucking tracheotomy?"

"I figured that if I had one of them, when I went to drink booze, it would shoot right out my throat. I wasn't willing to have the stiff arms like Vollis. But I didn't mind walking around spewing like a fountain when my liver called up collect."

I jerked my head for Bayward to follow me inside where, I hoped, Raylou still kept the rubbing alcohol. I said, "You aren't going to stitch that up yourself."

"I was hoping *you* would," he said. He walked behind me. Bayward said, "I know where you got them turtles. I know you stoled them turtles. And I could turn you in for the re-ward, unless you stitch me up. I'll sign a paper saying I won't sign a paper, if you stitch me up. Man can weld, man can stitch up a friend."

I bumbled beneath the bathroom sink, Bayward standing beside me as if he'd been shot with a pellet gun. I found a small tube of Neosporin that expired 12/99, but my theory on all of the unguents was that they retained their medicinal properties fine if left capped in a cool, dark environment. I found a cache of hotel soap bars, most of which flaked sullenly in their waxlike wrappers; a short plastic bottle of witch hazel; a brand-new cardboard sleeve of old-fashioned wood-stick cotton swabs; an empty bottle of hydrogen peroxide; about four full cans of athlete's-foot spray I kept buying drunk when I thought I didn't have any— and which I forgot to use anyway; a one-can–sized greasy brown paper bag of what was either septic-tank cleaner or rat poison.

Bayward stepped over me, flipped down the toilet lid, and sat down. He stuck his finger over the drill hole, as if it mattered, and said, "From what I can make out, if I'd've not passed out completely, I could've drilled the hole all the way through to my stomach tube. Then I would've got my intended result, you know."

"I don't know," I said. "I didn't pay attention to the anatomy parts of drawing class in college. And in high school, that formaldehyde smell masked what flasks I brought in. So I didn't pay attention in biology, either. Hold on." I reached into the back and found some bobby pins and metal hair rollers, which must've been left over from when we bought the house from Mr. Coomer. I, of course, went directly into remembering the old Dial-a-Style sign out front of Ms. Gorman's place, which made me go directly into my father's voice: We won't call you Harper because that sounds like a woman's name, like *Harper's Bazaar*—Harper's bizarre, Harper's bizarre, Harper's bizarre.

"If you find an old bottle of vodka down there, I hear that works as a topical," Bayward said. "Any of the old liquors works as topicals."

I pulled out a half-empty box of Virginia Slims Ultra Light Menthols and realized that Raylou hid a vice I'd long suspected, but that thought vanished immediately after I unburped a green Tupperware lettuce saver to find one letter addressed to my wife, postmarked February 20. I looked up at Bayward and said, "Go look under the kitchen sink, man. I'm thinking I saw some alcohol down there last time I looked. I know for a fact I used to keep wine corks down there. Worst comes to worst, we can just plug you up until we get down to a drugstore."

Bayward stepped over me and shuffled out of the bathroom. I opened up the no-return-addressed letter and read, "Hey Raylou—I did the same thing to my husband, by the way, so he'd finish his second novel. Good work!"

It was handwritten, and signed only "CB," without even periods in between the letters. Oh, it was some flowery writing, too, all loopy, gigantic, and graceful. I put the letter back in the lettuce container, positioned it back, and called out to Bayward, "You find anything?"

From the echo that emitted, I could tell that he yelled straight into the pipes how Dial antibacterial hand soap contained sodium chloride, which, to him, sounded like a good topical.

12

MY NEIGHBOR POOLE didn't fill front-yard cages with the normal fowl or mammal: No guinea hens, mixed-breed cuts, rabbits, chickens, or bobcats huddled inside four ill-matched enclosures. I drove back and forth a good dozen times, nosy, feigning to really have chores and reasons to travel between our plot of Ember Glow and, say, the closest sawmill or junkyard twenty miles away. No imprisoned fox or groundhog or armadillo stared back at me, ever, and since the four new cages stood at the edge of my right-of-way granite drive, I noticed how Poole had poured cement slabs down before stobbing down pens that ranged from barred lemur-house zoo habitats all the way down to short hurricane-fence–sided kennel runs.

I finally pulled off to the edge of his front yard, and kept the Citroën running in case he came out with a shotgun again. Poole must've sensed my presence. He limped out from behind one of the added-on parts of his original shingle-sided abode and barked out, "It's about time you asked me what I got or what I'm getting."

He didn't have a firearm. He didn't have a shirt, either, and I noticed right away that he either suffered chicken pox or acne.

Because I always kept a Rolodex of excuses queued up in my brain—one of the leftover habits from the booze years—I said, "Hey, Poole. The UPS guy didn't leave a package for me over here, did he? I've been expecting a shipment. Never can trust people when they say they've shipped something."

I went on and on before Poole said, "If he did, I would've ripped it open see you got any calamine lotion for this." He clawed at his chest and approached the best cage. "Gall-dang fire ants. But I'm about to change all that." He opened the door and stepped in, kind of bounced on the cement floor.

"You getting some animals?"

Poole said, "Come stand in here, Harp, tell me you think it'll hold."

I turned off my ignition and closed the flimsy door should anyone need to drive by. No one, of course, would need to go the quarter mile up to my house. Raylou sold her face jugs at some kind of clay festival down in Edgefield. Every man who found it necessary to monitor my sobriety either worked, or attended one of those AA Shake-a-Thons.

I walked into the cage as Poole stepped out. He closed the barred door behind me. I heard the latch turn, but concentrated on not losing my temper or patience. "What is this, about twelve-by-twelve-by-twelve? Man, you could house howler monkeys in here. Please tell me you aren't getting a troop of howlers. They make some noise," but I didn't go into that ubiquitous "that wouldn't be good for my recovery." I'd learned to attach that last phrase to about anything. If Raylou wanted me to take out the garbage, do the dishes, fold towels, clean the gutters, check her CHECK ENGINE light, write letters of apology to the Republican Party about my ice sculptures of prominent Southern politicians melting down at that fund-raiser to look like various historical fiends, feed the kidnapped snapping turtles, or grind coffee, I only had to say, "That wouldn't be good for my recovery, Raylou. That'll remind me of how I used to always drink while undergoing those acts," et cetera.

Poole said, "I believe it's about that size. I don't need the high so much, but I'm thinking I'll need the wide. I still ain't so sure about the length of they noses."

Talking to Poole, like talking to most anyone within about a two-hundred-mile radius, felt like a game of Twenty Questions. "You getting an elephant?"

Poole walked over to the next cage, one that stood four feet tall. "So I went around driving to all these rich neighborhoods over in Greenville, you know. And then when that worked, I took to places like Anderson, Due West, Forty-Five, and Gruel. My trick worked just like I planned, you know. Stupid people."

I said, "Okay. I've seen enough of this cage. You can let me out."

"Everybody's got the fire ants nowadays. You can't kill the things off. Oh, people try covering the mounds with oatmeal or grits, thinking the workers will take it down to the queen and she'll explode eventually once she takes a drink, but that's a lie. A big lie."

I thought, Hearing "take a drink" isn't good for my recovery.

"I don't know if it come to me in a dream, or what. But I knew no one had tried it yet. I copied up some flyers. I set them in people's mailboxes. I would've done one for you if you had something other than an all-rock yard. I waited. Sure enough, they succumbed to curiosity. That's what'll happen to people lost their family pets and small children in a fire-ant mound, you know."

I jiggled the door. I reached around and tried to pull up a clasp. "The one good thing about living on a flat expanse of granite, up there" — I pointed in the direction of my house — "is that we don't get fire ants. Or termites."

"I advised people to get out their silver change — silver dimes, silver quarters, silver dollars — and place them all over the mounds at dusk. I said that the workers come and nibble on the change, and contact a poison from it that they hand off to the queen. Well, I just made that up. But then I drove up to these people's houses at night — I keep a bunch of newspapers rolled up in the car in case I get caught by the po-lice and I just have to say I'm the newspaper deliverer, you know — and walked right up into their yards and plucked off silver coins like it was manna."

I jiggled. I said, "I don't believe you. Let me out of here. I get claustrophobia."

Poole sauntered over and pulled the clasp in the opposite direction than I'd been maneuvering. "Wasn't locked. You supposed to be some kinda artist. I'd've thought you could figure a lock out," he said. "Anyway, yeah, I wrote that once the fire ants was gone, people could take their silver back to a coin shop and turn it back in. Thing is, I found out that people thought the ants drug the dimes and whatnot down into the queen's den. So they went and got more. And then I *made* more."

I looked at his chest and surmised that they were fire-ant bites. "That's a good scam," I said. "I'd be proud of that one, myself."

"It won't last, though. People will catch on sooner or later. That's the way with people — they catch on."

I walked toward my truck. I started to say that I needed to call up NASA and see if I could get a ride on the next shuttle back to planet Earth. "Okay. Well. I guess I'll see you next time."

"I never answered your question," Poole said. He spread out his arms. "I took all that silver I stole and sold it off. Then I got me a man going down to one them countries down there, smuggling me back some anteaters. Now that I got the people thinking about fire ants all the time, I'm figuring the time's right."

I kept looking at Poole, but I thought about "a man going down to one them countries down there," and thought about Kumi. I thought, *That's* why Kumi's part of this grand scheme. I knew he was more than mere caricature—besides being a slam poet, he's an exotic-animal smuggler.

I needed a drink. If it took me either more or less than twelve steps back to my truck, I would've taken it for a sign.

It didn't.

I drove home and stood in my yard, looking at half of the dozen welded public-art angels I'd finished. When the phone rang inside my Quonset hut studio I walked in, figuring it was Raylou calling on the hour to make sure I'd not thrown potatoes in the bathtub or corn in the Crock-Pot to make homemade booze. I answered with my standard primal scream, then hung up when the voice on the other end wasn't my wife's or old booze therapist's.

When it rang again, I let the answering machine pick up. "Hello. I hope I have the right number. If this is Harper"—he seemed to be shuffling papers to find my last name—"Spillman, please call Southern Hex. My driver needs directions."

Southern Hex was a nut-and-bolt outfit down in Jacksonville, but I didn't know it at the time. You got a neighbor with plans for raising and working anteaters, a man with cages in his yard big enough to house slaves, and some strange voice on the answering machine wants you to call Southern Hex—as if there weren't enough hexes daily in South Carolina—and it's enough to make you either drink or lock your doors. I'd not had any art supplies to finish my twelve twelve-foot angels in more than ten days.

According to Joe at nearby Joe's Nuts, the economy still declined, steel mills laid off workers, and the nuts and bolts being manufactured in Taiwan or wherever melted altogether in the presence of a match, much less my Clarke 220T mig.

I mashed PLAY and listened to the voice again to see if I could detect some kind of practical joke. It didn't sound like Vollis or Delay. It didn't sound like missing Bayward. It certainly wasn't Raylou, unless she got drunk herself and talked some face-jug collector friend of hers to call me.

I thought, My father wouldn't call me Harper because it sounded too much like the old lady's magazine. It sounded too much like Harper Brothers office-supply store, and real men didn't sell pastel reams of typewriter paper. I thought, the infamous Natchez Trace pirates Big Harp and Little Harp wouldn't be afraid to take on Southern Hex. I thought, Harpo Marx wouldn't be afraid of Southern Hex.

I peeped out of the Quonset hut's sliding metal door and saw no one. I closed it shut as possible, lodged rebar in the handle to lock myself in, and dialed the number. The same man answered with a hearty "Southern Hex." I'm talking it came close to "Southern Hex!" like maybe he worked part-time at a radio station that specialized in heavy metal.

I conjured up my best I-drink-roadkill-blood-for-breakfast voice and said, "I'm returning your call even though it's taking time out of my day returning calls that I never summoned myself." I didn't know what it meant. I think another drunk said a similar statement in the one or two outpatient-rehab meetings I attended before the insurance company decided against my going. That other drunk explained what it was like when the bottle called up in the middle of the night.

"This Mr. Spillman?! Hey, I'm trying to find your location of business. This here's Lang Langley down at Southern Hex. I'm the owner. Your predicament came across my desk—and your story—and I figured I could help you out, man. I got a load of hex nuts on the road as we speak, so's you can finish up your sculpture. If I could just get some directions for my driver."

I said, of course, "Came across your desk? How would you know about me?"

"I ain't got no idea. See, I'm the CEO of Southern Hex down in Jacksonville. We supply most hex nuts from Louisiana to Virginia, Florida to Kentucky." It sounded like he was calling from inside a work-filled warehouse, sure enough. "I got you eight tons of nuts coming your way, free of charge. I can take it off taxes, like giving my shirts to Goodwill."

I listened hard and tried to make out if this man was Poole down the driveway, maybe on a cell phone, rattling his own cage. I said, "Did my wife call you? Did a guy named Joe from Joe's Nuts call and say he couldn't get my art supplies?"

"It came across my desk," Lang Langley said. "If you could give me some directions. My man's tried Mapquest, but he says that Mapquest sucks, unless to get to your house he needs to drive from Jacksonville to the Outer Banks, then left to the Smoky Mountains, then back south somehow."

I tried to think of a logical route from Jacksonville to Ember Glow. The path Lang Langley explained didn't seem that off the mark, really. I said, "Do you have your driver on the other line or something?"

Lang Langley paused. He said, "Yeah. I'll call him right after we hang up." I heard more noise in the background. "He tells me he's on something called Old Old Ember Glow Road and Old Old Old Due West."

I envisioned the driver's location. "Well, that's closer than being on Old Old *Old* Ember Glow and Old Old Old *Old* Due West, I suppose." I unlocked my Quonset-hut door and looked out. No one stood in my so-called yard. "Listen. I can wait for my regular nut order to show up. These commissioned angels aren't due to be delivered until mid-November. They want them before Christmas, really, I'm thinking."

Lang Langley said, "Old Old Old Due West." He said, "I can tell from your voice you think this is some kind of trick. Let me say this: Maybe I, too, once had a little drinking problem, back in the day. I'm just trying to help out my comrades going through the same thing."

Not that I've ever been a full-fledged card-carrying follower of the communists, but anyone in the South who used the term "comrade" was okay by me. I gave out directions the best I could in the state I was in, and ended it with "Turn right on an unmarked rock driveway at the corner of a house that either has empty cages in the yard, or cages filled with anteaters."

Lang Langley didn't seem either impressed or surprised.

I won't deny that perhaps my wife Raylou attended a number of arts-and-crafts shows during my decade-plus-long binge in order to sell face jugs she built and fired in the groundhog kiln, that she needed to stay in touch with new and old collectors alike from Mississippi to southern Virginia, that maybe I didn't keep track and chose not to remember. But it seemed that since I'd sobered up, she found ways to load up her clay works and drive them all over the place for weekend festivals. I called her cell phone and said, "Hey, where are you? What day is it? When're you coming back? I know how you've probably got somebody watching my every move, making sure I don't fall off the wagon. And I know all about how you got old man Poole to say he's stocking his cages with anteaters, and how you're putting that Southern Hex on me. But that doesn't scare me. I know all about anteaters. They don't have any teeth. Big claws and no teeth. I'm used to that. Did I ever tell you about my uncle Lester? And I know all about hexes, too, by the way. I was brought up in South Carolina, goddamn it."

I would've said some other things but her voice mail beeped The End. I walked outside and stared at my last angel, noticed how her wings showed more sky than I liked, and made a note to fill them in better. Poole walked up my driveway scuffling, whistling—get this—either that recurrent dirgelike section of Shostakovich's String Quartet Number 8 in C Minor, or a slowed-down version of any song by the Ramones, I couldn't tell. Poole called out, "You ain't seen a driver up here ain't from UPS, Federal Express, U.S. Postal, Roadway, Yellow, Greenwood Motor Lines, Thurston. I'm talking a driver, a truck, a blank trailer no writing. Probably a black fellow behind the wheel."

In my head I cataloged every nearby impromptu weapon: slag hammers, that piece of rebar, some tongs beside Raylou's raku pit. "Ha ha," I said. "You making fun of me?"

"I'm serious as all get-out, neighbor. He's supposed to be here today. I had to go down my bomb shelter, check out cracks. Thought maybe I missed the fellow."

We both turned when we heard a truck's air brakes release, then the grumble of its engine in first gear. "Maybe that's him there," I said.

The semi made its way up my wide rock driveway and when the driver saw us he pulled his horn twice. I waved for no good reason. When he turned his wheels somewhat, I made out SOUTHERN HEX on the door panel and said to Poole, "I believe this one's for me." On the off chance that someone like, oh,

Lucifer, appeared on my plot of land, I said to Poole—and for a second there I thought about asking him his first name, do the handshake and all, seeing as I'd never known any way to identify him other than his mailbox's advertising, which over the years had also been "Pool," "Poo," "Po," and, my favorite week in Glow Ember, "ole"—"Hang out here with me while I deal with this guy. I'm pretty sure there won't be trouble."

A man who ended up being Lang Langley himself hopped out of the cab and said, "I was japing you, Harper. I'm one of those 'hands-on' CEOs. I kind of knew where you lived, and was just making sure you were home. I'd already driven by the house and all, but it took me about six miles down the road to find a place to turn around right." He stood only about five-five but took giant steps, like a bull rider acting nonchalant striding out of the ring as his nemesis charges. Lang Langley stuck out his hand, nodded at Poole, and then shaded his eyes to view my works in progress. "These are what's going up down in Birmingham, huh? They'll look good. You figuring they're going to string Christmas lights on them as kind of a pathway for people to get from the warehouse district into revitalized Five Points South?"

I said, "Tell me again how you found out about my sculptures." I needed someone to confess accidentally that Raylou had an all-encompassing master plan.

Poole said, "Y'all need any help, I ain't got nothing else to do 'less my man shows up from wherever below Mexico."

Lang Langley wore a trucker's hat with a Rebel flag on it, and what appeared to be a suit not bought at S&K, Sears, JCPenney's, or the Men's Wearhouse. He said, "I got two hand trucks and a dolly. Let's get this load off. I got a hundred gross of bolts I need to deliver up to a man in North Carolina who quit drinking and took up a hobby. He's making a bridge from Point A to Point B. Did you know that there are actual towns named that somewhere up there near the Tennessee border? What were those Founding Fathers thinking about?"

Lang Langley unlatched the trailer door and slid it up and open. He pulled out the long metal conveyor ramp and walked into the full trailer, slid two hand trucks down, then slid a box of hex nuts after. I said, "Is this all about free advertising? No offense, but I don't want a little plaque at the bottom of my sculptures with 'Material Provided by Southern Hex' or whatever down there."

Lang Langley grunted and slid another box down. Poole grabbed the first and set it on the lip of the hand truck. I took the other hand truck and waited. Langley said, "I don't want to cast any aspersions, Harper, but you must've not grown up in a family full of clichés. You must've never heard the one about the gift horse."

I thought about how during my serious drinking days I would've never questioned every person's actions or supposed motives. In the old days, I'd've thanked Lang Langley for two hours, and made sure he drank a bottle of bourbon with me before I got out the mig welder and somehow burned myself gravely.

In the old days, I surrounded myself with men and women who, I'm sure, preordered up not only anteaters, but colobus monkeys, wombats, and sloths. Such irrational needs seemed normal to me back then. Perhaps my memory failed, but more than likely my wife probably got a captain of the steel industry to donate something in years past without my scrutinizing his or her intent. Like flange beams. Or screw anchors. Crimper pigtails. Rod clamps and nut washers.

I said, "I'm thankful, Mr. Langley. It's just that I want to know some things that I can't leave be. Please just call me Harp, by the way."

"Don't think, Harp. You have to stop thinking," Lang Langley said.

We unloaded the last case of hex nuts. When Lang Langley backed his eighteen-wheeler out of my driveway, Poole said, "If I'd've stopped thinking, fire ants would take over the world." He spit. "I guess we'd be through with cockroaches, though, if fire ants took over. And stray dogs."

I said, "People."

Raylou returned. She said that, if she weren't a pseudo-converted Quaker, she'd swear on a Bible that she had nothing to do with Southern Hex, that she'd never heard of Lang Langley, and that no face jug—collecting men or women made a pass at her. Like most of our life together, she kept eye contact, stood upright, then went straight to her studio and got on the potter's wheel.

I said, of course, "What? Quaker?" But when I asked her about Mr. Poole's anteaters — and they showed up mysteriously on the same night that Raylou returned, I believe — she nearly stammered, then feigned swallowing wrong. I squinted and turned my neck a notch in order to let her know I had my doubts as to her honesty, mostly-silent-and-somewhat-pacifist Quaker that she was or not.

But it's not about the anteaters anyway. Or the philanthropist with a semi full of hex nuts. Or marital secrets that might have been condoned by both Pavlov and Skinner.

I heard a commotion all the way down the quaquaversal slope of our existence and cut off my welder. What sounds did anteaters make? I thought to myself. Raylou returned telephone messages she'd gotten over the previous three or six days to customers who wanted specialized face jugs with crooked eyeballs, swollen cheeks, freakish freckles, a chin that could open a beer bottle. These weren't the sounds of any mammal I'd ever encountered—grunts so low that I thought another eighteen-wheeler low-geared it up the drive, and pitches so high that every dog in a ten-mile range probably cocked its head.

I set my mig down and wandered to Poole's house where, sure enough, four anteaters occupied four cages. These weren't the pygmy-variety anteaters, either. Not that I had had the time to research my neighbor's new pets, but it seemed that his bootlegger somehow smuggled in the largest anteaters this side of the Mesozoic era. They looked like freakishly long German shepherds hobbling around in search of an exit.

Poole stood there shirtless, looking at his business venture. I said, "Good God, man, what was that noise?"

He said, "I told you. I told you about them things. I could tell on your face you didn't believe me. I told you."

"Man," I said. "I'll give you this one, Poole. I don't know how you pulled it off."

Then that noise occurred again, from inside his house. Poole said, "You better go home now. Come on back tomorrow."

My first thought was that he watched some kind of horror movie, and that he'd connected a good ten or twelve speakers to his TV. I said, "What the hell's that noise?" The anteaters didn't seem affected. Maybe they had great senses of smell, but not much hearing. Like I said, I'd done no research.

Poole turned around and yelled, "I'll be in, in a minute. Hold on." He turned back to me. "It ain't what you think."

Again, I'd lived up the hill from Poole more than a decade. I'd never seen a wife—I remembered his mentioning a better half once, but that turned out a lie — or child out in the yard. I'd seen prospective customers come by to ask about lawn mowers, washing machines, Radio Flyer sleds, buckets of Leyland cypresses, piles of bark mulch, rebuilt Schwinns, fifty-five-gallon-drum ham smokers, rusted gas-station signs, rusted gliders, rusted lengths of rebar that might've been mine originally but I never took inventory, cardboard boxes of Rust-Oleum, and the occasional wrecked sedan. I said, "Don't think I don't live all the way out here nowhere without a pistol and a cell phone," which might've been true, though Raylou was in charge of the phone ever since I didn't fully understand "roaming charges," and the .38 I got once to shoot up car hoods for a sculpture ended up far off my property somewhere when I evidently mistook it for a boomerang.

The sound emitted again, and Poole called back, "I'm picking the oranges, girl. They ain't there inside the pantry."

I looked at the anteaters. One stuck its snout outside the bars of the cage and shifted its weight from side to side. "It sounds to me like you have some cages inside. I think you have a woman held against her will inside."

"Well, come on, then," Poole said. "She ain't gone like a stranger in the house, but if you got to know." Then, turning toward his front door, he said, "Maybe it'll help with your heart," though I'm sure he meant "art."

Poole's shingle-sided house, which must've come in third place to the Winchester house, then mine, in terms of built-on additions, held heart-pine hardwood floors throughout. And they were noticeable because no furniture stood in the first two dens we entered. The walls held scars not caused by cracking plaster, for none of the fissures appeared from the ceiling to about chest level. We walked into the kitchen, a room with a wood stove, a Formica-topped table, two chairs, and an apparatus that seemed half playpen, half high chair. I said, "You have a nice place," because I remembered that people uttered such things. "When was this place built, the twenties?" I thought, And the thirties, forties, fifties, et cetera.

"She'll want a special orange," Poole said. He lifted the wooden lid of a vegetable bin and handed me two round new potatoes. He reached in the sink and got a paring knife for me. "Just peel off the skin and make it round as possible."

The wailing occurred again from maybe three rooms away, down a hall. "Is that your wife?"

"My little sister. I ain't ever married, though I tode you that oncet. You'll understand soon."

I wanted a drink something bad. I peeled, but searched the glass-doored cupboards for a likely booze cache. Poole dropped his potatoes, not much larger than Ping-Pong balls, on the table and pulled a jar of Tang off of the ancient refrigerator, a neck-high Coolerator brand. Needless to say, the Tang looked older than his kitchen appliances.

The house smelled faintly of natural gas, baby powder, and bacon grease. Poole shook Tang granules on the potatoes. I said, "What're we doing? Are these for the anteaters?"

He said, "Arthette." He handed me the jar and nodded once for me to follow his lead.

I said, "Arthette. That's a cool name," and walked behind him to where, finally, only a whimper emanated.

Now, it's no secret that DNA disasters run rampant in parts of the South. If it's not relatives coupling, it's tainted groundwater, lead in the moonshine, syphilis, adult chicken pox, uncured ham, toxin-bloated fish, and/or plain bad luck. If it's not pure cause-and-effect, it's an administered hex. Poole led me into a small room where his baby sister, who somehow had survived to the age of thirty, lay on a makeshift hospital bed, her body all limbs and gigantic head. Her mouth agape revealed—I'll be the first to admit that I considered post-acute withdrawal syndrome here, that maybe I hallucinated this part—two long incisors rooted in the roof of her mouth. She wore pajama bottoms, but a light blue work shirt with CAROLINA WASTE stitched over one pocket, and PAYTON on the other.

"Here you go, Arthette," Poole said. He handed over one Tang-covered potato, which she grasped like any other wild animal might. To me he said, "It's cheaper to buy her dollar shirts from the flea market and throw them away than to wash them. I've had a bunch, mostly from this joint Carolina Waste. Yesterday she went by Jason, I believe. Day before that, Jaycee, one word. Day before that, J. C., like initials I used to keep track. I got no idea what Carolina Waste does, but they got themselves a mess of employees." Arthette chewed three or four times, then let out the noise and stuck her left arm my way.

I said, "Hey, Arthette," as if I spoke to a newborn, or a questionable stray.

"Give her a orange, Harp Spillman. She don't bite. She can stick her mouth onto you like a leech, but she don't bite." He said, "Not that I'd have it any other way, but you can see how come I'm always trying to make a dollar. Keeping Arthette costs some money. The anteaters might make us enough for real medicine, ain't that right, Arthette?"

I didn't mean to say, "There's no god or human who could cure this plague," aloud.

I don't know if, through evolution, cement's gotten weaker or anteaters' claws have turned to a compound just this side of a diamond cutter. Poole showed up at my house a few days after my encounter with Arthette, asking me if I'd seen his herd. Raylou turned off the switch to her electric wheel, washed her hands in a drywall bucket of water, and came over to where Poole and I stood. I'd been welding my hex-nut–laden angels nonstop, alone, without the help and aggravation of Bayward. Anyway, Poole looked like he'd not slept in a couple days, and Raylou said, "Hey, Mr. Poole. Harp told me all about your sister. You should've let us known a long time ago. We could watch after her when you have things to do."

I'm not proud to say I thought *Shutup, Shutup, Shutup, Shutup, Raylou* the entire time she spoke.

Poole said, "I don't want to burden the already-burdened, ma'am. It ain't been a secret around Ember Glow you had your life filled up with worry and wrought, what with the husband's drinking."

Did I disappear? Was I no longer standing in front of these people? I said, "I haven't seen them. They couldn't have gone far, though. Anteater can't walk but about, what, a mile an hour at most?"

Poole shook his head sideways. "And they ain't hard to track, neither. It ain't like they got a common print. I guess they made it to the road, though, and stayed on it a while. And I've called up my people, but they say they don't think they dogs would know what to follow unless a anteater smells like a coon, fox, rabbit, or other dog."

Raylou said, "I used to work in a home for autistic adults a long time ago. And they weren't like the ones they make movies about, either. I wouldn't be scared of your sister. Harp and I could handle it fine, if you need to be away for a day or two."

Poole looked at my wife about like I did, as if she'd landed on Ember Glow from another solar system. "That's kind of you.

199

I might take y'all up on it. Right now I got to round up the anteaters. I got too much investment to let them take off on a adventure like they probably used to down in the jungles."

Raylou took off her denim apron. She pulled her hair back in a couple twists to knot it perfectly, and said, "I can't do anything until my jugs get leather-hard. I'll go inside and make some soup. Harp, you and Mr. Poole get going now."

Mr. Poole stared at my wife's boobs, as I would have, too, had I not known about how jugs needed to dry leather-hard. I said, "Well," but couldn't think of an excuse. Poole didn't chime in how he could track them alone, et cetera. I said, "Let me turn off my welder."

"Seems to me we could just visit nearby fire-ant mounds, if that's what attracts them," Poole said. We walked toward my old refrigeration truck, parked behind the Quonset hut. "Good thing I tricked all those people into throwing out silver change. I know where the bad yards are, you know."

I looked at the back of my beautiful and do-gooder wife's head as she slid the glass door open into our den. To Poole I said, "I got some rope around here someplace. I guess we'll need some rope."

"Anteater's head's too sloped. It's like a cone. No rope could hold them from slipping out, they decide to walk backwards."

I thought, This would be a good time to pack up a thermos full of bourbon and Coke. Gin and tonic. Vodka and orange juice. Vodka and grapefruit juice. Rum and Pepsi. Rum and soda. Moonshine and peach nectar. Scotch and Dr Pepper. I thought, We could have some fun.

Poole and I drove five miles an hour, his head out the window searching for disturbed underbrush. He said he'd once seen a show about bounty hunters, and another about FBI men.

Poole said that, between the time of his birth and that of having to nurse Arthette, his father used to take him bow hunting and sometimes they followed blood drops for half a day.

We found the first dead anteater on the side of the road, evidently hit by a passing car on Old Ember Glow Road a half mile from Poole's yard, which meant, more than likely, someone driving around lost. We found the second one in the back of a pickup truck parked in the gravel lot in front of Joker Ray Coker's Pay Now country store. Three men stood looking down at it, and driving up, I knew what we'd find.

The man who shot it said, "I thought it was a rabid coyote. It ain't no coyote. What the hell is this thing?"

Another man said, "They've been experimenting again," but he didn't offer further documentation.

Poole started crying. We were out of my truck, and I said, "It was his pet," to the men. "It's an anteater."

When Poole reached down to pull the anteater out, the hunter said, "Hold on, now, Poach. I don't know where you're from, but this-here mount-to-be's mine."

I started to say, "I wouldn't do that if I were you," or "We can pretend we're in a civilized land," but before I could do so, Poole had the man's head down against the bed liner with one hand, and the anteater's claws up to his face with the other.

Poole said, "These claws hold diseases you've never known." No one around asked for him to explain what he meant. No one went for the rifle perched in the cab, either. Poole released the man, draped the dead anteater across his shoulder, and walked back to my idling truck. Over his shoulder, he might've said, "This Poole don't drain."

The hunter said, "That's all right, Cuz. More them where they came from, brother."

I thought, Definitely moonshine and peach nectar.

Poole didn't talk on the way back to pick up the first dead anteater. Not that I'm a mind reader, but I could tell that he understood it as useless to search out the other two escapees. We pulled into his yard to find Arthette and my wife sitting straight up in metal lawn chairs, in front of the still-locked cages. Raylou said that, although Arthette couldn't speak verbally, she caught on to sign language. My wife said, "Watch," and we did as the two women went through dirt, air, fire, and water, then pain, fear, sadness, and want. "That'll get you through about any day, knowing those words," Raylou said.

Poole said, "I suspect everything happens for a reason," then excused himself inside to search out a good knife, a scoop, some foam rubber, and catgut. His sister signed "want" and stared at the nearest cage. I knew that I would lick my own rocky land later that night, following the trail between house and workshop, where I probably spilled a couple gallons of booze over the years.

13

MY WIFE SAT ME DOWN across from her in the kitchen and said that she needed to make a confession. Raylou asked me how long we'd been married, how long we lived together before that, how long we dated, how long we had known each other from when our easels nearly touched in college. I took this entire line of questioning for a trick, of course. Somehow I skipped ahead in the conversation and foresaw my not paying enough attention to Raylou over the years, and that she had met, fallen in love, and carried on an affair with another face-jug clay artist from someplace so small that it would make our homestead look like a bustling and cultural mecca. I wouldn't have blamed her.

I answered correctly. I said, "Thirteen years. Three years. Three years. One year."

Raylou dropped homemade wagon-wheel pasta into boiling water two at a time. The previous fall she had built a raised garden using railroad ties and scrap lumber, bought bags of topsoil on sale down at Rudy Haulbrook's nursery, hoed in mucked horse manure from a stable at the foot of Table Rock, and extended the roof on her own studio to the other side of the kiln in order to make a shade garden. There she planted purple basil, rosemary, lavender, chives, marjoram, mint that always wanted to take over, and more basil. She said it would save us money, not having to buy dried herbs in the nearest organic-food store which, I figured, might've been in Asheville some fifty miles away on the map, a good eighty on back roads. I never got out a calculator, but as infrequently as we ate homemade pasta with homegrown basil, and as much as it cost Raylou in fancy dirt, boundaries, awning, and labor, our break-even point might occur about the same time we left Ember Glow in order to help colonize one of Jupiter's moons.

My wife looked at me in a way that she might stare at someone driving a European car with a pro-NRA bumper sticker before she veered her steering wheel and ran that person off the road. She said, "Rhetorical, Harp. I know how long. What I'm getting at is, I want you to understand how long I've kept this secret bottled up inside me. And it's time to let you know. Before I die or something."

I felt my eyes wet up. "Are you sick? Goddamn it, did you go to the doctor without my knowing and something's wrong? I told you that hanging around that kiln caused you to breathe vapors."

Raylou turned down the burner, lifted the pot, and poured her pasta into a rather useless ceramic colander. "It's not that bad. It won't be that bad for you, I'm betting. But as the years go by—and as I've watched you be so good about your stopping drinking—I feel guiltier." She said, "Hey, will you chop up this basil I picked today? Chop it up fine." She handed me a cutting board, a good Henckels butcher knife, and a fistful of herbs.

I said, "Go on."

Understand that I feared she might ask me to tell some old secret of mine, something I'd have to make up altogether seeing as up until I quit drinking I kind of worked on blackout mode.

"This will take a while," she said. "Hurry up with that chopping." She poured some jarred alfredo sauce into the original pot, slung out half-drained pasta into it, and stirred with a wooden spoon. I couldn't remember if the spoon was home-carved or not. I clenched the basil in a fist and added it.

I said, "I hope this doesn't cause some kind of fight. Indigestion isn't good for my recovery, you know." That was a new one—Raylou had pretty much told me to stop every other "not good for my recovery" excuse.

She sat down. She slid a bowl—another handmade, beautifully glazed bowl—my way and slopped pasta in it. "This story starts before we met. I went to high school, as you know, outside the middle of nowhere eastern Tennessee because of the foster parents. It only lasted my junior and senior years, but for a while our school's mascot was the cottonmouth. Our sad sports teams were the Fighting Cottonmouths. Our homecoming queen was Miss Cottonmouth. All of that. Anyway, as you can probably gather, I wasn't the most spirited girl in school. I didn't give a damn if we won a game, or even played. But for those two years, in my mind, I was the most gung ho fan there was. I even beat out the cheerleaders."

I said, "Please don't tell me you were voted Miss Cottonmouth, and that Mr. Cottonmouth knocked you up and there's a child out there somewhere—Baby Cottonmouth—who's found you finally and wants to come live with us." I started to say, "It wouldn't be good for my recovery," but figured that Raylou would intuit all that.

"No. Shut up for a minute. No, I discovered weed, and I'd—all by myself—smoke a couple joints, get cottonmouth like no one else in all of Cocke County, and giggle my way through football, basketball, and baseball games. I'd sit up in the stands, usually surrounded by about a hundred empty candy-bar wrappers, and yell like crazy. Cottonmouth for the Cottonmouths, you know."

I thought, of course, What's so bad about all of this so far, except the pronunciation of her county? Raylou actually let this information weigh on her mind for one, three, three, then thirteen years? I said, "This is when they made you go to that white-flight private school."

"Yeah. Okay. Well, up there in the mountains there were plenty of places to grow pot. And I did. I kept up a patch the entire time we were in college, too. I'd go back home, harvest it up, then bring it back down to Florida. I didn't want you to know I kind of had an addiction, so I never offered you any. And, if you can remember, you already had enough problems with the liquor. The whole time we knew each other, right on up until we bought this place, I was either slightly buzzed, or officially buzzed. You, I have a feeling, thought I drank like you did." Raylou stopped in order to pick out most of the basil from her meal. "If we had a video camera of everything, you'd see that most of the time I carried the same glass around all night, or the same bottle. Then I'd go out back by myself and take a toke or two off the very first thing any ceramicist-to-be makes in Pottery 101—a pipe."

I didn't mind the slant of the conversation so far. I said, "In Sculpture 101 we do a self-portrait with a huge dick. I used a Slinky for mine."

"This is *my* story," Raylou said. "You can talk when I'm finished. You can scream and yell. I'm prepared for it. Okay, so I smoked dope throughout high school without anyone knowing, and then in art school, and right on up while we lived together. Do you remember how you never really wanted to move here?

206

Maybe you're used to it now, but you didn't want to move to South Carolina in the first place, and certainly not to a plot of land that had no soil, just this big flat granite slab we live on."

I said, "I remember. I know what you mean. Call me crazy, but I thought perhaps we should live within a thousand miles of a gallery that might represent our work. But we've turned out okay."

"I wanted to move here because I'd been secretly seeing a therapist down in Florida, and she said maybe I should move to a place where I couldn't grow marijuana, for one, and couldn't get it so easily, for the other."

"And now that you have a raised-bed garden you want to grow pot," I said. "Big deal. So what? Who's going to find out, all the way out here? In the history of the universe, this doesn't mean anything."

"I haven't smoked pot since we moved here, Harp. I've always wanted to, but I started drinking more until I realized that I needed to be sober to keep an eye on you. I don't want to grow pot in the garden, no."

I said, "What, then? I don't get your point." I still tried to figure out how Raylou might turn this entire anecdote into her cheating on me. I said, "One of those other face-jug artist guys who spends all his time at art festivals wants to come up here and live with us so he can stop smoking pot, too."

I got up to get some water from the spigot. My wife said, "I think our land might have some significance when it comes to latitude or longitude. A group of people are coming to check it out. They're bringing compasses and magnets, and some kind of other New Age shit."

I said, "As long as they don't stay."

"Oh. And that commission you're working on for the city of Birmingham? I kind of made that up. You caught me on that one. I mean, you got it, but you never applied for it. *I applied for it in hopes that you'd get back to work and quit drinking so much before it killed you.*"

I said, "Say that again?"

She said, "I bought a blueberry cheesecake yesterday."

It's not like I didn't know. My thoughts and actions from the ages of about twenty-five to thirty-eight came and went, existing in a foggy, murky, wind-driven echo-chamber part of my brain. I'll admit that months earlier, when I came back home from the first night of outpatient rehab and Raylou told me I'd gotten a call about the commission, I played along, pretending to remember sending off color studies, a prospectus, and timetable. But when I went back to my studio to unearth all of my records — even drunk, I tended to photocopy everything, or make notes in a memo pad, or blurt out what I'd done all day into a handheld tape recorder — I found nothing concerning giant angels, the city of Birmingham, or hex nuts to buy. As a matter of fact I uncovered a nightstand memo pad from a Holiday Inn in Bay Minette with a nearly illegible "Fear people who only talk about George and Lurlene Wallace, then promise to send money later" scrawled on it in blue ballpoint, probably from a time when Raylou sat around a booth surrounded by her scary heads. It wasn't likely that I would take on a giant art project, with knowledge that I'd have to hire a lawyer to get paid in full.

But that was nothing.

I did the dishes by hand. I couldn't believe that my wife could be so conniving — so-called converted Quakers, as much as I had ever dug up, didn't go behind the backs of their husbands. I said, "Wait a minute. You mean to tell me that we didn't have to live all this time on a piece of rock that makes the moon seem habitable? Let me get this straight—as I recall, out of all the places we could've moved this was my last choice and your first—we only moved here because you thought it would make you stop wanting to smoke dope? Goddamn, woman, you could've taken up drinking with me. You could've smoked cigarettes and pretended. Here we've lived for more than a few years..."

"Thirteen. You got it right, earlier."

"...for a long time, without so much as friends, really. And no neighbor for a quarter mile, then another mile. I know it's quaint and everything for a near–folk artist to wipe with a corn-cob in between firing face jugs, but goddamn. It's not the place to be if you want to sell giant public sculptures. Or giant private sculptures to rich people who own big houses. *Giant sculptures.*"

"I don't blame you for wanting to kill me," Raylou said. She got up from the table, took off her shirt, and handed me the butcher knife. "I won't fight back. I would understand if you stabbed me in the heart, Harp. 'Heart, Harp.' That's hard to say."

She didn't cry. My wife didn't raise her voice. She did everything right, as usual, and I had no other choice but to change the subject to the lesser of two tricks, the sculpture project. I said, "You know that I didn't want to say anything, but of course I didn't remember sending out anything to those people in Alabama. It's real, though, right? I'm not just spending all my time and money making giant angels that I'll have to try to sell for ten grand each or whatever to people I'll never have connections with seeing as we decided to live on another planet here in South Carolina."

Raylou set the knife on the table. She unbuttoned her jeans and half zipped them down. "Oh, it's real. It's been hell trying to keep those fuckers from contacting you. Half the time my cell phone rings, it isn't for me, Harp. And I'm out of excuses. The guy in charge wants to visit and check your progress."

Dr. Vince Vance, as far as I could remember, said a good drunk's head doesn't clear for six months, that the first 180 days is the worst, that some kind of beast-voice takes over and tries to talk you into partaking of only one tiny jigger. So I couldn't, technically, respond one way or another to my wife and trust my language or action. Or to anybody, especially myself. I said the only thing that I *could* say, namely, "Hey, I think my other head might be able to work. And my genes might be dried up enough to not produce a fetal-alcohol-syndrome little Spillman."

Raylou zipped her pants back up. She put on her blouse. I didn't understand why. "You think I'd raise a kid in this godforsaken place? It should be against the law. What're you thinking?"

I looked out the window. I opened the refrigerator and retrieved our snapping turtles' chicken necks. I set them down on an enamelware platter, then separated them, counting one to twelve. "This is one of those reality shows I keep hearing about, isn't it? This is one of those shows we could watch seven days a week if we had a satellite dish."

"The man's name is Charlie Baynes. I think he likes to go by CB. Like the trucker radio. He's showing up tomorrow to check on your progress, and I think to pay up half the money as long as you don't screw up."

"More like City of Birmingham. I'm started to piece it together, dear heart."

Then I did a stupid thing. I placed the enamelware platter of chicken necks down on the counter, thought about how I wanted a cigarette for the first time in a week, and subconsciously went to take the imaginary Lucky Strike from my lips.

I touched my mouth with my hand. Evidently I licked my lips soon thereafter, often, not thinking.

Salmonella poisoning can occur from handling an iguana, then licking your hands before washing them. Little kids might get an Easter chick, accidentally stick the chick's head in their mouths, and contract salmonella. But mostly one gets the disease from eating raw or undercooked chicken, or from cutting up chicken on a chopping block, forgetting to scrub said block, then chopping up raw vegetables in the same place and eating them.

Oh, the symptoms aren't difficult to identify: In most cases, the affected individual can scream right through the bathroom door, "Goddamn it to hell, you're trying to kill me, keeping uncooked chicken around for your stupid snapping turtles," right through abdominal cramps and all that emanates from such seizures, which I won't go into.

Pet turtles, by the way, have been cited as the second-leading cause of salmonella poisoning—usually those little green things that kids paint up with fingernail polish. Then lick their hands.

"You ought to be more careful" was Raylou's advice. I could've been used for a doorstop; that's how curled up on the floor I had gotten. I wedged myself up against the toilet so close that if a freak fetishist came by, he might ask why I didn't marry it. "This isn't the best time to make a first impression, what with Charlie Baynes showing up later today."

Raylou knocked on the door. "I've done some research on this thing. You want to hear it? I hate to admit it, but you might like one of the remedies."

I thought about her the night before, shirtless, her pants ready to slip off. For the very first time in my life, I wished that

I'd gone to a regular state-supported college, studied something like finance or accounting, and gotten a job as a banker, or financial planner. At least then—even if I got poisoned—I'd live in some town big enough to host a hospital. I said, "Go get that knife and stab me right in the ear, Raylou. Come in here and kill me. Go down to Mr. Poole's place, borrow one of his guns, and shoot me in the temple, please."

"From everything I've come across, antibiotics don't seem to work," Raylou said. "Weird, but antibiotics somehow make it last longer." She shoved the door open, which I thought I'd adequately blocked. "You can have a diet of yogurt for about the next seventy-two hours. That puts some other kind of bacteria in your digestive tract and helps kill off the bad bacteria." I envisioned tiny microbes running up and down my alimentary canal, fighting. I kind of got stuck thinking about an old bathroom tile commercial I used to see as a child. "Or you can fast."

I said, "Feed me some raw pork. I might as well get trichinosis while I'm down here." I said, "Open up the cabinet and hand me a bottle of Rid-X."

"The other option's a liquid diet, Harp. Nothing but liquid. And from what I read, some people in the medical profession believe that a good hard bourbon might kill it off. I'm not sure who these people are, but I read it on the Internet. They said beer doesn't work because of the hops and barley, but bourbon will work. They said vodka won't work because of the potatoes. Don't ask me why."

I got all my strength possible and barely got my torso bent to the letter C. I looked up at my wife and said, "I realize that I must've done a lot of things to you. And I now realize that you were hurt. You can have this entire rock we live on. Just let me live. I'll go off and never bother you again."

My wife said, "I didn't read anything about hallucinations or irrational behavior. Do you want a big bourbon and water or not? I still have some stashed away."

She didn't smile. Raylou didn't have her arms crossed over her midsection. She stood there as beautiful as any hand-chiseled marble statue carved by a real artist. When was the last time I saw her from this perspective? I thought to myself. I said, "I don't want bourbon. But I tell you what—for some reason I want some jalapeños diced up in some chopped Vienna sausages. With pickle relish. And some good mayonnaise."

"That's my man," Raylou said. "Your old hangover recipe. Poor man's pâté." She backed out of the door. "You're on your way to recovery."

I think she meant it two ways.

Charlie Baynes didn't show up, miraculously and surprise-surprise, until I had fully recovered from food poisoning. Fortunately, he showed up about thirty minutes before the first of the outright freaks appeared, a loose band of hopeless ex-hippies and hippie wannabes—there seemed to be a lost generation in there somewhere, which I would be proud and confident to label "my generation," by the way—with their compasses, tie-dye, dowsing sticks, crystals, beads, hemp clothing, turquoise, healing herbs, headbands, leather-fringed jackets, Earth shoes, yoga mats, peasant skirts, Birkenstocks, and JERRY LIVES bumper stickers plastered all over their VW buses, VW Bugs, and one odd gas-saving and logical hybrid.

Raylou took them into the house and promised me that she wouldn't let them wander or be seen until I finished my work with Charlie Baynes. An hour before he even showed up, I said to her, "Tell me, again, what I'm supposed to say to the guy.

Seeing as I never applied for the commission, I'm not sure what I never promised to do."

"Mid-November for delivery. A hundred twenty-five grand, I think. You're responsible for getting the work there."

Upon introduction, Baynes was a deceivingly likable Alabaman who wore a straw fedora and a seersucker jacket. He might've been either forty or sixty-five years old, and smiled nonstop. When he arrived, I stood in the middle of the yard feigning interest in the snapping turtles, all of which defied that Darwinian rule that a caged turtle will not grow if confined to a small cage. These snappers bulked up to real prizewinners, and for a still-cloudy-minded moment I daydreamed about renting the things out to movie companies that specialized in Cajun thrillers, et cetera.

"I take it you're Mr. Spillman?" Baynes said when he got out of his rental car. He took off his hat like some kind of Southern aristocrat, then shaded his eyes and looked at what angels I had looming near the Quonset hut. "Good God, man, if you're not, then I'll hire you on to *be* Mr. Spillman."

I said, "Hey there, Mr. Baynes." I left the turtle hole and met him halfway to my studio. "I'm the guilty one." We shook hands. Well, I shook hands and he gave me some kind of thing at the end of his wrist not unlike a pound of Raylou's homemade pasta. I thought, Bureaucrat in charge of buying public artworks. I thought, Man who would rather be in charge of purchasing watercolors for old-money, tasteless, three-home-owning clients in need of an interior decorator down in Charleston, Savannah, Key West, Santa Fe, or Tempe. I said, "Here we are in Ember Glow. I hope you didn't have a problem finding the place."

"I drove north until I smelled it, then east until I stepped in it," Charlie Baynes said.

Uh-oh. This wasn't going to be good for my recovery, I thought. "Say you're from Birmingham, huh? They still calling it the Pittsburgh of the South? What's the story with having a giant statue of Vulva in the middle of town? You got something like that, I don't know why you need a bunch of angels."

"Vulcan," Baynes said. "It's Vulcan, the Roman god of the forge. But I'm not from Birmingham. I'm from Gulf Shores originally. I still call Gulf Shores home nine months out of the year. Right on the water. My work takes me to Birmingham, Mr. Spillman. That's all. And where must you go for inspiration? Certainly it can't be this place." He turned his head around more than 180 degrees and actually sniffed.

We stood in front of the first angel I had finished, which had begun to rust appropriately. Believe me when what I say next might be one of the only truths about myself that I know without doubt: I detest those little artist statements printed out on thick paper and hung near the entrance of a gallery show, or displayed in a program of sorts, or in a literary magazine when the middle part's devoted to selected pieces of one painter, et cetera. But I found it necessary to say, "My sculptures reflect both the steadfastness of mankind and, paradoxically, its inevitable deterioration. I want the works to endure, yet to change on an almost-daily basis." I thought to myself, of course, *You're a fucking idiot, Harp.*

Charlie Baynes stared up. I cocked my ear down Ember Glow toward Poole's house. What I thought at first was the sound of a Gatling gun—maybe a troop of hunters on the trail of the two missing anteaters—ended up being the caravan of Volkswagens coming our way. "This isn't exactly what I envisioned when you sent us the prospectus," he said. Baynes reached into his coat pocket and pulled out the letter I never wrote, the color studies I never drew up. He leaned my way and showed them.

I'll give Raylou this: For someone who immersed herself in what might be considered only one slight rung above folk art, she had the drawing abilities of a goddamn superrealist. She had found my own sketches for works I planned, but man, she overdid it when it came to how said works might end up. I said to Baynes, "Well, they looked like that on the day that I finished them, but then the rust takes over. If I welded these sculptures in a place like the Australian outback, or the Sahara, that's what they'd look like for a long period of time. No humidity, you know. But here in South Carolina — or in Birmingham, for that matter — they're going to slowly develop a patina of sorts, buddy."

I felt defensive, of course, and it didn't help that the puttering sounds neared. Sometimes at night back when I drank a quart of bourbon per day, I could hear my pulse in my ears similarly, because of the arrhythmia. "You kind of have a woman's handwriting," Baynes said. "Here where you signed everything and left us that P.S., you kind of have a woman's handwriting."

I looked down at where my wife had forged my signature. She'd added, "Every town's in need of more angels, big or small." I made a note to ask her later if she meant big or small towns, or big or small angels. I said, "My regular handwriting's indecipherable." I yelled out over all the noise coming up my wide driveway. "Sometimes I get in touch with my other side so people can understand what I mean."

I think Baynes said, "Well, this'll have to do." I think he said, "Another Sherman won't be able to burn these down, though they'll look that way what with the Christmas lights."

The first ex-hippie got out of the passenger side and said to no one in particular, "You can feel the hot spots. You can feel the deep-mantle lateral shear-wave velocity gradients." The first hippie wannabe got out of the driver's side and said, "I hope they have a backpacking store nearby so I can get some Atsko Sno-Seal Beeswax All-Season Leather Protection for my Vasque Sun-downers with Gore-Tex liners."

Raylou came out quickly and waved for everyone to follow her inside. Except for Charlie Baynes and me. I said, "My wife doesn't have a problem taking in strangers."

Baynes said, "I used to have a stupid little dog I got from the Humane Society that was the same way. I finally taught him how to beg, and roll over. Maybe you should try the same."

I would've punched him then, but I stood relatively sober, and therefore almost clearheaded, and therefore rational, and therefore understood that I needed to wait until I got paid in full before finding a way to deeply hurt the haughty little fuck. Plus, sober, I didn't want to make a bad impression on my wife's new visitors even though, I felt sure, it would be wonderful, finally, for my goddamn recovery.

14

MY FATHER'S IRISH TRAVELER mistress Ms. Gorman, I found out later, ran the Dial-a-Style beauty salon and fixed my mother's hair twice a month. The cement-block business, a three-seater, must've been a front for other things, for it remained hidden way out on two-lane Pick Road, which dead-ended into a creek that fed the Savannah River after Georgia authorities voted to never fix their side of a questionable wooden bridge. In retrospect, my mother had to go slightly out of her way to the Dial-a-Style, which could only have meant that she probably suspected my father's dalliance.

"I lived with a bouffant atop my brain from 1977 to 1979 back when it hadn't been in style for ten years," my mother said. "You remember. Dial-a-Style my ass. Every Irish Traveler woman down there looked like *I Dream of Jeannie*. That girl on *Gilligan's Island*. Jackie Kennedy. Whoever posed for the Mr. Bubbles box of bubble bath."

This was over the telephone. I'd not talked to my mother since taking my wife down to meet her thirteen years earlier a couple days after our impromptu wedding ceremony. Like I've always contended, the noncommunicative nature of our relationship stemmed from Mom's inability to believe that I knew nothing of Dad's affair, plus her incessant presumption that any man named Spillman could only turn into another petty and ceaseless philanderer, no matter what the evidence. I said into the receiver, "I remember that big sign out front of the Dial-a-Style. Like a rotary phone where you could turn it to pageboy, or that haircut that looked like a nuclear bomb exploded your bangs. And then the Peter Pan look."

My wife turned her head toward me and squinched her eyebrows, the international facial expression for "Who's that?" Raylou flipped through a gardening book too fast, as if in search of the plot. I mouthed "Mom" and shrugged my shoulders.

"Yeah. Yeah, like any one of those Irish Traveler women knew how to cut another hairdo. Those bitches didn't know shit."

In my mind, I calculated my mother's age. She wasn't quite old enough for classic dementia. Maybe she suffered from a postmenopausal syndrome akin to Tourette's. Even when my father packed up and left for New Orleans with Ms. Gorman, my mother didn't go on a cussing binge. I said, "So what's on your mind? Raylou and I are still together, by the way, and I don't run around on her. I quit drinking. Raylou has a slew of people across North America and Europe who collect her face jugs. I have public art standing in a number of cities and just got a commission for Birmingham, Alabama, I'm working on."

"Good," my mother said. "Your father and I were married for almost fifteen years before he took to foreign snatch. So there's still time for you to become a true Spillman."

Raylou set down the book, opened the end-table drawer, and took out a pack of Lucky Strikes that I hadn't touched in two weeks. She held a cigarette lengthwise in her open palm, sprang her arm like a catapult, and caught the thing in her mouth after it flipped a few times midair. "What're you doing?" I asked my wife.

My mother said, "I watched a fascinating show on the influx of nutria and armadillos down in Louisiana, which made me think of your fucking father, which made me think of you. Where the hell's this Ember Glow where you live? I called Information about twenty times before the stupid man on the other end figured out I wasn't saying 'sputum,' and then I got you. And then I thought that, by now, you'd invite me up seeing as I'm retired from teaching those goddamn little chalk-eaters. And I have a new hairdo. I've convinced myself that if you look me blankly in the face and don't recognize me at first, it's because I have a new hairdo instead of that son-of-a-bitch beehive made me look like those two women singers up in Athens."

I didn't ask my mother how she ever came across the B-52's. Me—since I'd gone to outpatient rehab for two meetings before the insurance company said I was cured or hopeless, either one, so they wouldn't reimburse my efforts at sobriety and I quit drinking on my own—I only listened to other people intent on regenerating their livers, and about a thousand books-on-tape from Southern writers who cheated death eight times. I veered my eyes away from Raylou and said, "Okay. Well, okay. Can you still drive, or do you need me to come down there and get you?"

I held the phone away from my ear as my mother went into a stream-of-consciousness curse that embarrassed me. She finished it up by saying, "I got a van, and I got equipment. I got almost enough backers, and I got people."

I told her that I seemed to miss something in the conversation. I said, "People for what?"

I listened as my mother exhaled smoke, something she didn't do when bringing me up alone as the only *gaje* within about a two-mile radius. She said, "I've spent the last twelve years studying up on it. Thank God for the invention of the VCR. We never did get a movie house within twenty miles of the house, Harp. Anyway, I've watched them all, I took a college course in the mail and through conference calls out to my professors at Southern Cal, and I've finally figured out how to make a movie."

At that moment I wished that Raylou and I had a speaker-phone feature so she could listen in. I said, "Wait. You took a film class at the University of Southern California?"

She exhaled again, then stomped. I heard a Zippo click and rasp appropriately. "Southern California Junior Film College. I might have those words turned around. Some such crap. Anyway, I successfully completed the program. My major's in Directing. My minor's Best Boy."

I shouldn't have said anything about how she should've either majored or minored in Visual Effects, or Negative Cutting, in keeping with her rage against the Dial-a-Style.

My mother hadn't shown up for more than five minutes with her head in a buzz cut a half-centimeter all over when Raylou decided to pipe up, "You know. I have an idea for you. Why don't you try a documentary on Harp here? You can do a documentary that'll be multilayered as can be. First off, you got him doing his twelve-foot angel sculptures. Then you got his constant struggle with staying off the liquor. If some of his new friends show up and you get to interview them, I see Sundance Film Festival in your future."

I looked at my wife and, just in case she couldn't interpret my expression, said, "I'll kill you." But what she said was true:

Since I'd quit drinking, quit going to rehab, and quit going to AA meetings, the rehab participants and AA victims took to coming my way. Sometimes I thought that they checked up on my progress, but most of the time I felt as though they felt safer at our little compound on a twenty-acre rounded piece of granite, far from liquor stores and bars. I imagined a documentary wherein my part-time helper Bayward went into detail about how he tried to perform a self-inflicted tracheotomy so beer would shoot out his throat before reaching his bloodstream. I daydreamed about Vollis, Delay, and Kumi trying to explain how they discovered a questionable orthopedic surgeon down in Costa Rica who fused their elbow joints together so they couldn't bring a drink to their lips. I said to my mother, "You don't want to make a documentary about everyday people doing nothing. It would be boring and a waste of cellulite."

"It's celluloid," my mother said, taking suitcase after suitcase out of her Dodge van. "Damn. First test in History and Terminology class." She looked around at the Quonset hut I used for a studio, Raylou's work shed and adjacent kiln, the clear expanse of smooth granite between anything man-made standing. "Not many trees around here," she said. "Wouldn't have a problem with lighting." She reached down, picked up a suitcase, and put it back in the van. "Okay. I'd say it's about a good time for a drink, but I won't do that. When in Ember Glow, you know. I believe Marty would act thusly, too. Marty and Francis Ford. Frank. F.F. Spike. Quentin's another story, though."

I thought, *If this were a movie, my mother and I would undergo an awkward hug while Raylou looked off at the horizon.* "Did you actually get taught by those directors somewhere along the line? Do you know them somehow?"

"This'll work out perfectly. Great idea, Raylou," my mother said. "Listen. I've got to be up front on this. I know I said, 'When in Ember Glow,' but this old cinematographer could use a drink. Are you sure you quit, Harp? You're named after a by-God Irish lager, among other things."

I said, "There's nothing here. If you brought your own, fine. It ain't going to bother me."

Raylou grabbed two suitcases to haul inside the house and said, "We've got bourbon and vodka, I think, Ms. Spillman. You come on in and I'll fix you up."

Where? I thought. Where's the booze? Since I had quit, I hadn't gone on any scavenger hunts, but believe me when I say I knew every inch of fiberglass insulation and its underside in the old days of Raylou hiding. I said to my mother, "You were going to say something about being up front."

We walked a straight line to the house. I didn't point out the snapping-turtle pond off slashdicular between Raylou's work space and our sliding glass door for fear that she might possess certain suicidal tendencies and dive in.

We sat in our den. My mother looked surprisingly young for a woman nearing sixty, a woman whose only husband ran off with a jack–Irish Traveler who used to operate the Dial-a-Style, a woman who must've lost all reason to live if she succumbed to throwing away hard-earned retirement money to the Southern California Junior Film College correspondence course. She'd lost weight, but looked more wiry than I ever remembered. Her baldish head didn't make her appear the chemo survivor, the concentration-camp victim, the Citadel plebe, or the alien from another planet as much as it did, well, maybe an older and savvy California woman involved in the movie industry.

"I'm neither ashamed nor proud of it. I was going to make a feature film about your father running away like he did. And I was going to let the guy have it. Kind of like a modern-day Job, you know. But now that I see you, Harp"—she made a see-through square with her thumbs and index fingers, like a camera lens, I supposed—"and with Raylou's suggestion, I can see how I can turn this all around."

It sounded like an earthquake occurred in the guest bedroom, bottle shaking against bottle. I tried to envision where my wife hid the booze over all these dry days. Or months. Decades. I said, "As long as you don't need my help, do what you want. I have a thing against movies. And it's not like I'm some kind of theater snob, either. I have a thing against actors every which way."

As Raylou came out carrying Old Crow so old that it came in one of those embossed bottles, my mother said, "You look exactly like your father when he was thirty-eight. As a matter of fact, that's when he left us. Oh I foresee all kinds of possibilities in a documentary, kind of like a cross between *Fahrenheit 9/11* when it comes to showing how stupid you are—I mean your *father* was—and, oh, I don't know. Let me think back to the syllabus we had second semester at the junior film college." My mother flashed those fingers my way again. "I can see a multi-layered before-and-after, then-and-now, the-acorn-doesn't-fall-far kind of movie, with a ton of voice-overs provided by yours truly."

I didn't like the sound of this, of course. It's not how I ever imagined a reunion with my odd, obsessed mother. My wife said, "The bourbon's old, but the mixer's new. What'll you have with this, Ms. Spillman?"

"I've got it! A cross between that, and maybe a little-known film we saw on Rube Goldberg and his ways." To Raylou, my mother said, "I'll take it straight out of the bottle, if no one else is joining me. And please call me Ansel."

Raylou walked a wide half circle from my reach and handed my mother the untapped Old Crow. A woman whose name I'd always known to be Margaret. Margie. Peggy. Peg.

My Quaker wife met her fellow parishioners in their own eight-by-twelve outbuildings Sunday mornings, and maybe once or twice had them over to our house, though I tried to be busy and/or off our property. She always asked that I tiptoe, that I don't fire up the mig welder, that I perhaps use this time to take a long, long quiet walk far away from our house. There might've been ten of them in all of South Carolina, spread out. Raylou and her pacifists required a boatload of quiet.

I brought this up when my mother — or Ansel — said that she wanted to work in cycles that ran seventy-two hours, with one day off in between. I'd mentioned that we couldn't work on Sundays if Raylou hosted her mutes. "I don't have much use for Quakers," my mother said. "I'd've liked to've gone to a Quaker school, though, just to beat everybody up. You have to understand, I like *action!*"

I thought to myself, How long could it take to do this documentary? She would watch me weld for a minute or two, ask some questions; watch Raylou form a face jug, ask her some questions; then maybe undergo that ubiquitous voice-over to rant about how her own husband, my father, never had any ambitions outside of grading eggs and peaches for his job with the South Carolina ag department before he ran off with a younger woman who couldn't dial but one style.

My mother said, "I really need to hire on someone to run a

second camera, or at least hold a boom mike." This was kind of late on that first night, and the booze hadn't seemed to've affected Ansel.

Raylou said, "You know, we could do this between the three of us. When you're shooting Harp, I could hold the microphone, and vice versa. On top of that, Harp and I both learned how to run a camera and do lights back in college. It doesn't take a rocket scientist." Raylou kept talking to a point above my head. I wasn't sure, and tried to retrace the evening backwards, but she might've excused herself to the bathroom and smoked some pot in there. "I'm not saying anything about your correspondence degree from that junior film college, Ansel, but honestly I think that some of those places where mentally challenged adults go in the daytime to string beads? — they've let them run the lights for their yearly Christmas pageants."

She had definitely hit a bowl or two, probably with a ceramic pipe she made in between face jugs that took her thirty minutes to form, which she sold for upwards of $300. Back in my more politically incorrect drinking days I might've pointed out that adult retardates had been known to fetch top dollar on their face jugs, too. I said, "I have enough to deal with right now. I'm not even sure I'm all that hip to someone putting my mug on film. There are people out there who might be looking for me, you know."

My mother didn't say, "Oh, come on and humor me." She didn't say, "Well, this is a fine welcome after all these years of silence." She got up from her seat and said, "Well, this little cinematographer needs to visit the editing room to unreel a spool."

I looked at my wife when Mom got out of earshot. "You've been smoking pot again, haven't you? I can tell. Don't try to hide a high from an old drunk, Raylou."

226

She giggled. She said, "First off, do you think your mother's film will ever be seen by anyone? Give it a break, Harp. This might be the highlight of her life. And you want to take it away? Check your ego in the Green Room, man. And second, it's your mom who gave me the pot, back when you were pretending to need something back in the room where I had the bourbon hidden. There's a chapter in the latest etiquette books that says it's proper and right to smoke dope if it's offered by an older family member. It keeps everybody from feeling uncomfortable."

I looked at my wife — I'd forgotten that when she got stoned her eyebrows kind of arched up like a clown's, like a McDonald's sign, like the wings on my giant welded angels out in the yard and inside the Quonset hut. I said, "I'll love you tomorrow, but I want to go on record as saying this is trouble."

My mother came back and said, "False alarm." She grabbed her bottle and sat back down. "Oops, there it is again. *Take Two.*" She walked faster to the bathroom this time.

"A big mistake," I said.

"No one. What're the chances?"

I unboxed a new wooden crate of shiny nuts from Southern Hex, stood back, and stared at the frame I'd built of cold-bent rebar. My mother stepped in closer to me and said, "Unlike most artists, Harp Spillman doesn't hold his thumb up to the work in progress."

I laughed and said, "Cut!" like that. "That's just stupid, Mom. Is there any way you can go back and add the commentary later? And let me know what it is you plan to let out of your mouth."

Raylou dropped the boom mike down to rest on our granite lawn. She said, "That *was* kind of dumb, Ansel, I hate to say."

My mother made no promises, but said, "And...action!" like

she'd seen in the movies, I supposed. I pulled the trigger on my mig and beaded a nut down low, then another and another. In the distance, wild dogs barked, and then a flock of ducks passed over. I felt the camera angle up toward the sky. I said, "The trick to these things is getting them heavy enough to remain sturdy, but balanced so they don't tip over while I'm working. And I want enough negative space to create the illusion of the angel being nearly airborne."

This time my mother yelled, "Cut." She said, "Okay. You weren't good at direction when you were a kid, but I let you slide seeing as it was your father's fault. But you're an adult now. Hell, you're old enough to leave your wife."

Raylou said, "Thanks."

I said, "See? I told you."

I circled the half angel and my mother operated the camera about two inches from my face, which, luckily, couldn't be seen for the welder's mask. She said, "So. When your father left you for that skank gypsy, what did you think, Harp? Was that when you decided to become an artist—because your brilliant mother supported you, and helped nurture your talent, and urged you to follow your dream even though she couldn't afford to get her hair fixed right in a proper hairdo?"

I said, "Most of that's correct. I think my mother really only wanted to see the pretty colors all swirl together while she smoked dope in secret."

My mother said quieter, "Yes. Yes. That'll keep an audience riveted." I pulled the trigger again. Over the hiss, my mother said, "How's about that father of yours. Do you think you received your alcoholism through him genetically, or did you start drinking hard early on in life as a means of trying to forget what an asshole he was and still is?" I didn't answer. I continued working, reaching down for new nuts, standing back half crouched, trying not to think about how I would soon invest in a series of massage-therapy sessions, or at least a case of Doan's Backache Pills. My mother said, "I'll take that for a yes."

Raylou kept the mike above my head, and my mother shot for a good half hour in silence. Finally, I set the trigger down and pulled up my mask to get a look at the sculpture. My mother released her handheld camera. I said, "Maybe it would be a good time to go film Raylou. I'll hold the mike. You probably have enough footage that you can cut and splice together."

We went through the same format, pretty much. I held the mike, Raylou sat down at her electric wheel, and my mother said out loud, "Raylou, do you truly believe that Harp received his alcoholism genetically, or that he began drinking at the age of thirteen because his father left a stable household in order to navigate the strange choppy waters off the Gulf of Poontang?"

I leaned the microphone up against Raylou's groundhog kiln. She started laughing. I said, "Are you intent on making an X-rated film? You need to watch your language a bit, Mom, if you ask me. I don't care what those correspondence-course directors say, even art-house movie joints have some sense of decorum, from what I hear."

"Cut," my mother said. She set the camera down on the hard rock of our acreage. "Don't y'all have any friends or anything?" She swept her arm around. "I need some people to tell me some stories, man. Y'all obviously can't do it."

My mother left her equipment on the ground and walked back to the house as if marching toward a spank-needy child. I said to my wife, "I told you this wouldn't work out. She was kind of nutty way back when. That kind of behavior doesn't reverse itself."

Raylou shrugged. She said, "I'm betting it won't take her another twenty-four hours to understand there's no story here."

Those same ducks, I was pretty sure, flew back overhead in the opposite direction. My mother yelled out, "What the hell are these things?" and I looked to see that she'd almost stepped into the snapping-turtle pond.

I said, "Never mind those things. It's a long story that involves Raylou getting too involved with rescuing animals she thinks are being tortured by biologists."

"Biotoxicologists!" Raylou called out. "Hey, now, that might be—"

"Hurry up and bring the camera!" my mother yelled out. "Leave the microphone for now. Hey, when these things have their necks stretched out, they kind of look like...Good God, man, talk about your *father*." She said, "I got a whole new idea. Take One, baby, Take One!"

What my mother decided to shoot ended up—I'll give her this—kind of a good idea. She took a real liking to the twelve cooters—all of them now weighing in at about twenty or thirty pounds apiece, their necks able to stretch out nearly eighteen inches—and filmed them burrowing down in the mud, gnawing on chicken necks, sticking their heads out of the water like prehistoric periscopes. My mother said, "I think I could merely dub some Bartók over the film—maybe some Shostakovich—and then market this documentary to schools so they can get their students to understand biology *and* music. I'll call it something like...damn, what're those words for a turtle's shell? There's a top and a bottom word."

My wife said, "There are copperheads around here, too. A few rattlesnakes. You'd have to go further south to find cottonmouths. I'm thinking you could do a whole series of short shorts involving, you know, God's scary creatures of the South."

I said, "We got fire ants, and the neighbor down the hill tried to smuggle in some anteaters from Central America or someplace, but they all got loose. At least two of them, from what I understand, are now mounted."

We sat in mesh chairs that rolled up and fit in a bag Raylou got somewhere. We sat in the Quonset hut, surrounded by what angels I had finished, drinking coffee. My mother and Raylou ate dry, dry homemade scones that I wouldn't touch seeing as I figured they'd remind me of the days of pretzels and beer. My mother said, "You know, it's really not all that bad here in Ember Glow. There sure isn't the hustle and bustle like there is where you were brought up, Harp."

My hometown might've held 2,000 residents. There may be nothing more selfish than a committed drunk become a committed recoverer, which may explain why I said, "Don't think about moving up here."

Raylou said, "Harp. That's not very nice." To my mother she said, "You can come up here anytime you want."

"Hollywood East," my mother said. She rubbed at her scalp a few times like a kid might rub a balloon to urge static. "No, I was just being polite. I'll keep my home base right there near the Dial-a-Style so I can remember why I'm on this planet every day."

I cleared my throat. I got up, rummaged through a drawer of old washers, and found a pack of Camels I'd stashed for such mornings when I felt lost without bourbon, and said, "Is your reason on the planet to make sure everyone knows what Dad did twenty-five years ago? I mean, that first documentary you started—the one about how I looked like him, and I was destined to act like him—to be honest, I thought it was plain mean-spirited. And kind of presumptuous."

Raylou got up and said she wanted to throw a couple dozen face jugs, that she needed to chop oak for the kiln, that she'd bought a new shingle hammer she thought might work best for cracking up old porcelain plates used for scary teeth. I think she felt uncomfortable. I think she thought it necessary for my mother and me to have some kind of long-time-coming talk, maybe for my mother to admit some wrongdoing in her child-rearing skills, or me to confess that I should've forged contact years earlier, before the era of correspondence courses, when my mother had no hobbies or use for family members.

I kept eye contact. I said, "He was here not so long ago, and told me that y'all talked. That you had some kind of code ring for your telephone."

When my mother opened her mouth wide, I thought she started to admit some kind of shortcomings on her part, or that she wanted to say how she admired how I broke the Spillman family drinking problem. The sound that came out of her throat, though, sounded more like one of those trick cellophane-and-cardboard disks kids put in their mouths to talk like the speech-afflicted. Or it sounded like that death rattle.

I said, "What?"

My mother pointed at her chest twice. She pointed at half a scone—and later on I would point out to anyone that, outside of a cheap way of killing yourself, scones were better used as tent stakes—then to her throat. Of all things, my mother got up out of her chair and walked quickly to my twelve-gallon wet-dry Shop-

Vac. She made that noise some more and stamped her feet. On her face I read — frustration? discomfort? some kind of existential dread? — until she finally eeked out, "Choking."

She was the one to turn on the switch. Me, I jumped up like a good son and tried to figure out how to perform that Heimlich maneuver without touching my mother's breasts because, well, I had enough nightmares.

My mother shoved the black nozzle in her own mouth, tightened her lips around the business end, and unclogged her air passage. It's an image I knew that I would never escape, even with daily visits to a certified psychoanalyst with training in hypnosis to eradicate Oedipus syndromes. I screamed out for help, but by the time Raylou showed up the vacuum's hose half snaked around by itself on the floor, a chunk of scone stuck to the plastic attachment, and I stood there cradling my mother's abdomen from behind.

Raylou said, "I knew y'all would patch things up. I wish I had this on film. I didn't want to say anything before, but you don't need all the cursing and violence."

I let go of my mother. Later on I would think about how most people would thank a son for having a Shop-Vac at the ready, for my at least attempting to heave at her diaphragm. "Lucky thing I don't wear dentures," my mother said. She went back to her chair. "If you end up with your teeth falling out someday, Harp, you can blame it on your father's gummy side of the family. Maybe that's why he ran off with Flora Gorman. It wasn't for her hair, believe me. Maybe her having retractable teeth played a part in it all. I saw it before. There in the Dial-a-Style, I saw her have to apply another strip of that gum glue." My mother laughed and laughed, reached in her pocket, and pulled out a four-inch clay pipe I supposed that Raylou gave her. "Now that I think about it, your daddy's mistress looked about like those snapping turtles when it comes to smiles."

Then, like any good sniper, she left the premises within five minutes while Raylou went back in the house, while I stood in my studio making mental lists as to what I needed to do next. My mother packed up her van and drove in reverse straight down Ember Glow without as much an invitation to come see the final cut of whatever it was she shot. I realized that, in the movies, I would probably have a voice-over saying, "What just happened?" or "I hope to hell this is all a dream," or "This isn't good for my recovery."

I locked the door to the Quonset hut. At the snapping-turtle pond, I tried not to think of my father's mistress from years ago. Inside, while my wife took orders for her face jugs over the Internet, I turned on the television. One of those cable channels had a Three Stooges marathon going. Another showed a Marx Brothers film. The Atlanta station showed Laurel and Hardy, and the Cartoon Network offered up the Roadrunner.

Nothing seemed funny.

I turned to the independent-film channel. A German man and woman, their faces in close-up, talked about the good and essential symbiotic nature of termite mounds. There were subtitles. I think it was the man who tried to make some kind of connection with Schopenhauer. I turned to the all-animal channel, and — I'll meet God or Satan insistent that something more powerful than I planned this all along — a man doing a voice-over explained that there were many differences between land tortoises and aquatic turtles, but that both depended on sturdy plastrons and carapaces. A woman came over the film and pointed out how, although it's not common, snapping turtles have been known to be monogamous, and that one pair stayed together over fifteen years.

I thought about postacute withdrawal syndrome.

I turned back to the cartoon channel.

15

I WENT OUT LOOKING for all of my unofficial handlers on the six-month anniversary of liver regeneration, a humid, near-unbearable mid-August day. I'd not seen Bayward in more than a month, Vollis and Delay Sucks for a couple weeks. Kumi, as far as I knew, never came back from Costa Rica in order to receive use of his elbows again. I'd gotten to that unfortunate point where I didn't pity drunks as much as I shook my head and looked down on them, which pissed me off immeasurably seeing as, to be honest, I knew deep down that commitment was commitment, no matter what. The term "backsliders" kept cropping up in the front of my brain. I gave no slack whatsoever. Raylou told me, "You can't judge them, Harp. If they turned to drinking again, you can't judge them. From what I've read, they're probably undergoing a guilt unknown to most men, even the everyday adulterer."

From what *I* had read, the six-month point was when ex-drunks finally turned a corner in terms of straight and clear thinking. I said to Raylou, "I ain't going out trying to find them cheating on their wives. Hell, I don't even know if Vollis or Delay *have* wives. Bayward's wife—goddamn, she locked herself in a room a long time ago, from what I understand. He told me one time that she only comes out to watch reruns of *Dynasty* and *Dallas* on their good TV."

My wife said, "You're not listening to what I'm saying." On my six-month anniversary, she said, "You go do what you want, but I want to go on record as saying I don't think it's a good idea for you to enter the doors of a bunch of local bars. The little beast-voice in your head's going to tell you it's all right to sit down, that it's all right to try drinking one bourbon, that it's all right to stop by the liquor store on the way home, and then you're going to be right where you ended up the day before Valentine's Day."

I tried to erase the image of my crawling around on the hard floor of my Quonset-hut studio, confused, wondering what Ray-lou talked about when she was talking about the snapping turtles she was off to rescue; I tried to eradicate that morning when I, four or five weeks into a balls-out binge, hoped desperately that I'd not really concocted ice sculptures that would only get me on the long, long Republican Party hit list.

"I'm going down to the Alcohell Club clubhouse where they used to hang out, first. Then I'll drive around to all of those industrial vacuum cleaners that Delay Sucks takes care of, to see if he's working. I'll drop by that art school, but I think they're in between sessions and there's no need for Vollis to drive a bus. As for Bayward, I can go back by the rehab clinic and see if he's still enrolled in outpatient. And I can ask Vince Vance what's up and kind of gloat that I did all this without spending twenty-three hours a day drinking coffee, smoking cigarettes, and eating stale doughnuts while listening to the same hammerheads talk about waking up in jail, the hospital, or halfway up a roadside oak tree. Then, if I don't find them at any of those places, I'll start hitting the bars."

Raylou looked at her watch. She didn't ask, "Can I go with you?" or "What time do you think you'll be back?" or "Can you stop by the grocery store on your way home and pick up some bread?" or "Did you see the news this morning where there are going to be roadblocks set up all over the place looking for drunk drivers?" or "Can you stop by the pawnshop on your way home and pick up a pistol and some bullets for me so I can go ahead and shoot myself should you start drinking again?" like in the old days. Raylou said, "If I'm not home when you get back, I've gone to deliver some face jugs up to Tryon. The gallery's sold out, and they want another ten or twelve."

I could tell by the look on her face that she wanted me to go along with her. In the old days, I would've jumped right in the passenger side of her step van, lugging along a quart of Old Crow, a mini-cooler of ice, a liter of Coke. I said, "I'd go with you, but I don't think it would be good for my recovery," of course.

Raylou didn't shake her head sideways. She looked me in the eye, walked by me in a way that invaded my personal space, and tapped my chest with her palm three times. I don't think I underwent auditory hallucinations of a chicken peckering around our den. I'm pretty sure it was Raylou clucking her tongue against the roof of her mouth. She shrugged, then handed me the keys to the old Citroën.

I drove straight to Carolina Behavior, but didn't see Bayward's moped in the parking lot. I didn't want to run into Vince Vance because I knew that he'd start telling me that even though I'd not had a drop in six months, I still needed to go to meetings, seeing as they were the only thing that worked, even though that wasn't close to the truth, et cetera. I looked around for Delay's truck, or Vollis's beat-up cone-bashing vehicle with the orange smears on the fender. Nothing.

Then I went out to downtown Travelers Rest and slowed down in front of Shaky's coffee place, but there was a CLOSED sign out front, which made me wonder if Shaky himself had rejoined the bourbon brigade. The last thing I wanted to do was find my old obnoxious teammates at the Alcohell Club playing Drunken Jeopardy, fighting over who first yelled out "What is Heaven Hill?" when asked to think up synonyms for "Utopia Mound" or "Nirvana Hummock" questions.

I got to the door and walked in in midtestimonial, some reformed holier-than-thou self-righteous guy wearing a commemorative blue-chip medallion the size of a Frisbee around his neck. No one looked my way, and through the smoke I noticed how the regular seat for Bayward was empty. The speaker said, "You can't just up and decide to stop diarrhea, either! Let's say you been squirting nonstop for a week 'cause you ate something wrong down at that new Honduras or Guatemala or Red Lobster restaurant. You can come back from the bathroom all you want saying, 'I promise that's the last time ever' to your wife, but it ain't gone be the last time. And it's the same way with the liquor. I don't care what you think or how strong you got the willpower, no matter how many times you say you gone quit, there you go again: Instead of heading back to the toilet like the diarrheaholic, you heading back to the bar. Or the liquor cabinet. The red dot store. Who in here right now — show of hands — can say he promised to quit drinking, and it worked without the help of good brothers like us? Show of hands."

I didn't mean to scream out, "I did," loudly, but it came out. "I did, and I didn't have to wear a goofball necklace to let everybody know." Then I said, "Anyone here seen a couple guys can't bend their elbows, and another fellow with a self-inflicted trachea scar? If you see them, could you mention that Harp Spillman's worried about them?" but I'll admit that I was halfway out the door and running to my car during that second part, in case anyone wanted to strap me down for a lie-detector test, force me to undergo a brainwashing technique best known to pre-religious cult followers, or go the safe route and plain lynch me on site.

Someone called out after me, "The Lord blessed thee! Come back soon!" which got me stuck thinking, "And thee thou, thoo," because I was such an idiot.

I drove around slowly in the heat, thinking to myself, Where would I go if I tried to hide out from people who thought I had everything under control?

There was but one answer in the upper half of South Carolina.

I drove straight to the nearest scary drinking establishment, a place called Scatterbrain's halfway between Pickens and Brevard. Let me say this: Scatterbrain's used to be called plain Bob's Place or Don's Bar or Ron's Saloon, I forget. No one called it that after the owner lost an unforeseen one-sided duel back in the early 1970s over one of the finer, lesser-known rules concerning cockfighting. They say that Bob, Don, or Ron's brain matter was equally split by a wooden support in the back middle of the establishment, then splattered on what had been a whitewashed expanse of foot-wide pine planks. The place closed down until someone rented it out for an election-night party for President Carter, and then Don, Bob, or Ron's widow — a woman whose enunciation I could never understand, but finally talked myself into hearing her refer to herself as Rowena — decided to make a go of it all over again, this time without illegal activities that involved farm animals. She understood that the area needed a near-wholesome meeting place. She kept the wooden support — a poor-woman's stripper's pole—rearranged the location of the beer cooler, and called the centerpiece of the place Scatterbrain's Stem. I had heard her say things in the past like, "Man, wha'chew eat for lunch that's stinky? Go stand all way over there Scatterbrain's Stem."

Bayward's moped, adorned with the owlalope I'd given him months earlier, stood nearly upright off to the side of Scatterbrain's, far from both the road and the outhouse Rowena never bothered to tear down. And a school bus from the South Carolina Secretary of Education's School of the Arts and History jutted off there on the side, too.

It wasn't eleven in the morning yet. I walked in to find a man behind the bar whom I'd never seen. My old buddies weren't inside, which made me wonder if Bayward helped the boys out inside the outhouse, an image I couldn't shake, so to speak. There would be another patron coming in right after me, seeing as — up until this point I thought it could've been coincidence—Raylou or someone had hired a detective to follow me around. All morning I'd checked my rearview to find a lime green Ford Maverick back in the distance, usually about a hundred yards behind my car. Some psychologist should do an experiment on how dumb a person would have to be to set up shop as a professional tailer who worked out of a glaring goddamn singleton car no one outside of a blind man might drive.

I said to the man behind the bar, "I'll take water. I'm waiting for some people."

He said, "I ain't seen you in here a long time." He said, "Knock your head on something? You know we can't serve nothing clear without getting accused. Brown or yeller, that's all we got. You want brown or yeller?"

It came back to me. Scatterbrain's only served bourbon and beer, nothing in between.

I looked up at the short ceiling, not seven feet high. Back before Bob, Don, or Ron misinterpreted the rules of cockfighting—sometime between needing a church key to open a beer can and the advent of the pop-top—somebody thought it would look good to glue pull-tab rings up there. At the yearly barbecue, Rowena held a guess-how-many-are-up-there contest, the number changing from year to year due to college kids coming down on scavenger hunts, fights that involved someone starting a roundhouse punch too high and slicing off half his knuckles, et cetera. I looked back at the bartender, who I realized was Rowena's son Timmy—a man who used a goat's foreleg and cloven hoof for a roach clip—and said, "Brown."

"Now you're talking," he said. "Where you been, man? Goddamn, I 'member you coming in here so fucked-up we used to take bets. You the artist, right?"

He placed a glass of Jim Beam in front of me.

I said, "That bus out back, and that moped. Where are those guys? That's who I came here to meet up with."

Timmy might've been thirty-five years old. He wore a light blue work shirt that read CAROLINA WASTE above the right pocket, TICK above the left—the same company that Mr. Poole's little sister wore that time I went over to look at his anteaters—and kept his hair slicked back with, I imagined, a homemade hair gel akin to lard.

I looked down at the bourbon and thought about how I needed those naked pictures of all those women who'd be disappointed in my drinking again, viz., Raylou.

The door opened and in walked, I assumed, the detective.

242

He said to his assembled audience of Timmy and me, "Hot-damn. I didn't expect the ceiling. I'm about to have a flashback of a pet hedgehog I almost spray-painted silver one time."

Timmy said, "Brown or yeller."

The man sat down right next to me and looked at my glass. He said, "Silver. I said silver. He was already brown."

I said, "Is that a Maverick or a Pinto you're driving?"

He said, "I'll have what he's having," to Timmy.

Timmy poured. He did his job and said, "Y'all want to keep a tab?"

I said, "I know you're following me around. Tell my wife she's wasting her money having you follow me around."

Timmy said to me, "You talking about Vollis and Delay and Bayward and that black dude what talks funny? They off in the north slope woods cropping ginseng. At least that's what they say. I don't know about y'all, but I heard people call it a lot of things, but not ginseng."

"I don't know what you're talking about, man," my detective said to either Timmy, me, or both of us. He drank his bourbon in one good gulp—this one act gave me a metallic taste in my mouth, and I'm pretty sure I kind of shuddered both internally and visibly—and said, "It's a Maverick." He didn't answer the rest of my question.

I said to Timmy, "Tell them I need to see them when they get back." I tried to think up a fake name but couldn't. I said, "Tell Bayward and those guys that Harp's looking for them."

Timmy turned around to look for a pencil and paper. I got up to set some money down next to my untouched bourbon, but the man next to me grabbed my forearm. He said, "It's not your wife that hired me on, unless your wife's named Karl. I'm pretty sure the guy's named Karl." He lowered his head and eased toward me. For a second I thought the guy wanted to kiss. "Grab your drink and come outside a minute. You'll want to hear this."

I thought, Karl, Karl, Karl. I thought, Who do I know named Karl? I said to Timmy, "We're going out on the porch," which really wasn't but a slab of cement blocks haphazardly set down in front. I took my drink and held it tightly. Outside I said, "Karl. Karl rings a bell."

Off in the woods it sounded like a bear rolled down the hill. Then I heard Kumi's voice blurting out, "Do not bruise the ginseng! We must not hurt the ginseng!" and either Vollis or Delay Sucks saying, "My goldurn muscles are gone."

"I don't think it would be wise for me to tell you my real name. I don't know you at all. Let me say this, though: I think I got hired on to follow you around, see what you do and where you go, then report back. I'm getting paid a lot of money for this, which can only make me think that it's someone serious enough to later hire on a real professional to get you to stop whatever it is you do." He drank half of his second drink.

I said, "Are you a traitor?"

"It depends," he said. "What I'm saying is, I don't do work for the big guy wanting to hurt the little guy. Somewhere along the line I made some decisions about who needed help more. So I guess I'm a traitor, you know."

One of the other ex-drunks rolled down the hill, screaming. I said, "Karl. I remember who Karl's got to be." I lifted the drink up to my nose and sniffed it. "That dickhead at the Republican National Committee party who got so mad at me."

"The man who hired me out to look at you said his name was Lark. I figured out right away that it was a code name, and that he probably didn't have enough imagination to come up with anything outside of simple dyslexia. So Karl, more than likely."

I'm pretty sure we both stood there trying to think up other configurations of L-A-R-K. Me, I tried to think up scrambled letters for T-R-A-I-T-O-R, couldn't, but then thought of how T-R-A-D-E-R could be turned around to "Retard," which made enough sense for me. I said, "I appreciate your honesty," though I didn't believe him; I still figured that Raylou sent someone after me so I wouldn't drink. I said, "When you see Karl, tell him I might've *ordered* a drink, but I only sniffed it."

I didn't think that I would ever look forward to seeing the Elbow Boys and Bayward show up en masse, but I did. They wandered up to the front of Scatterbrain's, covered in poison-ivy vines, brambles, red clay, and briars, all four of them swinging their arms freely like regular trudging fools. They looked at me in surprise, of course, and Traitor or Trader said, "I'm going back inside. You'll see me later, because I do have to do my job," in a whisper.

"Well, well, well," I said. "Looks like some old friends of mine either lied to me, or took a trip down to Costa Rica to get the pins taken out."

Kumi hugged me and said, "How long did you last, my brother! I see you now enjoy the drink again! We, too, could not hold back, *because we are powerless* to the alcohol!"

Bayward said, "I got to tell you — it's like goddamn diarrhea. You ever tried to hold back the diarrhea attack?"

Vollis patted me on the back and said, "Welcome home, Harp. We've missed you."

I opened the door to inside Scatterbrain's and said, "I'm not drinking, you idiots. I'm just holding this thing, like a test. I'm making a point to myself."

They walked in single file and Delay Sucks said, "Uh-huh. Testing yourself. I know that feeling. Sometimes when I'm on the job cleaning out my vacuums, I test how long I can keep the nozzle on my crotch." He held his arms up and showed off his muscles. "We didn't have to go to Costa Rica, thanks to Kumi finding out a few things."

Inside, Timmy stared at the ceiling, one index finger in midair, counting pull tabs. My detective sat in a ladder-back chair away from the bar, his bourbon poised atop his knee. He seemed to stare at the wall. Vollis said, "The three of us decided we didn't want to pay up five hundred ten dollars and sixty-five cents apiece on roundtrip airfare, not to mention the twenty or thirty dollars a night at a crappy motel, plus the two hundred and sixty-seven dollars each that Dr. Sanchez of San José said he needed to take out our elbow pins right there outpatient in his office."

Timmy said, "Goddamn it," and looked at Vollis. He pointed back in the air and said, "One, two, three, four," stabbing at the ceiling like a stargazer.

Peripherally I watched a man who would, in later years when I told the story, become a *hit man* more than a detective. Bayward, Kumi, and Delay sat down at the bar and ordered both yellow and brown. "So Kumi goes all the way out there to get his elbows back, and come to find out Dr. Sanchez has a *brother* who's an orthopedic surgeon, *too*, right here in South Carolina. He couldn't quite get a job down in his home country — something about test results and qualifications — but he got one not eighty miles from us, Harp. He's working out of Graywood Emergency Regional Memorial. Well, long story short, we went down there a few weeks ago, got him to do a little conference call with his brother, and the next thing you know we're all flexing muscles like the old days. And I guess we got to thank you for that idea about the elbow chastity belt. We figure we're all going on one last binge until you're done with the angels—and you can take your time, if you know what I mean—and then you can weld us up some protective gear."

I thought, I cannot wait for my head to fully clear. I put my still-full bourbon down on the bar. "What's your story, Bayward? Where've you been?"

Bayward wouldn't look me in the eye. He said, "They always say that honesty's good. Well, you got to where you were boring, Harp. I'm sorry. I told Vince Vance all about it, and he said that *you* weren't good for *my* recovery."

My supposed tailer started laughing all by himself. I said, "Shut up, lime green Maverick."

Kumi said, "It was my idea to harvest the ginseng. I met men from Japan in Costa Rica say they want the ginseng. My idea!"

"I'm just glad to have use of my elbows back," Delay said. "I didn't realize how much I missed whittling. And I guess I can type again. I been thinking about writing a story."

I promise I wasn't watching Timmy count ceiling beer pull-tab rings. Delay, Vollis, Kumi—and then even the traitor got up and looked at me—kept jerking their heads up as I listened to them. "What're you looking at?" Vollis said. "That's kind of annoying."

I said, "What?"

"You keep slashing your eyes upward. Like you're not making eye contact. Your eyes keep going up like you're looking for specters. Or angels. Or the sky to fall."

I thought, *I'm officially sober.* I said, "I need to go home."

16

RAYLOU SAT IN A RUSTED metal glider on the side of Poole's yard. I drove up sober, even though I took the full glass of bourbon along with me. I'm talking I hit country curves like a slalom racer, for I had a feeling that things might be awry at home. Would Machiavellian Republican hit men be awaiting me and mine? Would my wife vote with the ex-Elbowites and Bayward in regards to my new boring personality, and thus be halfway done with moving out? I told myself somewhere between Dacusville and Ember Glow that if she left me alone with those angels and snapping turtles, then it was a sign for me to go ahead and start back filling up the liver. I told myself somewhere on Old Old Old Due West Road that if Raylou stuck with me — even though I tended to repeat myself, that I tended to stare at my beads too long on the angels, that I screamed in my sleep, that I woke up feeling guilty for dreaming drunk — then I could partake of the good four fingers of Jim Beam I'd been hanging out with since entering Scatterbrain's.

When I saw Raylou peripherally, I hit the brakes so hard my bourbon blew right out of the glass and onto the dashboard. I got out and said, "Where the hell did all that kudzu come from on the long side of our property? I was just going down the back road and noticed about two acres of the stuff traveling up our rock."

This was true. I remembered Raylou getting the roots or seeds up in Sylva during that arts-fair thing, and I remembered her planting the shoots, but I figured they died off mostly. Poole had mentioned them down on his corner, but the vines looked dead. I'd not taken any root of kudzu capsules, or chewed on any of the original source since that one time what seemed years ago.

Raylou got up off the glider and said, "Mr. Poole's sister died. Arthette died."

I had to think for a minute. I had forgotten the woman's real name, and could only think of her as "Payton" with that Carolina Waste work shirt she wore. "Oh, man," I said. "What happened?"

Raylou said, "I smell bourbon. Have you been drinking? I'm not judging you any, Harp."

I said, "It's only on my hands and pants leg. I still haven't tasted any." We stood in Poole's side yard, amid empty anteater cages and shoots of stray forsythia that rooted down in the last plots of soil before the rock mound proper. From inside the house Poole let out long mournful wails, then talked, I supposed, to dead Arthette.

"He came up to the house looking for you. He wants to bury her over there in the side yard, but he wants to know if he can trade something off with you for one of the angels."

Jesus Christ, I thought. Poole came outside, wearing a suit. He said, "I guess you heard the news," to me.

I said, of course, "I'm awfully sorry," and then realized it wasn't the occasion to just say "Poole" at the end of the statement. I said, "All this time we've been neighbors, I've always called you Poole. I don't even know your first name."

"It's Arthur."

What else could it be? I said, "I'm awfully sorry, Arthur. Raylou and I want to tell you how we think you're nearly a saint, having taken care of your sister all these years." I'd never read any of those etiquette books. I didn't get a newspaper and have access to a Dear Abby, and how she might handle such a situation.

"I'mo need help shoveling out a grave."

I said, "I'm here for that," which I was. I kind of wished that I'd never taken to art, that I'd've become a writer. Shoveling a grave with a neighbor seemed to be a perfect occasion to find a story.

Raylou said, "I'm going to take the car back up to our house, Harp. I'll make y'all some supper." To Arthur Poole she said, "Do you want me to make any calls, Mr. Poole? Do you have any relatives you want me to contact, or the newspaper for an obituary?"

This is me: I thought about how Arthur Poole wasn't going to use a shovel, seeing as he wore a suit. I'd never seen a man dig a hole wearing a suit, outside of maybe one spadeful of dirt when a new building site got christened.

Poole said, "I guess I better call Social Security one day. She got a disability check, you know. No. It'd probably be best if you didn't call anyone."

Raylou said, "Well, if you think of anyone, write down a note to yourself. When I come back in a couple hours, you can give me their names and I'll call up." She kissed me on the cheek, got in the Citroën, let out a "Shoo-whee!" when she smelled the spilled bourbon, and drove up to our house.

Arthur Poole leaned a shovel my way. He said, "It's times like this I wish I'd've marked Momma and Daddy. My little brother. All them dogs that come by back when I was a boy. I hope we don't accidentally dig them up."

For as rocky as my land was up at the top of Ember Glow—or as *rock*, I guess—Arthur Poole's was loamy. Digging in his soil was not dissimilar to digging the upper reaches of a Carolina beach. Whereas I thought I'd have to find a sledgehammer, rent a bulldozer, and hire out a man who knew how to use an auger, I barely needed to give the shovel foot pressure before it sank right down. Arthur Poole stood beside me, his head bobbing along somewhat toward the ground. I didn't know if he suffered from palsy or Parkinson's, or if he—like Timmy at Scatterbrain's—took note mentally of what bodies he'd submerged in the past, and where. I had already dug out a nice four-by-eight rectangle two feet deep before Arthur Poole said, "You got a good wife."

I said, "Man. Have you ever had a geologist out here? I'd like to know why my land's pure rock, and yours might as well be sold off for talcum powder."

We had Arthette laid out in a beautiful dovetailed pine coffin, the lid closed, that Poole had fashioned beforehand. I'm talking this casket could've won Best in Show at one of Raylou's arts-and-crafts festivals. "Forty years ago it wasn't like this," Poole said. "It's acause your land's melting up there, and the tiny, tiny sand particles get swept down here by rain and wind. A thousand years from now, or maybe ten to twenty, your place will be flat, and my land will be up high like a giant dune, you know."

I reached down and pulled out a long strand of hair from the soil that looked exactly like what I pulled out of the shower drain most mornings. I reached down and pulled out a gold loop ear-ring that I automatically identified as one that Raylou lost some twelve years earlier, then put both in my pocket. I said, "I believe you're right." I continued shoveling effortlessly until Arthur Poole said, "That should be about level with the rest." He said, "I can't remember how I put down Momma and Daddy by my-self. I don't remember just dropping the box straight down hard."

I said, "Let me run up to my studio. I got some rope up there. We can shimmy your sister right down gently."

Arthur Poole sat on top of the coffin. He said, "I wasn't think-ing ahead when I smoked the last of my rope. I appreciate it."

I started to set the shovel on the ground, then picked it up to use as a staff of sorts. During the long walk up, I felt the grit beneath my shoes slough off. In my mind I imagined wearing emery boards on my feet and slowly filing my homestead down to a flat expanse, then a bowl. In time, the rain would fill up the hollowed spot, and we could live amongst the turtles, swimming happily, in full anticipation of someone throwing a chicken neck our way.

At the top of the path, I found my wife standing next to my current angel. Raylou wore my welder's mask and still held the mig, though it wasn't firing. I thought, *What the hell is she doing?* I thought, *This makes sense — I didn't even remember fin-ishing off numbers three through about nine.* I called out, "Hey. Hey, Raylou," and jogged up the last of the incline.

She didn't turn my way. For a split second, I expected her to drop the trigger, lift up the mask, and then I would find it not to be Raylou — that it might be Bayward, or Joe from Joe's Nuts, maybe Vince Vance, even my insane mother. In my mind, I saw stupid Charlie Baynes at work, finishing up my project because he had no faith that I might. I imagined Lucifer himself beneath the mask, that maybe I'd sold my soul somewhere along the line à la Robert Johnson at the crossroads, et cetera, and then — worse — that Karl guy from the Republican Party.

Raylou pivoted the mask atop her head. She didn't smile. "Caught me," she said. "I'm sorry, Harp."

I said, "What the hell are you doing? You don't see me over there molding out face jugs."

She shook her head from side to side. Tears rolled down her face. "I just want us out of here faster," she said, then bent down on her haunches. "We can't get out of here soon enough."

I bent down and put my arms around my wife. Was she having a nervous breakdown? Had all that time with my being drunk finally caught up with her? Was she somehow in league with the green Maverick fucker? Did she no longer find reason for being on this planet? I said, "I came up here to get some rope."

She started laughing and said, "I wasn't going to hang myself, I don't think."

We lowered Arthette. Her brother either said a prayer or a poem for the occasion, I couldn't tell which. When I was a kid, my mother once stood over a buried dead cat that wasn't really ours, a yellow tom that spent most of his time on that same path that my father and Flora Gorman took for blackberries. The cat got hit by one of the Irish Travelers on the day the men scattered around to paint naïve people's asphalt driveways. My mom said, "There once was a cat named McGruder / Who wooed a nude Manx in Bermuda / The nude thought it shrewd to be wooed in the nude / But McGruder was shrewder and screwed her."

I figured out later on that my mom might've been venting somewhat, that she might've been substituting McGruder and the bitch-cat for my father running off to New Orleans.

Anyway, Raylou and I stood there with rope burns on our palms tingling when Poole bowed his head. This was before I shoveled dirt on top. "Lord, we don't understand why You make some of us live in pain. We don't know why You give some creatures the IQ of a stick. Arthette didn't know You, 'cause you forgot to make her brain. And as far as I'm concerned, You can come down here and suck my dick."

Raylou said, "Amen."

I didn't, seeing as lightning struck our immediate surroundings more times than I could ever count. I said, "You are a good brother, Arthur Poole. I never had an older brother, but if I did I would have wanted him to be as loyal as you are."

Poole stood there beside the mound of dirt yet to be redelivered into the hole. He said, "I tell you what I'mo do—if it's too much trouble getting me one them angels to put on Arthette's grave, what say y'all promise to give me the turtles should y'all ever leave."

I didn't want to say, "Bubba, I get more than ten grand each for those angels, and I can't just hand them over like party favors for the dead." I said, "I'll make her an angel when I'm done with this commission I'm working on. It might have to be a little smaller."

"I'd just as soon have the turtles," Poole said. "Ain't nothing going to dig her up, I don't think, unless some ants settle atop her and those last two anteaters come back from wherever they went to hide."

"The turtles are yours," Raylou said. We stood there silent a moment. The sun eased down below the horizon. At first I

254

thought I heard my stomach growling, then Raylou's and Poole's. Then I convinced myself it to be kudzu growing from the edge of his property, toward mine. "I saved them from being poisoned daily, but you can probably find them a reason to live and be useful otherwise."

Poole turned his head in the direction of my house. He sniffed the air. "Y'all need any work shirts? I got a whole pile of clean unworn work shirts back in Arthette's room. I doubt I got any with 'Harp' or 'Raylou' on them, but I got a good one man by the moniker of 'Worm' used to wear, and another some old boy named 'Roach.' Both of them worked at a lawn-care company. Maybe that's why, don't ask me. Anyway, I got a slew the things. Hey, where's that supper you were talking all high and mighty about?"

Raylou said, "Oh. Oh, I forgot. Our oven's not working," to cover the fact that she'd spent her time finishing up my angels.

On our walk back home, armed with our rope, Raylou said, "If we lived closer to a town, we could order up pizza. We could run down to a barbecue joint and pick up a couple quarts of hash and loaf bread. In a regular town I could probably walk onto the square and find a bakery that sold blueberry pies — I've always found blueberry pies to be comforting at a time of loss. We could find the deli section of a good grocery store and come back with quarts of macaroni salad and that green pistachio stuff with marshmallows and Cool Whip and pineapple. Banana pudding. Baked beans, coleslaw, potato salad. A tray of cold cuts."

I looked at her silhouette as we walked. We were two nearing-forty idiots on — as far as I could tell — incongruent planes of keeping secrets and telling lies. I said, "I'm six months in and there's no one around to talk about it. So we're going to have to talk about something else. I think you know what subject I'm going to broach."

"Watergate salad. That's what that gelled pistachio stuff is called."

"You're going to have to sit down and tell me some things, Ray. No bullshit, either. If you're jonesing for pot again, let me know. We can either get you into my rehab place or, what the fuck—*smoke the shit more,* for all I care. I owe you about twenty years of getting wasted."

When we got to the house, Raylou went inside and turned on the floodlights. She took me by the hand and led me to the drunkards' clubhouse. "I'm not going to leave you or anything like that, Harp," she said. "I can't believe what I'm about to say, either."

Was she carrying on an affair with the guy in the green Maverick? What about that Cherokee guy up in the tree at the campground outside Sylva? I said, "What?"

"Are you sure there's no way you couldn't drink responsibly? Are you sure you can't have a couple bourbons every once in a while without going on a yearlong binge?"

Was I no longer funny? I thought. Was I no longer charmingly reckless?

I said, "Not from everything I've read."

Raylou took my hands. "I might have made some mistakes."

I didn't get it, of course. Down Ember Glow, we heard Arthur Poole either cry out, wailing unabashedly, or call his missing anteaters.

The snooper showed up around midnight. I still sat in the clubhouse. Raylou had long ago gone inside, fired up—I supposed—

a ceramic pipe, and set to fixing some kind of dish for Poole. When I heard the car come up, I peeked out one of the windowless holes in my structure and made a mental note as to where the closest piece of rebar stood, or the shovel. I underwent flashbacks of the last time this happened. Off in the distance, I heard Bayward's moped zipping down the back roads at twenty miles an hour.

The detective didn't seem armed. He stood at the door — just stood there — as if wondering whether to knock. I leaned in and listened. Then he looked down the driveway as Bayward's tiny light began an ascent up the granite. I boomed out, "What do you think you're doing, Traitor?" or "Trader," like that.

He jumped visibly and looked back to the Quonset hut. "My name's not Traitor," he said. "Forget about my ever mentioning that I might be a traitor. My being called 'Traitor' would be what linguists would call an appositive."

I stepped out of the clubhouse. Bayward veered his moped off to the flattest part of the land and kicked down his stand. By the way Bayward moved, I could tell I was in no trouble, as if I couldn't've figured that out myself what with a fellow bringing up what linguists say to each other. But it *did* get me thinking about what the hell an appositive was, and whether he had used one earlier. That's the trick of a good detective, I thought — getting you to wander all the way back to tenth-grade English in your mind.

I said, "Boys. Lovely evening out tonight," as if I were on the set of one of those faux Southern movies. "Y'all hear about old man Poole's sister dying?"

Bayward said, "Hey Harp, I come to tell you that this-here man's one of us. Well, except he drinks like crazy and didn't get his arms fused at the elbow, and doesn't have to drive a moped because of too many DUIs and whatnot."

I yelled in at the house, "Come on out here, Raylou. Come on out here and see firsthand what you've connived again." I didn't mean to sound foreboding or anything; I just liked the way my voice came out all drawly in the midnight air. For the first time I'd ever noticed, there was a slight echo, too—maybe off the kudzu growing a foot and a half per day. "Here comes another one of your angel messengers to reveal something I need to know or do."

The man who tailed me all the way to Scatterbrain's pulled out his wallet and unleashed a driver's license. He handed it over. "My real name's Ronald Wilson. Just like Reagan's first two names. That's how I can gain their trust. Up until these gigs I got snooping into other people's business—and let me tell you right now that business is good under this particular administration, and has been since right after rational citizens started questioning our president and senators and congresspeople—I ran a little business of my own, taking care of office plants. Literally, I mean. I watered accountants' potted begonias and such."

Raylou came out wearing an oven mitt.

I said, "Yeah, yeah, yeah."

Raylou said, "Hello." She looked down the slope and said, "Cool car. Hey, you want some ginger ale, YooHoo, coffee, sweet tea, RC Cola, Cheerwine, Dr Pepper, Mr. Pibb…" She listed off every drink I'd cached during my nondrinking tenure, soft drinks that couldn't rightly be mixed with bourbon.

"Good job, Ray," I said. "Pretending that this guy must be from the Alcohell Club, or the rehab center."

Bayward said, "Hey, Ms. Raylou. Vollis and Brinson Sucks

have their elbows back, case you ain't heard. And they didn't have to go back to Costa Rica."

Raylou said, "What's going on?"

Ronald Wilson said, "I just want to go on record as saying I warned y'all. That's it. One day you'll probably read about my death in some kind of weird tragic accidental explosion, but I want to go on record as saying it'll be a hit squad that did it. Bottom line for you, Spillman, is this: Count on being audited for the rest of your life when there's a dumb puppet president with henchmen in charge. That's all I got to say. My job is to report back to them and say you've done something unpatriotic so they can bring you into court somehow. Or worse. I don't know what all else is going on in your life, but don't say I didn't warn you."

Ronald Wilson left, and I stood there wondering if "don't say I didn't warn you" was a double negative, another tenth-grade English assignment. Bayward said, "We got him liquored up and he said pretty much the same thing to us. You wouldn't believe how strong Vollis is with the use of elbows. He pinned that old boy right up against the side of the outhouse and made him talk."

Raylou, out of nowhere—after telling Bayward how much we've missed his presence, after inviting him to sleep on our couch—said, "I hope the dermatologist isn't on the side of the bad guys."

I tried to think back if I missed part of the conversation, or if my wife spoke in code. I said, "What?"

"Oh. Nothing. I guess I forgot to tell you that I made an appointment at a skin doctor. It's nothing, really."

Down Ember Glow, Poole wailed some more. I went into my Quonset hut to finish up Raylou's angels, trying not to think about what other sculptures I may or may not have constructed over the years, what other mishaps I might have avoided through luck or design. Stacked to the left of the studio were about two gross work shirts, neatly folded, mostly dark blue and cotton, both long- and short-sleeved, but some pinstriped brown or green. The one on top was once owned by a man named Ron who worked at Stinky's Septic.

17

MY WIFE SAID THE PLACE sold bruise cream. The pharmacist made it up himself, supposedly, one batch at a time. He advertised that the salve would eradicate hematomas in half their normal life spans, something about cold and heat and agents that worked either for or against broken capillaries at required and crucial times. The pharmacist worked out of a clapboard mill village home on the outskirts of the medical community, both figuratively and literally. The regular hospital stood at the hub. Orthopedic surgeons, pediatricians, internists, oncologists, and the like kept their offices in a three-block-deep area around the hospital in strip-mall–like buildings. Then came the chiropractors and massage therapists and acupuncturists. I'm sure a couple aromatherapists holed up next, perhaps a witch doctor and faith healer, and then this guy named Max, a man with a regular degree from a normal pharmacy school, who gave up pushing the likes of Xanax, Prozac, Loritab, and Vicodin ten years earlier in order to sell bruise cream and other homeopathic remedies, a man who somehow took on the moniker "Dr." Max.

Before driving thirty miles into town I said to Raylou, "While I'm there, you want me to pick up any snake-oil medicine?"

She looked like she'd shoved her face into a garbage disposal, the business end of a coffee-bean grinder, or had it tenderized by an old-timey butcher. Raylou looked like she went through a windshield twice. The day before she'd gone down to this same area — maybe a block from Max's place — to a dermatologist who specialized in an outpatient laser technique that cured or healed or eclipsed something called spider veins. Raylou said she got these spider veins from working too close to a kiln for twenty years. To that, of course, I said, "I've never noticed any veins showing on your face."

"Maybe it's because you don't pay attention to me very often," she said. "Maybe all those years you were drunk kept your vision blurred."

If I'd've said, at one point or another in our marriage, "Say — look at all those *spider veins* on your cheeks and neck," I'm sure Raylou wouldn't have been much more rational.

According to my wife, a shaky little pudgy guy named Treen never fully explained the aftereffects of his laser application, that her entire face minus the chin would turn into a purple black skinscape, that her pores would actually ooze blood, and so on. She said he kept turning around and jacking up the machine's velocity. When she came out of the back room, the receptionist actually dropped her mouth open and said, "Oh my God! I've never seen *this* happen before!"

She drove home with an eyeholed paper bag on her head — and she never thanked me for keeping the car a mess filled with about everything from found-metal farm-implement parts I could use later in a sculpture to petrified box turtles I rescued crossing the road then kind of forgot to release atop where we lived — embarrassed by her visage. You'd think she would have let me take a couple pictures of her, in case we needed to sue the dermatologist, but Raylou said rightly that if her face never healed she'd be Exhibit A there on the stand and would need no Polaroids.

When Raylou got home banged up, I unfortunately laughed and said, "I told you. I've been reading up on this little procedure on the Internet while you were gone. If they can't *find* the broken capillaries, then they surge down harder to *make* them burst. I told you you didn't have spider veins."

Some of this is true. I'd looked on the Internet, and I read about the procedure, but there was none of that "can't find" and "make" stuff. But I wouldn't've been surprised. Back when I was a kid, I insisted that my finger was broken—though looking back, it probably only got sprained, which is exactly what the doctor prognosticated—until finally the guy bent my index finger back all the way until we heard a big crack. My mother wasn't in the examining room. The doctor looked me straight in the face until I quit screaming, then said, "Maybe this'll teach you not to point things out with such conviction," which I didn't fully understand.

And then my wife got on the Internet herself, looked up everything from malpractice to voodoo spells, and somehow, along the way, encountered the questionable last-resort "bruise cream." I told her to hold off until morning—that perhaps her port-wine face might fade down to something that geisha, clown, or corpse makeup might hide—and Raylou agreed. Then the next dawn, as she felt around the bedroom for either an X-Acto knife to slit her swollen eyes so she could see, or a pistol to shoot herself in the head, I put on my pants, got out the address to Max's Apothecare, and slowly drove back roads for forty minutes before hitting two-lane Highway 183, which took me to 25, which took me into town.

I walked right up to the counter and, not thinking ahead, blurted out, "My wife needs some bruise cream to hide the welts on her face." Behind me, waiting for a concoction of black cohosh, dong quai, and other secret-ingredients-hot-flash elixir, a woman said, "I read somewhere that a wife beater's best friend these days is the local homeopath who makes bruise cream." I didn't know if she said, "You should be drug by your testicles throughout town!" to me or Dr. Max.

When she burst into horrendous sobs, I went back outside to my car and got another paper sack so she could breathe into it. Dr. Max said, "I'll put some extra chasteberry in here to help with the mood swings."

He looked at me, closed his eyes, and nodded, as if to say that we must be patient and understanding. I looked behind him into what used to be a breakfast nook from when Max's Apothecare wasn't a business. Like the ex-den waiting room where I stood with Ms. Hot Flash, he had it adorned with indigo-colored bottles and a collection of antiquated mortars and pestles. I said just above a whisper, "My wife had an unfortunate collision with a dermatologist."

Dr. Max measured something in a beaker. He whispered back, "Did he laser?"

I shook my head. I heard him right, but shook my head. "Not that I know of. I think he might've held her hand, but I guess we'll find out should she become pregnant or get the clap."

The homeopathic pharmacist closed his eyes, stuck out his lips, and nodded patience again. He told me to have a seat, and that he'd be right with me. The hormonal woman had the bag nearly over her head. I underwent flashbacks from the day before, then to a bad joke I remembered hearing more than once.

I sat down, opened a free trade magazine called *Herbal Times*, and turned straight to an advertisement of a bucktoothed man named Rodney who held tantric-sex seminars all over the country. On the verso page was an article titled "Laughter's *Not* the Best Medicine."

I said to the woman, "I didn't hit my wife. She works around a kiln about every other day, and she says the sudden heat caused spider veins."

The woman calmed herself and breathed evenly. She said, "I apologize. At first I was kidding with you, but then something came over me and I went with it. I've been watching too many talk shows." She stood up and stretched her lower back. "Dr. Max," she called out. He still held a beaker up close to his face and peered over half rims. "Do you know of any good therapists who could help me get over my hatred for men in general and my ex-husband, father, and brothers in particular? And brothers-in-law? Plus our politicians?"

I looked down at the free magazine. I thought, I'm going to kill Raylou when I get home. I thought, *This isn't good for my recovery*—which I found myself thinking four hundred times every day now, in regards to any situation. Dr. Max said, "The only one I know is a man. So that might be defeating the purpose. Fellow by the name of Sibley over on Hope Street. I don't think his address is an accident."

She sat back down and said, "Maybe I could talk to his wife. Maybe he could talk to her, and things rub off, you know, and then I could talk to her."

Dr. Max didn't answer. I looked past him toward the mortars and pestles lined up. I felt pretty confident that one of them was really a bong in disguise. He said, "Give him a go." Then he poured into a bottle and said, "I got you ready."

I turned the page to an article on the importance of flying insects to our outlook on life. The woman got up, paid, and didn't turn back toward me and say anything. I looked out the open venetian blind and saw her get into a new Mercedes. Dr. Max said to me, "If she would exchange those high heels for some fisherman sandals, everyone involved would be happier. Fisher*woman* sandals." He said, "Okay. Bruise cream. I can tell by the look on your face that you think this is just another hokey placebo. Am I right or am I right?"

I stood up and walked my six or so steps to his counter. I said, "Uh-huh."

"You think that the power of the brain will help diminish the swelling and discoloration."

I said, "To tell you the truth, I got other things to think about. I'd been on a good twenty-year drunk, and I quit. So to be honest, I think there are more urgent matters going on when compared to spider veins and laser."

Dr. Max picked up a putty knife and shoved it into an industrial-sized mayonnaise jar. The door opened and another woman came in, looking much like the last one. Max said to her, "Good morning, Becky."

She fanned herself with an actual honest-to-goodness Asian bamboo fan, just like in the movies. "I need to get a setting on my air conditioner somewhere past 'Arctic.' Goddamn it to hell." She looked at me and screamed, "What're you looking at?"

I said, of course, "If you wear more comfortable shoes, it'll make everyone involved happier."

"Tell me your name," Dr. Max said to me.

I thought he needed to write down Raylou's name for the

prescription or something. "My name's Harp Spillman, but my wife's Raylou Hewell. It's kind of hard to say. You'd think she'd've taken my name when we got married, but she wanted to keep her own."

"Good for her," said new hot flasher Becky.

"Raylou Hewell, like the face-jug artist?" said Dr. Max.

I said, "Uh-huh."

"I got a bunch of her work," he said. "I used to have some of them up here" — he pointed behind him to the shelf — "but I think they scared off some of my customers, you know."

"Good, good, good," said Becky. "All well and good. Have you got my medicine ready yet? I called it in so I wouldn't have to stand around sweating. I used to keep a row of orange Fiestaware teapots in my kitchen until I found out they were radioactive, but that doesn't mean that I have to talk about it all the time in front of strangers just so everyone will feel sorry for me."

I wanted a drink more than anything else. I looked around his shelves and tried to find some codeine-and-alcohol–loaded cough syrup. Dr. Max left his putty knife stuck in whatever secret ingredient he had back there for bruise cream. For no apparent reason, I began laughing, shook my head, and went to pat Becky's shoulder a few times. She jumped out of the way and glared at me. I laughed harder.

Dr. Max handed over a bottle of hormone treatment to Becky. He said, "I'll put it on your tab."

I laughed and laughed and said, "Engine coolant might help you out."

Dr. Max looked at Becky and said, "Don't mind him. He's going through delirium tremens." Becky left and the pharmacist said, "Are you lactose-intolerant, Harp?"

I quit laughing. "No sir."

"If you get pricked by a holly bush, or a big thorn—like a briar—do you break out in a huge rash all over your body?"

"No. I try to stay clear of those kinds of things, though."

He got out the putty knife and scooped goo into a clean marble mortar. "Good. You might want to buy some milk thistle for your liver, man." I looked at him and smiled. He said, "That was a little homeopathic joke that goes around a place like this."

I said, "From what I've seen, you might need some humor in a place like this."

He set down the knife and said, "Has Raylou been keeping ice on her face since the laser procedure?"

I didn't know. I said, "I told her to. I told her to put ice on her face for the first twenty-four hours."

"Good. Ice for maybe two days, actually, and then heat. She'll end up about the same. And if her face is bleeding, she can put some regular petroleum jelly on it." He cleaned off the knife and recapped whatever he'd first scooped out. "What you're going through now, I don't want to cheat you more so on something that may or may not work."

I shrugged. "She's going to be pissed if I don't bring something back. Believe me. Raylou's more levelheaded than anyone I know, but she's got reason to believe I don't follow through some times."

Dr. Max looked at his watch. He said, "Some days it seems like 4:20 will never come." He reached below the counter and handed me a small tube of something called emu oil.

"This supposed to fade her skin back to normal?"

"How many bruised emus have you ever seen?"

I smiled and nodded. About as many as I'd seen bruised turkey vultures, I thought, and turkey-vulture cream would've done the trick about as well. Because I'd been accused of having selective hearing since I met Raylou in art school, I couldn't be sure if the homeopathic druggist said, "Tell your wife she's got a big fan here" or "Try not to be such an unsympathetic jerk when you get home" as the door shut behind me.

Raylou spent a few hours turning mirrors around while I trekked for a panacea. She deliberately smudged the sliding glass door going out to her kiln, my Quonset-hut studio, the outbuilding designed for my drunkard friends meeting haphazardly who couldn't hack AA. Raylou ventured outside at some point—I wouldn't ask if she put a bag over her head, and knew that chances of seeing anyone way out where we lived atop a granite mound so barren Le Petit Prince would've felt at home—walked all the way down to where the kudzu crept, pruned off large leaves, and covered the snapping-turtle pond's surface so as not to accidentally glimpse her own reflection.

I got out of the car to find her seated in a ladder-back chair turned to the corner. I said, "Nice guy down there at the weird pharmacy. Mean clientele, but a nice druggist."

"Just put the bruise cream on the floor and kick it over this way. I don't want you to see me."

"It's not that bad. You'll be barely able to notice it in a few days," I said. I took the minuscule tube of emu oil out of my watch pocket, walked over, and set it over Raylou's shoulder, onto her lap. I spied down to the book she read—which she tried to close immediately—and only made out the chapter heading on the top page: "How to Deal with It When There's No Doubt He's Right," from one of those self-help books I thought Raylou burned during our last cleanup. "What the hell are you reading?"

She turned the book over and said, "Please leave the room, Harp. I'm not kidding." She pushed me back with her left arm and leaned her face forward, over the book, into her thighs.

I said, "The pharmacist dude's name was Dr. Max. He was one of *those* guys, like an ex-hippie without a last name. I'm betting if you took up yoga or tai chi, he'd be right there in the back row. Anyway, he said you should put this emu oil on your face lightly three times a day, in between ice packs. Don't sit in the sun. Do not operate heavy machinery or farm equipment."

I added that last part on, of course, hoping to get a laugh. Back when I drank a quart of bourbon a day and tried to operate a mig welder sculpting, I often told myself that I might be drunk, but at least I wasn't driving a bulldozer or steamroller. Raylou picked up her book and cradled it into her chest, then walked backwards into the bedroom. On the way, she said, "I don't want any of that 'I told you so' crap. Promise me one thing: You won't say 'I told you so,' even if my face never turns back regular. I wouldn't blame you if you left me, and you wouldn't even have to say why. I would know."

I didn't laugh out loud. I felt myself smiling, though. I said, "I bet that chapter you're in the middle of turns out to be really long." Then I heard the click of the lock. I got up close to the door and said, "Hey, you want me to make some lunch? I suddenly feel like making a big old blackberry jam sandwich and rubbing it all over my face. Hey, after you get that emu oil slathered on your cheeks all slimy, let's you and me go to the video store and get *Ghostbusters*, or *The Blob*." I said, "I don't know how much you paid for your elective surgery, but I would've punched you in the face for five dollars in the name of spider veins."

Let me say right here that I quit kidding around when I heard my wife crying. I would never know if that's what her self-help book said to do, but I understood Raylou well enough to know that she didn't become emotional, normally, though she did on both the 2000 and 2004 election nights, which, wrongly, I blamed on early stages of menopause. She finally blurted out from the other room, "I have a whole new line of face jugs to make, now. From this point on, I'll commit myself to making face jugs for the deformed."

I had to go outside on that one, I started laughing so hard thinking about face jugs with acne or port-wine stains being bought by their real-life counterparts. It didn't occur to me then that maybe my six months–plus of sobriety brought on a certain giddiness that wasn't socially acceptable, that the rebirth of my liver caused me to undergo an odd and inexorable condition that consisted of objurgatory, vituperative thoughts and statements.

Somehow, too, my vocabulary returned.

From outside our bedroom window I yelled to Raylou, "Hey, if you have any of that bruise cream left over, maybe we can send it to Mikhail Gorbachev over there in Russia."

And my knowledge of twentieth-century history.

I spent the next two days welding on my latest twelve-foot angel constructed entirely of hex nuts. I went inside every couple hours and yelled out to Raylou hiding in the bedroom, bathroom, her office space, and an added-on room we never finished out or figured why we needed it in the first place. This is not my imagination: Every time I walked in, every time I said something like, "Hey, Raylou, you want me to learn how to make some crepes and slide them under the door?" the first muffled thing I heard from her side was, "Hold on a second." She was talking to someone on the telephone, is what I'm saying.

Then she'd tell me to go back outside and finish my work,

that she was fine, that the bruises still existed but the swelling had gone down considerably. I'd say okay, I'd say for her to flash the floodlights if she needed me, I'd say that I was making a new pot of coffee, et cetera. Then I would go back outside and use a piece of rebar to sling out kudzu leaves from the snapping-turtle pond out front in order to see our pets better, in order to make sure they ate the chicken necks I threw in every night. I walked over to Raylou's work shed, opened up her kiln door, and stuck my head in to look at the empty shelves. I picked up every face jug she had lined up. I dropped china plates out back so she'd have a collection of broken teeth from which to choose should her face heal up enough to work again. In my Quonset hut I found an old windup wristwatch with a second hand and timed how long I could stare directly into the sun. I put on my felt-soled boots and climbed on top of the Quonset hut to inspect metal seams, wondered how long it would take me to learn the guitar, listened to AM radio preachers talk about how everyone was doomed, reread a physics textbook in hopes that something might click, reread aphorisms from *The Charvaka* and Schopenhauer, and practiced yodeling.

I fired up the mig welder, attached a nut or two, then went back to *anything else*, basically, which had always been my work habit, drunk or not.

Finally I tiptoed back into the house, got a drinking glass from the cupboard, snuck up to the bedroom door, and played poor-man's detective. Although her voice was muffled, I felt sure that I made out this one-sided conversation: "Okay...I agree... I'll do that...Well, I'm worried because sometimes he doesn't take change very well..." Then she laughed like crazy and said, "I'll be in touch soon...I don't know when I can see you again 'cause I don't want to scare people..."

I think she was saying something about up-front earnest money when I put my shoulder to the door, took it off the jamb, and found Raylou seated on the bed with two ice bags tied onto her face with a summer scarf. The telephone rested on her lap, on top of that self-help book, and I said, "So what're you doing, Raylou? Let me guess what was going on with the man on the other end of that conversation: Gee, maybe it went a little like 'Your husband's an idiot...You need to leave him as soon as possible...Let's meet at the motel room...You won't scare the desk clerk...' I can't figure out the thing about earnest money, unless you're buying the motel."

Raylou looked like one of the Three Stooges in blackface, with a toothache. She said, "Why are you carrying that empty glass? We keep the water and whatnot in the kitchen."

I said, "I heard it *all*, Raylou. You can't get out of this. Hey— did you really go to a dermatologist, or did your up-till-now secret boyfriend beat you up? I know I haven't been the best husband, but I never raised a hand to you. I might've been drunk all the time—and maybe you should be thankful I couldn't stand up. I bet there's nothing in your book about that."

I tried not to hyperventilate, and got caught up thinking about that first woman in the homeopathic drugstore as Raylou said, "The door appears to be irreparable."

When she laughed, I said, "This ain't funny, goddamn it."

"It was supposed to be a surprise, Harp. I have a CD that's maturing in a couple weeks. If my face heals right, and if you finish up your commissioned angels, and if you stay sober, then I was thinking about buying this antebellum place with a big old wraparound porch. It needs work, but the time seems right. It needs a lot of work, really—but I've been thinking that your staying sober might depend on a long project."

I looked down at that book of hers. "So this thing says that when he's right, you find him a big project without even asking? I don't like this idea at all."

Raylou got up and stuck her arms out smiling. She kissed me so hard, I felt the chill off of her cheeks. "You have to be more flexible, Harp. I'm not trying to benagle you. Actually, it's almost *only* a wraparound porch. The house is on its way of falling in on itself, but the porch's still solid. This place is down in the town of Gruel. And Gruel's revitalized itself. I've also got some earnest money down on a storefront on the square, too, in case we ever want to run a little gallery."

I didn't pay much attention to that last part. I tried to think if "benagle" was a real word, and wondered where I'd heard it before. Then I busied myself trying to think up a joke that involved a fixer-upper house and bruise cream. I asked my wife if she needed more ice, and went out to my studio in search of wood putty and screws.

When I looked up at the tall metal angel standing near the entrance of my Quonset hut, I said to it, "Shut up." I said, "It says in *The Charvaka*, 'What could be better than a brown-eyed woman with large breasts?'" I forgot about the broken door, about the wraparound-porch project, and didn't think about having to greet customers sober in a small-town art gallery. I fired up the mig welder and bent down for a handful of new nuts donated to me by Southern Hex, appropriately. This particular angel, I knew, would one day stand proud and different than the others, down in Birmingham, though passersby might not understand that she pointed for them to trudge blindly and trust their instincts.

I kind of felt drunk and disoriented.

I am not too proud to admit that I felt some changes going on inside my head right about this time. I felt as if things went backwards. In the past, I could remember people's names without stalling or running an alphabetical mental Rolodex through my mind. I'm talking about people I met drunk at a party one year, then didn't see again until the following party. Since right about the same time Raylou volunteered to have her face *defaced*, though, I found myself grasping at the simplest words and concepts. "Man, I'm worn out. I've been pulling the trigger on the mig welder so long that I've lost feeling in that part of the body that hangs off your arm and holds five digits that separates us from other life-forms seeing as we can use it to grasp, thus hold tools," I might say before Raylou offered up, "Your hand?"

And to be honest I had felt this way maybe about four weeks into not drinking, but it had progressed with each month. When my wife finally emerged from the bedroom without feeling like the Elephant Woman, she said, "It's not all that much a surprise about this place I want us to buy, Harp. I mean, we talked about it a bunch about a year ago. And then I started thinking about what you said a couple months ago—about how maybe we cheated ourselves by living so far from civilization. For me, it's a good folksy story to have a face-jug artist out in a place like here in Ember Glow. But I've been thinking that you were right—you need contacts. You need some action. The town of Gruel, from what I hear, has upwards of six hundred people living there now. There's a bunch of gurus running some kind of colony. And you got Forty-Five not far down the road. And from there you got Columbia. And in Columbia you can take a plane to Cincinnati, then to D.C., then to New York or back to Atlanta, if you needed something cultural."

We sat in our stone yard. Down the hill, Arthur Poole called out, again, to his missing anteaters. He still held hope. I said to Raylou, "Your face is healing nicely," which it was.

"I told you that bruise cream would work. You need to go back to Apothecare and apologize to Dr. Max."

I nodded. It had been six days since I'd bought the stuff. "Yes, I do. I need to go right over there and say something about how your face might've taken upwards of seven days to bleach back out, but his amazing wonder cream did it in a miraculous six."

This might've been about noon. The snapping turtles hunkered down as was their wont midday. Raylou said again, "You need to go back to Apothecare and apologize to Dr. Max."

I looked at her hard in the eyes. Maybe that bruise cream ate through her frontal lobes. "I heard you the first time."

"I wasn't sure if you did. Sometimes I don't think you're listening." She pointed toward my latest sculpture nearly finished. "That one came out different than the others. She looks like she has actual boobs. You know what—when you go to apologize to Dr. Max, why don't you take some pictures of your work down there? Maybe he'd be interested in buying something for out front. If he collects face jugs, maybe he'll collect your sculptures, too."

I trusted my wife. She'd put up with me for too long not to understand what I needed. The sun stood directly above our heads. We cast little shadow. Her skin, now minus the spider veins, blended with a cloud off to the west. I said, "I'll be back in a couple hours, unless you know that whatever you got schemed up might take longer."

Raylou said, "You'll be back before I have a good half-dozen face jugs ready to turn leather-hard." She said, "A rosacea series, maybe with their eyes slanted up as if they remembered scenes and events that they experienced before. As if something overly familiar occurred again."

I thought, She's testing me. I said, "Déjà vu."

Raylou said, "We talked about this last night."

A man sat in my old chair, thumbing through *Herbal Times* backwards. He looked up without moving his head. Dr. Max wasn't behind the counter. Instead of one of those order-up bells, a tiny gong the size of a silver thirty-day AA chip set atop a GENTLY STROKE FOR SERVICE handwritten card. I thought to myself, There's got to be some kind of brothel joke in there somewhere. When Dr. Max returns, I'll say something funny about the sign.

I sat down in the other chair and looked at the rows and rows of herbal supplements running down the wall. The man next to me said, "He's out back picking something. I forget what. He hasn't been gone long."

I said, "Thanks." I said, "Hey, man, check out the picture of the dude who offers up tantric-sex seminars. I'm no expert, but it seems to me that if you trust your bedroom problems to this guy, you might want to get a full-fledged psychiatrist to help you delve into your childhood."

He turned pages correctly and said, "Yeah, I checked him out last week when I was here."

He looked like a normal guy, maybe nearing forty. I said, "I came here last week for some bruise cream for my wife. Sure enough the bruise faded away, but I have a funny feeling it would've done so anyway without my paying thirty-nine bucks."

"Tantric," he said. "Tantric. Tantric. Tan. Trick. Tan. Trick." He got louder, and his voice reached some high notes. I imagined one of those menopausal women coming in here brandishing a mace or cat-o'-nine-tails and taking out both of us.

I thought, Uh-oh. I said, "Bruise cream. Next thing you know these homeopathic places will offer up freckle remover. A little something offered up by Sherwin-Williams better known as 'tan paint.'"

"Tan trick. Tan trick. Tan trick," the man said, and I understood that we slightly worked together in a word-association kind of way.

I thought, *This isn't so bad.* I thought, *I really should get out more often and mingle with normal people going about their daily routines.*

Dr. Max came back in, looked at me, and said, "Harp Spillman. Raylou's husband." To the other man he said, "Okay. I got you set up." He shook a special amber bottle the size of a fire extinguisher and said, "You're going to need to drink about eight ounces of this every morning. In all my years of homeopathic medicine, I've only dealt with one other patient who needed this stuff, but it worked for him. As a matter of fact, he's our senator now."

The man got up, paid, and left, still chanting. I had heard somewhere that there was a patient-pharmacist confidentiality clause written down somewhere, but that didn't stop me from saying, "What the hell's wrong with that guy? He started off acting normal, but then..."

"Oh. He'll be all right. Probably," Dr. Max said. "So did the bruise cream work? I got on the Internet after you left and ordered up three more face jugs from your wife. Man, she's got a talent."

I started wondering who my two senators were at the moment. I figured them to be Republicans. I figured that I hadn't voted for either, but I didn't remember ever seeing a man on the stump suffering echolalia, unless saying "compassionate conservative" whenever possible counted. I said, "Her face is fine."

"Does she need some more? If she needs more emu oil, I'll swing you a deal. That little tube should've been enough."

"No. No, no," I said.

"Do you remember why you came here?" Dr. Max asked me.

Let me say right now that I knew without a doubt that Raylou'd called ahead, that she'd tipped off the druggist. I said, "Look. Yes, I do. The drinking took its toll, as they say." I could feel the words well up inside my throat, terms I had never used before and must've read somewhere along the line. "Ginsenoside concentration for perceptual focus and memory storage. Nutrients to the brain via blood flow. Something to cut through cholesterol and triglycerides, through pollutants, pesticides, booze, and old fillings in my teeth." I went on and on, as if in a trance. I mentioned free radicals. I came up with atherosclerotic plaques. I said, "Is it hot in here, or is it me?"

"My women usually show up about now," Dr. Max said. "I keep the air turned down so they know they're not crazy."

I said, "Raylou thinks my memory might not be what it used to be. Evidently I worked for twenty years on some kind of autopilot. Evidently I interacted with people, because I actually finished and sold my work."

Dr. Max hit the tiny gong lightly three times. He closed his eyes and wrinkled his forehead. He asked me if I really wanted to remember everything. I shrugged and said I might as well give it a try. He handed me a white sack he'd already filled before I showed up and told me not to stand in the sun for long periods of time. He told me not to smoke, unless the tobacco was untainted. When I pulled out my wallet, Dr. Max held up his palm in the international no charge way. When I reached the door I noticed a gumball machine, the proceeds of which went directly to victims of confusion, plain victims of confusion.

18

I FINISHED THE FINAL ANGEL a month ahead of time. I sand-blasted each one, then sprayed them down with a coat of WD-40. Then I rented a forklift and flatbed truck with six wheels, loaded it up all by myself, and made it to the first underpass on I-85. No one bothered to notice that perhaps the twelve-foot angels, added to the five- or six-foot-high truck bed, might not clear most overhead bridges. It wasn't close. I illegally turned around on the interstate, drove the wrong way until I found a flat spot in the median, and came back home. I found Raylou on the telephone. She held up a finger toward me — looking back, I guess she showed some relief on her face — hung up, and said, "What channel's the news channel?"

She turned on the television. A reporter east of Atlanta stood on the roadside in front of a burning truck similar to the one I parked in our yard minutes earlier. I said, "Hotdamn, that looks like my truck outside."

The reporter said, "Eyewitnesses say it looked like the truck was hit with a missile. We have here," she looked down at her notes as the camera widened, "Claude Snoddy, who was about a mile behind the truck when it exploded. What can you tell us, Mr. Snoddy?"

I said to Raylou, "That bullet was meant for me."

She said, "Shhh."

Claude Snoddy looked into the camera and said, "I was about a mile behind the truck when it exploded. I seen a flash across the sky, and I thought it was only one them big spotlights car dealers run at night, you know. Then I thought UFO. I said to my wife, 'Hand me my sunglasses.' I got me some prescription sunglasses. We were on our way to the game, you know. Funny thing was—me and Momma told our friends to look out for us on the TV. I guess we got our wish."

The reporter said, "Right now there's still a lot of confusion as to just what happened. The truck was carrying propane cylinders, from what we understand. So far there's no report on the condition of the driver."

The camera operator panned behind the reporter to show a charred and melting husk of a vehicle. The driver, to all eyes outside of an untrained television journalist, didn't survive the explosion, obviously.

I said, "Those mean-ass Republicans." I said, "They've been watching my progress and keeping tabs. And they fired a Scud missile at some poor fucker *not* transporting twelve angels down to Birmingham."

Raylou stared at the television. She said, "You have to quit being so paranoid. What happened to you, anyway? Why're you back here?"

I thought, Why is it that no one wanted to go down to Birmingham with me? Bayward begged off, as did the ex-Elbow Boys. Raylou said she needed to finish up a hundred face jugs for the upcoming annual meeting of the American Society of Plastic Surgeons—ASPS, I'm not making this shit up—with snakes wrapped around the odd-shaped noses of each jug. I said slowly, "Yes. Yes, that's a good question, Raylou. Why *am* I back here. I guess that must surprise about everybody." I walked over to the telephone and hit REDIAL. I said, "Maybe whoever you were talking to when I came in will be just as surprised as you were. I didn't take a close look at the calendar today." The phone rang twice. "And I haven't been keeping up with all the new holidays they got out, but maybe today is *Surprise!* Day."

It should've been, I guess. My mother answered the phone. She said, "Hey, Raylou," like that. Because we lived nowhere, I didn't think about anyone having caller ID.

I said, "Surprise, surprise, surprise," in the best Gomer Pyle rendition I could muster. I felt myself shaking. "I guess you didn't expect to hear from me again, Mother."

"Oh, thank God," she said. "I thought for a minute that was you burned up on the highway. Raylou called me—I guess she told you the secret—and I was watching CNN."

Raylou said, "It was supposed to be a secret."

I said to both wife and mother, "What secret?"

My mother said, "Oh. Nothing."

Raylou yelled out, "Go ahead and tell him, Ansel. He won't believe me." I think she mumbled "Paranoid bastard," there at the end. I think my mother did also.

On the television, the CNN reporter said, "And now we're going back to our nation's capital for a live news conference, already in progress."

The sad, clueless mouthpiece paid by our nation's taxpayers looked straight into the camera and said, "We're upping to Code Orange until we have some conclusive evidence."

I thought, You'd think he could come up with a better verb than "upping." I thought, *How am I going to trust my wife and the people around me, ever?* I said to my mom, "Okay. It wasn't me. I have to go now."

She said, "My documentary on the turtles is going to be showing at a number of independent-film festivals," but I figured she lied.

"Okay. I have to go now."

"Let me talk to Raylou again. This whole you're-not-really-dead thing has me confused as to what we're going to do."

"Okay. I have to go now, really. I'll see you sometime." I hung up and looked at my wife.

"We were all going to go down to Birmingham and surprise you. That's it. Your mother and father were going to be there, and they knew about each other going to be there. Your mom didn't mind, because she says she's got an idea for another documentary. Your father wants to make amends so he doesn't have to drive around tricking people into passing him on back roads. Bayward, Kumi, Vollis, and Delay Sucks wanted to go down there because they feel as though they helped make the angels. Did you know that Brinson Delay is a licensed helicopter pilot? We were going to rent a helicopter so he could fly us over your sculptures and see them from the sky. Anyway, Vollis was going to hijack his school's school bus and take us down there as a group. I'd been on the phone making last-minute plans, but then your mother called in the middle of it all, and now you're back here, and everyone's supposed to be showing up tomorrow. It's a long story."

Boy did I feel like an idiot, of course. I said, "Did you get those spider veins erased from your cheeks because of this?"

"No. You're not that important, Harp."

On the television, the coverage went back to I-85. Firemen stood in the road. The truck no longer burned. The reporter said, "A spokesman from Hartsfield International says their radar picked up nothing on the screen, and a spokesman from the Georgia SBI says that, more than likely, one of the propane cylinders was defective. We'll keep you posted."

Then she did that "back to you in the studio" thing, and the news shifted to what went on in Hollywood the night before.

I called Charlie Baynes down in Birmingham to tell him I'd pay the City of Birmingham back ten grand if he found a way to come pick up the angels. I said, because I couldn't think of anything else, "My wife, my therapist, and I have come to the conclusion that a long, tension-filled road trip wouldn't be good for my recovery. I'm sorry."

Baynes said the only thing he *could* say, namely, "I should've known not to count on a South Carolinian for being on time or getting the job done. Y'all started the war on the wrong date, and you gave up too early."

Here was my first thought when he finally paused: I'm glad that those drunk friends of mine got their elbows back in commission so they can help me beat shit out of this pompous little old-money fuck. But because half of my money wouldn't show up until delivery, I said, "Well, you know how it is. I had to go back and run a bead on a couple of the angels in order to strengthen their nuts."

"I wouldn't know," he said. To someone else in his office he said, "You know, I won't even consider giving grants to a watercolorist unless it's a scene from Charleston's Battery." To me he said, "Well, tell me what I need to do."

I bit my bottom lip. I looked around the den for a stray bottle of booze. I said, "You'll have to rent a couple trucks, probably. I'll have people here to help load up. You just need a driver, I guess, who can read a map." I didn't say anything about the Republican conspiracy. "You're a big boy. I bet you can drive a truck."

He said, "Don't think I can't." And then he said, and I quote, "Ta-ta."

Bayward's owlalope had worsened over the ten-mile-an-hour rides. He'd duct-taped the head back on, I supposed, unless he only wanted it to appear to own a choke collar. The feathers on its chest had blown off, plus some of the skin, to reveal a chicken-wire and burlap inner construction. I stepped out of the clubhouse and said, "You know about those Republicans trying to kill me? Were you in on that, too?"

He dismounted and said, "I've gone one whole week without a drink. I ain't too proud to admit that I'd been lying to y'all all these times. I'd maybe make it one day — or thirty-six hours — but I just couldn't ever get over that quaquaversal hump."

"Quit using that word. I'll buy you a pint of whiskey if you quit using that word." I felt my voice rising and kind of thought about Harold Pinter's *The Dumbwaiter*, Samuel Beckett's *Krapp's Last Tape*, and any of those other theater-of-the-absurd productions I had to see when I took an elective called You Are Here outside of art school.

Bayward looked up in the air. He said, "What's got into you? You drinking again? Vince Vance said that you might go and celebrate by going out and having 'just one drink.' That's how he said it, too: 'Just one drink.' He says it happens all the time. Then that one drink on the first day turns into two drinks the next, then four the next, then a bunch. He says it's a downright equation."

I shook my head. "I need some help. I got all the angels ready to go—by the way, I know all about how y'all were going down there to surprise me or whatever—and now I've decided not to drive them down. They're coming to pick them up, and I need y'all to help me load them in their trucks." I told him about the overpasses. I told him about the truck afire on I-85.

Bayward raised his hand. Then he dropped it down and looked at his wristwatch. "No problemo," he said.

Raylou came out of the house, and she and Bayward looked up at the sky, then back to me. Bayward said, "Vollis could drive them down. He had an idea a while back about going to hijack the school bus anyways, take out some them bench seats, and slide your angels right up in there lengthaways. I'm figuring you can get a good six or eight in there—one this way, one the other. Like a box of hawksbill knives. Or fish."

"There you go," Raylou said. "That'll save you ten thousand dollars, Harp. Okay. It looks like my job's finished here. Thank you very much for your patience and attention." She bowed. Her face looked about as alabaster as ever, like marble with the veins bleached out. I felt myself get an erection for the first time I could remember.

"You need to go," I said to Bayward. I remembered having a thought pass between my eyes not long before, something about using the bus for the delivery. No one would've believed me if I mentioned it at this point, though, while my eyes shot up at invisible specters flying above. "Well, no, you don't need to go, but Raylou and I have to go inside for a while. If Vollis shows up in

286

the bus, I'll pay y'all to take out those seats. No. Wait. No. I don't want to see y'all mixed up in this, and getting killed."

Bayward smiled as if he understood. Michael Heatherly came up the drive in his UPS truck, asked if Raylou was ready to mail off her jugs, apologized for nothing, and said, "I almost forgot. I got a package for y'all."

When we opened it up—and this was a box big enough to hold a bag of nickels from the U.S. Treasury—we found inside what appeared to be straight out of those dominatrix catalogs: six black harnesses with protruding metal spikes, and metal mouth bits. A note on top read, "It'll be easier to walk the snappers if they wear these."

My pecker went back down immediately.

Later that afternoon Bayward came out from Raylou's kiln yard with a casserole dish. Me, I'd taken a nap on the cement floor of my Quonset hut, kind of like old times. I didn't even know that Bayward still hung around. "I was working on the wheel and almost had a pot come up in my hands. Then the thing just half flattened out all on itself. But that gave me an idea—I'mo make a bedpan. When I glaze the thing, I'll draw a bull's-eye in the middle."

I don't want to come off as some kind of soothsayer predictor or anything, a prognosticator in regards to raison d'être and setting goals and finding one's true path in life, but I looked at Bayward's expression and understood that he would leave both itinerant roofing and brown liquor from this point forward. I said, "You son of a bitch. You've got a mission. If you'd've ever gone to any of those stupid craft shows that Raylou has to slog through sometimes, you'd know that people will pay upwards of forty dollars for a vessel like this, just to have around the house as a conversation piece. They'll use it for ashtrays — hey, do you have a cigarette by any chance? I'm out — or candy dishes, or paper-clip holders, and then tell people to get their hands out of the bedpan." I said to Bayward, "Go inside and show Raylou."

Vollis drove up in the school bus. I could tell that he tried to look unsurprised at my being alive. He got out and said, "So where's the crescent wrench?"

I looked at him hard and tried not to allow my eyes to slant upward. "I don't know what you're talking about," I said. "What would you need a crescent wrench for?"

Raylou came out carrying Bayward's bedpan saying, "And then when you finally do get the hang of lifting clay up correctly, you can make matching urinals."

"I thought we had to take the seats out of the bus in order to stack your angels inside."

"How would you know that?" I said. "And why are you not asking why I'm even here? You know I left in the truck early this morning." Vollis looked at my wife. I said, "Don't look at Raylou," and started laughing. When he started actually wringing his hands — just like in the movies — I noticed burn marks up and down his inner forearms. "You helped make the angels, too, didn't you? When did you work on the goddamn things?"

Vollis shrugged. "When Raylou wasn't. You might want to go to a doctor and get you some kind of amphetamines. Go back down to that Dr. Max guy and get you a higher-powered herb supplement. When I signed up for this gig unofficially, I didn't know you was going to be asleep so much."

Everyone told me to go away, that they would be able to load angels better without my jittery self pacing around. "Go for a drive," Raylou said. "Go look around the area and come up with some ideas. Go see if Joe ever got any more nuts in."

I said, "All right," because, sure enough, I felt the pangs of having to let go of my angels besetting me. And I had "Que Sera, Sera" running through my head. Raylou, I imagined, choreographed yet another scene for me to undergo, some type of important, relevant give-and-take that she deemed necessary.

But then Charlie Baynes indeed drove right up on our land. He blew the horn twice, got out, and said, "Guess what handle I chose? Guess! It's 350 miles from Birmingham to here, and every trucker listening in on the CB — coincidence? CB? City of Birmingham? Charlie Baynes? — felt right at home talking to yours truly disguised as 'Calamity Baynes.' Get it? CB again? Those truckers are *rich* in stories, I tell you."

This was a new Charlie Baynes, I could tell. I stood there with my friends. We had Arthur Poole's hoists and come-alongs and hydraulic lifts scattered around the yard. I said, "Aren't you supposed to have a license to drive an eighteen-wheeler?"

Bayward said to Baynes, "Are you of the gay persuasion? Not that I judge you any. But are you full of gay? How many gay truckers are out there, I wonder. This is a new one on me."

I didn't have time to explain things to Bayward. Raylou took him inside on the pretense that she needed help with some snacks. Charlie Baynes said, "You don't need an official license if you have friends in the highway patrol. Or friends who work closely with the highway patrol."

I said, "My father?"

"I'm supposed to say nothing. Anyway, what I do want to say is this, Mr. Spillman: There will be no need to reimburse me or Birmingham. It was worth the experience. *I* should be paying *you.*"

He looked up in the sky in search of whatever my eyes involuntarily detected. I said, "Goddamn it. Up until now, I almost didn't mind thinking about your getting shelled out on the highway. Now I can't do it."

We loaded my angels on their backs and atop one another, tighter than a boxcar filled with flour. We ate some odd sandwiches that Raylou brought out that, I felt sure, included kudzu leaves instead of spinach or romaine.

I thought about how it was a mindless drive from Ember Glow to Birmingham, once you navigate the snaky one-and-a-half–lane macadam paths between our house and the closest on-ramp for the interstate. As for Atlanta, for me, the safest route is right through the center of the city—not that circle of death known as the Perimeter—at about eighty miles an hour. It's like driving through the wall of a hurricane, then experiencing the inner-city calm, then wading back through the far wall. In the old days, drunk—and I'm not proud of this, of course—I once drove from Ember Glow to Atlanta, got on I-20, passed Birmingham, and entered Jackson, Mississippi, in about the same time it took me to listen to a Johnny Cash CD three times, filled only with that one song about being married in a fever hotter than a pepper sprout. In Jackson, a block from one of those Jitney Jungle grocery stores, another block from Belhaven College that once had a mascot called the Clansman but deep down everyone thought "klansman" when they said it, and down the way from Miss Eudora Welty's house, I spent a week welding an abstract life-size Senator Trent Lott, but from what I heard someone stole it soon thereafter using a Mississippi bulldozer—i.e., a mule. Everyone knew that it had been a fraternity prank, and that the pledges sledgehammered Lott to pieces and used his nuts-and-bolts body as a foundation for a barbecue pit. I didn't care. I got paid by some arts patrons from Germany, just the same. But even back then, ten years earlier and drunker than a bird dog surrounded by doves, I felt a certain paranoia and didn't trust going home in the same direction.

When it was time for Charlie Baynes to leave, I said, "I want you to follow me. Just trust my paranoia on this one. Anyone want to ride shotgun with me, or with Charlie in the truck?" I opened the driver's door to the Citroën. Bayward, inexplicably, said he'd drive with Charlie Baynes. I said, "This might take halfway into the night," and cranked my little car.

We drove twenty miles in the wrong direction. We stopped at someplace called Aunt Sue's—a tourist trap somewhere near Table Rock and Caesar's Head made up of linked log-cabin specialty shops whose owners sold geodes, I LOVE JESUS signs fashioned with a wood-burning kit, I LOVE JESUS flags, arrowheads, candles, and hand-churned ice cream—so that I could study my comrades' eyes. A woman wearing a giant bow on her chest always hammered away on a pipe organ out front, playing "I'll Fly Away" about every other song. Raylou and I had come here once to see chain-saw artists sculpt cords of oak. The runner-up did a nice totem pole of the disciples, if it matters. The winner didn't even crank up his McCulloch after he insisted that an image of the Virgin Mary appeared in the bark and he couldn't, in his heart, maim a vision.

Anyway, I had no scientific evidence, but my intuition told me that a ton of Midwesterners stopped here on their way to drop off wayward sons and daughters at Bob Jones University, and I also predicted that a mercenary branch of the Republican Party probably didn't suspect an ice-sculpting trickster to be hanging out in the parking lot. I kept my car running, looked up to Charlie Baynes, and said, "So far so good?"

"Hit the road, Jackie," he sang.

We took Highway 11 and followed the lower Blue Ridge to our north, the flat red clay below us. In the rearview, I saw Charlie Baynes hand a telephone over to Bayward, then Bayward hand it back. I watched as they took turns on the CB, too.

I reached behind my seat and pulled out my gym bag, set it on the passenger seat, and unzipped the top flap. Instead of pulling out Lucky Strikes, though, I extracted things I never packed: a rabbit's foot, a black cloth voodoo doll, some worry beads, and a can of Mace. There was also a note that read, "Mr. Poole said I should stick a gun in here, but I know how you dream at night. I love you. Raylou."

I pushed the dashboard lighter. Then I got a bad song stuck in my head that I couldn't place and turned on the AM radio. I thought, *How in the world did she know that I would lead the angels on a serpentine path back to Birmingham? How did she know that I would change my mind about Charlie Baynes and feel guilty should he get killed?*

We forged our way from western South Carolina to the northeast tip near Charlotte, then drove south, bypassed the state capital, and either divided or skirted the brilliant outposts of North, Neeses, Norway, and Denmark. At the intersection of 321 and 78, I pulled over in front of a one-man barbecue stand. Charlie Baynes eased the truck to a stop and left it running, rolled down his window, and said, "Breaker one-nine, we have twelve angels probably thinking they've been sent to Hell."

I stood beside my car and yelled for Bayward to get out. To Baynes I said, "Sorry about the roundabout loop, but I just wanted to make sure we weren't being followed or tracked."

"Ten-four, good buddy," he said. He blew his horn again.

"All you have to do from here is take a left on 78, drive about thirty or forty miles to I-95, drive south to Brunswick, then take 82 across south Georgia until you hit Columbus. From there, take 280 right into Birmingham. If you have to stop and sleep, I'd try a well-lit truck stop right around Waycross."

Bayward got in my car. Charlie Baynes said, "Goddamn, I almost forgot," and handed a sealed envelope down to me that I opened immediately to make sure the check was right. He said, "I won't be needing sleep. I got *some pills* along the way. Oh, these wonderful truck drivers!"

I thought, *And you have angels behind you*, but didn't say it, seeing as it would've been overly symbolic, sentimental, and hyperbolic. I said, "Let me know if those things get bolted down okay at y'all's unveiling."

Then I got in the car and took a right, barely skirting the Savannah River nuclear site most of the way home, which took almost three hours. Bayward didn't say anything. He either slept, or feigned sleeping, until I pulled up the long, wide driveway. Raylou and Vollis and Kumi sat on lawn chairs, beside the snapping-turtle habitat. I got out and waved my check. "Cheated death again," I said.

Bayward got out. He said, "Finally," and I don't think it was my imagination that his dialect came out a little different sounding than normal. He said, "Finally" in a way that sounded — if I closed my eyes — too much like Charlie Baynes.

"Finally is right, Harp," Vollis said. "Our job is done here. We can finally offer some explanations, boys."

I said to Raylou, "Let's celebrate. YooHoo for everyone on me." I had heard Vollis, but I didn't want to know what he meant.

"Maybe we're emissaries from a World of Good as opposed to the World of Hurt, taking away available booze from the poor people who want it. Stockpiling until our members of Congress agree to finance stem-cell research better and in such a way that faulty, scarred, and fatty livers can be easily repaired through the wonders of modern scientific breakthroughs." Vollis spoke slower than usual, in a measured, melodic voice. My wife didn't make eye contact with anyone, and I assumed she'd been smoking pot for the nine hours I had been gone. "You see, we've only been in your life for eight or nine months, officially. That's a tiny portion of our collective lives added up, you understand. You have no idea what Brinson Sucks and Bayward and I did for our 140-plus years on this planet. For example, Bayward wasn't always a roofer. He only became a roofer after he fell victim to the bottle. Before that he trained some champion steeplechase horses up in Tryon. And Brinson Sucks once had a promising career as a book critic early on, after he served our country. It only took his reaming six books in a row that eventually won Pulitzer Prizes and National Book Awards before he gave it all up. As a functioning drunkard, Harp—and even in the throes of recovery and remission—you don't know how to show any inquisitiveness, or perhaps the word's 'inquisitorialness,' about other members of Homo sapiens working and breathing around you. I don't judge you for that. We've all been there."

I turned to look at Bayward and Delay. They paid attention. Delay said, "Maybe I was a little jealous of people who wrote good novels, I'll admit now."

Bayward said, "I wasn't yet thirty when something in me give off the smell of fear, and them horses lost all respect in my abilities."

"So perhaps we're emissaries, you don't know," Vollis continued. "Maybe we're just moving around from one town to the next, helping out whomever we see struggling. Maybe we got giant grants from the Centers for Disease Control, or the National Institutes of Health. Perhaps we're wealthy billionaire philanthropists who trained with Lee Strasberg and Uta Hagen back in our salad days, and now we travel around Method acting so well that our chosen subjects think of us only as bus driver, vacuum operator, and hopeless moped rider."

I thought to say, "Are you, at this very moment, preparing for a role in Sartre's *No Exit*? I saw *No Exit* when I was in college. And now I'm living it." But I felt ashamed for making so many presumptions, and for a second felt as though I might cry—though looking back, I'm sure it was because of sleep deprivation. And I might've gotten *No Exit* confused with *Nausea*.

"And then there's Raylou," Vollis said. He arched his back and looked into the clear night sky. "I don't think you even know about her. Do you know how much she gave up in regards to her own career so that you wouldn't make a fool out of yourself in public had y'all lived in a town with a population over three and a half? Now it's down to three, what with Arthette dead. Your wife could've been right up there with the Limogeses of the world when it came to pottery. With the Hulls and McCoys. But she turned to those goddamn face jugs, seeing as it fit the part. You live with a man consumed with the liquor demon, you make liquor-demon vessels. Sometimes you make me sick, Harp. I mean it. Sometimes you burn my balls."

I thought, *I'll kill you, motherfucker.* I said, "Good. Fine and dandy. I guess I had this coming. You didn't mention your past, Vollis. While you're skewering me, what's your story? And what about Kumi? Where's he, anyway?"

Raylou said, "I knew it. You didn't pay attention in contemporary art history, honey."

"Kumi's really a slam poet. We just like having him around, though lately he's not been around due to winning the state and regional slam-off. He's getting ready for nationals," Vollis said. "My name's not really Vollis. And twenty years ago I was an artist with a real name and reputation, you dumb, lucky son of a bitch. And then I disappeared. I was too young to take it." He lit a cigarette, the first I had seen him smoke in months. "I seemed to have the choice of real death or fake death. Let me say right now that no life-insurance policy played a part in my decision."

That last sentence sounded funny to me. Did he not have a life-insurance policy, or did he have one and faked death anyway? I said, "And now you go to the studios at that South Carolina School for the Arts and History, and touch up student drawings. And you're Santa Claus to boot. Maybe even Jesus." I handed Raylou the check, told my friends that they could use the guest bedroom, couch, or Quonset hut, and took my wife inside by the hand.

No one else made a move.

In bed, naked Raylou put a finger to her lips and whispered, "I will tell you this: Much of what's happened to you, I'll admit that I planned all along. But I didn't foresee the wrath of the Republican dude, or the snapping-turtle biotoxicologist woman, or your father showing up unannounced, or your mother and her documentary, or Arthette's death, or the anteater project, or —"

I said, "I don't want to know. I know enough. I don't want to know. I know enough. I choose nothing."

"You smell like Lava Soap. Or Goop Hand Cleaner. You smell like what I remember my father smelling like."

I thought, This is not a good sign vis-à-vis psychoanalysis. In the den I heard someone say, "Well, let's get on it. Oxford, England, or Oxford, Mississippi?"

I awoke to find the house empty of people, except for Raylou back in the bedroom. A note on the kitchen table signed by Vollis read, "Sorry about being honest and hard with you, but I knew you could take it. Congratulations. I enjoyed the sculptures."

I said, "Weird fuckers" out loud.

The kudzu my wife planted back in February or thereabouts had, indeed, taken strong root at the base of our property, on the edge of Arthur Poole's land. It's not like it grew a few hundred feet over the previous few days, but it had grown enough for me to notice that, probably by the end of the next summer, it would take over our house unless I spent a few hours each day with a can of kerosene and a few sharp pairs of hedge clippers. I crossed over some of the braver shoots that found their way creeping toward my Quonset hut, opened the door, and stared inside at what I had left: the welder, a box of press clippings from earlier public-art pieces, not enough hex nuts to damage the plate-glass windows of the South Carolina Republican Party headquarters at 1508 Lady Street in Columbia, or a local one at 1 Chick Springs Road in Greenville. I opened work cabinets to find them empty, though I expected, for some reason, to see full bottles of bourbon.

"I cleaned up while you were gone," Raylou said. "I've made some decisions, as I guess you know."

After that long tirade given to me from Vollis not ten hours earlier I expected Raylou to announce her intention to leave me. I said, "Yep." I tried to think up something a little more philosophical, a little more I-don't-blame-you-at-all-and-I'm-sorry. "Well."

"I'm kind of scared, to tell you the truth," my wife said. "And I still can't tell if you're clearheaded enough to know when fear is a good and necessary thing to possess and acknowledge."

I said, "Goddamn you—you've had time to practice a speech. Give me a minute to think up something to say." I don't know why the only thing that cropped into the front of my brain came from the first pages of Flann O'Brien's *At Swim-Two-Birds*: "Who are my future cronies, where our mad carousels?" I thought, *When the fuck did I ever read that crazy novel?* I said, "Go on. Wait. No. Go on."

Raylou shifted her weight from one foot to the other. "I went ahead and put earnest money down for that house in Gruel, and the storefront. And I'd like for us to move down there eventually. After everything settles down. When you're ready. The town's not much, the locals make Bayward seem normal, and the new-comers moving in tend toward New Age, but it's nice. It'll be easier. And from what I understand, the town's been a refuge for people on the run since the Civil War. People there don't offer up information to strangers. They protect each other."

I said, "Do I need to graze on the kudzu? I'm not drinking. I know that you thought I'd drink, but I didn't drink. I smelled it that one time. I drove it around, but I didn't drink."

"The new house has about the same amount of land, but it's *land*. I mean, there's soil. We could put in a garden and everything and start over. If we had a garden, what would you want to grow, Harp?"

"Potatoes for vodka. Corn for bourbon." I noticed how a bird had gotten in and befouled my floor. "Grapes, wine. Rice, saki. Juniper berries, gin. Hops and barley, beer." I paused a few seconds. "Coffee beans, crème de cacao. Peaches and apples, brandy and cider. There's no way I'm going to move, at least for another few years."

"Your mother showed the first unedited version of her documentary at some kind of pre–film festival over at Clemson. It was kind of like when actors sit around and read a play out loud so the writer can hear what's wrong. In this case, would-be directors sit in and discuss what needs to be cut, and so on. The biotoxicologist happened to be there. That's who's been calling us up, and sending us weird things in the mail. Your mother told me about meeting this woman, et cetera, and how the woman seemed genuinely interested in the turtles. So your mother gave out our address and phone number. I told her what had happened because of that. She said, and I quote, 'Oops.' She said, and I quote, 'Looks like my next documentary might be some kind of murder mystery.' If you move with me to Gruel, we need to not leave a forwarding address for a few reasons."

I sat down on the floor. "Ha ha ha ha. All of your little Rube Goldberg devices went haywire. I still don't see why, instead of all the prearranged hoops that both of us had to go through, you didn't just come out and say, 'Hey, Harp, if you don't quit drinking, I'll leave you, and then you'll die alone.' Did you get me the ice-sculpture job in the first place? I can't remember."

"It started a year before that, even. You don't want to know."

"But you knew I'd do something stupid with those ice sculptures, that I'd get in trouble."

"I sat down with Vince Vance and we made up a list of things that you would likely do, and what the outcome could be. DUI didn't seem a choice: You were always such a functioning drunk that you could talk a cop out of giving you a Breathalyzer. The list went on. I finally understood that there was only one group of people in America who would not give you a break whatsoever — that they had memories like mules. Which is, as they say, ironic. Well, except an elephant has a long memory, too."

I asked Raylou about the guy driving the green Maverick, and about every other person who'd shown up since Valentine's

Day. More of her answers came out "Don't know" than any proud and self-proclaimed Rube Goldberg aficionado should've admitted. I said, "Gruel. Grewwww-ulllll. Is there a scrap-metal place near it?"

"Yep."

"A good bakery where I can fill up on doughnuts when I'm craving booze?"

"Uh-huh."

"An army-navy surplus store so I can get a DON'T TREAD ON ME flag to fly on our property?"

"There is."

I didn't believe her, of course. I thought about saying I couldn't live anywhere without a barbecue shack with a petting zoo off to the side, only to hear her say, "Of course!" like that, but didn't.

I didn't ask Raylou if she'd put our own house on the market, if she contacted a moving company, if we should worry about a SCUD missile attack, or if the kudzu—as she planned—would eventually take over the premises in such a way that all of my enemies would go insane tracking me down.

I trusted her. Almost. Maybe.

19

I'D NEVER BEEN ONE to profess publicly a solid belief in the cyclical nature of existence, the Hegelian dialectic, ashes to ashes and dust to dust, what goes around comes around, karma, or the infinite and benevolent wisdom of a Creator. If anything, I sided with the Trickster belief of the Native Americans: a being that brings order out of chaos, only to reimpose the chaos. Nevertheless, I had to rethink my worldview somewhat when Raylou came home from a young real-estate agent she contracted who happened to be friends with Dr. Max, the bruise-cream guy. This Realtor once studied drama at the South Carolina Secretary of Education's School of the Arts and History; he was a land salesman who came back to South Carolina after a disastrous attempt to make it in New York as a stage actor, turned to drinking hard between the occasional local TV commercial, and finally deemed Vince Vance his savior.

"There's too much coincidence in this life," Raylou said. "Even way out here away from everyone else, the world's too tiny."

"I'd like to take it to the bowling alley someday," I said. "So does this guy think he can sell our place?"

We sat in our den, five days after I heard from Charlie Baynes that all went well, that the workmen praised my ability to have holes at the angels' bases, and that they got erected properly and secured tightly down there in Birmingham. The check had already cleared, I should say, but because I didn't trust either the bank or the City of Birmingham—plus I wondered why they'd offer up a real check in the first place, seeing as everyone involved knew I'd be snuffed out mysteriously, somehow—I cleared out most of my checking account and took the money in hundred-dollar bills.

"Get this: His name's Jason Grimm, so his business card has 'The Reaper of Real Estate' down there below his phone number. Get it?"

I didn't want to move. I didn't want to go out and drum up sculpture business, either. For some reason I felt like I could sit at Raylou's wheel, make some pots, and not get dizzy. I said, "I get it."

"Here's the most important connection: Grimm's somehow a nephew by marriage of the same guy we bought our house from." Raylou might've made acquaintance with one of those Nature's Amphetamine products. She seemed more animated than usual. "You remember how Jinks Coomer wanted to go out to Nevada and hook up with scientists because he knew something about barren landscapes? Well, that didn't work out, of course. Jason Grimm talked to Coomer at a family reunion. Or a funeral. Anyway, the Coomer guy evidently said that his biggest mistake ever was moving away from his family homestead. And he wants it back no matter what the price. And on top of that, we have the New Age people wanting to move here for the magnetism."

I said, "Yeah, yeah, yeah." This was only another big loopy trick, I figured. "Let me guess: Coomer discovered the real

Fountain of Youth and made a fortune. And now he fears that he'll get caught with the scam, so he wants to take all his money out of the bank and come back to hide."

"Better," said Raylou. "Or worse. He got in on the ground level of those goddamn glaze-your-own-pot chains. He made some big bucks and now wants to come back here to retire. It was called Glazy Eyes."

Glazy-fucking-Eyes, I thought. We bought our house, and would sell it back to someone who could use the help of my old friends. "Perfect. Everyone will be happy and prosperous and needed and helped."

Raylou said, "Whatever. Now get your sorry crybaby, feeling-sorry-for-yourself ass off that suitcase of money and let's go meet some new citizens down in Gruel."

I didn't say, "Denizens."

The snapping turtles disappeared in the middle of the night without a torrential rain to float them to the enclosure's edge. What I'm saying is, someone took the things without our hearing a ruckus. I went down to Poole's house and knocked on the door. He said, "I didn't hear no car come by. I *did* hear a voice say 'Watch your step,' but I took it to be my sister talking from the grave again. Maybe it was people careful not to trip on the kudzu."

I said, "Maybe it was." And then I heard all of Arthur Poole's statement and said, "What? What's that about Arthette?"

"Nothing new. I mean, nothing the rest of the dead family don't do in their spare time—I think it was my daddy who one night came into the bedroom all dead to tell me 'Forget the ants and clean the septic tank.' That's what I'm working on now. Inventing a self-cleaning septic system. By the by, you promised me them turtles."

303

I said, "I guess you know by now that Raylou wants to move. I finished up that last project, and Raylou's pining for a bigger town."

What else would Poole say but, "I been knowing that"? He said, "I been knowing that since he made it big with Glazy Eyes. Old Coomer thinks someone out there's gone see his life as special and want to write a book about him. So he wants to cover his tracks, you know — like he got too good for us up here. He gone buy back his house just to tear it down and let the kudzu take over the spot. Which is fine by me. I didn't like his family in the first place, bunch of jacklegs. They say them Coomers got kicked out of Irish Travelers for lying too much. You ever hear of them? If you know a Irish Traveler, then you know it takes a lot to get kicked out."

I looked at a contraption in Poole's yard that looked like a cross between a moonshine still and one of Delay Sucks's industrial vacuums. "That the septic-tank cleaner?"

"No. That's my one-man rocket ship to make the aliens feel welcome."

Raylou said, "Ansel called. She didn't want to bother us. She's taking the biotoxicologist and turtles on tour with her to every independent-film festival in the country as some kind of stunt. I wrote down where she'd be. For some reason she seemed intent on making sure I had it down correctly, but she also said that there was a Web site in the works. She seemed pretty pleased that there's a stop down in New Orleans."

I said, "Did you know that Mr. Coomer's going to tear this place down if we move out?"

"No, he's not. He's moving back in. He told me he wants to keep the kiln and get to work."

I wanted a drink. I wanted some Kahlúa, because it started off like "kiln." I said, "Well, maybe you're not in the loop as much as you think."

"He can't tear this place down. It's our first real home. *I'll* tear it down just so he can't. Glazy-eyed motherfucker."

And then she fell apart. Raylou set down a spiral notebook that she'd been keeping To Dos in, crouched on the floor, and cried. She shook. It scared me. I kneeled down there with her and said, "It's okay. In a few years we won't even think of this place unless something really bad happens and we say, 'Well, it could've been worse; it could've been Ember Glow.' Come on. Get up. Let's you and me pack up some things in the step van and drive down to the new place. Hell, I know that I haven't been all that gung ho about it, but I'm excited to move. I really am. I want to plant some peppers and tomatoes. You can't make booze out of peppers and tomatoes."

Raylou breathed in starts. She said, "Bloody Mary mix."

I didn't call Bayward, Vollis, or Brinson Delay Sucks, for I knew that one of those mechanical voices would come on to relate to me that "That number is no longer a working number," et cetera. I never knew Kumi's number, but figured that if I should ever want to get in touch with him I only needed to find the closest poetry-slam competition. I said, "Come on. I want to go see this place you're talking so high and mighty about, this Gruel town."

I didn't say, "What do you think about how face jug–collecting people in the near future are going to say 'Raylou Hewell from Gruel' and how it might have the same onomatopoeic properties as a word like 'ooze.'"

Do not think that I just sat around pouting, like my wife accused. Raylou told me to sit in the Quonset hut, or the playhouse, and work on some new ideas. She said, "The angels brought you luck and renewed faith in yourself. Now it's probably time for you to start thinking secular. It's time for you to make some statements, if you ask me. That's what artists do. And I know that you can say to me, 'Well, bitch, what kind of statement are you making with face jugs?' The answer's this: Plastic surgeons should've stuck to saving lives. Anyway, Vince Vance says your brain cells should be back in place and working overtime. So it's time to think."

I might've imagined most of that monologue of hers, which would indeed prove that my brain cells worked overtime. I said, "For starters, I wouldn't call you a bitch, and you know that. Take that part back."

I didn't ask any more questions. I asked my wife to tell me when to pack my suitcase, and I promised to sit around trying to think up some new projects. I even got on the computer and looked up a bunch of sites dealing with art fellowships, commissions, grants, and whatnot. Raylou drove around doing whatever she needed to do to make us happy in the long run, I guess.

I answered the telephone one afternoon, for some reason, and the real-estate agent Jason Grimm said, "This is not going to be good news. The people selling both the storefront and the house are backing out. These are two separate families, too, which I guess Raylou told you about. Anyway, something happened, and they got spooked. I feel bad about all this. Tell Raylou to give me a call, and I'll get that earnest-money check back in the mail to you."

I said, "I know this is either Ronald Wilson, or Karl, or Vollis," et cetera. I said, "You can't trick me again," and hung up. In my idea/color-study notebook, on my lap, I made a note not to pick up the telephone again, or at least until I didn't yearn for bourbon hourly, which was a feeling I thought would've left me by this point.

I didn't tell Raylou about my conversation with the supposed Jason Grimm for a few reasons, some paranoid and the others selfish. She came home later that day and said, "Did you get some good work done?" She said, "I promise that our new life will be better. Vince Vance says that we'll be undergoing a 'geographical cure' that doesn't work for everyone, but he has faith in us."

I said, "Yes."

It took only two weeks for the earnest-money check to come back, and Raylou opened the envelope without mentioning it to me. For those two weeks, Raylou kind of went about her business, as did I, during this whole time. Understand that it neared Christmas. We kind of missed Thanksgiving, and though neither of us celebrated the virgin birth—but I admit I kind of liked Mary's temerity and vision and ability to bluff—Raylou wanted to bring her Quaker friends over to sit around in silence. Seeing as I had never met any of them before, I said, "I think that'll be a grand idea." To be honest, I felt as though Raylou tried to bluff me—she always talked about meeting these folks Sunday mornings, or how they came to our house when I just happened to be off somewhere. I said, "Since we're moving to Gruel, it might be proper to have them over one last time, and give them directions to this new house with the wraparound porch you're talking so high and gleeful about."

We sat in the den with the television on, my rabbit-ears-of-hangers pointing all over the place because of the half-working and suspect satellite dish. Raylou said, "Shit. Oh, you don't know how I hate to have to tell you what I'm about to tell you, Harp."

I played dumb. It didn't take much. I said, "Don't tell me you lied about the army-navy surplus store, the scrap-metal outfit, the bakery, and the barbecue joint with a petting zoo attached. Please don't tell me you lied."

Raylou sat forward on an ottoman. "I know that you already know about this, pinhead, because I talked to Grimm and he told me about talking to you. He said the conversation took some curious turns there at the end, and I told him he didn't have to explain. I told him you had a distrustful streak."

"Did you get the check back?"

"I got it, I tore it up, and I'm taking it for a sign. I'll use the money for lawn-care products when the vines creep too close."

When the phone rang, I didn't answer. I looked at the muted television set and thought, *That* looks familiar, for about three seconds. The answering machine picked up and Charlie Baynes yelled, "Turn on CNN! Oh, wait—you probably don't get CNN. Do you get CNN? Anyway, turn on one of the news channels now."

I picked up and said, "Hey, Charlie. I got it on." To Raylou I said, "Hey, could you turn the volume up?" And that's when I recognized my angels. To Charlie I said, "Uh-oh. I'm somehow going to get charged as an accessory, aren't I?" I said, "I'll call you back."

Now, I don't want to make any presumptions or assumptions, but the reporter down in Birmingham was the same person who told America about the SCUD missiles hitting that truck filled with propane cylinders. Maybe there was only one CNN reporter covering all of the South. Raylou stood five feet from the TV and I leaned forward. The woman said, "These statues have only been up about a month, from what we understand. They're supposed to be angels, and I guess with some imagination you can see the wings and the halos. From what authorities have told us so far, one of the victims left a note behind for her parents to find. And a friend of one of the victims told me that this collective death wish had been posted on the Web."

I said, "Those are my angels. I can't believe that they actually strung Christmas lights all over the things. I bet no one ever strung Christmas lights on the Venus de Milo."

I wasn't thinking straight. I promise that I knew the history of the sculpture, from Aegean island Menos, to cave, to Turkish farmer finding the thing back in 1820. That there wouldn't be any Christmas lights on a sculpture chiseled in 120 B.C. Raylou said, "Shhh."

The cameraman panned the entire area down what I assumed was Thirty-second Street North in Birmingham. The giant Sloss Furnaces furnaces stood in the background like heavy alien spacecraft. The reporter said, "So far, we know that ten vehicles crashed at high speeds into the angels, and that each car held between four and six teenagers. No one on the ground has admitted to a death count, but from what I can see from here — counting sheets and tarps that have been placed over windshields and car windows — I would be surprised if the death count reaches somewhere between forty and sixty."

I didn't say, "Nice obvious math, reporter woman." I said, "If I would've known, I would've never welded the things, you know."

And it was Raylou who said, "We're going to have people from the media calling here. I wouldn't be surprised if they came to the door, Harp. I'll take care of it. You just take a book or two and stow away in the bedroom for a few days." She reached for the bookshelf and pulled out her copy of *Being and Nothingness*. *When did we get a copy of that*, I wondered. "All of this isn't going to be good for your recovery. This should be thick enough."

I balanced the book on my knee. On the television, people ran and screamed and cried, "Oh my baby, oh my baby." Aerial shots from a helicopter showed the disaster area. Two of my angels still stood, near the entrance to Sloss Furnaces. The other ten lay on the ground, still pretty much intact—maybe in twenty or thirty years, I would be able to commend myself on the welding job—with cars rammed into their cement bases.

"The twelve angels—if you look at them long enough, they indeed do appear to resemble angels—have only been up since around Thanksgiving, Carol," an off-camera news anchor in the Atlanta studio said. "Birmingham officials had strung lights on them for Christmas, and from what we can gather—if we can get our cameraman to zoom in—they were to be adorned with red hearts in celebration of Valentine's Day, come February."

The camera showed two men holding a sheet up to the driver's side of a four-door sedan. The anchorwoman said, "Do we have any more information on the nine-eleven call?"

I said, probably inappropriately, "Detroit needs to invent a radiator that doesn't spill antifreeze all over the place during a crash."

"Officials won't go into much detail about the alleged call, but from what we understand, this isn't the first time the statues have been involved in controversy. We know this much: We've learned that many people think it was a waste of taxpayers' money. And then there's a radical group whose members want public displays of Christmas abolished altogether—these are some of the same people dead-set against the Ten Commandments inside courthouses and schools here in Alabama—and they had a plan thwarted to steal the statues a week after they were erected.

But from what we understand today, though—and it almost seems too coincidental, if not impossible, beyond the willing suspension of disbelief—unhappy young people—lonely, depressed teenagers, people who felt as though they were all alone in this world—could not fathom one more Christmas, Valentine's Day, or the upcoming St. Patrick's Day celebration where city officials planned to spray the angels green..."

The reporter said directly to a helicopter pilot, "These aerial shots are being provided by local station WBRC-TV's Chopper 6. Hey, Brinson, see if you can get a shot of the Vulcan statue overlooking all of this destruction. Vulcan, to our viewers, is the Roman god of fire and forge, and he has overlooked the city of Birmingham since 1904. The sculpture is cast iron, and stands 56 feet on top of a 124-foot pedestal. In 1949 the city placed a torch of sorts in Vulcan's hand, which was lit green when there were no traffic fatalities, but red when someone died in a car accident. But the torch was removed in 1999 during renovations." The helicopter's camera pointed over to Vulcan atop Vulcan Park. "I would assume that the red light would be on right now if it were still functioning as such a beacon."

I looked at Raylou. I looked at Raylou, then up at the ceiling involuntarily. The helicopter pilot said, "This isn't Brinson Delay, Carol."

20

HERE'S ONE THING I learned about remaining sober: It's not always good to understand what's going on in the world daily. It's not beneficial to make connections, understand motives, and ultimately admit defeat. I hid inside the house for the rest of December and all of January. I'm talking I didn't take the worn path to the Quonset hut. I didn't look out the windows. I read Sartre, then I read Heidegger, then I read a bunch of bad books about conspiracy theories. Raylou indeed took care of the telephone calls that came in. Sometimes, if the bedroom door was cracked, I heard her tell people that they could find me living with the gauchos on the Argentine-Chilean border. She told people that I could be found atop Mount Everest, or in the lowest part of Death Valley. The Bermuda Triangle seemed to be her favorite destination for journalists to track me down for an exclusive interview.

Raylou said daily, "It's a good thing we never moved. This is a sign. When things settle down, we'll remain right here, Harp."

I said daily, "'It would be impossible, for example, to define being as a *presence* since *absence* too discloses being, since not to be *there* means still to be.'" Or "'If character is essentially *for oth-*

ers, it can not be distinguished from the body as we have described it.'" Or "'A dull and inescapable nausea perpetually reveals my body to my consciousness.'" Or "'Let us note first that no matter how absorbed I am in my reading, I do not for all that cease making the world come into being.'" All from Sartre. I had a million of them, and I understood exactly zero of what the guy wrote down.

But I had an inkling: I figured out that nothing made sense, nothing mattered, and that spending a fucking lifetime trying to figure out causes, effects, and that which probably occurred through pure-tee chance meant spending a fucking lifetime confused and somewhat pessimistic about the entire ordeal.

So this happened: The telephone calls dwindled. People got kidnapped, or ran away from their grooms-to-be, Hollywood couples split up, and CNN forgot about what ended up only being two teenagers killed and fourteen injured when they crashed into my angels. Raylou got back to work in her studio after receiving a commission to throw a bunch of face jugs and accompanying face mugs for a chain of independent microbreweries. Each day I got up and put on one of Arthette's used work shirts. I kept a notebook on my lap, but thought of nothing.

Then the telephone rang exactly one year after I woke up on the cement floor of the Quonset hut. I didn't answer. I'd been in the middle of looking down at my shirt pocket for an hour—it read x.x. for the name. Did it stand for someone who went back to his old ways, like an ex ex-husband, or an ex-ex-drunk? Did it stand for a cartoon character's eyes when he got drunk or died? Was the shirt once owned by a man twice the radical thinker of Malcolm X? This particular shirt had no corresponding place-of-employment patch parallel to X.X. There wasn't even a discolored rectangle above the right pocket. Maybe X.X.

was self-employed, I decided. Maybe he got tired of every other company he'd worked for and finally went out on his own.

I got up and turned up the volume to the answering machine, finally, for I figured it would be Vince Vance congratulating me, or whoever Brinson Delay Sucks, Kumi, Vollis, Ronald Wilson, the anteater hunters in front of Joker Ray Coker's Pay Now convenience store, or Charlie Baynes really were.

A gruff-voiced male on the other end said, "I'm trying to reach Harp's Pill Man."

I said to myself, "Harp's Pill Man." Why had I not seen my name as such over all these years? Like I had a private drug dealer, or pharmacist.

"This is Buddy Etheridge at the Carolina Arts Council Association, and I'm trying to reach Harp's Pill Man. I'm calling about seeing if you'd be interested in doing some work in bronze. We have a group of donors who've committed some money—a *lot* of money—for four larger-than-life bronzes..."

The answering machine beeped. I walked to the door and looked down at the empty snapping-turtle pit. "Hey, Raylou, do you know anyone named Buddy Etheridge at the arts council?" I yelled.

My beautiful wife turned around from her wheel and smiled. She wore a bandanna, and a sweatshirt with the sleeves cut off right at the elbows. She said, "Hey, you're almost outside. I love you, Harp."

"I love you, too, Raylou. I love you, too, Raylou Hewell, who almost moved to Gruel."

"Yeah, I know him. Good guy. Sounds like he smokes about five packs a day."

The phone rang again. I said, "The phone's ringing again. Come on in here when you get a chance."

"This is Buddy Etheridge again, calling for Harp's Pill Man. I hope I have the right number. Anyway, these donors want two sculptures at either end of I-95—one on the North and South Carolina border, and one at the South Carolina–Georgia border. And then again, two sculptures on I-85 at both ends."

Raylou walked in the door and said, "Pick it up."

"No way. I'm going to listen first," I said.

"This is going to end up being about a million-dollar project, and we have a deal on the use of Sloss Furnaces down in Alabama, I don't know if you're aware that they open the furnaces once a month for artists to work there—the whole reason I know about you and your work is because my cousin—" The machine beeped off again.

"This is another trick," I said. "I love you like I said, Raylou, but believe me when I say I don't need another project in order to stay sober for another year."

"If I chose to perform another intervention, I wouldn't come up with a bronze project. You said a long time ago that you wouldn't do a bronze. You made a big deal about it. I remember an interview somebody had with you, and you said you'd never, ever, ever do a bronze."

I fucking hated bronze. I hated most artists who worked in bronze, for they weren't much more than bad portraitists with a ton of money to throw away after they screwed up. I said, "Have you ever thought that maybe I was *drunk* when I said that?"

Buddy Etheridge called again and said, "The four sculptures can all be pretty much the same—they're supposed to be of John C. Calhoun, who almost made it all the way to president of the United States. Oh, wait a minute—I'm lost in my narrative—I'm Charlie Baynes's cousin. He told me all about you. Anyway, a group of John C. Calhoun's relatives are backing this project, I think mostly because they're pissed off that there are more Strom Thurmond statues in the state than of their great-great-great-great whatever he was."

"Pick it up," Raylou said. "I promise that I had nothing to do with this one. This one's all yours, pal."

Buddy Etheridge said, "Anyway. Here's my number. I'll try to call you again, but if you want to call me it's—" And then the machine broke off again.

I said, "He'll call back."

Raylou smirked. She shook her head. She sat down on the floor, holding a fettling knife in one hand and a sponge in the other. I looked past her, out the window, and in my mind saw both the latest outbuilding and my Quonset hut, all lined with shelf after shelf of bourbon. I envisioned glass shelves, like at a nice hotel bar, and mirrors behind the shelves. I daydreamed about a kindly slick-haired bartender who would talk about baseball trades, the *Farmer's Almanac*, and explain all of those damn books I read while hiding from the outside world more than usual.

I quit staring at the telephone about an hour later. I still didn't trust calling Information, then getting the man on the telephone only to have him say, "Listen, about those angels you made a couple months back. I'm writing an article for *Car and Driver*," or whatever.

Raylou sat with me. I didn't count, but about every two minutes she insisted that her days of planning convoluted ways to redirect my life were over. "If the phone rings again, I'll get it. And if it's Buddy, you can talk to him yourself. You can do this now."

I said, "Deal."

"But, again, you once said you'd never do a bronze. So if you take up this project, I don't want to hear you whining about it for a year."

Evidently Raylou didn't take all the electives outside of art school like I did. "If I do *four* bronzes, then I'm still telling the truth. If I only do *two* bronze sculptures, I'm still telling the truth. There's a difference, in the math world, between '*a*' and '*four*.' Or '*two*.' I'll never do *a* bronze; I'll do a *slew* of bronzes."

Raylou got up and pulled me off the chair. She held my hand and led me to the bedroom. She said something about how she was proud of my choosing nothing over booze. Raylou said, "I mean, I guess I thought you could've done it if you took some kind of drug that put you in a coma for an entire year."

Harp's Pill Man, I thought. I thought, John C. Calhoun ran for office on the Nullifier ticket. He probably printed up some shirts for his campaign workers, their names on the left breast pocket, nothing on the right.

ACKNOWLEDGMENTS

Hey whip-smart editor Adrienne Brodeur, hey putting-for-birdie agent Liz Darhansoff, hey Benthamite André Bernard, hey Job-like managing editor David Hough, hey to everyone else at wonderful and generous Harcourt; to Joe Thompson for tips on Fire; to David Rice for views on Ice; to my students at the South Carolina Governor's School for the Arts and Humanities for working hard, writing well, and watching closely; to Glenda Guion for unknowingly giving me info on New Age apothecaries, groundhog kilns, and for feeding me oatmeal pies, RC Colas, YooHoos, and Pepsis over a long stretch, with love.